A KNACK FOR METAL AND BONE

The Knack Series Book 1

KIM McDOUGALL

Hardcover ISBN: 978-1-990570-56-8
Paperback ISBN: 978-1-990570-48-3
eBook ISBN: 978-1-990570-47-6

Version 6
FICTION / Fantasy / Epic
FICTION / Fantasy / Action & Adventure
FICTION / Fantasy / Romance

This one's for my husband, Louis, whose
yearning to retire encourages me every day.

1

A KNACK FOR OBFUSCATION

From A CRACK OF AN ALLEY between three-story townhouses, Conall watched. His buyer lived in the home across the road, but he wasn't going anywhere near it until he was certain that nobody was watching him watch the house.

It isn't paranoia if they're really out to get you.

The neighborhood was clean and quiet, exactly the kind of place where you'd expect someone who collected priceless mechs to live. And it just so happened that he had a priceless piece of mech prancing on his shoulder right now. The metal lizard let out a stuttering *ca-ca-ca*, and Conall poked it until it settled down.

After a month on the road together, he'd become used to its odd noises and jerky movements. The damned thing had no off button and no thera chip that he could find to deactivate it. It had no discernible power source of any kind because it wasn't just a mech, it was a *pneuma* mech crafted by the legendary Harry Hightower, a mech mage who was long dead but whose artifacts lingered on. Pneuma was an archaic word that literally translated to "that which is breathed." The lizard was a creation of metal and heart, something that thousands of standard mechs working in the streets and homes of New Torwood could never boast. Some collectors even believed the pneumas had souls. Conall didn't know if they were wise or foolish in this assumption. He only knew that he couldn't turn the saints-damned thing off, and when he'd tried to stuff it in his pack, it made an even bigger racket. Better to endure the pinch of its claws on his shoulder and hope it would stay quiet.

One of the lizard's back legs ended in a broken stub, but apart from that, it was a striking piece of mech art, with an undulating body of copper and brass rings, a dog-like face with a sharp brass muzzle and green gems for eyes. Its reticulated tail wrapped around Conall's neck, and the metal coil was a comfortable weight. Every inch of it was etched with filigree lines that were both beautiful and practical as they represented a language of magic that only a master mech mage would understand.

Dr. Renata had paid Conall twice his normal fee to find this pneuma in the southern city of Dowchester and bring it to New Torwood. Or at least her agent had paid him half as a goodwill deposit. The lizard had been a difficult treasure to find and the journey north had nearly killed him twice. He'd been following the river and was caught in a spring flood. Then only a week ago, as he neared the city, a lone gaunt had found him while he slept. Only his wolf instincts had saved him that time.

But tonight Conall would collect the rest of his fee, and all the hardship would be worth it. The money would keep him in provisions for a year. That meant a whole year before he had to venture into the city to take on another job.

He rubbed a finger along the lizard's head and it leaned into his touch. Part of him—a very small part—would be sorry to see it go.

The lizard seemed to watch the world with curiosity, and he could almost believe the wild stories about Harry Hightower creations. And then the lizard would stutter and flail its metal tail, and he would dismiss the idea as foolish and fantastical.

Certainly, Dr. Renata thought the lizard was special. He just hoped she knew about the stutter and the broken leg. He was paid to track it down, not fix it.

Conall continued to study the doctor's house. At this time of year, the estival sun filled the city with a weak but inexhaustible light for twenty-one hours a day, and it dropped deep shadows into the street between the three story homes.

A dark figure skittered along those shadows. Conall pulled back into the safety of the alley.

The figure was too small to be an adult human, so either a child or an elf. It used the shadows like a pro, creeping from window to window on silent feet, then stopping at the doctor's house to check the ground floor latches. They were secure and the would-be thief moved on.

The street fell still again. Conall waited and watched. His wolf made his restlessness known, like an itch under his skin. Garou understood waiting, but he didn't like being confined inside the city.

There are monsters in the Meadows, Conall told the wolf.

There are worse monsters here, Garou said. *And it stinks.*

Conall couldn't argue with that. Even here in Hightown, the odor was oppressive to his sensitive nose. It smelled of rot and sweat and excrement—the scents of too many people too closely confined.

Let us be done with human business and run free, brother. Garou pushed a little with his power to remind Conall that he could force a shift whenever he wanted. It was an empty threat, brought on by boredom more than anger or agitation. Garou had only forced a shift on him once and they were both still paying for that transgression.

Conall glanced over the rooftops. One block to the north, stone merlons of a massive wall were silhouetted against the darkening sky. The wall was an amazing feat of engineering that circled New Torwood City to keep out monsters that roamed the Meadows.

Above the wall's peak, a copper dome glinted in the dull sunlight as Talos lurched by. Only the top of his head and eyes were visible above the stone. Twice a day, the giant mech circled the city with slow, grinding steps. He was a better timekeeper than the summer sun. If Talos was rounding the northern edge of town, that meant it was almost midnight. The sun would soon dip below the horizon. It never got truly dark this far north, but dusk would turn the world flat and gray and make hiding much easier.

He waited.

There was no drawn out sunset. The city was simply plunged into shadow as if a god had dropped a blanket over his favorite pet's cage.

It was time.

Conall gathered his magic about him like a cloak of shadows and pushed away from the alley. His knack was a minor talent for obfuscation, not disguise really, or even camouflage. Just the ability to be ignored when he wanted it, a useful bit of magic when the senior city keepers would still recognize him as a traitor and deserter.

He crossed the road. The lizard mech chittered in his ear. He poked it. The damned thing needed to stay quiet a while longer. He wasn't planning on announcing his arrival.

Standing on the front stoop of the doctor's house, he examined the door. It had the sturdy lock of someone with wealth to protect. His favorite kind. From his pack, he pulled out a mech shaped like a feather with fine, metal barbs on each side. He slid it into the keyhole and pressed the button on the handle. It made a faint whirring sound as the barbs extended to fit the keyhole. He turned it and the tumbler clicked.

Here's hoping the doc isn't mistrustful enough for a dead-bolt too.

He pushed and the door opened a crack.

Excellent.

He took a moment to put away the lock pick and listen for a shuffle of feet. Nothing. The doctor was an elderly widow according to his sources. She slept alone and kept minimal staff. Even the butler would be asleep at this hour.

He slipped inside. Curtains covered the windows, but the fading light found chinks in that armor. Garou snorted at the closed, musty smell of the place.

Conall crept across the foyer to the grand staircase, and stole up the stairs, touching nothing. Halfway up, a board creaked. He froze and tightened his knack around him. One heartbeat. Two heartbeats…ten heartbeats later, the house was still silent. He crept on.

It would have been easier to make an appointment to meet Dr. Renata during normal business hours, but then she could have alerted city guards and had them waiting when he arrived. No, it was better to meet on his terms. She'd get her precious mech. He'd get his money. And the keepers would still be out one traitor. He'd slip away from the city before anyone knew he'd been there.

In the upper hall, only one room had double doors. It had to be the master bedroom. The door opened on well-oiled hinges. That was the nice thing about breaking into stately homes. They were always free of clutter, dust and rusty hinges.

The doctor's bedroom was darker than the hall. The windows were shuttered and heavily shrouded. He shut the door anyway and paused with his back to it until his eyes adjusted. The room was steeped in a heavy perfume that, to his wolf senses, smelled like flowers left to rot in a vase. Ticking and clicking sounds came from all around. The wolf growled in the back of his mind until Conall's night eyes adjusted to the gloom.

Mechs filled every surface in the room. Clocks and perpetual motion machines. Birds, dogs, and cats with glowing gemstone eyes. Vehicles with spinning wheels. Even a humanoid automaton whose head stuttered left and right with a quirky tick.

Creepy as fuck.

Garou whined in agreement.

A rustle of bedsheets confirmed his mark was in her bed.

The mech lizard plucked at his vest with sharp claws.

Conall stepped forward. A plush rug muffled his footsteps. Two feet from the end of the bed, the bedclothes rasped, and a small voice said, "Who's there?"

Conall paused. He'd meant to wake her, but now that he had…She sounded frail and lost.

"I can see you." Her voice cut through the darkness like a whip.

Okay, maybe not so frail.

"I brought your mech."

"Commander West." It wasn't a question. She shifted in the bed. He heard the flick of a thera lighter and the bedside lamp came on, filling the room with purple light.

Dr. Renata sat up in a bed of silk linens and over-stuffed pillows. Her dark hair, shot through with gray, was loose around her shoulders. The color of her eyes was lost in the dim light, but they bored into him.

"Not Commander," he said. "Not anymore. Just Conall."

"I expected you tomorrow. At my office." She didn't seem surprised to see him and that made his skin prickle as if fur were about to burst from his pores. Inside his cage of flesh, the wolf howled a warning.

"I'm sorry. I don't like hospitals." He tried to smile, but was aware that his smile was too feral to be reassuring.

He didn't like this. Not at all. Dr. Renata watched him with a frown and her tone reminded him of his old school mistress after he'd been caught stealing test sheets.

The lizard mech opened its mouth. "Ca-ca-ca!"

Dr. Renata sucked in a breath.

"Is that it? Let me see." She swung her legs over the edge of the bed and landed on bare feet. A long blue night-dress covered her from chin to ankles. She crossed the space between them and stood before him without fear, despite the fact that he was a strange man dressed in hunting leathers who had breached the sanctity of her bedroom in the middle of the night.

Dr. Renata had eyes only for the mech.

Something was very wrong. Conall stared at her outstretched hand. He'd lived too long in the Meadows where silence and stillness meant a predator was nearby. But she was just a tiny woman. He was the one with the power here.

"Payment first." His voice sounded like he'd been chewing on charcoal. He hadn't spoken to another human in weeks.

"Of course." She took a few steps back to claim a pouch of coins from the bedside table and handed it to him. His fist closed over the pouch.

She had the payment ready, Garou whined.

Conall wanted to run from the house. The wolf wanted him to keep running until they'd left the city far behind.

"It's a big sum, but worth it." She plucked the mech lizard from his shoulder. The long tail scraped his neck as she drew it away. "Not that you'll get the chance to spend it. Oh, well. Perhaps the magistrate will donate your effects to the orphans." She was turning away, gazing at her prized mech.

"Donate?"

Shit.

His wolf had already bypassed slower human reactions and urged his feet toward freedom when the dressing room door banged open and three guards rushed out.

From years of battling gaunts during the uprising, Conall and Garou had perfected a technique to blend their abilities. Conall had strength, agility and the long reach of human arms. Garou's heightened senses made him preternaturally aware of his surroundings. They put all those talents to use as the guards tried to grab him. He ducked under the first guard's clumsy attempt, and by the time he'd spun to face the next, he'd unsheathed his air blades.

The blades had cost him a small fortune. They were titanium with handles custom made to fit his grip. A runnel ran along each flat edge where thera chips could be fitted to ignite the mech mage runes that were etched into the metal. A sharp whipping motion of both wrists ignited the thera chips and the blades hummed in his hands. The magic caused a thin layer of air to heat and vibrate around the knives. The vibrations were inhumanly fast and let the blades tear through flesh, bone and sinew like they were gossamer.

The guard had a longer sword, but it was only steel and when he hit an air blade, the recoil sent him sprawling with a cry of pain.

The bedroom door slammed shut and Conall whirled to face the next opponent. This man was taller, broader in the chest and had the scars of a seasoned soldier.

"I know you." He pointed the tip of his blade at Conall's chest. "You're that traitor who killed his own general. They'll hang you." He spat, but it was more for effect as only a tiny spray hit the ground in front of Conall.

"I'll thank you not to dirty my floors like that!" The old doctor sounded cross, but not scared. Both men ignored her.

Conall circled the big man, keeping the others in his sight. One was down. The other waited for his chance to wade into the fight. Dr. Renata watched from the safety of the far side of the bed, her precious mech clutched in her hands.

"You weren't at the Battle of Algid Pass were you?" Conall asked. He feinted left, trying to see if the big man would fall for the ruse and open himself up to a fatal jab. He didn't.

"I was not." The guard puffed out his chest. "I fought on the eastern front with the forty-third. What does it matter?"

Conall lunged again, jabbing, feinting, looking for weakness in this behemoth of a man.

"Because if you'd been at Algid Pass, you'd be thanking me for killing General Naylor, not trying to skewer me."

"Doubtful." The guard grinned, displaying an impressive array of blackened and broken teeth.

Conall could see there was no way out of this fight. The third guard was rousing. He could never beat back all of them and make an escape.

Release me, brother. I will tear out their throats. And I can run faster than any man.

Conall was seriously considering this tactic when a bolt hit him in the shoulder. He looked up to see Dr. Renata holding an antique rail gun. Her lips were pressed in a grim line, but there was merriment in her eyes.

He looked down at the dart protruding from his shoulder.

"Bitch shot me!" was what he tried to say, but it came out in a slurred garble. His fingers went numb and he dropped his blades. The wolf howled, but he sounded very far away.

Conall's knees buckled, and as he crumpled to the ground, the last thing he heard was the *ca-ca-ca* of the mech lizard.

2

A GIANT LEAP

Rowan stood on the wall that surrounded New Torwood City and watched a cat cross the grasslands. Silhouetted against the midnight sun, the train of wind-powered cars really did look like a caterpillar, but white sails made it part butterfly too.

The cat sailed west, away from the city, and Rowan bit down on a sudden rush of envy.

Phalian launched from her shoulder and flitted into the great expanse of sky, but only for about a dozen yards before the wind buffeted him. The little mech bird returned to her shoulder and clicked his metal wings in irritation.

"You know you have to be careful up here. That wind can be fierce." She patted him with the tip of a finger as she gazed at the amazing vista spread out before her. The Meadows went on for miles in an endless sea of grass that shimmered green and gold until it met the Ubruulen Mountain Range far to the north, their jagged peaks like teeth that had rent the horizon.

It was beautiful, majestic…and empty.

New Torwood City wasn't on the way to anywhere. It held little strategic significance for the bigger cities to the south, and so it was mostly left out of squabbles over land and resources. You could see its gray walls from the old Kanta Highway that wayfarers still used to cross the Meadows, but you had to be very foolish or very brave to make that journey. Which were they, the ones riding the cat?

Brave, she decided. Brave and lucky.

The only way she ever saw the outside world was when she came up here. The wall was her refuge from the endless functions, galas and state dinners that Regent Atherton expected her to attend.

She was supposed to be at one such gala in less than an hour.

Screw that plan.

She had real work to do. And besides, the day was too bright and warm to be stuck inside chatting with some stiff ambassador from the southern cities. When he discovered she was gone, the regent would reprimand her, of course, but he couldn't punish her. She'd learned that golden rule many years ago, when she was a lonely, unruly child. And once she'd learned it, she'd refused to be stuffed back into her princess ballgown again.

Six stories above the busy streets, she could forget that stifling life.

She pressed her hands to the wall. Her left, fully human hand wore a black fingerless glove. The sunbaked stone was hot under her touch. The fingertips of her right hand were even more sensitive though they were fully gloved in supple black leather. The glove hid the mech prosthetic, gifted to her by Uncle Hermie after the horrific childhood incident that caused the amputation of her arm half-way to her elbow. It also dampened the hypersensitivity of the mech fingers, otherwise she'd go mad from the constant onslaught of sensory input from the hand.

Anything mage-made—whether stone, metal or wood—brought a reaction from her mech touch. Even now, as she leaned on the wall, it sent magic deep into the stones, tracing mortar lines like neural pathways, and pinging back information about the wall's health and stability.

Rowan patted the stones. All was well with her city's mighty fortress.

She opened a pouch on her tool belt and pulled out a timepiece made of brass gears and cogs arranged as much for their aesthetics as for functionality. The longest arm ticked off the last seconds before nine o'clock. Rowan counted with it.

Three, two, one…

Talos appeared in the distance. Right on time.

He was a mech marvel. Seventy-six feet tall, he could rest his chin on the wall if he wanted to. Of course, he didn't. He was just an automaton, a pneuma creation that Harry Hightower gifted to the city founders, but he was from an age when mech mages could create true marvels from metal, gears and wires.

For nearly three centuries, Talos had guarded the walls of New Torwood with measured steps. And Rowan was the only mechanic left who could fix him when he broke down.

As she watched his approach, she leaned too far over the short wall, and Phalian fluttered at her shoulder, pushing her back to safety.

"Okay, okay! I just wanted to get a good look. Does he seem to be limping to you?"

The mech bird said, "TWEET!"

"Go look."

He flew off with a whir of metal wings, zipped around Talos's head, then dove and circled the automaton's knees. Through Phalian, Rowan could sense an unhealthy grinding of gears inside the giant mech.

She whistled for Phalian to return and scrutinized Talos. The ground beneath him was packed tighter than stone after centuries of his massive feet pounding out the path each day. His left foot lifted and slammed down. Right foot lifted, paused, and fell.

Yes, he was definitely limping.

She'd come out this morning for routine maintenance, but this was going to take longer.

Oh, well. She grinned fiercely as she got ready to leap. This was so much more fun than a boring old palace party.

Talos was only a hundred feet away now. Phalian clacked his wings near her ear. He hated this part. If Rowan was honest, part of her did too, but mostly, she found it exhilarating. She was never more alive than when she hopped the two-foot gap between the wall and Talos's shoulder.

As he came alongside, she sucked in a breath and leaped.

Don't look down. Don't look down.

She looked down.

The drop was sixty-six feet to hard ground. Her stomach twisted. Her foot slipped on Talos's epaulette. A sudden gust of wind tugged her off balance.

Phalian said, "SQUAWK!"

Rowan grabbed for an unobtrusive metal handle sticking out of Talos's shoulder. Her mech fingers locked around the handle and she hung on.

Talos lurched onward, oblivious to his new passenger. Rowan fished a key from her pocket and fitted it into the lock in the small door on the side of his neck. She scrambled inside, and her feet found the rungs of a ladder as easily as slipping on a favorite pair of boots.

"Are you coming?" She held out a hand. Phalian didn't like flying inside Talos. Too many moving parts. As he hopped onto Rowan's hand, gears shifted. Metal wings retracted and front legs extended. His beak flipped on a cog to become a snout at the same time as a wiry tail unwound from his other end. The transformation from bird to mouse took only seconds, then he sat back on his hind legs, begging.

"Fine." She pulled back a flap on her glove just above her wrist and twisted a small lever. A circular disk about the diameter of a walnut retracted on her mech arm to reveal a port with metal contacts. Phalian scurried onto the port, his tiny feet clicking into place on the contacts, and he lay still.

Rowan gave him a little tug, then satisfied that he was locked into his charging cradle, she descended into the inner workings of the greatest automaton ever created.

The familiar tang of warm metal and grease enveloped her. The pneumatic hiss of pumps and the *tick-tick-tick* of perpetual gears was the music she heard in her dreams. The space was dark, cramped, hot, and as comforting as home.

She laid her mech hand on the metal wall, just below a seam of rivets. Its magic pushed outward, and Rowan could sense the whole machine—spots where the metal was stressed, old rivets that were starting to rust, places where grease had caked in the cogs, making them squeal as they turned. She followed the flow of kinetic magic from his lifting foot, up the shaft to the hydraulics that pumped knees and hips, and all the way to the glowing heart in his chest.

That heart was the real marvel, a pneuma creation of the most powerful mech mage in New Torwood's history, Harry Hightower. It was a living organ of magic and mech that no one in three centuries had been able to duplicate.

The heart lit the inside of the mech in a faint orange glow. It was the only light Rowan had to work with, but it was enough. She continued down the ladder that ran along Talos's chest wall, stopping twice to pull a grease gun from her pack and squeeze some onto cranky gears.

She kept descending until she'd reached his right hip. Careful not to dislodge Phalian, she removed her glove and placed her bare mech fingers on the metal frame just above the massive joint as its hydraulic gears pumped it up and down. With her eyes closed, she concentrated on the current of magic flowing through Talos. In her mind, she saw it as a stream of tiny lights in a river of energy. And in reality, Talos did have a sort of blood stream. An ichor pumped magic from his unique heart through all the connecting pistons and tubes and back to the heart to be resaturated with magic again. It was an unending ebb and flow of power. Rowan didn't even know what the ichor was made of or how the heart renewed its magic with every pass. She only knew that it worked. For now. If his heart failed or his ichor drained away, Talos would take his last step because there was no mech mage in New Torwood who could equal Harry Hightower's mastery.

Luckily, for Rowan, Talos's repairs were always mechanical and she never needed to fiddle with the glowing heart or main arteries.

Today she sensed a blockage somewhere behind the hip joint.

She tapped Phalian gently with one finger. The mouse detached from his cradle.

"Go see what's blocking it."

"SQUEAK!"

He didn't like the noise of the gears, but she had no other way to see behind the massive hip.

"Just a quick look," she coaxed.

Phalian scurried to the tip of her hand, and she lifted him up until he leapt from her fingers onto the hip's frame. He circled the ball joint even as the massive pistons rose and fell. Seconds later, Rowan saw the cause of the limp. A bird had started to build a nest on the pump that engaged the joint. The bird had abandoned the project, probably because of the noise and heat, but the nest was blocking the pump and causing it to overheat.

Phalian tugged at a wedged stick. When it came free, he let it drop to collect in Talos's foot. More debris stuck to the pump's bellows, but it was too dangerous for Phalian to attempt a retrieval, and she called him back. Phalian scampered over her arm to latch into his cradle. She gave him a little pat. He'd done well.

Apart from the blocked pump, she had another problem. If a bird had made its way inside the mech, that meant there was a rivet missing somewhere, a bolt hole big enough for a songbird to enter.

Talos really needed a thorough cleaning and tune-up. She'd have to petition the Regent's Council to let her shut him down. The council ministers wouldn't be happy. There was no help for it though. The work needed to be done and soon. For now, she would fix the limp and maybe get home in time to make a late appearance at the gala. That ought to appease old Atherton.

Rowan timed the rise and fall of Talos's leg. As the shaft of the thigh bone rose, she reached around to grab the rest of the bird's nest from the pump. Sticks and grass came away in her hand, but the shaft fell again before she'd cleared it completely.

The pump hissed as a gear ground around a stick. She couldn't reach it, not without getting her fingers mashed.

She'd have to zap it.

When the shaft rose again, she primed magic in her fingertips. It was risky. Galvanic magic could ignite grease and set the whole mech on fire. But her aim was precise, as was her control. She let a little galvanic missile zing out and snatch the bird's nest from its perch. It fell thirty feet to land in Talos's heel.

The giant mech hadn't lost a step. A hiss of steam rose from the hydraulic pump. The hip's ball joint moved freely now. She gave it some grease, then pressed her mech arm to the metal, urging Talos's flow of magic to settle back into a healthy rhythm. His lurching gait smoothed out.

She spent the next two hours climbing around the internal rigging until she'd found the missing rivet and a hole big enough to let in a bird.

When she finally leapt from Talos's shoulder back to the wall, Dale was waiting for her. It was odd to see them on the wall. Although Dale technically held the rank of commander, they'd been a ranger not a keeper, and only keepers patrolled the top of the wall.

Wind tossed their black curls as Dale leaned against a parapet, the picture of ease. If she didn't know them better, she'd think they were slacking, but Dale was the regent's personal secretary. They didn't slack. They'd fought during the last gaunt uprising. And before that, they'd been a companion to Rowan's brother, Ethan. She'd known Dale since they were children, and she'd never seen them up here.

"Watch your step, Princess." Dale pushed from the wall with easy grace.

"Don't call me that." She brushed a hand across her sweaty forehead.

"Sure thing, Princess." They pointed to her brow and grinned. "You just smeared grease across your face. It's a good look."

"Shut up." There was no real animosity in her tone. She pulled a cloth from her pack and wiped her face. "What are you doing here?"

"I wanted to be the one to deliver this." They held out an envelope with a broken seal.

"You're reading my mail now?"

Dale's grin spread even wider. "It's not mail. It's orders."

"Orders?" She took it and slipped out the notice. The official crest of the New Torwood City Rangers was stamped at the top of the page. Her brain raced through the text, but she already knew what it said.

Princess Rowan Elizabeth Cecilia Andula is commanded to appear at the quartermaster's suite at 07:00 on June 22 for outfitting and preparations to join Squad 54.

The wind tried to pluck the letter from her hand, and she gripped it tightly, as tightly as shock and disbelief were now gripping her heart.

Every citizen of New Torwood was obliged to serve in the military for a minimum of two years. They could either become keepers to guard the palace and patrol the city streets or become rangers and go outside the walls to guard the produce farms and the thera farms that supplied the city.

Rowan was going outside.

She squeezed the paper in her fist. "Squad 54? Who's the commander of that?"

Dale shrugged. "Dunno. It's a retired squad. My old squad, in fact. I guess you'll find out who's in charge tomorrow."

Tomorrow. She could barely believe it.

Rowan was going outside.

The orders were only ten years too late. She should have been drafted when she was eighteen, but the regent had refused. For years. Now, at twenty-eight, Rowan would be the oldest raw recruit on the squad.

"Welcome to the club." Dale squeezed her shoulder. Phalian launched from his cradle, transformed into a bird, and pecked at Dale's fingers.

"Well, shit." Rowan shook her head, but couldn't hide a grin.

"That's 'Well, shit, Commander' to you," Dale said, smiling and shaking out their mech-pecked fingers.

3

THE WOLF OF ALGID PASS

Instead OF HAULING HIM TO THE dungeon under the palace, the keepers dumped Conall in a small apartment with bars on the windows. It was still a prison, but one for treasured guests.

Curious.

Things became even more curious when a troupe of servants brought in a bath and filled it with hot water. He didn't need to be forced into the bath, even though two keepers stood guard inside his room to be sure he didn't turn his razor into a weapon. Living wild usually meant bathing in cold runoff and shaving was a luxury. He hadn't seen his own face since he left Dowchester over a month ago.

After the bath, he dressed in the nondescript clothes that were left for him. Food had also been left. At first he only picked at it, but the wolf encouraged him to eat.

This could be our last food for days. Wolf logic.

So he ate and he studied the scene outside the barred windows that looked down on a dismal storage shed somewhere behind the keepers' barracks.

And he waited.

Some hours later, two more keepers entered his room. They jerked him out of his chair and roughly shackled his hands behind his back.

"Where are we going?"

No one answered. Instead, he was marched out of the room and through the dark palace halls until they reached the grand doors of the council chambers. The doors opened, and the keepers shoved him through. He stumbled into a large room with light filtering through high stained-glass windows.

Harry Hightower's famous Infinity Clock ticked away on the wall farthest from the door. It didn't actually tell time, not in any measurable way, but it was a splendor cast in copper, silver and gold, as stars, planets and moons shifted and whirled in a graceful and unending dance. Its only music was a quiet *tick-tick-tick* as it counted the seconds to some destiny that only its creator understood.

Beneath the Infinity Clock and bathed in the light of the stained glass, eleven ministers sat at a long table.

Conall was having a bad case of déjà vu. Ten years ago he'd stood on this very spot, facing a similar cast of unsmiling men and women, while he'd tried to convince them that General Naylor was unfit for command.

Conall's eyes roamed clockwise around the table.

Regent Faustus Atherton was as ageless as ever, with gray hair that seemed cast from steel and dead blue eyes. The eyes of a shark, if that shark dressed in frippery. He wore a high collar and an elaborately knotted lace cravat, with more lace poking out of his waistcoat at the wrists. The coat was brushed velvet in a deep burgundy. Ropes of braided gold were draped around his neck, and he wore large gaudy rings on every finger.

Saints, I hope that fashion statement doesn't catch on.

Garou didn't respond. He was still sneezing at the clouds of perfume in the room.

The empty chair beside the regent was reserved for the absent heir to the throne. Next to that sat a minister who was unfamiliar to him, but looked enough like Rufus Hayes, the old Minister of the Purse, that it had to be his brother or son. The Minister of Guilds was also an unknown. Dr. Renata glared at him from the next chair. Had he known she was on the council, he would never have taken her job. The rest of the ministers were slightly older versions of the men and women who'd once listened to Conall's plea to have General Naylor removed before he got his platoon killed.

They watched him with unfeeling gazes.

The only other person in the room was a blank-faced scribe who sat in the corner, looking austere in the high-collared black uniform. He was already memorizing the proceedings. Later he would record them efficiently and precisely and file the event with the Temple of the Word.

The keeper who'd dragged Conall through the palace shoved him one last time for good measure. Conall didn't give him the satisfaction of reacting, even as he staggered toward the grand table.

The shackles on his wrists pinched. The foolish guards believed tight rings would hold him. He itched with the need to shift. It would be so easy. Shed his clothes, his shackles, and his human morality. The predator in him wouldn't see it as murder if he took a few lives while escaping.

Someone grabbed his hands from behind—someone with a familiar scent that soothed his snarling wolf.

"Just listen to what they have to say," Dale whispered as they unlocked the shackles. That voice spoke right to the wolf and the beast shivered.

A friend's voice. An ally.

Commander Dale Bellamy had lived through the Battle of Algid Pass, the one where hundreds of lives had been lost unnecessarily because this council of old biddies had ignored Conall's warning. Dale had been a lowly maven back then, third in command in Conall's squad, but while Conall had escaped in his wolf skin, Dale had stayed to pick up the pieces, to care for his squad like a good officer. Had he stayed with the rangers, Conall would have promoted Dale to full striker for their actions during that battle. As it was, Dale hadn't needed his support. They'd worked their way up the chain of command with diligence to become commander.

Dale had always been detail oriented. An arranger and an enabler. After their years in the service, they'd turned that talent into a career in the palace and now sat at the right hand of the regent. Conall didn't begrudge them that success, even if it meant working alongside a corrupt system. Dale had always been too altruistic for their own good. Ten years ago, they'd probably thought they could change that system from within. Conall wondered if they still thought that way.

Dale stepped back as Conall rubbed his sore wrists. The room was silent except for the Infinity Clock's ticking. The councilors seemed at ease, bored even, but under the cloying perfume, the wolf could smell fear in the air. They weren't used to dealing with shifters, at least not one who openly acknowledged his animal half. There were shifters in the upper classes, a couple in the palace even, but they kept their secrets, and if they enjoyed long weekends at their hunt cabins outside the city, no one asked too many questions. The upper elites could do whatever they pleased, as long as they did it discreetly.

Conall let the wolf shine from his eyes for just a moment. A small current went through the room. The Minister of the Purse clenched his hands together. Another minister leaned back in his chair, making it creak. It was enough to satisfy the wolf.

I'm watching you, he said. *I have big teeth and strong claws. If you push too hard, this human skin won't hold me back.*

The Minister of Foreign Affairs spoke first. "Thank you for joining us, Mr. West."

"It's Commander West." He'd denied his rank and title before, but in front of this crowd, he'd use every weapon he had.

"Only because you never stood trial for desertion and murder. You were stripped of your rank in absentia."

"Is that what I'm here for now? A trial? It seems like you've already convicted me."

The minister frowned. Deep lines appeared around her thin mouth. Unlike the regent, her dress was almost austere. She wore a black blouse and her straight black hair was cut short. Like many in New Torwood, she had the pale but earthen complexion of a northerner. Conall couldn't remember her name. Deiffer? Keiffer? Yes, Keiffer. Stella Keiffer. Not that it mattered. The ministers were as interchangeable as stale bread. But why was the Minister of Foreign Affairs leading this hearing? Why not the Minister of Defense, General Kranson? After all, Conall's crimes were of a military nature.

"A trial, yes." Minister Keiffer shuffled papers as if his interruption had been an inconvenience. "A trial is still a possibility. That will depend on you."

She sorted through her papers until she found the right one, then began to read, tapping one finger against her chin as she listed his offenses.

"Desertion, misappropriation of military supplies, corruption of rangers under your command, insubordination, and…oh, yes, murder." She glanced at General Kranson who frowned and bobbed his head with every accusation.

Keiffer leaned forward. Her dark eyes bored into Conall. "You murdered your commanding officer. Is that correct?"

"General Naylor was unfit for command. I warned this council about him. Other generals warned you about him. Naylor was crazy. He was obsessed with killing gaunts at all cost. But the council didn't listen."

"So you killed him."

"He shot his own men."

"He shot deserters."

"He shot soldiers who were scared, underfed and without ammunition. We had no chance against the wave of gaunts coming through the pass. We should have fallen back. Naylor shot anyone who ran, but as far as I'm concerned, he murdered more men and women than the deserters. He's responsible for the deaths of hundreds of good rangers."

"And so you killed him." She was back to that. There was no point denying it.

"Yes. I did."

"And then you deserted your post."

Conall ground his back teeth. He took a long breath to calm himself before he spoke.

"Only after I led the few survivors to Camp Norsap. Then I left."

"Because you knew *murderers* aren't tolerated in the ranks."

The wolf huffed in his mind. Keiffer was careful not to mention his shifter status. Technically it was illegal to discriminate based on a person's magic, but shifters were barely tolerated in society and actively discouraged from continuing military service after their two mandatory years.

Conall had kept his wolf a secret. It had been his dream to be a lifer, a career ranger who served in far-flung outposts, fighting gaunts, titans and northern raiders to keep his home city safe. General Naylor's actions had cut that dream short.

He glared at the impassive faces around the room. They all knew he should have been pardoned for taking down the mad general. His soldiers lauded him for it. One general had even publicly praised him for keeping his squad alive, against all odds and with great personal sacrifice.

If only he hadn't done it as a wolf.

Minister Keiffer shuffled her papers again. She lifted one sheet and nodded to Dale. They walked over to retrieve it and delivered it to Conall.

Their eyes were dark and sent unspoken messages.

Something else was going on here. Conall wished he'd had a chance to speak to Dale in private before the hearing.

He took the sheet and read it. Then he read it again, and a third time just to be sure his eyes weren't playing tricks on him.

The council was going to pardon him, and return his rank of commander, if he went on one mission.

It seemed too good to be true.

He lowered the page and squinted at Keiffer.

"What's the mission?"

The minister frowned. "A simple reconnaissance. A group of scientists went silent in the Meadows, northeast of Oxeye Outpost. They check in every evening by graphium, but we haven't heard from them in two days. This is the last communication we received."

Dale retrieved another sheet and gave it to Conall. He read a few lines of the report. It was a standard check-in with notes about provisions needed for the next supply run.

"We don't expect anything is amiss," Keiffer continued, "because the communications officer had complained about graphium problems the day before, but…"

All the ministers were still as statues. The wolf sensed agitation rippling through them.

"But?"

Keiffer sighed. "But the scientists are a delegation from Dowchester. We must do everything in our power to assure their safety."

Ah, that was why Foreign Affairs was involved.

Relations between New Torwood and the cities to the south had always been shaky. Recently, Dowchester's government had reached out with diplomacy. It was no secret that they wanted to increase trade in thera with New Torwood. The council would have been delighted to expand their market in the magic mineral, but trust between two ancient rivals didn't come easily. Smaller non-trade delegations such as an exchange in the arts and sciences could go a long way toward making new friends, but not if New Torwood let those delegations get eaten by monsters.

The scientists were important enough that the council ministers were willing to pardon one of the ranger's most notorious traitors in order to find them.

Conall read the mission again. "So I drive into the Meadows, check on some scientists and come home? Too easy. What's the catch?"

Keiffer's lips spread in a bland smile. "Perhaps to one such as yourself, traveling through gaunt-infested country is easy, but I assure you there is no catch. Except..."

Here it was. The thing that would make this mission impossible.

"The science camp is in Eklridge Oasis."

Conall knew the place. It was some two-thousand miles northeast of the city. Not an easy journey, but not impossible.

"And," Keiffer paused until Conall looked up from the documents in his hands. "You will have certain, ah, *precious* cargo along with you. Princess Rowan will be your mechanic."

A princess? In the wilds? Not going to happen.

He could barely keep himself alive out there. He wouldn't be responsible for some untrained, spoiled brat. He glanced at Dale. They gave a curt nod with lips pressed thin. They thought it was a good idea?

Conall ground his teeth. A growl rumbled in his chest as he tried to sort through his choices. He really had no choice though, did he? Either he took the mission or they hanged him.

He didn't like ultimatums, so he pushed them to see how much they would give.

"Fine, but I have some requirements."

Keiffer opened her mouth, but Conall continued before she could voice her protest.

"I want a full squad. Ten rangers. I don't care who they are, but I want Bretta Tyendi as my second."

Keiffer closed her mouth and looked to the regent. Atherton's shoulders rose as he heaved a sigh.

General Kranson spoke up first. "Striker Tyendi is no longer in active service."

"I don't care." Conall crossed his arms.

"We can't force a free citizen into military service," the general said. "But if she is willing to go, I have no objections. Is that the end of your list of demands, *Commander* West?" He leaned on the rank, as if to remind Conall that he kept it at the pleasure of this council. Conall knew General Kranson only by reputation. He was known to be harsh but fair. He'd been one of the voices who called for the removal of General Naylor, but that didn't mean he'd support his killer.

Conall tried to act relaxed, but the wolf wasn't buying any of this. Garou was ready to run. Neither of them truly believed the council would just let him walk out of there a free man.

"Just one more demand," he said with a tight grin. "I want a cook on the squad. A good one."

He might have imagined it, but he thought Kranson's eyes twinkled with humor as he announced, "Done. See the quartermaster for your supplies."

"Wonderful!" Regent Atherton clapped his hands once and rose. "My secretary, Dale Shannock, will make certain you have everything you need for the journey. And good luck, Commander West."

Conall FOLLOWED DALE DOWN THE COLD stone stairs. Everything about this palace was cold, like a forgotten corpse lying on a slab. The only good thing about his new mission was that he'd be out in the Meadows again.

"What's this really about?" he asked.

Dale shushed him.

"Not here."

Two keepers in uniform came up from the landing below. The four of them had to shuffle and squeeze to cross paths in the spiral staircase. The soldiers were heading up to the palace ramparts. The keepers had it easy. Their only real enemy was boredom. Not like the rangers who went beyond the wall to face gaunts and titans.

And they wanted him to take a princess along for the ride.

At the ground floor, Dale pushed through an open doorway to the bustling kit hall where the quartermaster and his aides were doling out uniforms, weapons and food rations. Conall entered the line to get his kit, but Dale pulled him outside, then through the courtyard to a small supply shed. They shut the door and put their back to it. The only light came through a dirty window, and it fell on Dale's profile. Their dark hair contrasted starkly with pale skin but made the deep circles under their eyes stand out.

Conall remembered a time when Dale's complexion had been more robust, when their lean frame had been more muscle than bone.

Too much time behind a desk. The wolf sniffed. *They smell frail.*

"You're not going to run, are you?" Dale asked.

"I'm not going to run."

Conall hadn't actually been sure of that until he'd said it. If he was honest with himself, he was tired of running. Sneaking in and out of the city was a young man's game. Not that he wanted to come back here to live. He'd been too long in the Meadows to put back on the hair shirt that was city life.

But it would be nice to be free, truly free, without always keeping himself guarded.

"Here. I managed to save your things when they brought you in." Dale picked up a small leather pack and crossbow. Conall rifled through the pack until he found the air blades. Those were too expensive to replace. He also noted the fat purse from Dr. Renata. That was something.

"Thanks." He slung the bow over his shoulder.

"And I have this for you." He held out a thick folder. Conall flipped through the pages. The first one was proof of his rank and command.

"You'll get your pardon when you return," Dale said.

"You really believe that?"

Dale shrugged. "There was a scribe recording it. You have a case, if they don't honor it."

Conall huffed out a laugh. He wouldn't have much of a case if they shot him.

He kept reading.

The second sheet listed names of the scientists at Eklridge Oasis. A brief report followed, outlining the work they were engaged in. The camp was called the Nursery, and the scientists were studying a group of female gaunts and their offspring.

"Dangerous work," he muttered. He'd read the full report later, but he went back to the list of names and scanned it.

"Myron Wrede isn't on this list and he wasn't in the council chambers today. Has he been replaced as Minister of Science?" Conall tapped the page. Wrede was a fanatic. If there were a major discovery happening anywhere that was connected to New Torwood, he'd be part of it.

"Wrede?" Dale frowned. "He's out in the field for sure, but not at the oasis as far as I know."

If this delegation of scientists was important to the council, Myron Wrede would have his hand in their affairs.

Conall studied the file and rubbed his jaw. It had been broken the first year of the war and never healed properly. It still ached when he spent too much time grinding his teeth in frustration. He closed the folder.

"Tell me the truth, what's this really about?"

Dale wouldn't look him in the eye. It was one of the reasons his old friend wouldn't play poker. They had a terrible tell.

"I don't know. I tried to find out. But it all seems above board."

"They're hiding something."

Dale nodded. They both knew the council would have no qualms about commuting his sentence for murder. Some people still thought he was a hero for what he'd done. Even the desertion charge could be explained away. But they'd never forgive him for being a shifter.

Something about this whole mission just stank like a week-old kill.

He opened the folder, studied the map and frowned. The Nursery was a ten-day journey from New Torwood, but only three days north of Oxeye Ranger Outpost.

"Why don't they send a patrol from Oxeye? They'd reach the scientists a full week before us."

Dale shook their head. "Gangra outbreak at the thera farm and the outpost. They have no one to send."

Gangra was bad. Apart from the fact that it killed half of those it infected, it also meant that they wouldn't be able to re-supply at the ranger outpost.

"And this princess?" Conall grumbled. "The council can't be serious. What the hell am I supposed to do with her?"

"She's actually a pretty terrific mechanic. Give her a chance."

Conall grunted. It wasn't an agreement. He trusted Dale's judgment, but a princess? That was a recipe for disaster.

Dale handed him another folder.

"Here's your squad and your list of approved supplies. I arranged for three cats to take you out. And since I know you like to be thorough, I added briefs on each of your squad members that include all military background and their known knacks."

Conall raised an eyebrow at that. A person's knack was private. They didn't have to reveal it when enlisting. But Dale was a canny sort. They had other ways of finding things out.

At the top of the list of names was the squad number. Fifty-four. His old squad number. It had been retired after Algid Pass, when all but a few of them had been killed. Dale had been one of those survivors. Bretta too.

Conall pointed out the number and Dale shrugged. Conall shook his head as if it were a bad joke. He flicked through the character briefs. He'd be sure to study them before they left, but for now he read through the names and ranks of his new squad. Striker Tyendi's name was top of the list.

"You knew I'd ask for Bretta."

Dale smiled. "Of course. And I knew you'd want a full squad. And a decent cook." They grinned and Conall spied the Dale he remembered from years before. "I picked the best I could find from those who are on leave or on palace duty. The medic is a keeper, not a ranger, but by all accounts, he's good in a fight."

Conall nodded and thanked them. He didn't recognize any of the other names on the squad except for Ranger Clementine Tyendi, Bretta's little sister. Saints, she'd been a child the last time he saw her. Could she really be old enough for military service?

The last name on the list stood out: Maven Mechanic Rowan Andula. Maven was third in rank after commander and striker. It usually took years for a ranger to make that rank.

"They made her Maven?" Conall's claws were close to the surface, as if they might burst from his fingers and shred the paper.

"It wouldn't do for royalty to be non-commissioned."

"Of course not. That would be about as foolish as letting a princess go into the wilds." He ran a hand over his face. When was the last time he'd slept? "Let's get this done then. I need to go see Bretta."

4

FRIENDS IN LOW PLACES

An hour later, Conall walked away from the palace wearing his new uniform. It wasn't actually new. The quartermaster recycled everything. The light gray pants were well worn. Conall didn't mind. They were comfortable and stretched with his long stride. The summer weight jacket was patched but the repairs were disguised by the mottled light gray, dark gray and tan weave. The uniform had probably been taken off a dead ranger, but since Conall was a dead man walking until he'd completed the regent's mission, he decided that was fitting.

New Torwood City was built into a hillside. At the highest point, the palace looked over the vast Meadows. The streets wound downhill from there, passing through Hightown, Bailey, and Squall's End before eventually leading out Low Gate to the docks on the great Ikon River.

Conall wandered from the palace gates down King's Walk, the wide boulevard that cut through Hightown. The street was sleepy. Those with business in the palace were encouraged to take back roads and present themselves at smaller doors. Keepers patrolled King's Walk with officious regularity, discouraging the riffraff, and only a few nobles strolled along the cobblestones. Even errand mechs were notably absent.

As he moved farther from the palace, ostentatious townhouses flanked the street. These were the homes of wealthy merchants, doctors and guild masters. The real nobility, the ones who didn't need to work or to flaunt their wealth, had entire compounds tucked away on side streets. There was also one extravagant hotel for visiting dignitaries on King's Walk. It was so exclusive, it didn't even have a sign above the door. Everyone simply called it The Inn.

The solid granite facade, slate gray with bronze flecking, seemed to mock that lowly title. Conall had never been inside, but he could imagine that the rooms were as grand as anything in the palace.

As he passed The Inn, the keeper on door duty scowled, as if even Conall's imaginings were above his station. Conall turned his body to show off the four stripes on his shoulder. The keeper recognized the commander's insignia and lost the scowl. He stood taller and looked straight ahead.

That's right, keeper. You're doing a great job at saving the rich from the dangerous poor.

After The Inn, Conall turned off King's Walk and strolled down Baron Street with its high-end merchants—jewelers, tailors, mech mages and one apothecary. He spotted his tail immediately. Pausing to admire an elaborate display at a corner florist, he noted the dark figure lurking at the last intersection.

Garou made a *pfft* sound. *They don't trust you not to run.*

It was to be expected.

Dale had believed him when he'd said he wouldn't try to escape, but they also weren't stupid. Even so, Conall didn't like being followed. It felt too much like being hunted and wolves weren't prey.

He turned down the next street, then made another quick right. He was heading steadily south, but he ducked down alleys, to mix up his route and give his tail a good work out.

When he came to the Arcade, he stopped to watch an artist build a new mech installation. This part of town was only a few blocks from the King's Walk, but it was also a world away. Artists and musicians crowded the tiny bistros that lined the wide plaza where square footage was auctioned off to artists to showcase their talents. Wealthy patrons paid for the space, and it was a mark of high regard to have one's protégé attract attention.

Conall watched an artist link a series of curvy metal rods that looked like the arms of a titan squid. She was almost finished. He loitered until she slipped the thera chip into the mech and touched it with a lighter. The mech came alive. Its metal tentacles weaved back and forth in a mesmerizing pattern. They were made of different metals—copper, tin and brass—and they caught sunlight as they moved. The effect was stunning and the crowd applauded.

Garou thought it was a colossal waste of time.

You have no taste for the arts, my brother.

The wolf sniffed. *Can you eat it?*

No.

Then why bother?

Conall wasn't about to get into an argument with him about the merits of beauty and creativity. A crowd was gathering around the new installation. He spied his stalker on the edge of the Arcade and decided it was time to move on. He wrapped his knack around him and melted into the crowd.

He stopped again in Bailey, at the midtown market. Merchants had set up caravans or tents with the crumbling walls of the city's original fortifications at their backs. Bailey was less prosperous than Hightown, but at least he could find a decent meal without spending too much of Dr. Renata's hard earned money.

Garou smelled meat and his nose led them to a barbecue stall. Conall let his knack drop and got in line for a meal while he waited for his stalker to catch up. He didn't really want to lose his tail. He just wanted Dale to know that he could, if he chose to.

While he waited, he glanced around the market. Children ran between stalls. They looked grubby for merchants' kids. In fact, the whole market looked grubbier than he remembered. Awnings were faded and torn. A broken down wagon had been abandoned on the corner and a mech valet was stuck against it. The mech's wheels spun, but no one helped to untangle it.

When he got to the front of the line, he pointed to the skewers of seared meat warming over a low wood fire. "Is that chicken?"

The vendor shrugged. "Sure."

"I'll take three." It was probably rat or squirrel, but he'd eaten worse. He paid the man and leaned against the crumbling stone wall of the old bailey while he waited.

He'd finished the first two skewers before his tail came stumbling into the market square, frantically scanning the crowd.

He was a tall, lean guy with dark skin and close-cropped brown hair. He wore a keeper's uniform, similar to Conall's own, except the jacket was charcoal gray instead of camouflage. He had two stripes on his shoulder that marked him as a maven.

Conall made sure to be spotted before he disappeared again. The third time the poor tracker found him, he was heaving to catch his breath and Conall took pity.

He slipped up behind him. "A good rule to remember: the tail should never get ahead of the dog."

The stalker whipped around, panic clear on his face. His hands went for the knife on his belt. Conall let the wolf shine in his eyes.

"Stand down, Maven." He handed the kid the last skewer of meat. He took it hesitantly.

"Thanks." He held the skewer, but didn't take a bite.

"What's your name?"

"Noah, sir. That is…Maven Sommerton."

"The medic? You're on my squad. And they have you babysitting me?"

Noah shrugged. "I have no other orders until we leave tomorrow."

"Fine. But quit skulking around. If I'd wanted to give you the slip, I would have already."

"I'm sorry, sir." He looked embarrassed.

"Just try to keep up. And eat. It might be the last fresh meat you get for a while." He studied Noah while they rested. The kid was taller than him by a couple of inches, but lean. At twenty years old, his shoulders and neck had yet to thicken and his face was still round.

He's soft as a pup, Garou snorted.

A few years riding the Meadows or walking the wall will fix that.

He'd read the medic's file and the files of all his new squad before leaving the palace. Maven Sommerton *was* young, but according to his commanding officer, he was a first-rate medic. He had an unusual knack though, one that would be a blessing and a curse outside the city walls. Conall decided he could live with the curse if the rest helped to keep his rangers alive.

When Noah finished eating, Conall turned and headed through the market. His destination was right on the southern edge of Bailey where it merged with Squall's End. Noah followed in silence. At least the kid didn't chatter. That scored him some points with the wolf.

As they passed an alley, a beggar called out to him from the street corner. He was missing an eye and a leg and Conall wondered if he was a veteran of the gaunt uprising. Conall dropped a coin in his cup.

"Thank you, Commander."

Conall nodded and moved on. He'd never seen beggars in Bailey before. It wasn't the wealthiest section of town, but it had always been comfortably middle class. The businesses were honest and the residents busy with jobs that kept them fed and clothed.

His gaze sought out other telling details. Several shops were boarded up and dark. As always, errand mechs delivered messages and goods between shops, but even these seemed older and rustier than he remembered. He saw one limping along on three wheels.

He barely noticed the difference in atmosphere when they left Bailey for Squall's End.

The low part of town, near the docks, was exactly as he remembered it— noisy, smelly and packed with people and carts. And mechs were everywhere. They were popping out of the giant clock on the guard tower, waving banners in front of vendor stalls and endlessly underfoot as they rolled along the cobbles on errands for rich masters. Outside a tavern, a giant mech pounded out a tune on a piano. Women leaned out second-story windows, their breasts popping out of open robes.

"Hey, darling, need a good time?"

An extendable arm reached down to offer him a card, no doubt a discount coupon on the house's nightly rates. He waved it away.

"Sorry ladies but I need a hot meal and some rest more."

"I'm a hot meal." One lady blew him a kiss.

"And I'll let you rest…right here." The other laid a hand on her breast and winked.

He gave them a smile, then let himself fade a bit. The ladies' eyes slid off him and found another mark in Maven Sommerton. The mech arm nudged the card in his face.

"Um, thanks." Sommerton took it. The ladies whooped and threw kisses at him. A long feathery scarf dangled low enough to brush his cheeks, and the maven lowered his eyes.

Conall shook his head. The boy was as green as spring grass.

An errand mech bumped into Conall's legs. The knee-high robot spun its arms and squawked "Sorry! Move out! Sorry!"

Conall kicked it.

Damned mechs. His fade knack didn't work on them. That was the best part about living under the open sky of the Meadows. Fewer mechs. Of course, you had other things to deal with, things as silent as shadows that could kill you a dozen different ways. Still better than the city.

He picked up his pace and pushed through the crowd, not bothering to see if Sommerton had untangled himself from the ladies of the night.

They PASSED A DECEPTIVELY INNOCENT LOOKING garage that Conall recognized as an entrance to a tunnel that led to the vast underground neighborhood full of thieves, drug dealers and general low-lifes known as the Grotto. Two men sat outside the garage, pretending to be beggars, but were more likely guards and spies for the Blacksmith, the reclusive and somewhat legendary figure who ruled in Grotto, a place that even the keepers wouldn't go.

Noah eyed the garage and the beggars with a bit of disdain and a healthy dose of fear.

Conall clapped him on the shoulder. "Don't worry, we're not going in there." He continued another block and stopped in front of a teahouse.

The Fox's Cup was a little too close to Grotto to be respectable, but at least it was clean. It even had windows, a rarity in Squall's End, though they could easily be boarded up by a rolling garage door that came down to cover the entire front entrance in case of emergency. And in this part of town, emergency could mean fire, storm or riot.

"Wait here."

Noah looked ready to protest, but wisely bit it back and said only, "Yes, Commander." He turned his back to the teahouse and stood at parade rest, scanning the crowd.

Conall pushed open the heavy door and went inside. The noise of Squall's End faded as soon as the door closed behind him. The tearoom consisted of one large area with a few tables and chairs and a counter for taking orders.

Only three customers sat at tables—two together and one separately. A young woman filled honey jars behind the counter. Her frizzy dark red hair was pulled back in a ponytail. Freckles covered every inch of her dusky skin. Sounds of clanging dishes and muted voices floated from the kitchen behind her.

Conall stepped up to the counter. "Got anything stronger than tea in this place?"

The woman's head jerked up, her expression as shocked as if he'd pinched her. Then a huge grin spread across her face.

"Uncle Conall!" She scooted around the counter and threw her arms around him. The wolf rebelled at this assault, but Conall gave him a psychic swat on the nose.

Be calm. She's just a girl.

When was the last time he'd touched another human being? The keepers who had manhandled him out of Dr. Renata's house didn't count. And before that? He couldn't remember, so he let himself enjoy one bright moment of Clementine's hug before gently disentangling her.

"Is that how you greet your commanding officer?"

Clem's smile dimmed momentarily, then returned to its full wattage.

"Commander? Really? The rangers took you back?"

"They did. I leave tomorrow on a super-secret mission, and you're on my squad." He winked. "You and your sister, if she'll come."

Clem made a disgusted face.

Saints, she was so young. How could the council send such children out into the Meadows?

"Bretta's too old and fussy to be a ranger," Clem said. A loud bang came from the kitchen, then a shout. "And the ovens are acting up again. She'll never leave the teahouse."

A woman stormed through the swinging door from the kitchen. She was tall and broad shouldered with the pale, smoky complexion of a northerner. Straight dark hair was piled in a haphazard knot on top of her head with blunt ends sticking out at all angles. Conall had seen hair like that on a grizzly that had been hit by lightning.

She marched right up to Conall. The years had marked her with a few more lines around the eyes and a deep crease between her brows. She'd never been beautiful, but she could still be called striking.

She glared at him.

"Problem with your oven, I hear." He kept his voice low. The other customers were watching them. The woman pulled Clem's hand away from where it was still tucked into the crook of his arm. Then her frown turned into a wide smile and she kissed him on both cheeks.

"So good to see you," Bretta said quietly in his ear.

Conall grunted his appreciation.

Saints, I'm a half-wild thing, not fit for polite society. The wolf agreed with a snort, but he saw nothing wrong with that. Society was for weak wolves. They were a lone wolf and didn't need anyone.

Bretta pulled him to a chair. They all sat, but she nudged Clem. "Get us something to drink. The good stuff. This is a moment to celebrate!"

Clem scurried off.

"She's so grown up, I almost didn't recognize her," Conall said.

"It's been five years, old man. Girls turn into women in five years."

He didn't tell her that he'd been to the city several times in those years. He hadn't visited, and he wouldn't have come this time either, if not for the circumstances. He'd told himself that visiting friends only put them in danger when the keepers were always on the lookout for him. But the truth was, it got harder every year. The people he knew went on with their lives, got married, had children, ran businesses, and he just…was. He came and went, hiding from keepers in the city and rangers in the Meadows, but always hiding.

Clem returned with a brown clay jug and two matching cups.

"I'll leave you two to catch up. Gus needs help in the kitchen." Clem made an exaggerated salute at Conall, snapping her heels together, then turned and marched to the kitchen.

Bretta popped the cork and poured a creamy liquor into each cup. Conall raised his and sniffed. It smelled strongly of cinnamon and nutmeg—expensive spices that had to be traded from down south.

Bretta lifted her drink. "To reunions!" They touched cups. Conall gulped the liquor. It burned like sweet fire down his throat. He coughed. Bretta grinned.

"We call it Fox's Milk. Gus makes it from his grandmother's recipe."

"Smooth." Conall choked out, then he held his cup out for more.

Bretta poured them both another. He lifted his cup and drained it.

"How is the old coot anyway?"

Gus had been with them at the Battle of Algid Pass. He was the best camp cook Conall had ever met. After that campaign, he'd given up his ranger commission. A lot of them had.

"Same old Gus. He's been slow-roasted over the fire all these years. He's never going to spoil."

"I heard you finally married him."

"Yeah, well. I thought I'd better make an honest man out of him." She flashed a grin.

"I'm sorry I missed the wedding. I bet it was one hell of a party."

Bretta poured two more cups. "It was. I drank my poor groom under the table." She paused. "That begs the question though, you missed our wedding, so why are you here now? It must be important."

"I have a commission. A mission, really."

Bretta raised her cup. "To new missions!"

They drank in companionable silence. That was one thing he always liked about Bretta. She could do silence. His wolf liked her too. She was pack. Not mate, but pack nonetheless.

Eventually the stillness went on too long even for Conall.

"Aren't you going to ask me about the mission?"

Bretta shook her head.

"Questions just make you run."

"I'm not running. I'm legit this time. I have orders from the council and everything."

"Orders?"

"That's right. They're sending me into the Meadows. Clem is on my squad list."

"Shit." Bretta grabbed the towel that had been slung over her shoulder and twisted it around her knuckles. "I wanted her to be a keeper, to stay close to home. But Mauro's been filling her head with adventures."

"Who's Mauro?"

"Oh, just some ranger she fancies." Bretta slumped into her chair. "I should have guessed this was coming. It just feels too soon, you know? She's just a kid."

"She's older than we were on our first campaign."

"Yeah, but I was mature for my age and you were born old."

"You should come with us. Keep her safe." Conall dared to smile.

"Go with you? Are you serious?"

"As serious as pie. I need a second and I don't trust anyone else."

"What's the mission."

"Reconnoiter with a research team. They're set up in Eklridge Oasis."

"That's a long drive into the Meadows."

Conall nodded. Bretta knew the terrain as well as he did. In their days on the squad, they'd hunted gaunts all over that area. "The council lost contact with the scientists. It's probably just a graphium malfunction, but they have an agreement with the Governor of Dowchester. The team is from down south. We're supposed to be hosting them."

Bretta didn't seem convinced.

"There's more. This is our squad." He handed her the list of names. Bretta read it. Her eyes widened on the last name. Her hand fell to the table, still holding the sheet.

"What the hell have you gotten yourself into?"

"I asked Dale the same thing. They're looking into it."

"You saw Dale? How?"

"I saw the whole council. Seems a job I did for a nice, little old lady was a setup. They were waiting for me."

Bretta's hand went to her lips as she mouthed a silent "Oh!"

"Don't worry. It's all been sorted. I go on this mission and they'll cancel the bounty on my head."

"I don't like it."

"Me neither. But I don't see that I have a choice." He nodded toward the door where Sommerton's back could be seen through the glass. "I'm sure he's not the only eyes they have on me. And besides, I'm tired of running."

Bretta mulled that over. "But you know, they'll never let you back into the rangers. Not really. They want you for this mission for whatever reason." She waved a hand in the air. "But they won't welcome you back with open arms."

"I'm not looking for a hug. I just want the bounty on my head gone. Are you in?"

"Of course I am! Do you think I'd let my little sister go out into the wilds with a rogue like you? Not a chance. Come on. Let's go tell Gus. He won't be happy, but he'll have to run things while I'm gone." She planted her palms on the table and pushed upward.

A keeper came through the door and headed straight for the counter. Clem served him and while he waited for his tea, he turned to scan the room.

Conall cursed under his breath. The wolf perked up.

Is this someone I can eat?

No. Just an old friend.

"Hey, I know you." The keeper pointed at Conall. "You're a dead man!"

Conall stood and moved his chair away to make room for a fight.

"Dolan! Stand down!" Bretta said, but the soldier raised his truncheon, the weapon of choice for the keepers who were often sent into unruly crowds. He lunged, but the wolf's reflexes were faster and Conall sidestepped the blow, grabbing the truncheon as it sailed past him. He twisted the man's arm behind his back, and pushed his head down until his cheek pressed against the table. It happened in a fraction of a second.

"You always were a little slow, Dolan."

"Enough! Conall, let him up." Bretta was using her no-nonsense voice. Conall jerked Dolan's arm once more, just to hear him squeal, then let go.

"I think I'll hang onto this." He hefted the truncheon. "I'll give it to your commanding officer and let him know how easily I took it off you."

Dolan scowled. Conall had never seen any other expression on his face. They'd fought together years ago. Dolan had been wounded early in the war, not badly, but enough to have him transferred to the keepers, which was what he'd always wanted—a cushy job inside the city walls where the gaunts couldn't get him.

Coward.

Dolan rubbed his shoulder. "He's got a bounty on 'im. Five thousand chips."

"The bounty's been canceled," Bretta said.

"I don't believe you."

"And I don't care." Bretta grabbed the truncheon and handed it back to him. Clem put his mug on the counter.

"Now take your tea. It's on the house, but get the hell out."

Dolan picked up the mug. He pointed at each of them with the truncheon. "I'm going to check up on this. If you're lying, I'll be back with friends."

"You don't have any friends," Conall said to Dolan's back as he left.

"You'd better be sure the council's offer is genuine," Bretta said. "He won't be the only one to recognize the famous Wolf of Algid Pass."

Conall nodded. He wasn't afraid of Dolan or his kind. But the cloying air of the city was making him itch, and despite his many unanswered questions about this mission, he longed for the freedom of the Meadows.

He gave Bretta's arm a squeeze. "We muster at the palace barracks tomorrow morning."

"We'll be there." She shot a grim glance at her little sister waiting on a new customer behind the counter.

5

SLEEPING GRACE

Where WAS THAT WRENCH? ROWAN ROSE from where she'd been squatting to sort through a bin of tools. With hands on hips, she scanned the room, then wiped a strand of loose hair from her face. She was sweaty, dirty and tired. Her squad was leaving in the morning and she was still scrambling to pack all her tools. Her tinker shop was never neat, but now it was a wreck as she sorted equipment to take with her. She'd be in charge of maintaining the mechs in general and the precious cats in particular. She'd heard rangers complain about how delicate the wind-powered cats could be. The quartermaster had issued her a set of mechanic's tools, but she'd taken one look at the pathetic bag of rusted wrenches and screwdrivers and decided she would bring her own.

She'd already read over the mission parameters. The night before the research camp went silent, the graphium operator had warned that their reception was spotty, so she packed a resonance booster. The problem could simply be that their thera chips were too small or badly synchronized to carry the graphium's signal all the way to the ranger outpost at Oxeye. A booster was a luxury that would take up a lot of room in her baggage, but she felt it was worth it.

Everything was packed, but for that last wrench. She had other wrenches, of course. A dozen of them. But this one fit into her mech hand's grip like it had been made for her.

From his perch on a high shelf, Phalian said, "SQUAWK!"

"Not now. I have to finish packing."

The bird screeched out a protest, and Rowan turned to see him prancing on her wrench.

"Oh."

Phalian cocked his head at a reproachful angle.

"Come on, now. Time to sleep. We have a big day tomorrow." She held up her mech arm. Phalian took off from the shelf and landed on her forearm as she opened his port. He shifted form in seconds and clicked into his cradle. She tucked the wrench into her trunk and gave the room one last look.

For nearly twenty years this shop had been more of a home to her than her suite of rooms in the palace. At first it had been nothing but an abandoned basement storeroom where a ten-year-old princess had come to be alone with her grief. The boxes in storage had been full of wonderful things—broken mechs, old lamps, books and more. She spent that first year after the accident hidden away here, making up whole new worlds from the junk—worlds far away from the palace, her comatose brother and her newly disabled arm.

Soon she began to tinker with the broken mechs and discovered that her prosthetic arm was strong enough to loosen even the most stubbornly rusted bolt. And it had a knack. This was a glorious surprise for the little girl who had always been a magical dud. Her mech fingertips could spark galvanic magic hot enough to solder metal, and when she touched anything mech-made, she could feel the flow of energy through its parts and sense any weakness in the structure in the same way one felt earthquake tremors underfoot.

The regent and his council had disapproved of her tinkering, of course. It wasn't a hobby fit for a princess. Luckily, Aunt Bella had stepped in and told them to leave her alone. Her exact words to the regent were "Do leave the child be or I'll sneak into your rooms one night, slice off your balls and leave them in the cup with your teeth."

Auntie had such a way with words.

But it had worked. The council had left her to grow up like a half wild thing, so long as she showed up for court ceremonies when they asked. And soon she even spurned those appearances. Some of the younger courtiers had never even met her, and she'd gained an almost mythical reputation, like the ghost that the servants swore haunted the west balconies.

But they didn't send myths or ghosts out to fight gaunts. They sent rangers. And Rowan was going with them. She could hardly contain her eagerness to get the mission underway.

Apart from guarding the city's food and thera supplies, rangers also took on specialized tasks like escorting dignitaries to and from the southern cities. Or like this mission—search and rescue for parties who got lost in the wilds.

Specialized rangers also hunted gaunts, the ghastly beasts that ran free in the Meadows. They kept watch in the north, waiting for the next swarm to come over the mountains. It had been nine years since the last gaunt uprising, but for many rangers the war was still a fresh memory.

Rowan had turned eighteen during that war and become eligible for military service. She'd petitioned the council to let her serve, but they'd denied her request. She was the spare heir, and with her brother caught in a mysterious coma, her safety became even more valuable to the council.

Nine years after the war ended, she'd given up hope of ever taking up military service, but here she was, kitting up for her first trip outside the walls. The regent's change of heart wasn't just unexpected, it was astonishing. She kept expecting some messenger to arrive with a note saying it had all been a mistake and really, the regent wanted her to cut the ribbon on some new tannery.

Her skin buzzed with the need to run. She wanted to leave now. Tonight. Before he changed his mind.

So far, she'd kept her nervous energy in check by packing, reading the mission parameters and visiting the quartermaster for her kit. As she tightened the buckle on her last pack, she realized all her preparations were done. Except for goodbyes, and then a long night of trying to sleep through the anticipation.

The door opened and Rowan's heart stopped when Dale came into her workshop.

"You're not here to take back my draft orders, are you?" she asked.

Dale raised an eyebrow. "No. Why would I?"

"Just checking."

Rowan walked over and hugged them.

"What's that for?"

"Just because." As the regent's secretary, Dale had influence. She suspected they were the driving force behind the decision to let her take military duty.

Dale frowned. Or smiled. They had an odd way of being able to do both at the same time with a smile that turned down at the corners.

"Yes, well. I just came to check that you're ready." They nodded toward the trunks.

"All packed," she confirmed.

"Good." Dale looked away, then patted down their pockets. If Rowan didn't know better, she'd say they were nervous. Dale never got nervous. They were the unflappable secretary of the realm, but tonight they definitely looked troubled.

"Regent Atherton is sending a scribe with your squad, for posterity, you understand. This is the first time a royal has taken military service."

Rowan felt a little of her bright eagerness fade. She crossed her arms. "No. Definitely not."

Scribes were nothing more than glorified snitches. She'd have her own little council spy with her at all times.

"It's not up for debate, Princess."

She hated when they called her that.

Dale sighed. "The regent was quite adamant. Besides, you won't even know the scribe is there."

"Unlikely." She'd been dealing with scribes all her life. They were a ubiquitous part of palace life. When she'd first taken up mechanics, reports of her new hobby made it into the rag newspapers, and she suspected the scribes of selling their stories, even though that went against the code of the Temple of the Word. Newspaper reporters started following her everywhere. She couldn't leave the palace without their pointed remarks about her life choices, her fashion choices, and her absence at court. The constant badgering became intrusive, until one day, the reporters disappeared. Rowan suspected Aunt Bella had something to do with that too, but she didn't ask. She was just happy to be able to carry out her duties as Talos's mechanic without a trail of obnoxious reporters following her.

She was never able to get rid of the scribes though. They lurked in a corner of every formal function to observe and later record their observations for the archives in the Temple. For posterity.

And now it seemed posterity was going to ruin her first ranger mission.

"And if I refuse?"

"There's still time to rescind your orders." Dale held out their hands, that same upside-down smile on their face. "Atherton's words, not mine."

Rowan clenched her mech fist around a discarded roll of wire. It made a sound like metal cogs snapping.

"Fine." Maybe if she was lucky the scribe would get eaten by a gaunt.

Dale seemed to want to say more, but Rowan wouldn't look at them. They headed for the door and paused.

"Rowan?"

She kept her back to them. "Yeah?"

"There's something else you should know."

"What?"

"I found out who your commander is." They paused long enough that Rowan looked up. "His name is Conall West."

The name sprang a little trap in her mind. It was familiar…

She gaped at Dale.

"Commander West? The Wolf of Algid Pass? You can't be serious."

"As serious as a saint's prayer."

The cogs in Rowan's mind whirred. Everyone knew the story of the wolf who'd saved his squad by tearing out the throat of the mad general. Over the years, it had become a legend. But Dale had actually been there.

"Is it true? Did he really do it?"

Dale nodded, their expression solemn.

"So he's really a shifter?"

Another nod.

And this was who the regent had decided to send her into the Meadows with?

Dale must have seen the agitation on her face. They crossed the space between them, but didn't touch her. Dale never touched her willingly, not since the night she'd lost her arm.

"He's a good commander, I promise. He'll keep you safe out there."

Rowan waited, but if Dale knew more, they weren't sharing. Finally, she nodded.

Wolves and scribes. The saints be damned. This didn't really change anything. She was still going outside the wall.

"You'll visit Ethan while I'm gone?" Despite the coma, Rowan felt that Ethan could sense when she was near. She didn't want him to feel abandoned.

Dale hesitated only a moment before answering. "Of course."

The EVENING NURSE WAS JUST FINISHING up when she arrived. He smiled quickly at Rowan as he did up the buttons on Ethan's pajama shirt, hiding scars that had once been three angry red claw marks dissecting his chest. Over the years, the scars had faded to delicate silvery lines, like etchings on a mech.

Nurse Grant finished dressing the prince and tucked the blanket around him. "He's all ready for you, Princess. Just gave him a bath and everything."

"Thank you."

Grant was one of many nurses and doctors who tended to her brother, but Rowan liked him best. He often sang to Ethan or told him funny stories, as if the prince might open his eyes and answer one day.

And Rowan never gave up hoping that he would.

Grant left, whistling a tune that would be better suited to a tavern than a sickroom. Rowan liked him for that too.

Auntie Bella was asleep in a stuffed chair by the window. Rowan crept over and shut the curtains, blocking out the continuous sun.

She ignored the lighter on the bedside table and lit the thera lamp with a flick of her mech fingers. The lamp's mantle caught with a bright white glow, then settled into the soft purple of lit thera.

She sat on the edge of Ethan's bed. For years after the attack, she'd been too nervous to come this close. Looking back on those times now, she wasn't sure if she'd been afraid *for* Ethan or afraid *of* Ethan. Would her presence somehow make his affliction worse? Or might he open his eyes and blame her for the months—and now years—lost to him?

Eventually, she'd put those feelings aside. It didn't matter what had happened all those years ago. It only mattered what she did now.

So she came every night to sit with him. She read aloud or just told him about her day.

Tonight she'd come to say goodbye.

She gripped his hand. It was warm and dry.

"I'm leaving tomorrow," she said quietly. She'd wake Auntie Bella soon but needed a few moments alone with Ethan first.

She brushed his damp hair across his brow. It was as red as ever, but dull, not the shining crown she remembered from their youth. Her hair had darkened too from strawberry to a burnished copper. They were both grown up. Grant had to shave Ethan nearly every day now. But to Rowan, Ethan seemed frozen in childhood. He would forever be that boy who loved to play at fighting gaunts or to sneak into the keepers' garage to sit in the cats and pretend they were racing through the Meadows.

"I just wanted to say goodbye and to tell you not to worry if you don't see me…" She stumbled a bit. He never saw her. "I mean if I don't come visit for the next few weeks. I'm finally going out with the rangers. Can you believe it? I wish you were coming with me. It's going to be such an adventure. But I'll tell you all about it when I get back. And you mustn't worry about me while I'm gone."

A snort from the corner of the room told Rowan that Auntie Bella was awake.

Auntie had two great talents. The first was the ability to sleep anywhere. She snored through state dinners and the ceremonial changing of the palace guards. She dozed through meetings with the Regent's Council and visits from foreign dignitaries. Rowan had never seen her actually sleep in her bed.

Auntie had come awake with a start. She'd been slumped in the overstuffed chair and now slid to the floor, landing with a thump in the middle of her voluminous skirts. She pushed back the tower of red hair that leaned to one side, and wiped her eyes.

"Fuckety-fuck. What time is it?"

Auntie's second talent was an astonishing and unwavering potty mouth.

"It's after nine. I'm just heading off to bed." Rowan held out a hand to help Bella stand. The old aunt creaked as she rose. She was the exact same height as Rowan. They stared at each other with the same blue eyes, though Bella's were heavily outlined and painted with eyeshadow. The skin on her cheeks was held up mostly by a thick layer of makeup. Her favorite deep burgundy lipstick had worn away, leaving only a thin outline on her mouth.

Like most court ladies, Bella favored long dresses in bright silks and satins that were imported from the southern cities at exorbitant prices. They were heavily embroidered with gold and silver thread that mimicked the resonance etchings on mechs. Each dress was worth more than most citizens of New Torwood made in a year.

"Hiding your wealth in a vault does no good," Auntie always said. "Better to flaunt it in their faces and remind the fuckers just who they're dealing with."

Rowan preferred sensible work pants and shirts, though she'd wear formal dress when the occasion called for it. Even if the ranger uniform didn't quite fit her, she'd been wearing it since she picked up her kit that morning. It was comfortable and suited her mood.

Bella frowned at the uniform.

"Are you still going along with this madness?"

Rowan ignored the comment. They'd already had this argument.

"Dale said they'd visit while I'm away. You will too, right?" She hated how her voice sounded so small and child-like.

"Of course I will. What else have I to do, anyway? I just don't understand what has always drawn you outside those walls."

Bella wasn't letting it go.

Rowan glanced at Ethan lying there, so still and pale. He had also been infected with the desire to go outside and it had landed him in a coma. The same adventure had taken Rowan's arm when she was nine. You'd think that would have cured her of any wanderlust. It hadn't.

"You know me, Auntie. If I have to sit all quiet and pretty for one more gala affair in the palace, I might stab someone with my shrimp fork."

Bella patted her arm. "Just don't hit an artery, dear. That makes such a mess."

Rowan's eyes suddenly warmed and blurred. She wasn't normally a crier. Too much grief too early in her life had weaned her of that habit. But saying goodbye to the only two people she truly loved was harder than she'd expected.

She threw her arms around Bella's neck again and breathed in her peculiar scent of lavender mixed with sherry. Bella suffered through her outburst for half a minute before squirming away. She'd never been one for extended displays of affection.

Rowan turned away and wiped her eyes.

Bella gripped her arm. Her expression under all that makeup was hard. "Just say the word and I'll get that pompous old bag of duck shit to rescind your orders."

"Don't you dare!" Rowan said. "You know I've wanted this for years."

"The pompous old bag of duck shit couldn't rescind the orders anyway," Regent Atherton said as he entered the room. Bella rolled her eyes, and he ignored her. It was a game they'd played for over fifty years, since the first time a young Faustus Atherton had asked the adolescent daughter of the king to dance, and Bella had told him to bugger off.

Atherton smiled at his old rival. "Princess Rowan's participation is crucial to this mission."

"Oh, Faustus, do fuck off," Bella said. "Can't you see we're having a family moment?"

"Charming." Atherton's lip curled like he smelled something foul. He was dressed as always, in formal attire—a blue velvet waistcoat, black pants with a stripe of blue silk up the outside seam and an elaborately knotted lace tie. His hair was swooped back from his forehead and held in place by some shiny cosmetic. Strings of gold hung on him like garlands.

He looked ridiculous.

Rowan's father, the late king, had never suffered through court fads. He'd favored comfort and sensibility over fashion. At any time, he could have stepped out of court for the market or the hunt and not seemed out of place.

When Atherton became regent, he'd inspired his court to dress like fourth century fops. Perhaps the costumes made him feel like a real king.

Rowan put that thought aside. It was unkind. Atherton had only ever had the best intentions for New Torwood and for her family.

"Regent Atherton, I'm glad you're here," Rowan said, ignoring Bella's snort. "I didn't expect to see you before I leave tomorrow."

Atherton ran a hand down his velvet lapel. "Yes, well. It has been a busy day. We have a delegation arriving from the south in a week. Much to prepare."

"I wanted to ask about that. I read the mission report. The scientists we are going to find are from Dowchester, is that right?"

Atherton lifted his chin and looked down at her. "It is."

"Is that why you're sending me? To act as an ambassador?"

"I am sending you because the mission needs a mechanic. Isn't that what you are?"

Rowan thought of all the times she'd begged him to leave her to her tinkering. He was throwing that back in her face now. She wouldn't let him belittle her. There was nothing wrong with being a mechanic.

She straightened her shoulders and met his gaze. "I am."

"Good. Because you make a terrible royal."

He was still mad about yesterday.

"I'm sorry I missed the gala. But I had good reason…"

Atherton held up his hand. "You always do, Princess. But I needed you yesterday. I'm just a lowly regent. The bigwigs from Dowchester wanted to meet royalty. And I need their money to run this city. It's not like I ask a lot of you, after all. If only you could…"

It was about that point Rowan tuned him out. She'd heard this lecture a hundred times before. Atherton must have seen her eyes glaze over because he paused mid-harangue. His shoulders slumped enough to throw off the line of his jacket.

"Well, never mind. It doesn't matter now." He smoothed two fingers over his shiny hair. "You got what you wanted. I just came to check on the prince." He gave Ethan a cursory glance. "And I see all is well. Good luck tomorrow, Princess." He paused in the doorway, and said, "Your father would be proud to see you in a ranger uniform."

Rowan tensed and the fingers of her mech arm tingled like they might burst into flame. This happened every time Atherton mentioned the old king. She didn't know why. The regent had always been kind to her. He didn't pretend to replace her father, he was more like a distant uncle. But there it was, she still balked whenever her father's name crossed his lips.

After Atherton left, Bella sat on the bed and brushed the hair from Ethan's brow.

"Really Rowan, I know he's a dick but you're twenty-eight years old, not a child. You need to show up at court more often. Give in a little and then when you take what you want, he won't even notice."

"You want me to be Atherton's figurehead."

"Don't be silly. I want you to learn to manipulate that little shit and all the ministers who kowtow to him. I want you to rule. You are the heir, after all."

"Don't ever say that! And especially not here. Ethan is the heir." Rowan's mech fist was clenched so hard, she could feel the joints creak.

"I didn't raise you to be simple-minded, child. Ethan hasn't been the heir in over fifteen years. Even if he does wake up, what will he be? A lost boy in a wasted man's body. Is that who you want ruling your city?"

Bella's words weren't just hurtful, they were shocking.

"How dare you say that?"

Bella reached across Ethan and took Rowan's flesh hand in hers.

"I know that's a harsh reality for you to face."

Rowan didn't know what to say. Ethan's recovery was not something they ever talked about. And now, on the eve of Rowan's first ranger mission, Bella was forcing her to confront it.

"I don't have time to discuss this now."

"I know, but while you're away, I want you to think about it. Will you do that?"

"I suppose we can talk about it when I return, if you insist."

"I do."

Bella smiled. She placed Rowan's hand on top of Ethan's and held them both. Rowan leaned over and kissed her brother's forehead. It was cold and dry. So were her eyes.

She rose. "Goodbye Auntie. I'll see you in a couple of weeks. If he wakes, tell him…tell him I'll be home soon."

Bella pursed her lips into a crinkled moue, but nodded. They both knew that Ethan wouldn't wake.

6

RANK AND FILE

The GRAY AND BROWN JACKET OF Rowan's new ranger uniform was too big around the bust and shoulders, and the pants bagged at the knees. She paired them with her favorite work boots that were scuffed so badly it was hard to tell if they'd originally been black or brown. Tucking her hair under the gray cap, she pulled the brim low over her eyes and studied the effect in the mirror. A mass of bright red hair stuck out the back. She looked like a fire beacon atop the castle walls. A fuzzy fire beacon.

She twisted her hair into a knot and stuffed in into the cap. That just made it look like an alien was about to birth from her brain. With a frustrated sigh, she tossed the cap on her dresser and rummaged in her pack for a pair of scissors. She pulled the mass of hair into a wad and tied it with the oldest ribbon she could find in her cupboard. Then, holding her breath, she hacked off the pony tail, leaving only an inch of hair. She held the lopped off length in one hand and a laugh bubbled up in her chest.

How long have I wanted to do that?

Phalian's wings whistled and clicked as he whirled around her head.

"Do you like it?"

"SQUAWK!"

She turned her head. The ends of her truncated ponytail stuck out like a thera sparkler, the kind they used to light as kids and wave around to spell their names with the sparkles.

Her heart did a little flip of regret but she purposefully ignored it. She tied her cut-off locks with another ribbon and tucked it into a drawer. It was only hair. It would grow back. She wasn't worried about looking good. She only wanted to fit in.

That was ridiculous, of course. Every member of the squad would know who she was. There was no hiding that. Still, she didn't have to flaunt her red Andulan hair in their faces. With her mech arm raised, she whistled for Phalian and he latched onto his charging port. She pulled her cap back on and admired the new look. It was…efficient. That was the best she could do.

It was time to meet her new squad.

She'd already had the crate of equipment and her pack of clothes delivered to the quartermaster, so she flung her lighter pack—the one with her essential tools and survival gear—over one shoulder and let herself out of her rooms. It was still early, well before the regent or other visiting nobles would be awake. She met only an elf page and a cleaning maid. They bobbed to her politely and hurried on their way. The palace staff were used to the princess's odd hours. And her odd clothes.

As she passed through the Grand Hall, the giant clock on the wall struck the half hour. It was a massive construction of gears and cogs that looked like an aerial view of the city. The hour hand was a circular disk that moved around the perimeter and was meant to represent Talos.

The single light gong meant it was five-thirty. She had thirty minutes to make it through the palace and across the keepers' quad to the mess hall. Yesterday, when she'd picked up her kit, the quartermaster had admonished her not to be late or Squad 54 would leave without her.

She ran down the long hallways with her pack dragging down one shoulder and her canteen slapping her thigh with every step.

The mess hall was nearly empty when she arrived. She poured tea from an urn on the sideboard, sat at one of the long tables, and waited. Keepers and rangers slowly trickled in to sit in pairs or alone at the tables. An unremarkable ranger lounged against a wall nearby. He leaned on his left shoulder, so she couldn't see his rank. His scowl said he wasn't one for small talk and her eyes slid past him. She heard two more soldiers enter from the far door. They spoke in a loud, carrying whisper, and she sank down a little on her bench.

"I'm telling you, the princess is on this detail."

"No way! I thought she never left the palace. Isn't she deformed or something?"

"Or something. She's probably crazy too. All those royals are. And I'll be there to document the auspicious moment when she gets eaten by a gaunt." The men laughed.

So she'd found her scribe. She turned to confirm her suspicions and recognized the scribe uniform: a plain black tunic with a high collar and a yellow armband to set him apart from soldiers in a battle. The scribe was short and stout with a round face and eyes nearly hidden in the folds of his eyelids. In the traditional scribe fashion, he wore his hair shaved at the back. A mech port had been implanted into his neck just below his right ear and a wire was plugged into the port. The wire snaked inside his shirt, presumably down his back to some recording mech.

The scribe was already puffing from the short walk through the keeper compound, and he seemed to be stuffed into his black scribe shirt as if it had been made for a much smaller man.

Rowan thought of the old adage about facing gaunts in the meadows: you don't have to run fast, just faster than the next person in line.

I can definitely outrun that jerk.

If the council was dumb enough to send an unfit scribe to follow her, despite her protests, then she wouldn't be responsible for what happened to him.

More soldiers entered the hall while the two men continued to gossip.

"Should be an easy mission," said the smaller man with the scribe. "They wouldn't put the precious heir in harm's way."

Rowan gripped her mug and tried to look like just another soldier.

People often spoke of "they or them" like some vague and almighty source of power. But Rowan knew that power well. The regent and his council. They were the omnipresent "they" who turned the cogs of industry, politics and the military in New Torwood City. And they weren't always of one mind. She had no doubt her commission had caused a fuss in the council chambers.

"But she's not really the heir, are you, Princess?" A tall, striking woman said from the doorway. A shorter, younger woman stood beside her. The tall woman wore the three stripes of a striker on her shoulder. Rowan rose and saluted awkwardly, nearly blinding herself with her own thumb.

Someone snickered.

She sensed Phalian ready to burst from his cradle and she locked her other hand over him, willing her heart to slow its furious beating.

You've got this. It'll get better. You can be a princess and *a mechanic* and *a ranger.*

She opened her eyes and addressed the officer. "I prefer to be known by my rank, ma'am. Maven Andula reporting for duty." She stopped short of tapping her heels together. She didn't need to be known as an eager beaver too.

The woman squinted, assessed her, then nodded. "I'm Striker Tyendi. You can call me Bretta, but only once we're outside the wall."

Rowan nodded hesitantly. She hadn't expected that. She'd heard rangers were more informal than keepers, but she'd expected more discipline. She'd *wanted* more discipline. Discipline meant she'd have something in common with her fellow rangers.

Bretta nodded toward the younger woman. "This is my sister, Clem. It's also her first mission. You two can braid hair or something."

Clem smiled. She was pretty, with reddish-brown hair that hung in long, springy coils. Her pale skin was almost completely masked by freckles. She bounced on her toes and had a perky smile.

Rowan hated perky people. Perky people generally wanted something from her—a position at court, a favor from the princess or a ray of reflected fame from hanging out with a royal. She turned away from the girl. She needed the others to take her seriously. There would be no hair braiding on this mission.

The two men who'd been talking smack about her stood at attention with eyes fixed on a distant point well past the walls of the mess hall. Bretta turned her attention to them. "Do I know you?" The smaller one shook his head vigorously. "Do I need to know you? Are you on this squad?"

"No, Striker!"

"Then get the fuck out of my face." She dropped the f-bomb with a light smile, as if she'd asked him in for tea. The man fled. Rowan instantly liked her. The striker reminded her of Auntie Bella.

Bretta focused on the scribe. He also shook his head, but it was a more ponderous and lazy gesture.

"Who are you?"

"Name's Orson. I'm here because they told me to be here." He slouched into his seat and wouldn't meet Bretta's eyes. She studied him for a long moment before turning away.

"All right. If anyone has a problem with this assignment, they can keep it to themselves. I'm not interested in your whining. Maven Andula is our mechanic. End of discussion. The rest of you, sound off. I want to know your rank and how you will be useful to me."

Bretta's sister started. "I'm Clementine Tyendi. You can call me Clem. This is my first mission. I'm a scout and a pretty good shot." She lifted the rail gun that was slung over her shoulder.

Bretta turned to the next ranger.

"Maven Medic Noah Sommerton, ma'am."

"Good." Bretta nodded and turned to the oldest ranger in the bunch.

"Hello Murdoch. Good to have you on board. Can you introduce yourself for the others?"

Murdoch grunted. "I'm the cook. Keep me alive and you get fed."

The next one was an elf, small as a child with delicate features and thin arms. A woolen hat, striped brown and red slouched on his head.

"Elias," he squeaked. "Scout and tracker."

"Don't be getting airs, elf," Murdoch grumbled. "He's the cook's help. He fetches things for me."

Somehow, Elias went even paler than his already alabaster skin.

"Don't be such an old curmudgeon, Murdoch." Striker Tyendi smiled at Elias. The elf stood taller, which wasn't much since he came only to the striker's elbow. "If Elias wants to be a tracker, we'll make that happen."

"As long as he fetches water when I ask." Murdoch's tone was gruff but it had no bite. Rowan had dealt with enough nasty people in her life to recognize them, and Murdoch seemed all bluster.

Bretta nodded to the elf and turned back to Orson. "What's your rank?"

Orson held up his arm with the yellow band. "I'm a civilian. All the scribes with ranger ranks are out on assignments, so don't expect me to salute. The council has asked me to document this mission, and here I am." His eyes slid to Rowan and back to Bretta.

"So you're a last-minute choice," Bretta said.

Orson scowled, then lifted his chin. "I'm a scribe." As if that made him holier than a saint.

"There are no spectators in my squad." Bretta pointed at him. "You come out into the Meadows with us, you're a ranger and I'll treat you as one. That means you carry your own weight. Got it?"

She made a point to glance at Orson's girth.

"Aye-aye, Striker, sir. Ma'am. Whatever." He licked his lips, leaving them glistening wet.

Rowan had already decided she disliked the scribe. Having him follow her around to detail what she ate and where she slept for the whole mission wouldn't help her win points with the others. And his appearance and general manner did nothing to endear him to her. Or Striker Tyendi, it seemed.

Bretta pinned the scribe with a glare. "I'm serious. You don't follow orders and the Meadows will be your final resting place." She had that whole school-teacher air of authority, complete with the raised eyebrow. Not that Rowan had ever known a school teacher. She'd been tutored by a stream of ancient scholars, but she imagined that's what teachers looked like.

Orson made a grudging sound that could have been a confirmation. Bretta turned to the next ranger.

"Lena Albright, ma'am. I'm a tracker."

Bretta smiled. "I read your record. Very impressive. Glad to have you on the team."

"Thank you, ma'am. Glad to be here." She didn't look glad. Her flaxen hair and wan complexion made her seem half ghost.

The next ranger was a tall, lanky guy, dark skinned and with short cropped brown hair. Rowan pegged him to be about twenty.

"Valko Mantik, ma'am." He saluted awkwardly.

"Is this your first mission, Ranger?"

"Second, ma'am!"

"Good. Try to stay alive."

"I will, ma'am!"

The last ranger was a huge blond kid, who couldn't possibly have been old enough for military service. He had baby fat cheeks and a puckered mouth like a dewy strawberry.

"Aug—gustus, s—s—ir. Er, ma'am. Augie Paddon I c—arry things."

Bretta eyed him up and down. "I'm sure you do. How old are you, Ranger?"

The kid turned red. "Eighteen, m…ma'am."

Bretta studied him for a minute. The kid fidgeted under her glare then started to hum a tune. Rowan thought it was *Ode to Joy*, a composition by an ancient composer that Auntie Bella favored. Odd choice for a young kid.

Striker Tyendi either decided that Augie wasn't lying about his age or that she would ignore the lie. She turned to face the door of the mess hall.

"Well, that's it then. Commander, is there anything else you want to know?"

Commander? When had he arrived?

The man who'd been leaning in the corner all this time uncrossed his arms and pushed away from the wall. Rowan had completely forgotten about him. He prowled into the middle of the room. Each step was deliberate and stealthy, yet completely natural. And how had she thought him plain? Now that he came into the light, Rowan saw a handsome if grizzled face, with sharp features softened by day-old stubble. Graying blond hair fell too long around his ears to be ranger regulation. Rowan felt strength coming off him that she hadn't noticed before. It made her mech fist clench reflexively.

"That'll do for now, Striker. My name's Commander Conall West. You lot will call me Commander. Striker Tyendi is right about the Meadows." He nodded his chin toward the window as if the great expanse of deadly grasslands was right outside. "There are a hundred ways to die out there, and it's not my job to protect you. My job is the mission. That's it. I won't be babying any of you. Follow orders, be smart and you'll stay alive."

There were a few nods and mumbles of "Yes, sir."

"Any questions?"

Rowan raised her mech hand. "Uh, sir. Commander?"

West turned his very blue eyes on her. "Yes, *Maven*." He somehow made her rank sound like a joke, and that killed all the butterflies in Rowan's stomach. She refused to be a joke to anyone, not even her commander. She'd been dealing with pompous men all her life. This one wouldn't faze her.

She took a breath and spoke clearly. "What is the mission exactly?"

The commander smiled. It was a cold, predator's smile.

"We're heading two thousand miles into the Meadows to track down a group of scientists who probably didn't have enough sense to charge the thera cells on their graphium. The rangers at Oxeye Station haven't heard from them in three days. We go in, we make sure they're alive, and we come home."

"And what if they're not alive, sir?" This from the medic.

The commander gave him a low stare. "Then we document the scene and come home with the bad news. Any more questions? Like what's on the lunch menu?"

"I prefer beef to pork," Orson said with a sly grin. "But bison will do in a pinch."

The commander favored him with a dead, flat stare. He held it long enough for the scribe's grin to wobble, then looked away to address the whole squad.

"We leave in half an hour. Anyone not at the garage by then will be left behind."

Most of the rangers fled. The commander's manner caused an instinctive fight or flight reaction. Rowan was sensitive to magic, or rather her mech arm was. It did strange things in its presence. Like clenching uncontrollably. Or extending her fingers as if they were surprised. Sometimes it just tingled. Right now, it was fisted so hard, she had to surreptitiously pry open her fingers with her other hand. It had never reacted that way before, except for that one time when the Minister of Guilds' husband turned into a badger during a state dinner. Rowan had been sitting right next to him and her mech arm reacted before she did, pinning the furry, spitting creature to the table when it went berserk and lunged for her throat.

And now it was reacting to the Wolf of Algid Pass.

She was still prying open her cramped hand when he came alongside and whispered in her ear.

"Maven Andula, a word please."

"Huh?" She jerked her eyes up to meet his. There was amusement there. Or perhaps mockery.

"Is something wrong?"

"Um, no." She dropped her mech fist, though it was still cramped. "Can I help you, Commander?" She put some royal ice into her tone.

Conall seemed to find that amusing too. A small smile quirked at the edge of his lips, though his eyes gave nothing away.

"Yes, you can. My caution before wasn't hyperbole, and it wasn't just for you. The Meadows are dangerous, and we have several greens with us on this mission."

"Greens...sir?" She remembered to throw the honorarium on at the last minute.

"Greens. Newbies. Call them what you want. I'm not happy about taking children out into the Meadows. I wasn't lying when I said there are a hundred ways to die out there. But I was lying about my responsibility. It is my job to keep you alive. You and *all* the others. I don't much care if you're a princess. Your life means the same as the others, no more, no less. Understood?"

"Of course...sir."

"And your rank, *Maven*? It means nothing to a grizzly bear or a gaunt. And it means nothing to me. You haven't earned it. Striker Tyendi has earned her rank. She has proven herself to me a dozen times. Your rank was given to you only because it looks bad to have a royal without an officer's title. But until you earn that maven stripe, you're just a drudge. That saints-damned elf outranks you as far as I'm concerned."

His gaze bore into hers and she felt like some predator was watching her—a predator that liked to play with his prey.

Her mech fingers suddenly relaxed. She reached out and tapped his nose.

"There's no need to huff and puff, commander. I get it. You're in charge."

He stared at her. A slow growl grumbled from his throat.

"Did you just fucking boop me?"

"Yes, sir. Commander, sir." She forced her lips to stay in a steady even line. *Don't smile. Don't frown. Keep him guessing.*

He leaned back and squinted at her.

"This is not a game, Princess. There will be no tea parties at the end of the road." His voice remained low, but the few rangers left in the hall were looking at them now.

"No tea parties. Got it. But you should know, I've been thumbing my nose at authority since I could buckle my own shoes. I'm also not an idiot.

I've never been in the Meadows, and you're clearly an experienced ranger. So I will listen to you, as long as you prove yourself to me too. *Commander.*"

She gave him a stiff salute and spun on her heel.

7

GREENS

Conall WATCHED FROM THE SHADOWS AS his squad packed the three cats they would be taking out. The trolley-like vehicles had three cars each, attached in a train. Each car had three benches and a cargo bed that were open to the elements on the sides and covered by a sturdy canopy. The eleven squad members could have fit on two cats, but Conall preferred they take two for transport and a third for their gear. Shit happened in the Meadows. Unexpected shit. Redundancy was important.

His scrutiny wasn't just to be sure his team loaded extra water, rations and weapons. He was assessing the squad and how they worked together. They weren't a team yet. Jobs were done twice or left undone because they had no rapport with each other. And there were some grumbles about the work required for extra provisions. That Orson character was particularly vocal in his protests.

"I'm not hauling water." He stood with his arms folded over his chest. "Scribes are too valuable for manual labor."

Conall wondered if he'd feel the same after two weeks on the road when they were stuck in the middle of the grasslands with no water for miles in any direction. He waited to see if he needed to intervene, but Bretta had the situation in hand.

"Are you going to drink water?" she asked. Orson glared, but refused to be drawn in. "It's at least a week's ride there and another week back," Bretta continued. "Think you can go that long without water? Because I don't see any reason to share with you if you're not going to help."

Orson hesitated a moment longer, then mumbled something under his

66

breath—probably a curse—before he picked up the gallon jugs and loaded them onto the cats.

Saints, they were all so green. And it was his job to keep them alive for the next two weeks. Two weeks, if they were lucky. Bretta's estimates were optimistic. It would take at least seven days to reach Eklridge Oasis. And that was if they didn't run into storms, raiders, or a pack of gaunts. Hopefully, they'd find the camp all in order and turn around the next day. If not? If they found the scientists killed by titans or gaunts or wolves? He hoped it would be wolves. At least they were efficient and there would be little left to bury.

You shouldn't bury the dead anyway, his wolf said. *Vultures need to eat too.*

Wolves were generous beasts.

Bretta barked out orders that kept the rangers jumping. Thank the saints for Bretta. She was equal parts drill sergeant and mother hen. If he played his cards right, he might not have to talk to any of the snot-nosed squadlings at all.

Other than Orson's constant grumbling, the rest of the squad worked quietly, if inefficiently.

Murdoch had served during the last gaunt uprising, nine years ago. He hadn't been with Conall's regiment, but he had a reputation for fighting bears bare-handed to protect his food stores. He looked cured—like an old leather that had been left out too long in the sun and rain. Conall didn't worry too much about him. Murdoch was a grumpy old curmudgeon, but he was a survivor. No doubt he could be dropped off anywhere in the Meadows and within half a day, he'd have a camp set up with a pot of boiled roots and some kind of meat stewing.

The elf scurried along behind him, carrying the heavier loads. Conall had never traveled with an elf before, since they'd only been allowed in the military in the last two years, but Elias was already proving his worth. He might have the stature of a pre-teen child, but Conall had just watched him hoist two five gallon water jugs at the same time. Those weighed upwards of forty pounds each.

Good to know. He could always find a use for strength.

The others worked with more or less competence. The princess was obsessive about her kit. She packed and repacked her tools at least three times.

Had she really bopped him on the nose like an unruly pup? Thinking about it still made him furious, but Garou thought the whole incident was hilarious.

She's feisty. Good mate material.

Don't even think about it. And what's with that ponytail? She looks like a firecracker about to explode.

The wolf snorted and sneezed, a gesture that Conall had learned was his version of laughter.

He forced his attention away from the fussy maven with the spray of shockingly red hair sticking out of her cap.

The medic rushed around trying to help everyone and mostly getting in the way. Lena and Clem loaded weapons and ammo. Valko followed Bretta around like a puppy, and the big, blond kid, Augie, stood near the front of the first cat looking lost.

Conall waited in the shadows of the garage until Bretta had all her chicks on board.

"We're ready, Commander." She gave him a nod, then stood beside the second cat. He glanced at the deployment of the squad and nodded his approval. Bretta had spread the experienced rangers among the greens.

Clem sat in the passenger seat of Bretta's cat, with Noah and Elias behind her. Conall made a show of circling the vehicle, checking the tires and the packed gear.

"Buckle in that pack, soldier!" He snapped, just to see Noah jump. "One good pothole and you'll lose all your gear. Is that what you want?"

"No, sir!" Noah fumbled with the rope that tied his pack to cleats on the cargo bed.

Lena drove the next car. She was older than him, maybe in her early forties. There were lines at the corner of her eyes, but he didn't think those were from a life of laughter. She didn't seem the type. And the bulge of muscle where her jaw met her ear told him she spent a lot of time with her teeth tightly clamped.

She has secrets, this one. You should watch her.

Conall ignored the wolf. Lena probably did have secrets. They all did. As long as she did her job, he didn't care what those secrets were.

Valko sat in the passenger seat as her second. His file was thin—no reprimands, but no commendations either. This was only his second foray into the Meadows. A rail gun sat on the floor by his feet.

"As soon as we leave the city, you keep that gun trained on the grass," Conall said. "You'll see titans coming, but there are plenty of predators who can hide in knee-high grass and pounce before you can raise a gun."

"Yes, sir!" Valko seemed confident. Conall sensed that it was all bravado. The kid would be tested soon enough. Only then would Conall know his true mettle.

Murdoch slouched in the seat behind Valko, surrounded by the cook's gear.

Conall moved onto the last cat. Orson lounged in the back seat, his boots propped on the edge of the door. Conall knocked his feet back inside the cat as he walked by.

"Ow!" Orson complained, but he straightened up when Conall glared at him. The princess sat up front. She stared out the windscreen as if they were already racing across the Meadows.

Augie, the giant child, filled the middle seat behind her. He hummed a quiet tune and fidgeted with a toggle on the pack by his feet. He had a dim, contented look, and Conall suspected he'd lied about his age in order to enlist. He couldn't be a day over sixteen, much too young to take up with the rangers. There had to be a story there—a reason why he was so desperate to leave the safety of home for the wilds of the Meadows. But Conall wasn't interested in stories. Stories wouldn't keep them alive out there.

Time for the kid to grow up.

"What's your name, ranger?" He snapped the words like a whip and let his wolf peek through his irises.

"A—Augie…Sir."

"No, it's not. You're Ranger Paddon."

The kid nodded. Two brights spots of red blazed on his cheeks.

"Say it."

"Ranger P—Paddon, sir!" His voice rose to soprano heights and he started to hum again.

"Quit the singing, Ranger! This isn't a cabaret!" He pointed out the garage door. "There are a dozen different monsters out there with hearing as good as a dog's. You plan to sing to them, ranger?"

"No, sir!" The kid was actually vibrating. Then he shot upward and hovered six inches off the bench.

"What the hell?" Orson grumbled from the back seat.

"Sorry, sir!"

Conall eyed the kid. That was one hell of a knack. He'd read his file, of course. His basic training sergeant had mentioned the levitating, but remarked that it only happened under duress. Conall had wanted to test him, to see how much stress was needed to push the kid over the edge. Apparently, not much.

He gripped Augie's arm. The boy recoiled and levitated even higher until his neck bent at a bad angle as his head pressed against the cat's roof.

Fucking council. They send me out to death's workshop with children and princesses and expect me to keep them alive.

"Settle down now, son." Bretta reached in from the other side of the cat and touched Augie's arm. Mother hen at her most motherly. Bretta could calm a situation with a few quiet words. She swore she didn't have an empathy knack. It was just the pure force of her personality that made people react to her. As far as Conall was concerned that *was* magic.

"You're safe here, Ranger." She spoke soothingly, as if she coddled a colicky baby.

When Augie was finally back in his seat, he looked sheepish. "S—Sorry, sir. It's a terrible knack. Mum says it's a bad habit that the rangers will fix. But don't worry, I only levitate when I'm nervous."

Conall showed the kid his teeth.

"Perfect. It's not like you'll find anything to be nervous about in the Meadows." He might have growled. Augie looked paralyzed with fear again, and Bretta shot Conall a dark look.

"Commander, why don't you continue with the cat inspections?" Bretta was still using her sweet-as-pie voice. "Augie and I will just have a little chat."

"Right."

By the time Conall finished the inspections, Bretta had rearranged the seating so Augie rode with her. Bretta would keep that little chick close.

Elias now perched on the bench behind Rowan.

"Fucking elf," Orson grumbled from the back seat. "He stinks. Am I going to have to put up with that stench for the whole journey?"

Privately, Conall agreed with the scribe. The elves had a peculiar odor, sweet and sort of sickly, like fruit left to rot in the sun. Publicly, he was about to slam the scribe, but Rowan beat him to it.

"You don't like it, you can run beside the cat, scribe. Just scream if you fall behind and maybe we'll hear you."

Orson glowered at her. "Scribes are sacrosanct. Even you, Princess, have no authority over me."

"Maybe not me. But Elias will be making your food. You like to eat, don't you?" She looked pointedly at his rotund middle. "It's never a good idea to piss off the cook."

Orson glanced at Elias. The elf's expression was smug. Orson grumbled some other nonsense, too low for anyone to hear and no one cared enough to make him repeat it.

Conall turned his back on the scribe. He liked the way Rowan had handled him. She'd clearly had experience dealing with jerks.

Even jerks in command, Garou reminded him.

As he approached the front of the vehicle, a bird mech flew from the front seat, circled the cat once and perched on the roof.

Conall pointed. "What in the saints' sinners is that?"

The mech opened its beak and said, "SQUAWK!"

Rowan chirped a response and the bird hopped onto her shoulder.

"Pets aren't allowed, Ranger."

"It's not a pet. It's more of a…an assistant. Trust me, Commander, you'll be glad for Phalian when we're stuck out there with a broken cat. He can get into the smallest space. Cuts repair time in half. I promise."

He glared at her and she smiled sweetly back at him. That wasn't how it was supposed to work. He was supposed to growl and she was supposed to cower.

She's fierce, Garou said.

Don't start with me.

Rowan's mech assistant suddenly shrank. Its wings retracted and a tail emerged. In seconds a mouse sat where the bird had been. It rubbed tiny metal paws against its nose, then scampered down her shoulder and locked itself into a port on the back of her wrist. It blended seamlessly with the black sheath that covered her mech arm.

Conall blinked. The wolf was intrigued. Rowan watched him with an expression that said she dared him to comment.

In truth, he'd worried about her disability. The Meadows were harsh for someone with four working limbs. But so far, the mech arm hadn't held her back, and he was intrigued to see what she could do with it.

You should tell her that, Garou said.

Not gonna happen. Not even a little bit.

The wolf snorted.

"Move over." Conall pointed to the driver's seat. "You're driving."

She hesitated for only a moment before sliding across the bench to take the steering wheel. Her mech hand was gloved in an odd black material like dull metal. The other hand was also gloved in black, but with the fingers cut out. She flexed her fingers around the wheel's grip.

"You know how to drive, right?"

"Of course." Her brows lowered over her eyes as she scanned the console.

"Let me guess, your chauffeur usually drives you."

Typical.

She tipped her nose in the air. "Actually, I like to walk in the city most days."

"Of course you do."

He settled back on the bench while she acquainted herself with the lights and pedals.

These were summer cats, wind-powered trolleys with fat rubber tires that could take on just about any terrain. They had no suspension to speak of. The squad would sit on hard benches for the duration of the journey. They weren't comfortable, but they were reliable. There was always wind in the Meadows, but if for whatever reason, the wind failed them, the cats could run on thera fuel cells too.

Rowan was hitting buttons on the console and the cat's sails started to unfurl.

Conall grinned. "You think we'll fit out the garage door like that?"

She scowled and hit the button again. "I've never driven a cat, just the thera cars in the city." They waited while the mechanical wings winched back into their pockets. Then she turned on the thera engine. It was noisy and slow, but it would get them through the city streets.

Bretta's cat was already out the door. Rowan jammed the gear shaft up and to the left and released the clutch. They lurched forward with a great grinding of gears.

Rowan shot him a savage grin. "Hold onto your breakfast, Commander."

Conall grunted as he was thrust back in his seat.

It was going to be a long trip.

8

SHIFTING GEARS

Every FIFTEEN-YEAR-OLD LEARNED TO DRIVE, EVEN Rowan, though she'd had few opportunities to practice. One of her rare joys was taking a thera car out of the palace, and racing around the city. Regent Atherton heartily disapproved of such behavior, and the palace garage attendants had been ordered not to let her near the cars. She still managed to sneak one out from time to time.

The meadow cat worked on the same principal as the town cars, though it was a more lumbering beast. The first few feet out of the garage were rough.

Rowan pressed the clutch, ready to change gears. The cat balked before she could release the accelerator too. She yanked on the gear shaft and winced as gears ground. They slowed to a near standstill as she tried to accelerate in second gear. The cat lurched like a drunk before catching enough steam to roll smoothly.

Beside her, the commander's head banged against the seat. His crossbow was braced on the floor between his ankles and he clung to it.

Rowan tried to shift to third and ground the gears again.

"Fuckety-fuck-fuck." She channeled Auntie Bella.

Conall hunkered down, no doubt trying to minimize the effects of whiplash, but a smile teased his expression. Maybe the wolf wasn't made of stone after all.

The traffic heading toward North Gate slowed and Rowan struggled to downshift as they came to an intersection. Bretta and the others rolled through the crossroads, but Rowan's cat stalled. She pounded on the wheel in frustration as she started the engine yet again.

"Try to relax," Conall said. "Tensing up only makes the transition from clutch to accelerator rougher."

"Thanks. I hadn't thought of that." She loved having someone explain mechanics to her, as if she hadn't been fixing machines since she was a child.

Conall grinned. He was enjoying her discomfort. Part of her wanted to make his ride even rougher, just to spite him, but pride wouldn't allow it. Instead, once she got them rolling and pushed the cat into second gear again, she released her knack. It ran along the wires and gears of the cat. Suddenly, she could sense how all the parts of the vehicle worked together. The clutch and accelerator barely kissed as they passed, like relay runners handing off a baton.

When the traffic cleared, their progress was smoother.

In truth, it wasn't her knack. Her mech arm did all the communing with the vehicle. She just reaped the benefits.

She squeezed the wheel and felt the machine respond to her needs. Everything inside her calmed. The tension left her shoulders and spine. Her feet easily found the right pedals and the cat drove on with a purr from its thera engine.

Conall nodded. "Good." It wasn't much of a compliment, but she'd take it.

His eyes never stopped scanning the crowded streets. This mission was dangerous, but all the monsters were outside the city wall and they hadn't passed through the gate yet. She wondered what other monsters Commander West was running from.

The crowd thinned as they neared North Gate, which was reserved for keepers and rangers. Unlike the other gates, there was no line of merchants and travelers waiting to get in or out. Their only delay was when Bretta handed over the squad's manifest and the gate guard counted heads in the cats to verify that all was in order. That manifest would be kept until they returned, and a roll call would be done again. The Meadows was a dangerous place. Not everyone who ventured out returned. Part of the gate commander's duty was to inform the next of kin for those who did not make it back.

The guard waved them through. Rowan easily slid the cat into first gear and headed outside the wall for only the third time in her life.

For nearly four hundred years, her family had ruled from the fortress attached to the north end of this wall. Tomasin Andula had risked everything to establish New Torwood. The old city was long gone by then, overrun by titans and gaunts. The people had scattered and lived in constant fear—fear of hunger and fear of monsters. But Tomasin grew tired of such a life. He knew they could do better. He moved his family east along the river, gathering to him an army of workers. Together they built a new city, with a wall tall enough to keep out the monsters.

Even if she wanted nothing to do with the running of the city, Rowan was proud of her ancestor's bravery and ingenuity. The wall was a true marvel that let life flourish in an otherwise harsh environment.

As the shadow of that wall fell behind them, Rowan peered backward hoping for one last glimpse of Talos, but the great automaton was around the south side at this time of day. From this vantage point, she couldn't even see the brass dome of his head above the wall.

A sudden and jagged longing hit her. She missed her Talos already. She missed her cozy tinker shop. And Auntie Bella. And her brother. She even missed her bedroom in the palace.

This is what homesickness feels like. No wonder they called it sickness. It felt like a stitch in her side and mild nausea from running too long in the heat. Phalian sensed her distress and unlatched from his cradle to run up her arm and sit on her shoulder.

She turned her attention back to the rumble of the cat. Mechs were always soothing. Their needs were easily understood. They wanted oil or wire or thera to keep going. A mech never complained about homesickness.

The energy moving through the cat steadied her, and the ache in Rowan's chest eased enough that she was able to enjoy the scenery.

Ahead, the Kanta Highway rolled out in an endless ribbon of brown. The fishy tang of the Ikon River blew over them though she couldn't see the water. It was somewhere to their right, but the ground swelled on either side of the road, filling her vision with tall grass that swayed and danced in the wind.

The other cats had stopped to wait for them. Rowan downshifted without hesitation.

"Let out the sails," Conall said. "Now we fly."

Rowan hit the button and the compartments on the cat's roof opened to let the great white wings unfurl. The thera engine automatically shut off, and within seconds, the wings snapped open and caught the wind. The cat raced forward, and the steering wheel was ripped from her grasp. It lurched sideways, kicking up dust and stalled.

"What are you doing?" Conall yelled.

"I don't know!" She flung her hands in the air.

He leaned over and grabbed the steering wheel, then her mech hand. He wrapped her black-gloved fingers around the wheel and gave them a squeeze. The hand's innumerable sensors felt the heat and strength of his grip.

"Don't let go again."

She licked her lips which were already dry from the wind. "Maybe you should drive."

"Do you know what a bison stampede looks like on the horizon? Or how the grass moves when gaunts are lurking, ready to attack?"

"No."

"Then you drive and I'll be the lookout."

Rowan peered behind her, looking for help, but Orson had stretched out in the last car and was fast asleep. Or pretending. Elias looked as freaked out as she felt. It would be too much to hope he could drive. The elf would barely see over the console.

"Fine." She released the brakes slowly and straightened out the cat. Wind buffeted them. She adjusted the wings to take advantage of this natural power, and they rolled forward. At least she no longer had to deal with the clutch.

She slowed to let the other cats pass, but Bretta waved her forward. It seemed they were to take the lead. Conall didn't comment. They'd obviously worked together closely in the past. Bretta had taken point inside the city, dealt with deployment of rangers in the cats and the guards at the gate. But once outside the wall, she automatically deferred to Conall. Rowan felt a little pang of envy that he and Bretta knew each other well enough to communicate without words.

The wind power was stronger than the thera engine and they moved away from the city at a good clip. She could feel Conall's eyes turning to her often. He probably thought she would panic with the speed of the cat. She wouldn't give him that satisfaction. She gripped the wheel tightly, but the new energy humming through the cat was vibrant. It tingled through her fingers and filled her with anticipation instead of dread. Instinctively, she knew when to adjust the wings. There was a slight vibration through the cat when they weren't in sync with the wind. She pulled a toggle to fine-tune them and the vibration eased.

Conall nodded as if he'd made up his mind about her, then he turned to the back seat.

"Elias, keep watch to the north. You see anything coming out of that grass, you let me know."

The elf shifted positions to better watch the Meadows. Conall loaded a bolt onto his crossbow and rested it across his knees with the arrow pointing to where the Ikon River snaked unseen through the grasses. It was more likely they'd be attacked by titans coming out of the water, and he was ready for them.

Without the rumble of the thera engine, the cat glided quietly over the hard-packed ground. The road ahead was empty and seemingly endless. She glanced behind them to see the other cats following at a safe distance. From high on the city wall, they had looked like undulating caterpillars. At ground level, with their sails stretched out like wings, they looked more like swans ready to fly.

They drove for hours, stopping only once for Murdoch to hand out dry rations. By late afternoon, the novelty of driving had worn off, but so had Rowan's nervousness. She could now divide her attention between the cat and the amazing landscape.

She'd expected the Meadows to be desolate—empty and silent. But as the cat bumped over the terrain, they were met by a cacophony of yips and chirps from unseen creatures. Cicadas filled the background with a constant, droning harmony. One bird's voice rose above all the others in a constant, screeching monologue, but Rowan couldn't see it in the tall grass.

She'd heard that the Meadows were filled with wonders from the ancient past. But only once did the frame of a building appear in the distance. Rowan was eager to gaze upon the marvels of a lost world, but as they drove by, she saw it was little more than a cement foundation with two standing walls.

Another misconception she'd had was that the Meadows were only grass. Yes, they drove through mile after mile of knee-high stalks that never seemed to stand still, but there were also patches of bare rock, and gullies where streams meandered toward the Ikon, collecting caribou, foxes and bears that watched the cat roll by with cautious eyes. Mountains lurked to the north, great beasts that seemed to swallow the sky.

Old mechs roamed the Meadows too, rusted automatons that had been lost or let loose by their masters in the city to wander without purpose. They sat where their thera chips had run out, slowly rusting away like relics from another age.

Some kind of massive flightless bird kept pace with their cat for a while. A smaller red bird rode on its back like a sultan on a plush palanquin. Phalian launched from her shoulder, transformed in midair and flew alongside them for about a mile until the giant bird stopped to peck at the ground. Phalian fluttered around the pair while the cat trundled on, then he zoomed in like a hummingbird and landed on his cradle again.

"You're going to lose that thing," Conall said.

Rowan hadn't really thought of it. Phalian always came back. Always.

"I don't think he's in much danger unless there's a predator around that eats mech."

"Animals aren't the only trouble we'll find out here." As he spoke, his eyes never stopped scanning the grasses. He pointed ahead and to the left. "Pull over there. We'll take a short break."

Thank the saints. Rowan had been sipping from her canteen all afternoon to combat the dehydrating wind and now her bladder was ready to burst.

The rangers climbed stiffly from the cats and stood in a loose circle in the road.

"Stretch your legs," Bretta said. "Get something to eat, but no one wanders."

"I've got to pee real bad." Clem hopped up and down.

Bretta frowned. "Stay within shouting distance. And take someone with you."

"I'll go," Rowan said. "I have to pee too."

Noah looked startled.

She winked at him. "What? Princesses pee too."

"Yeah," Clem said. "Did you think her pee just magically effervesces or something?"

Noah frowned. Beside him, Augie was turning a ripe shade of red.

"I…I didn't really think about it at all," Noah said.

"Well, maybe you should. Come on, Princess." Clem tugged on Rowan's arm.

As she passed them, Rowan whispered to Noah, "Sometimes, I even fart."

Bretta was grinning, but Conall kept his expression locked down tight.

Rowan had only a knife as a weapon, so she was happy to let Clem take the lead with her rail gun as they tramped through the long grass. Phalian flew on ahead. She couldn't actually see through his eyes, but he sent back impressions. If something big lurked out there, he'd send up an alarm.

A crunch of footsteps behind them told her Orson followed. So far, Rowan had steadfastly ignored the scribe, but Clem spun around and pointed the gun at his gut. "I have to pee. The princess does too. You don't need to document that for posterity. If you follow us, I'll shoot you."

Orson's brows came together. "Scribes are sacrosanct."

"You can tell that to the beetles eating your corpse." Clem jerked the gun at him. Orson's eyes narrowed, but he crossed his arms and stood his ground.

"Good dog. Stay." Clem backed away. Phalian zipped around Orson's head, and he swatted futilely at the mech before Rowan called him back.

A large boulder jutted from the grass ahead. Clem ducked behind it and tugged at Rowan to join her. They collapsed to the ground with their backs against the rock. Clem pressed a hand over her mouth to keep the sound of her giggle from traveling.

Phalian perched on the boulder and said, "TWEET!" That set Clem off again and she let out a burst of laughter that startled a cloud of buntings from their afternoon roost. They added to the noise with their gabbling as they flew away.

Clem finally got control of herself.

"Thanks for that." Rowan hiked a thumb back toward Orson.

"No problem. That was kind of fun. *Scribes are sacrosanct.* What an ass." She shook her head, then cocked it at an angle to stare at Rowan. "You know, you're not anything like what I imagined."

"Yeah. I get that a lot."

"When I was a little girl, I wanted to be a princess too."

"I get that a lot too."

Rowan's stomach clenched. Was this going to be one of those conversations? The kind where she had to feign magnanimity? Pretend to be honored by the desires of a little girl who knew nothing about what it was like to live in that shambling old palace. Clem quickly abolished all such thoughts when she handed the rail gun to Rowan.

"Here. Keep watch for a sec." She unbuttoned her pants, dancing from foot to foot. "I thought he'd never call a halt. Commander's got a bladder like an elephant."

Rowan turned her back as Clem squatted.

The fading light lit the grasslands like a sea of gold. Stalks waved in mesmerizing patterns and glinting highlights. Conall was right. It would be easy for a large creature to move unseen through that.

Clem rose and reached for the rail gun. "Your turn."

Rowan hesitated. Was that section of grass swaying differently? Her eyes locked on the unusual pattern, but the sparkling highlights had ruined her eyesight.

"What's the matter?" Clem asked. "Too shy to pee in front of someone else?"

Rowan, who'd had attendants wash her, dress her, and attend to all her needs since she was a child, had no such inhibitions.

"No. I thought I saw something."

Clem frowned and pointed the gun into the Meadows. They waited, not even daring to breathe. The wind flattened the grass for a moment. The stalks collapsed in an even wave of gold.

When nothing jumped out to eat them, Clem said. "Hurry up. We should get back."

Rowan squatted and did her business. Clem politely turned her back and continued to scan for predators.

"But seriously, I was a total fan-girl. I had the Princess Andula doll and everything. And I wore a black glove for weeks. Pretending I had a mech arm too."

Crouched in the shadows, Rowan listened to Clem with a sinking heart. Finally, she rose, tucked in her shirt and straightened her clothes. Clem was staring out at the Meadows, but she shot Rowan a shy smile.

She had to nip this fan-girl stuff in the bud.

"You weren't the only little girl to want a mech arm just like the princess. One girl from Bailey tried to cut off her own arm with a butcher knife. She was ten years old."

Clem gasped and her gun dipped as she turned to Rowan.

"What happened to her?"

"The wound got infected and she died. I wanted to go to her funeral but the regent wouldn't allow it."

Clem was silent. Her gaze returned to the dancing grasses.

"I guess you hate all that stuff, being a royal and in the spotlight all the time."

"It's not so bad." It really was, but Rowan had learned that no one wanted to hear that. "But out here, I want to be a ranger, nothing more. It's bad enough to have a scribe following me everywhere."

"I'm really sorry." Clem fiddled with the grip on her gun. "I'll try to tone down the princess talk."

"Thanks."

"Orson is an ass, though. I don't know how you put up with him poking his nose in your business all day."

"He's just doing his job. You get used to it. When I was younger, I was never allowed to be alone. A nurse even slept in my room at night."

"Really? That's awful. How did you…you know." Clem made a diddling motion near her crotch.

"Very quietly."

"I bet."

Rowan grinned. "This must be what they call 'girl talk.' I didn't realize it was so…"

"So fun?"

"So personal."

"Yeah, well, who else can you talk about this stuff with if not your girlfriends?"

Rowan smiled. "I never had a friend who was a girl. Unless you count my Auntie Bella."

"Huh." Clem scrutinized her in a way that made Rowan uncomfortable. "I guess I never thought about what life as a princess would really be like. I just thought it was all galas and fancy dresses. To a girl like me, growing up in Squall's End, it sounded like a lot of fun."

"It can be. But it can also be lonely and very boring." Rowan rubbed her mech hand. "That's why I took up tinkering. Strangely, when I'm fixing Talos, I'm more alone than ever, and yet I never feel lonely."

"Because you're good at your job. I get that. When you're good at something, it becomes like a friend that you always want to be with. That's why I'm opening my own shop as soon as my ranger service is finished."

They were walking now, heading back to the highway. Clem kept her rail gun primed and ready to shoot any rodent that might scuttle from behind the rocks.

"What kind of shop?" Rowan was genuinely curious. With her brick-red curls and brilliant blue eyes, Clem seemed a bit fey to Rowan, like she belonged among the exotic birds of the Meadows. She couldn't imagine the girl spending her days behind a shop counter.

"I'm a finder. Lost items, people. It's also what makes me a good sniper. My shots always find their mark."

"Wow. That's a great knack. I'm jealous."

They stopped for a moment at a spot where the land fell away at their feet, giving them a spectacular view of the Meadows.

"So what about you?" Clem asked. "What's your knack?"

Rowan held up her mech arm. Phalian took that as a sign and flew back to land on her wrist.

"My mech can do some pretty cool things, but I'm a magical dud."

"Huh. Who knew a princess would ever be jealous of me?"

"It's all about perspective."

"Still, your arm is pretty cool. And that bird too."

"His name is Phalian. And yeah, I wouldn't trade either of them for my own knack."

A soft sawing sound came from the Meadows. The women froze. Clem lifted the gun and squinted into the sun. Nothing moved except for the swaying stalks.

"There!" Rowan whispered. The grass shuddered and parted slightly before swallowing whatever moved stealthily through it.

"I see it." Clem's rail gun held only two projectiles, and they were cumbersome weapons to reload. As the grasses started to sway again, Rowan hoped Clem wasn't just bragging about her knack because something was coming. Fast.

With her eye pressed to the sight, Clem swiveled the gun to follow the creature's progression.

And fired.

9

IN THE SHADOW OF THE THREE SISTERS

Conall WATCHED THE TRAIL DOWN WHICH Clem, Rowan and the scribe had disappeared. When the scribe came back alone, he almost went into the Meadows after them, but he found Bretta watching the trail too. She gave him a nod and a smile. He could almost hear her admonishment to let the ducklings spread their wings. It was the only way they'd learn. And if she could let her little sister go off alone, Conall could too.

The scribe stepped into his path.

"A word, Commander West."

Conall nodded at him to speak.

"A scribe's duty is paramount and I cannot do that duty unless I have complete access to the royal."

The royal? He spoke about Rowan like she was a buffet table at a gala event.

"You're mad because she didn't let you watch her pee?"

Orson's mouth opened, then he thought better of the words that almost came out. He closed it, took a deep breath and tried again.

"One never knows when an event of great importance might occur. A titan could be ripping the royal to pieces right now!" He pointed into the meadows. "And there will be no record of her demise."

Garou growled. Conall's fists tightened and he wished they were around the scribe's thick neck.

"All I'm saying is that I need freedom to do my job. And it's your job as commander to see that freedom is granted."

Conall's nose twitched like he smelled something foul.

"You've already made it clear that I have no authority over you, and that's fine. But my job is not to make your job easier. I have a mission to complete and a squad to keep alive. That's it. If you need help to do your job, I'll note that in my report and I'm sure the council will sort it out for your next assignment."

Orson opened his mouth to argue, but Conall held up a hand.

"Save it." He spied Clem and Rowan returning. He was glad to see Clem's rail gun primed and her eyes scanning the fields. Rowan carried a derelict old mech in her arms.

"What is that?" he asked as they reached the cats.

"Clem shot it," Rowan said.

"I thought it was a hare or something Murdoch could cook."

Murdoch eyed the hunk of rusting metal covered in moss and sniffed. "I've cooked worse." He wandered away to board his cat.

Rowan hugged the mech. "He's kidding, right?"

"Probably," Conall said. "You keeping that thing? It's dead."

"It was moving before Clem shot it. It's a valet, I think. But a real antique."

Conall nodded toward the cat. "Stow it in the back, if you must, but hurry. We have a lot of road to burn before we make camp at the Three Sisters tonight."

As they drove down the Kanta Highway, Conall tried to dismiss the utter relief he'd felt when he'd seen the women return to the road. He told himself that the relief was mostly for Clem. After all, she was like a niece to him. Garou snorted at that thought. That was the problem with sharing your mind with a wolf. You could never lie to yourself.

Another TWO HOURS OF TRAVEL AND they were still on the old highway. It seemed to never change. The endless grass on either side was mesmerizing. Conall could see that Rowan was dazed as she drove.

"Slow down," he said. "There's a turn coming soon. We'll need to shut the sails."

Rowan squinted and leaned toward the windscreen. He knew she was thinking that the road ahead looked straight and unchanging. But the wolf's senses were sharper and Conall had traveled this way many times before.

He could already sense the tingle of resonance coming off the Three Sisters. They weren't far now.

Rowan slowed the cat to a stop at a track that bisected the highway. They quickly stowed the sails.

Conall turned in his seat to address the other two cats as well.

"Keep vigilant. This road is short, and we're unlikely to encounter any wildlife here, but I want everyone alert." He met a few wide eyes from the greens. Bretta's expression was pinched. She was feeling the pull of the Sisters too.

He motioned for Rowan to start the engine and they left the highway for a road that wasn't much wider than a deer track.

The beauty of the Meadows suddenly turned menacing.

The grass grew tall here, almost as tall as the cat's roof. And it closed around them. Conall could reach out and touch it.

A titan could drag Rowan from her seat and disappear before Conall ever got a shot off. That was silly, of course. Resonance from the Three Sisters would keep the titans away, but the image of Rowan being dragged off lingered with him.

"I thought we were going to follow the highway all the way to Oxeye," she said, not taking her eyes off the shifting shadows in the grass.

"We are, but it's not safe to sleep out in the open. It's not far now. Look." He pointed forward. The wall of grass on either side fell away and they emerged onto a wide, rocky plateau. Three tall spires jutted into the sky.

Rowan stopped the cat. The others pulled up alongside. Everyone gaped at the scene ahead.

"Is that the…" Rowan seemed at a loss for words.

Conall nodded and grinned. "The Three Sisters." The midnight sun lit them with dramatic highlights and shadows. They *did* look like three giant women standing in a field. One even seemed to be holding a basket. Another was slightly bent as if she had just stooped to gather the harvest. And they sparkled. Conall knew it was just the sun hitting bits of quartz in their makeup, but they looked like they were glowing from within.

Rowan's mouth fell open as she stared up at the five-story-high rock formations.

"I read about them, of course," she said, "but nothing that could prepare me for…for this."

He felt unreasonably happy for being the first one to show her such an incredible sight. But that happiness was an uncomfortable feeling for a lone wolf.

"Quit gaping at them, and park the cat," he growled. "We need to set up camp before dark."

"Sure thing, Commander. Don't get your panties in a twist."

Rowan rolled the cat into the shadow of the giant sisters.

At THIS TIME OF YEAR, THE sun shone for twenty-one hours a day. In the city, people went to bed and rose in daylight. They never experienced darkness. Conall knew darkness. In the Meadows night was short and sharp and brutal. Predators hunted. Prey hid. And gaunts went a little crazy.

They were fortunate to spend their first night in the shadow of the Three Sisters. It would be the last time they slept in safety until they returned to New Torwood.

Bretta already had duties divided up and the rangers were busy with camp chores, except for Noah, who stood with his back to the giant rock formations, gazing northward, where the sun was flirting with the edge of the Ubruulens.

"Was it really necessary to come so far out of our way to camp for the night?" he asked.

Garou snorted dismissively. *Greens.*

Conall rubbed the spot between his brows where he felt the weight of the world pressing down on him.

He may be green, but it's our job to teach him. Think of him as a pup. Pups don't ask dumb questions.

Conall ignored the wolf. Standing this close to the Three Sisters made him crotchety. Or more crotchety than usual.

"You'll want these rocks at your back when the sun sets," Conall said. "The grass can hide a full grown bison titan."

Noah turned toward the meadows that now shone like gold in the waning light.

"You think there are titans this close to the city?"

"We left the protection of the keepers as soon as we lost sight of the city walls," Conall said. "But don't worry. The Three Sisters sit on a crossing of two ley-lines. Can you feel it?"

He held a hand to the stones. Noah did too, and his eyes widened.

"You have a sensitivity to resonance."

Noah nodded.

"Animals are much more attuned to it than any human. Gaunts and titans even more so. None will come within a mile of the Sisters."

Bretta called Noah over to help Augie fill the water jugs from a small stream that ran below the Sisters. The others were also busy. Murdoch and Elias were setting up a small camp kitchen. They'd have a hot meal tonight. It might be their last for a while. Rowan and Clem left the camp to find whatever firewood was available. Conall had to stop himself from following them. Again.

You work yourself up for no reason, Garou said. *This is sacred ground. Nothing will harm them here.*

Still, he was almost glad when Orson rose from the back of a cat and trailed after them.

Bretta was watching Conall as he watched the girls leave.

"Saints have mercy on him if he tries to watch them pee again."

"Not too much mercy," Conall said.

Bretta laughed and swatted him on the shoulder. "Murdoch says supper's in thirty." She left him to his vigil. He watched the trail until the women returned, each carrying an armful of wood. It wasn't enough for a decent fire, and Murdoch told them to stow it in the cat for later.

"I got the thera stove going anyway," he said.

Conall followed the cook back to camp where he saw that in less than an hour, Murdoch had set up a kitchen and cooked a stew from their rations. Now he slouched on a stool nearby, looking like a pile of wilted rags. The stove radiated little heat and just enough light to see faces as the sun finally dipped behind the northern peaks.

Lena and Valko were on watch but the others congregated around the thera stove, and Elias handed out bowls.

The wolf wasn't the only one who thought their lunch of bison jerky and trail mix seemed like a lifetime ago. Rowan accepted her bowl and immediately tucked into it.

"Good, yes?" said the elf.

"Really good." Rowan spoke with her mouth full. Such a graceful princess. Elias grinned and handed Conall his ration. The wolf let out a satisfied grunt as he took his first bite. The dark broth was thickened with potato and squash. Chunks of some red meat floated with carrots, peas and herbs. Conall thought he tasted rosemary and a hint of nutmeg, both decadent spices for a simple camp stew.

Oh, yes, Dale had fulfilled their promise when he recruited Murdoch as their camp cook.

The others were as hungry as he was and ate in silence, except for Augie who'd already finished his meal and he hummed quietly. He was too polite to ask for seconds, but Elias took his empty bowl and refilled it anyway. The humming stopped as Augie tucked into his second meal.

Good to know there was one thing that kept the kid quiet—food.

Orson didn't join the group. He sat outside the stove's glow with his back against one of the stone sisters. His legs were laid out flat in front of him, and his hands rested in his lap, palms up. A slack jaw let his mouth hang open and his eyes were unfocused. If it weren't for the subtle twitching of his fingers, Conall would have thought him dead.

Clem pointed her fork at him. "Creepy bastard."

"He's recording." Conall had seen scribes do this before. Normally, they went into seclusion before falling into a trance to record the day's events, but he'd seen it happen a few times when the scribe felt an urgency to have facts secured. He suspected that Orson would prefer some privacy while his brain rendered his report to whatever mech device scribes used to store data, but he was probably too afraid to venture far from camp alone.

"So what is he recording?" Clem asked. "We drove down the highway. There was grass. We drove some more. There was more grass. Very exciting."

"Future generations will be riveted by that tale," Noah said. "Maybe you should have let him watch you pee."

Clem flung a piece of carrot at him. Noah caught it and grinned as he popped it into his mouth.

Orson finished transcribing and came to join them. If he'd heard their teasing, he didn't remark on it. He took his bowl from Elias and sat slightly apart from the squad.

Elias handed out small mugs and Conall was surprised that Murdoch rose to pour a drink for each of them from a large water bladder. Until now, he'd let Elias do all the serving.

Murdoch wasn't much taller than the elf, but he was stout as a barrel. A black beard peppered with gray hid his lips, just as bushy brows nearly obscured his eyes. As he poured water into Rowan's cup, his eyes twinkled.

"A fine vintage for the lady."

Rowan smiled at his teasing, but when she took a sip, she nearly choked. "That's not water!"

Murdoch winked as he poured some into Conall's cup.

Conall took a sip. It was wine. A strong, velvety red.

"Where did you get this?"

"It's a knack," Murdoch said. "Not one I share openly. But it's not every day you get to dine in the shadow of the great Sisters."

Bretta and Murdoch shared an amused look at the stunned faces of the squad. She'd served a time with Murdoch during the war. She must have known.

Conall considered refusing the drink, for all of them. The squad watched, waiting for his verdict. Finally, he lifted his cup high. "To Murdoch and his very welcome knack."

"Did you really turn water into wine?" Rowan took another sip.

Murdoch raised the water bladder as if to answer Conall's toast.

"So you're basically god," Clem said.

"Something like that." Murdoch winked.

Conall sipped the wine. It was stronger than a normal vintage. Garou stifled a sneeze. He never understood the humans' desire to poison themselves.

"Don't think that means you get to drink to excess on this little party," Conall said. "One cup only. Everyone will take a watch shift tonight and I need you all alert."

"Yes, Commander!" Clem gave a mocking salute then took a deep drink from her mug.

With a bit of alcohol in their bellies, the squad members loosened up. Conversation started to flow, which was exactly why he'd allowed it. These rangers needed to learn to act as a unit. They needed to care for each other in a way that was as intimate as family. They couldn't do that if they remained strangers. It was a lesson he'd learned in the war. Fear and respect could only take a squad so far. Loyalty would bolster soldiers when all else failed.

But the war had ended a long time ago. He'd spent the intervening years traveling as a lone wolf. Just sitting here with a group, made him slightly antsy. He wasn't confident that he could sharpen this squad into a fighting unit. But he had to try.

It would help if you paid attention to what they're saying. Garou snorted.

As if you're any less of a lone wolf than me.

But Conall turned his focus outward. Clem was telling the tale about the first time Bretta came home from the war and devoured an entire roast pig. She had a gift for storytelling and even Augie forgot to hum while she spoke.

Bretta retaliated with stories of Clem as a child.

"Well, Clem was a royal wannabe. She even had the Princess Andula action figure. How does that make you feel now that you've met the real princess?"

Bretta's words weren't mocking, but Conall glanced at Rowan, worried that she would feel the sting of being called out.

And why would you care if her feelings are hurt?

He ignored the wolf's commentary.

A conspiring look passed between Rowan and Clem, and Clem said, "You can't embarrass me, Sis. I already confessed my fan-girl tendencies to Rowan. She's cool with it, aren't you?"

"Very cool."

Another silent communication passed between the two.

Isn't that interesting. Maybe there's hope for these squadlings after all.

That feeling of goodwill lasted only until Orson cut in.

"You're an action figure!" He laughed and pressed his index and middle fingers to the ground, making them walk toward Rowan. "Look at me. I'm a princess with a stick up my ass!"

Clem rolled her eyes. She stood up and tripped over Orson's hands.

"Ow!" He stuck a finger in his mouth, then shook it out. "Clumsy oaf."

"I'm so sorry." Clem gave him a wide, innocent smile. "I have big feet and they're always tripping over stupid things."

Unlike her sister, Clem was petite. All eyes went to her tiny feet.

"Bitch." Orson stuck his hand under his armpit.

"Puckered duck ass." Clem smiled down on the scribe.

"That's enough." Conall's voice rumbled like thunder. "Clem, sit down."

"Can't, Commander. I'm on watch." She grabbed her rail gun and gave a little finger wave to Orson before heading out to relieve Lena.

Rowan cleared her throat. "I'd like to address the titan in the room." All eyes turned to her. "You all have lives, families and friends back in New Torwood. So do I. But out here in the Meadows we have only each other. I'm here to keep the cats rolling. If they fail, we fail and then it won't matter that I'm a princess. So please, call me Rowan or Maven or even 'hey you' but not Princess. Only the mission matters."

Conall looked around the group. They were solemn, but heads bobbed in agreement.

Lena arrived and immediately headed for the food, then sat cross-legged in front of the thcra stove with her bowl in her lap. The conversation had lulled. Conall was thinking about ordering everyone to their bedrolls when Orson broke the silence.

"So what exactly is the mission, Commander?"

Conall glanced at the scribe with a frown. "You know already. We're going to check on a bunch of science nerds who can't figure out how to use a graphium."

"Seems a bit sketch to me. Why send a whole squad from the city when the Oxeye Outpost is closer?"

"The council believes it is necessary." Conall kept his tone quiet and even, as if speaking to a child. "The scientists are from one of the big cities down south. Dowchester, I believe. New Torwood is supposed to be hosting them."

"And what kind of hosts would we be if we let them get eaten by gaunts. Is that it?" Orson finished for him. "We're trying to avoid a diplomatic situation?"

"Something like that."

"Just seems like a lot of fuss for nothing," grumbled Orson. "I mean if their graphium is busted, they'll get a new one with their next shipment of food, won't they? And if not, well, we're just an overpaid burial team."

"Do you ever shut up?" Lena asked. "I mean seriously. Don't you ever get tired of the sound of your own voice?" This outburst was unexpected from the tracker who hadn't spoken more than two words since leaving the city.

Orson's black eyes blazed. "Do you ever get tired of being a whiny old hag? I bet you've never even been laid, have you." He dropped that little bomb, then sat back against the rock with a self-satisfied grin.

Lena looked stunned. Her face seemed extra pale in the starlight. After a moment of frozen silence, she scrambled to her feet and took off into the night.

Bretta rose to go after her but stopped to kick Orson on the leg.

"Ow!"

"You're a jerk. Her wife just died." Bretta followed Lena, and in a moment Conall heard her low voice trying to soothe the upset tracker.

Orson rubbed his leg. His wide eyes looked at the faces around the thera stove but he found no sympathy. "What? How was I supposed to know?"

Conall turned to him. "You have been a disruption since we left the city. From now on, you'll hold your tongue. You speak to my rangers only when necessary."

"You can't command me." Orson looked smug. "Scribes are outside your purview. Remember, *Commander*?"

The stress of the situation was too much for Augie. His humming ratcheted up a notch and he hovered a couple of inches off the ground. The mech bird launched into the air and circled Rowan's head.

Orson sat back with a sly grin, confident in his scribe's armor, and pleased with the chaos he'd fostered.

"Would you like to sleep outside my purview too?" Conall's tone was soft, almost a whisper and he pointed to the darkness of the Meadows. Orson's grin melted "We'll be camping in the open tomorrow and every night after," Conall continued. "There is safety only in numbers. If you insist on being an outsider, I will treat you like one."

Orson glanced outside the ring of the Three Sisters. He licked his lips.

"Fine. Whatever."

"I believe you owe Tracker Albright an apology." Conall couldn't command the scribe, but his tone made it clear he wasn't asking.

Orson scowled. He mumbled something that might have been "I'm sorry."

"Tomorrow, you can apologize again when she's close enough to hear you."

Orson glared at him, but nodded.

Conall sighed. He'd lost control of things this night.

"Augie, settle down please."

Augie thumped to the ground. Noah gripped his shoulder and whispered into his ear. The humming fizzled out.

The kid's singing was starting to wear on Conall's nerves. It seemed to always be there in the background, like a tiny mosquito buzzing in his ear. He rubbed his forehead. If he'd hoped to forge camaraderie among the squad, he'd failed.

He ordered everyone to sleep, except those on watch. Tomorrow they might have to face gaunts or titans, and they were nowhere near ready.

10

Meadow Larks

They LEFT THE RELATIVE SAFETY OF the Three Sisters at midmorning and returned to the highway. They would follow the Ikon River for another two days until it widened into Lake Oxeye. In the last ten years, a thera farming town had been built along its banks with a ranger outpost to protect it. Despite the warnings of an epidemic in the town, Conall planned to stop in Oxeye for news before turning north.

Bretta's cat had the lead, followed by Lena with Valko as look out. Rowan drove the third cat and Conall kept his crossbow armed and lying across his knees. Periodically, he turned in his seat to be sure nothing snuck up on them from behind, but mostly he kept his sights trained on the small rise of land between the road and river.

Lena's cat kicked up dust about three hundred yards ahead. Valko leaned sideways with one foot on the dashboard. His gun drooped in his hand.

"Damned foolish green," Conall muttered. They were getting complacent. The warm sun and constant rumble of the road beneath their wheels would do that.

Conall reached for the vox on the cat's dashboard. He flicked it open to the channel that would broadcast to the entire squad.

"Wake the hell up," he snarled. "This isn't a Sunday drive in the park. There are titans in that river that can crush your cat with their fists. Stay awake. Stay alert or we'll leave your body at the side of the road for the vultures."

He slammed the vox back into its cradle. Ahead, Valko jerked upright in his seat and his gun swung toward the river.

"Idiot probably doesn't even have it primed."

"You have a very unusual leadership style, Commander," Rowan said. "Like the only tool in your bag is a hammer."

"It gets the job done. And I'm not here to coddle anyone."

"I see that."

Rowan returned her attention to the road as they drove around a tumble of old mech debris.

He *was* a hammer, and he wanted to drive home the point. His sole job was to keep the squad alive and return them in one piece. He was about to belabor that point once more, but motion caught his eye. He swung the crossbow around as a creature crested the river bank. Rowan saw it at the same time, and the cat swerved as the creature heaved itself onto the edge of the road.

It looked like an otter, but with a piggish snout and upward curving tusks. And it had to weigh fifty pounds at least. Its long, sleek body slithered along the bank, following their caravan for a while. Conall turned in his seat to keep the crossbow trained on it, but the beast lost interest when a meadow lark swooped past its nose. A paw whipped out and swiped the bird from the sky.

"What is it?" Rowan's head swiveled to see behind them.

"Eyes on the road, Maven. It's just a fisher rat looking for an easy meal."

She nodded, but didn't seem mollified. The pink fingers of her left hand squeezed and released the steering wheel. It was a nervous gesture that the mech hand didn't copy.

Conall had a sudden and fleeting image of her in court dress. Did she have matching white lacy gloves to cover the mech? That seemed wrong somehow. She was pretty enough that he could imagine her in such a dress, but she seemed so…perfect in the ranger fatigues, black gloves and all.

Garou sniggered in his mind.

What's your problem, brother?

The wolf let his amusement be felt. *It's been a long time since you imagined a woman in any kind of dress.*

I'm only curious about the mech. That's all.

Of course.

They DROVE EASTWARD FOR TWO DAYS. The sun flirted around the edges of the Meadows, crawling west during the day, dipping below the Ubruulens for a brief night and then continuing east into morning. At midday of their third day on the road, the sun hung over the southern horizon. Shadows from stunted trees and mech driftwood stretched across the road like fingers reaching from the Ikon River to pull unsuspecting travelers into its depth.

The shifting light was mesmerizing and Conall barked into the vox several times to keep the others alert. Finally, Bretta's voice came over the vox. She sang a bawdy song about a girl who lost her knickers in Grotto and found them hanging on the clock in old Bailey. The music was tinny coming over the vox, but it helped to keep the others alert.

When she finished, Augie took over the serenade. The young ranger seemed to know only one song—an ancient piece of symphony that children still learned to play on the piano. Unfortunately, Augie didn't know the words.

"Da-da-da-da, da-da-DAAAA-da-da," he hummed. Granted, he had a lovely tone and seemed to be able to mimic an entire orchestra. When he concluded, there was a brief silence with only the flap of the cat sails to break it. Then Augie launched into song again.

"Doesn't he know any other tune," Orson grumbled from the back seat.

"I like it." Elias sat forward and started humming along with Augie. Rowan joined in. Soon they could hear the tune, not just through the vox, but drifting back to them from the cats ahead as the entire squad became a choir.

They call to all the predators and scare away the prey, Garou groused.

At times like this—when he was tired and tense—Conall found it difficult to separate Garou's will from his own. The wolf's agitation was a constant irritation, like his mind was cushioned in nettles. And Garou didn't always understand the nuances of the human psyche. Conall's jaw clenched as he bit back the command for the squad to be silent. The predators already knew they were there, and maybe the singing would keep his team alert.

Eventually, the song petered out. Rowan slowed their cat as she saw the others stopped at a wooden bridge ahead. Lena and Clem were already lowering the sails.

Bretta hopped out and jogged over to them.

"We made good time. This is Station Four. You want to drive on? Or are we stopping?" She pointed to the side of the road by the bridge where a natural spring had been tapped. There were a handful of these stations along the highway, but the next one was another two-hour ride down the road.

"No. We'll rest here. Make sure someone's on point at the bridge while we eat." Conall unfolded his legs from the cramped cat. His hamstrings were tight and he longed for a run. Odd how he could walk thousands of miles through the Meadows without tiring, but a couple of days on a cat had him feeling like an old man.

Rowan jumped lithely from the driver seat and immediately did a quick tour of all three vehicles. She dragged her mech hand along the side of each cat while she checked their tires for possible punctures. He had to admit, the princess took her duties as mechanic seriously.

Murdoch and Elias were already doling out lunch from their food stores. They wouldn't be stopping long enough to cook, so lunch was cured sausage and hard cheese.

Garou gave a sneezing snort when Elias handed Conall his share.

Smells like feet left in sweaty boots for too long.

That's how you know it's good.

Conall took a bite to confirm it. The cheese melted on his tongue and perfectly complemented the savory sausage. Even Garou was appeased.

Augie chewed and hummed, his eyes focused inward. Conall was going to have to teach the kid vigilance. Sure they had posted a watch, but a ranger never left his safety entirely in someone else's hands.

"Augie, eyes out!"

Augie's head jerked up. He choked on his sausage and coughed, turning red. Conall thumped him on his back. No way this kid was going to survive out here. When Augie's coughing slowed, Conall said, "Stay alert."

Augie nodded vigorously.

Rowan sat with one hip in the driver seat and one leg dangling over the edge of their cat. Her mech bird soared and dove, then swooped in a loop around the cat before taking off again. While she ate, Rowan scanned the line of grass beside the road. Good. At least the maven had some sense.

The rest of the squad sat on the cat benches or leaned against the vehicles as they ate. Only Valko and Clem stood near the bridge. Valko kept his rail gun pointed toward the right riverbank, while Clem surveyed the left.

The bridge spanned a tributary that flowed with a swift current toward the great Ikon River. The water rushing under the bridge was dark and deep and hid its secrets well. Upstream a tumble of rocks made a short waterfall and the sound seemed to fill the entire Meadows.

Bretta finished her meal first. She jumped out of the cat, took a gun from the back seat and relieved Clem so she could eat.

Conall watched as Clem sauntered back to the cats. She threw a comment to her sister over her shoulder. With the rush of the waterfall, Conall didn't hear the comment, but assumed it was offensive when Bretta flipped her the bird. The striker grinned and shook her head. Her rail gun hung from a strap on her shoulder.

She never had the chance to raise it.

A titan launched from the river and swatted her with one massive flipper. Bretta screamed as she hit the ground a dozen yards away.

Conall was up and running, even as he nocked a bolt into his crossbow. Clem turned to face the titan.

Six hundred years ago, some god or demon had opened a valve on a leyline and let magic pour into the world. They called it the Resurgence. Doors to other worlds opened and closed—brief flashes that broke time and space. Otherworldly creatures came through those breaks. Monstrous creatures. Many of them took up residence in the mighty Ikon River. Giant squid, sharks and seals attacked any ship that dared to travel in their home, but some land animals appeared too. Bison-like beasts that were carnivorous killing machines, and smaller monsters like the fisher rat.

Then some time during the lost ages, while humans struggled to barely survive, magic receded, but the damage was done. The landscape and the creatures thriving within it were forever changed.

This titan was a walrus-like monster, twice the size of a normal walrus and with a maw of sharp teeth meant for rending flesh. Rolls of fat undulated as it pulled itself higher onto land. Razor sharp whiskers twitched on its leathery cheeks. Triple chins worked up and down as its jaw worked like an old man chewing his gums.

"Well, aren't you a cutie pie." Clem raised her gun and primed it. The titan roared, covering her in a spray of spittle.

She threw an arm over her face. "Gah! What a stench!"

"Clem, watch out!" Conall's words were too late. The titan undulated up the road, moving much faster than he could believe. It swatted Clem before she got a shot off.

Conall barely recorded the sizzling sound of Valko's rail gun as he shot the titan twice. It didn't even flinch. Valko struggled to reload. Conall jumped in front of the beast and released an arrow. It hit blubber. The titan roared again, inches from his face.

Conall gagged. The rotting fish stench of its breath was a weapon as sharp as any blade. It burned his lungs and blurred his eyes as tears leaked down his face. He ducked under the massive flipper as he coughed and tried to suck in fresh air. More gunfire came from behind him as the others got into the fight.

He tossed the bow aside and reached for his air knives. They were each twelve inches of thera-infused metal, vibrating with a natural magic that made them sharp enough to skin a deer and hard enough to penetrate the bone armor of a gaunt. Or the blubber of a walrus titan.

Conall raised the blades and leaped onto the titan. Garou was howling to be released as he stabbed down. The blades sunk into blubber up to their grips. He pulled them out and stabbed again. The creature roared and turned to snap at him. Teeth gnashed inches from his face and the stench of rotting fish hammered him again.

Valko had reloaded the cumbersome rail gun and he pulled the trigger. The gun released a galvanic pulse and launched its metal bolt. It sank into the creature's thick hide.

Conall reared back and stabbed again. His hands were slick with blood, but he was barely doing any damage.

Another volley of bolts came from behind him. Clem had recovered and opened fire. Lena also wielded a rail gun. None of it would matter. The creature's protective layer of fat was too thick.

To Conall's surprise, Augie jumped onto the titan, brandishing an ordinary knife. His cheeks were flushed pink and his blond hair flopped over his forehead as he floated four feet off the ground and drove his knife into titan flesh. He twisted as the flipper lashed out and sliced at the creature's joint where limb met blubber, all the while chanting his favorite anthem.

The kid's brave at least.

Together they sliced off bits of titan. They'd take it down piece by piece if they had to. Even the damned mech bird got in on the fight, using its metal beak like a stinger. The titan roared and tried to bite the air where Phalian had been a moment before. Conall danced over and under its thrashing limbs.

Bretta woke up as the beast shifted its weight and crushed her leg. She screamed. And screamed. And then the scream changed pitch. It grew into a roar that rivaled the titan's.

Saints, no!

Garou joined Bretta with a predatory howl of rage, and Conall had to steel himself against shifting forms.

Bretta's face contorted, then exploded into white fur. Her uniform shredded as her body doubled in size. In seconds, where a woman had been trapped under a giant walrus, a polar bear now thrashed.

Conall yanked his blades from the titan's hide and leaped free of the beast, pulling Augie with him.

The polar bear that had been Bretta swiped a massive paw across the titan's back, raking its flesh with claws that left deep, bloody gashes.

During her years as a ranger, Bretta had kept her bear a secret. Even when a gaunt had nearly severed her arm, she hadn't shifted. Even when Conall couldn't contain his wolf, she'd stayed solidly human.

Because the military refused to allow shifters in their ranks and all Bretta wanted was to serve New Torwood.

Conall had known, of course. Just as she could sense the wolf inside him. It was this secret that had bonded them in the first place. Conall hadn't been able to keep his wolf under wraps, but Bretta had served her term without discovery and been released from military service with full honors. Honors that would be stripped from her now.

The guns had fallen silent. Most of the squad watched the match between titan and bear with shocked disbelief. Only Conall and Clem were unsurprised. And Orson, who stared with a scribe's unrelenting focus.

The bear slapped the titan with an open paw. The titan roared and bit down. An ursine scream was followed by a swipe from the other paw and the titan released its grip. Bear and walrus bobbed and danced, rending flesh with teeth and claws. The titan's jaws clamped down on Bretta's arm again.

"We have to do something!" Clem yelled into Conall's ear, and he shook his head. Guns and blades had done little damage. Even a polar bear was no match for the rage-fueled monster. Bretta's only move was to retreat and hope the beast couldn't follow.

But Bretta was no longer in control. The bear had taken over, and she had a berserker mentality. She wouldn't stop until one of them was dead.

Clem screamed at her sister to fall back. The bear ignored her. Bretta leaped at the titan and struck a solid blow, but it was obvious that she was tiring. Pink streaks of blood mottled her fur. Most of it was Bretta's. She launched another attack. The titan used its powerful head like a battering ram and knocked the bear aside. Bretta fell, kicking up dirt and stones. The titan's head shot forward and clamped jaws onto her foot.

The bear screamed.

Lena leaped away from the watching squad and bolted toward the fight. Conall bellowed after her, but the tracker either didn't hear or willfully ignored him. She landed on the titan's back and screamed one unintelligible curse as she pounded it with clenched fists.

Conall remembered the note in Lena's file about her unique knack a moment before the titan turned to glass.

In the sudden quiet, Augie's *Ode to Joy* sounded like a dirge.

11

A KNACK FOR CONSEQUENCE

Bretta WAS A BEAR SHIFTER. A *polar* bear shifter!

Rowan was still trying to wrap her head around that fact when the fight staggered to its unbelievable conclusion. Polar bears had been extinct for hundreds of years. She'd only ever seen one in a sketch and the drawing didn't do it justice. Even sitting, Bretta's head was three feet above Rowan's. The bear was making an odd noise somewhere between a mewl and growl as it pounded a massive fist on the titan.

The glass titan.

Rowan's brain was still stuck on the unlikely bear. She shifted gears and stared at the dead titan.

At least she thought it was dead. Its hide had become translucent white and reflective. Dead eyes stared at the blue sky. Rowan reached out her mech hand. The titan's skin didn't conduct. It was smooth and cold.

"Is that…?"

"Glass," Conall confirmed. "She turned it to glass." He nodded toward Lena who sat on top of the titan, pounding her fists on its slick back and weeping.

That was one hell of a knack.

Clem approached with hands outstretched. "Bretta, are you okay?"

Turning the titan to glass may have saved Bretta, but her foot was still stuck in its mouth. She thrashed and let out a moan.

"Bretta, look at me. It's Clem. You need to shift. Come on!"

Clem obviously had experience dealing with Bretta's bear. She babbled on, never getting too close, but the sound of her sister's voice finally unlocked something in Bretta's mind. She shrank. Fur seemed to mist away in rough patches. Her body twisted. Joints popped. Then the shift stopped. A gurgling roar erupted from her throat. She lay there in a horrific mound of flesh and fur that was neither woman nor bear. Her sides heaved.

"Should it take this long?" Rowan whispered with a hand held to her mouth.

Conall shook his head.

The mound of flesh twisted again, shrinking and finally morphing into the shape of a naked woman, panting in the dirt. Her foot slipped from the titan's jaws.

It too had turned to glass.

Bretta took one look at her transparent appendage, let out a strangled cry, and fainted.

Rowan ran forward, pulling off her ranger jacket to cover Bretta. Conall was already at her side, scanning her for wounds. Blood had spattered his face and arms. Sweat washed it down Bretta's cheeks in streaks.

"Is she hurt?" Rowan knelt and pressed the fingers of her left hand to Bretta's throat. Conall nodded. He seemed reluctant to touch her. The question was ridiculous anyway, more of a knee-jerk reaction on Rowan's part. Bretta's body was a mess of wounds—deep sucking punctures from the titan's teeth, scrapes and bruises that were already blossoming red under the skin. She winced with every shallow intake of breath. Her right arm was obviously broken above the wrist.

Conall assessed the injuries with a frown. "I don't understand it. The shift should have restored her."

His eyes landed on the glass foot. The color from her tawny skin seemed to leach away to porcelain below the knee and then transparent at the ankle.

Noah arrived, lugging his medical kit. He started barking orders for someone to light the thera stove and heat water.

Conall found his voice and gave his own commands. "Valko you're on watch." He looked around for Augie and found him floating beside a cat. "Knock it off, Ranger. I need you. You're on watch with Valko. Don't take your eyes off that water."

Augie dropped to the ground with a thud and scrambled for his rail gun. Conall continued to give orders.

"Elias get water for Noah. Clem, find a blanket. Rowan, help me move her." He bumped into Orson as he stepped around Bretta's body. A snarl erupted from his lips. "Get the hell out of my way scribe."

"It is my duty to docum…" That's as far as he got before Conall's fingers wrapped around his throat. He squeezed and Orson's eyes bulged. Conall gave him a shake like a wolf snapping a rabbit's neck, then thrust the scribe away.

Orson clutched his throat. "I'll report this! Scribes are sacrosanct!"

Conall ignored him. Clem returned with blankets and they all lifted Bretta onto one. Clem covered her with the second.

Bretta woke. "What h—happened?" Her teeth were chattering. Clem tucked the blanket more tightly around her.

Noah was unpacking his gear, his face a neutral mask of efficiency. "You were in a fight," he said. "But don't worry. I've got you." He pulled a small tin from his kit and opened it. It was full of thera chips. He sifted through them with a finger and chose one.

"Jocasta guide me," he prayed, then swallowed the chip.

Rowan had seen mech mages ingest thera before. The chips were pure magic. They boosted a mage's power before a difficult mech production. It had never occurred to her that others might use thera to boost their knacks. The side-effects of thera ingestion could be devastating. If Noah was using it, he must have believed Bretta's wounds were life-threatening.

Thera overdoses were common in New Torwood City. Rowan had tried it once, just for the experience. It had felt like she'd stuck her head right into a ley-line to drink the flow of unfiltered magic. She immediately understood how the feeling could be addicting.

She watched Noah pack away his tin of thera, wondering and worrying about how often he used it.

Noah met her eye, then looked at Clem and finally Conall whose expression was even more cantankerous than usual.

"I apologize for what you are about to witness," Noah said. "I can take away her pain, clean out any bacteria and urge her body to start the healing process, but my knack has an unusual side-effect."

"Do what you have to." Conall's eyes were dark and unreadable.

Clem had collapsed beside her sister. Tears formed rivulets through the dust on her face. She held onto Bretta's good hand and spoke in a low tone that was meant to be soothing, but was interrupted by her hiccupy sobs. Bretta was in shock. She stared wide-eyed at the blank slate of a sky. Her mouth opened and closed, but no sound came out.

Elias showed up with a small bowl of warm water.

"There's more coming." He handed it to Noah who indicated that the elf should give it to Rowan.

"Will you help me?"

"Of course." Rowan was better with mech than flesh, but she would do anything she could to help the striker.

"Start cleaning those wounds. Be gentle. I just need to get a better look so I know where to focus. I'm going to set her wrist first." He leaned toward the patient.

"Bretta, you have a broken arm. I'm going to straighten it. I'll take away as much of the pain as possible, but I need you to hold still. Do you understand?"

Bretta blinked but didn't respond. Her eyes were glassy pools of pain. Clem pressed her forehead to Bretta's temple and whispered words of comfort.

Noah sucked in a breath. He laid his hands on Bretta's arm, one on either side of the break, and closed his eyes. Rowan kept waiting for him to yank the bones straight, but he rested like that for a long time.

Bretta's shaking eased. When Noah opened his eyes, his dark skin had a sickly gray cast. Lines creased the edges of his mouth.

"Hold her." He bit out the words. Conall pressed down on Bretta's shoulders. Rowan held her hips flat to the ground. Noah jerked the broken bones into place. Bretta screamed and went limp.

Noah splinted the arm, then turned his attention to her chest. A bite wound leaked fluid on the left side. He laid his hand flat and closed his eyes again. He grunted and opened them.

"Is it her heart?" Clem asked.

"No. Just a couple of broken ribs." Noah wiped sweat from his brow with the back of his hand. "I eased the pain, but I can't do much for cracked ribs."

He turned his attention to the many puncture wounds, pressing a hand flat to each one, then moving on. Elias returned with a larger bowl of hot water and took the dirty one from Rowan.

"Can you bring fresh cold water too?" Rowan looked pointedly at the medic who was sweating profusely. Each examination of a wound seemed to take more out of him. His hands were shaking now. It might have been a trick of the Meadows light, but his face seemed cadaverous under the streaks of dust and sweat.

"Get out of my way." He snarled and shouldered Rowan. She fell backward on her butt as Noah moved on to the right-side wounds. Rowan picked herself up and decided not to take the slight personally since the medic was agitated.

Noah continued his catalogue of Bretta's wounds. He cleaned them, treated them with antiseptic and applied bandages. Only one was large enough to need stitches.

"Get me some thread." He pointed at his bag. When Rowan hesitated, he shoved her aside. "Never mind. I'll do it myself."

Rowan sat back on her heels and shot a glance at Conall. The commander stood with his arms crossed over his chest. He saw Rowan's concern, but only shook his head. It was some kind of warning, but Rowan didn't know what for.

By the time Noah finished, his lips were pressed into a thin line and his hands shook as he tied off the last stitch. His eyes had deepened from brown to nearly black and seemed sunken in his skull. He rose and stomped over to Valko, grabbed the rail gun from his hands and shot the two loaded bolts into the sky. Then he turned the gun around and smashed it on a nearby boulder. One of the rails flew off and landed in the grass. Noah beat the rock again and again as parts of gun cracked and scattered. When there was nothing left but the grip, he threw that into the river, raised his hands to the sky and let out a primal scream that echoed across the Meadows. The scream died away and he stalked into the grass away from the road.

Conall jerked his head at Valko. "Go with him. Make sure he doesn't hurt himself."

"Is that a reaction to thera?" Rowan asked.

"No." Conall rubbed his jaw as if it pained him. "That's his knack. He can take the pain away, but it has to go somewhere. Apparently, it turns into rage. Pity because he's a damn good medic."

They glanced down at Bretta. She seemed to be sleeping peacefully now.

"Help me lift her into a cat," Conall said. "We need to get away from the river."

"What about her?" Rowan glanced toward Lena. Sometime during Noah's treatment of Bretta, Lena had slipped off the glass beast. She sat with her back to the titan, legs splayed out in front of her and eyes fixed on blank space.

"She's a ranger," Conall said. "She'll snap out of it."

That wasn't exactly what Rowan meant. She'd meant, *What the hell are we going to do with the chick who turns people to glass?*

Every knack had its quirks, of course. But something like Augie's nervous floating or even Noah's raging blow-back couldn't compare to turning a titan to glass. That was mage-level magic. And clearly, Lena had little control over it.

But Conall had already turned away to lift Bretta to the cat and Rowan decided to keep her judgment to herself. For now.

The NEXT SAFE CAMP WAS TWO hours away. They hadn't planned to stop there, but with the events of the afternoon, Conall called a halt anyway.

This camp wasn't as secure as the Three Sisters. It was little more than a rocky plateau with a natural spring burbling up through a man-made fountain, but at least it was away from the river and free of grass. Nothing could sneak up on them. They parked the cats in a U formation to create a small protected camp.

Augie carried Bretta from the cat and laid her on blankets. There was no wood for a fire, but Murdoch lit the thera stove and Elias was soon doling out mugs of hot tea.

Noah sat sullenly with his knees drawn up to his chin. He'd been subdued since returning from his rampage into the Meadows. Lena refused to leave the cat and lay curled up on one of the benches.

Rowan brought tea for Bretta. Clem helped her sit up to drink. They propped her against a travel pack. She seemed in good spirits, despite the slight wheeze in her chest. Clem covered her in a blanket, but Bretta kicked it off.

"I have to see it."

Clem bit her lip, but she nodded and lifted the blanket from her sister's legs. While she'd been passed out, Rowan and Clem had managed to dress Bretta, but they hadn't dared to put a boot on the glass foot. They weren't sure how fragile it was and didn't want to risk breaking it. Instead, they'd wrapped it in bandages, which Clem now unraveled to reveal the shiny, transparent foot.

"Well, bugger the saints." Bretta's eyes widened. She lifted the foot and let it drop. It hit the pile of bandages with a thud.

"Does it hurt?" Clem asked.

"No." Bretta's face scrunched up. "I'm trying to wiggle my toes. I can *feel* them wiggling." But the toes ignored the message and remained still. Bretta slumped against her travel pack. She lifted the foot and let it drop again. Rowan winced, expecting the appendage to shatter. It didn't. Bretta thumped it again.

Lena chose that moment to approach. She seemed wan, like a ghost found wandering the Meadows.

"Striker Tyendi, I just want to say, I'm sorry. So very sorry."

Bretta grabbed her hand. Rowan moved to intervene, but the Striker bowed her head, touching her forehead to Lena's hand in the All-Saints prayer.

"You saved me. You have nothing to be sorry for. I was half a minute away from losing that fight. If you hadn't intervened, that fat walrus would be dining on my corpse at the bottom of the river right now."

Lena sniffled and wiped her eye. "It's just that…I can't always control it. I was trying to turn only the beast's heart, but as usual, my knack hit like lightning."

"As usual?" Rowan prompted.

Lena hung her head and gave a little nod. "It's why I joined the rangers again. I was never meant to be a lifer. I quit as soon as my two years of service was up. I got married. We had a farm south of the city." That thought made her raise her head and give a small smile. Then her expression turned dark again.

"She died. Or rather, I killed her. My wife. Freya." She didn't look at either of them. Need came off her in waves, like the smell of anxious sweat. Need to tell her tale to someone. "We'd been hassled by a juvenile gaunt for days. They sometimes hang around the farms in the fall when they've been kicked out of their clans. I thought it was the gaunt in the barn. Freya had been away at market…was supposed to be away for another two days, but she came home early to surprise me for our anniversary." She looked up helplessly. "It was dark." Her voice was barely above a whisper. "I thought she was a gaunt."

Oh, Jesus, Jupiter and Jocasta. Rowan's mech arm clutched Bretta's blanket as she invoked the saints.

Lena didn't finish her tale. She didn't have to.

"I joined the rangers again because staying at the farm was…painful." She pulled her hand from Bretta's grasp and flexed her fingers like she was working out a stiffness. "I swore I would never use my knack, and yet…here we are. Again."

Bretta patted her arm. "Well, when we finally do face the gaunts, I'll be glad that you have my back."

"There will be no fighting gaunts for you, Striker." Conall had snuck up on them again. Rowan jumped and scowled. He moved more quietly than any man his size had the right to.

"I'm going to put a collar with a bell on you," she muttered. He gave her a wry grin before sitting beside Bretta and taking her hand.

Bretta turned her head away. She knew what was coming.

"I'm sending you back." Conall's tone was firm—a commander's tone. Then he softened. "Brett, come on. Look at me. You know I have no choice. You need more medical attention than we can offer out here."

Bretta still wouldn't look at him. "You mean, I'll slow down the mission."

Conall sat back. "That too. But you know I don't give a saint's ass about the mission. It's you I'm worried about."

Bretta's chin quivered, but she held it together and nodded. "I know. I feel so stupid. Three years of war with the bloody gaunts, another two on patrol with the rangers, and I never shifted once. Not even to blow off steam. Now I panic in the face of an overgrown sea lion. Stupid, stupid." She wiped a hand across her eyes. "Clem, honey, could you get me another sweater from my pack?"

"Of course." Clem jumped up and headed for the packs loaded on the cat.

She shook her head, then gripped Conall's hand. "You'll watch out for Clem, right? There'll be looking at her now."

Conall nodded, but Rowan was confused.

"Clem? Why?"

Conall pitched his voice low. "Shifters aren't allowed to serve as rangers or keepers. It's not an advertised fact, but anyone known to be a shifter is quietly dismissed from service."

"But that's not fair. There are mages in service and even elves now." The law to admit them into the military had been passed just last year.

Bretta made a sour face. "Life's not fair, Princess."

Conall looked at her under hooded lids. "If only we knew someone in a position of authority who could effect change in the policy."

His words hit like a bullet. Is that what they thought? That she was someone in a position to make policy? That she willfully ignored the needs of the people of New Torwood so she could play at being a tinker? She looked at her squad mates for confirmation. Bretta wouldn't meet her eye, and Lena pretended to find something very interesting to look at in the grass. Rowan couldn't help feeling like they were ganging up on her, but they had no idea how the politics of the palace really worked. She had no power. No authority. The best she could hope for was to keep the regent's eye off her so she could live her life in peace.

Rather than open that debate, she changed the subject.

"Does that mean Clem's a shifter too?"

"No. We have different fathers. That's where my bear comes from." Bretta rubbed the knee above her glass foot as if it pained her.

"So, they'll leave her alone once they figure that out."

Conall shook his head. "They'll test her first. Throw her into every dangerous mission they can find in hopes of sparking her shift."

"Just so they can kick her out of service." Rowan's heart sank. It was unfair. She glanced at Orson who watched this exchange with his piggy scribe eyes. His report to the council would see Bretta discharged from ranger duty, even if her foot didn't handicap her. And if the others were right, it would mean the end of Clem's duty as well.

Bretta sighed. "I never wanted to be a ranger anyway. Not really. But I was a damn good one." She gripped Conall's hand. "Saved your ass a time or two."

Conall smiled. "You were. And you did. Now it's time to go home to Gus and the tearoom."

Clem returned with a sweater and helped Bretta into it. When she was settled again, Bretta turned to Lena and lifted her glass foot. "Is this permanent?"

Lena bit her lip and nodded.

Bretta swore.

"There's more," Lena said. "Glass is a nonconductor for magic. It acts as a nullifier. That's why your shift took so long. And why your wounds didn't heal as usual."

Bretta's face went blank as she considered the repercussions. Rowan saw the moment she realized that her world was suddenly very different—that something she had controlled all her life had now become uncontrollable. She let out a sigh, then winced and put a hand to her cracked ribs.

"I guess I'd better leave you all to it then." She squeezed Conall's hand and shook it. "You'll take care of my baby girl, right?"

Conall nodded. "Of course."

"Aw, come on," Clem said. "I'm not a baby, sis."

Bretta patted her cheek. "You are to me and you always will be."

Clem rolled her eyes so hard, Rowan thought they'd get lost in her skull.

"Please let me be the one to take her home," Lena said. "I shouldn't be out in the field."

"Denied," Conall said.

"But—"

"No." Conall held up a hand to refuse her request. "We need a good tracker on this trip. And even more important, we need your experience. The council sent me out here with four greens and a scribe to keep alive. You're staying. Valko will drive Bretta back to the city."

Lena looked like she'd protest again, then she nodded and seemed to wilt.

"Fine." She rose and went back to the cat where she sat on the back bench with her knees drawn up to her chest.

Rowan rose to let Bretta and Clem have a few minutes alone together. Conall didn't waste any time. He ordered Murdoch and Elias to redistribute their gear into two cats, leaving the third with enough provisions for the return trip to New Torwood City. Valko helped them shift crates. He wasn't happy about having his second tour as a ranger cut short.

While they waited for supplies to be moved around, Rowan decided to check the third cat's sail gear. It would be going home with Bretta, but she'd complained about it sticking and Rowan didn't want them to have any trouble on the way back to the city. She was applying grease to a rusted sail bracket, when Conall pulled her aside.

"I need a word."

"You can have several." Rowan smiled as she wiped her hands on a rag.

"With Bretta leaving, I need a new second in command. And you're it."

"Me? Why?"

"Lena is unstable. And Noah's attention will be elsewhere in a crisis. It has to be you."

She was a third choice. Not the most flattering endorsement.

"I'm promoting you to Striker, effective immediately." He touched her shoulder where the Maven stripes decorated her sleeve. "See Murdoch for a new stripe." He stood straight and gave her a curt salute. "Striker."

She couldn't decide if the wry smile half hidden under his beard was genuine. She saluted him back anyway.

"Commander."

12

REAPERS

Conall ORDERED THEM BACK ON THE road. They left the glass titan by the side of the bridge. It was too heavy to push back into the water. No doubt the next caravaners who came that way would think it was just another quirky bit of fun the Meadows had spat up.

The rest of the ride toward Oxeye Lake was more cramped. They'd redistributed the gear and passengers into the two remaining cats. As the new striker, Rowan drove in the lead. Clem acted as her lookout. Augie filled the second seat and Orson was forced into the back with the gear.

Lena drove Conall's cat. She was subdued, and he was happy to let her brood in silence.

Oxeye Lake was actually just a section of the Ikon River that bulged inland to form a large bay. The current slowed and the waters deepened. It was the perfect place to grow thera and the council had installed the farm after the last gaunt uprising.

Even before the Resurgence, the world had been on the verge of reshaping itself. The broken ley-lines poured magic into a crucible of war, famine and ecological disasters, forging new landscapes and new political powers. Humans discovered latent abilities that had been quaint family myths. Shapeshifters shifted for the first time. Witches turned to old grimoires that were no longer quirky relics from another age. Their spells worked. Other races, like the Enos elves, found new doorways from their worlds, and unearthly creatures followed them through these tears in the veil.

Magic became as important as oxygen and more valuable than gold.

For the northern dwellers of Old Torwood City, one new creature became more important than any other. The nacara mussel.

The fishermen of the great Ikon River thought they'd hit a goldmine delicacy when these enormous shellfish were first discovered. Their meat was sweet and tender, and even the smallest nacara grew to over two feet in length. The largest could be ten feet. The discarded nacara shells quickly became prized by artisans for their cobalt blue mother of pearl. They called it thera.

No one knew—not the fishermen, the artisans or the gastronomes who gobbled the new delicacy—that the nacre of these shells was more magically potent than anything on Earth except for a ley-line. The giant mussels leached magic into the water. Historians hypothesized that this magic surge caused rifts to open in the Ikon—portals that let otherworldly monsters such as titans and gaunts into their world.

Old Torwood City was overrun within months. The population scattered. If not for this fact, the value of the nacara's mother of pearl might have been understood sooner. As it was, the former residents of Old Torwood could do little to survive. Most fled for the overcrowded cities to the south. Others eked out an existence in the Meadows, fighting for every homestead they built and maintained.

They called it the Lost Ages. Humanity had tumbled from the peak of civilization to subsistence living. And their greatest loss was knowledge. Gone were the self-heating homes, the medicines, and the flying machines. Banks full of virtual money seemed like a joke. Giant unsinkable ships were nothing more than a cautionary tale, because all those ships had sunk during the Resurgence. The things humans had once taken for granted became stories, then myths.

For two hundred years the scattered people of Old Torwood barely survived in darkness and in fear.

Until Tomasin Andula and his friend, the mech mage Harry Hightower, built New Torwood City. Finally, humans had a refuge from titans and gaunts, a place where they could live without fear. A place where they could not only survive, but prosper.

It took another three hundred years for mech mages to understand the true power in thera. Then it became not just a curiosity but a necessity. The first thera farm had been established before Conall was born by the Theracine

Corporation, an entity whose board of directors had a lot of overlap with the Regent's Council. The new miracle substance was scraped from the shells of the giant nacara mussels and cut into chips to power devices of all sizes, from lamps to cats. Thera became the new currency. Chips were traded like gold coins.

Oddly, the meat of the nacara mussel turned out to be magically inert. It was still considered a delicacy, but a dangerous one. Occasionally, improperly prepared nacara meat caused a gastric infection known as gangra. It spread through the bloodstream and turned limbs gangrenous. Gangra was almost always fatal. Regardless of that risk, thera harvesters lived on nacara meat since it was a plentiful byproduct of the farms, and gangra was just one more hazard of the trade.

Dale had intimated that a gangra epidemic had hit Oxeye Outpost. It seemed improbable. Gangra was rare and not infectious. It would take a whole lot of bad nacara meat to shut down an entire town. But as they approached Oxeye, Conall was starting to believe Dale. Or at least believe that something terrible had hit the town.

Out on the water, the rigs that held the nacara farms were quiet. Rods jutted from the platforms at regular intervals. From a distance, they seemed like sticks, but Conall knew they were actually massive tree trunks. Some were four to six feet in diameter and would hang a hundred feet below the surface. Trees such as these didn't grow in the cooler Meadows. They'd been harvested at great expense from the jungles down south. The nacara mussels would latch onto the trunks and within four years, they would grow to eight feet in length.

"Should the rig be that quiet?" Lena asked. She'd slowed the cat down so they could all get a good look. The floating platforms were deserted.

"No. Something's wrong." Conall picked up his scope and studied the rig. There were no divers on the platform, no workers of any kind. Only one boat was moored to the side, but it also seemed abanandoned.

"They shut down the entire operation."

The boat moored to the rig bobbed gently in the waves. It wasn't a fishing vessel, but a harvester. On a normal day, divers would cut the ripe mussels from the trunks dangling in the water. The divers were called reapers because they were harvest professionals, but Conall had spent some time in thera camps and he knew they liked to pretend the name had a darker side. It gave a dirty, dangerous job a certain prestige. Only the strongest farmers became reapers. The rest worked the rigs or the processing plants.

Reapers would cut away the mussels with precision so they fell into nets that were pulled onto boats and taken upstream to the processing facilities in town. On any day, there would be a dozen or more such boats, waiting to catch the mussels.

Conall turned the scope upstream. There were no other vessels on the water. He returned his gaze to the lone boat. Several nets were piled on its deck. They seemed to contain nacara. He lowered the scope.

"They left in a hurry. There's a small fortune in thera sitting on that deck."

They continued westward. Conall was now worried about what they'd find in Oxeye. Garou couldn't stop snorting at the stench of rotting fish coming from the processing plants that they passed.

Lena pulled the cat to a stop outside the gates of the town. It was rare that gaunts would attack this far outside the Meadows, but it happened. The timber wall surrounding Oxeye wasn't as impenetrable as the stone wall of New Torwood, but an entire ranger platoon was garrisoned here and between the two, they kept the thera farmers safe. Mostly.

Conall stepped from the cat and approached the gates. They were double doors that could open wide enough for two cats to pass within. A smaller door to the right was used for foot traffic. Both were closed. No guards stood in the tower above.

Large white bags were piled beside the gate. As he approached, Conall saw what they were. Bodies. Wrapped in canvas and stacked like cord wood. In his mind, the wolf howled for the dead.

Jupiter and Jocasta. What in the saints happened here?

He pounded a fist on the smaller door. Nothing. He waited a moment, then pounded again. The top half of the door swung open to reveal a young ranger in uniform. His face was pale and sweaty. Dark eyes watched Conall warily, but the most striking feature on the young ranger was his nose. It was purple and the tip bent sideways like it might slide off his face at any moment. Blisters scored his cheeks and wept fluid.

Conall stepped back and pulled his scarf over his nose. The kid was in the last stages of the infection. How did he even have the strength to stand? The guard saw his reaction and started to cry.

"It's bad, right?"

"What happened, son?" Conall wanted to reach through the open door and console him. He was young, probably on his first ranger gig, and way out of his depth.

"I don't know." He wiped his eyes on his sleeve. "A few of the officers went down with gangra. No one thought anything of it. But then…then more got sick. Doctors say it mutilated or something."

"Mutated."

"Yeah, that. And now everyone's sick. Commander's dead. So are most of the officers. Town's shut down, Commander. Orders came in by graphium this morning. Full quarantine. We're not to let anyone in or out the gates." He looked behind him as if worried he might be overheard, then said in a quieter voice, "Whole town's been hit. Not a ranger or reaper left standing."

Damn the saints.

Dale had told him that the garrison had been hit hard, but Conall had expected to at least resupply before heading north into the Meadows, especially since he'd sent one of their cats home.

By now the rest of the squad had disembarked from the cats and stood behind him. Noah pushed through them to face the guard.

"Let me in. I can help." He was clutching his medical bag.

The ranger shook his head. "Can't do it, Maven. I have orders to keep these gates shut."

"That's ridiculous," Noah said. "Gangra isn't contagious. Quarantining isn't going to help anyone."

"Sorry, sir. I have my orders."

Noah looked like he was ready to break down the door. Then he got a good look at the guard.

"What the hell?" But the sight of the guard's infected face didn't deter him. Noah grabbed the door handle and tried to yank it open. The guard stepped back, his swollen eyes wide and leaking.

"Stand down, Maven." Conall pulled Noah away. The medic's eyes flashed with fire. Conall gripped his arm.

"This isn't run-of-the-mill gangra. You can't do anything to help them." He tilted his head toward the town. "The council will send someone to clean up this mess. We have another mission."

"Damn the mission!"

"You're not thinking." Conall squeezed his arm harder. "What if one of the squad gets hurt again? What if we find the scientists all sick? We need a medic and you're it."

Noah stared at him for a long moment. Conall hoped he wasn't stupid enough to challenge a direct order.

He wasn't. Noah was gritting his teeth so hard the sides of his jaw bulged, but he nodded once, then turned back for the cats.

Conall faced the guard again. "Is there any place we can resupply?"

The kid pointed north. "Halstead's. The old inn by the market crossroads. It might still be open, if anyone there is left alive." Then he shut the door in Conall's face.

"Everyone back to the cats," Conall shouted. "We're making one quick stop and then heading north."

The wolf's agitation rolled over him like a shiver. Garou was happy to be leaving the sick place.

13

INNKEEPER

Rowan PARKED THE CAT NEXT TO the only building in a wide, dusty clearing. The guard at the gate had said this was the market, but the square was empty. Maybe the market was seasonal? Or maybe the traders were staying away because of the quarantine in town.

Garbage was strewn about the area. A broken down wagon had been left to rot in the sun. The wind had tangled bits of cloth and brambles in its wheels. A mech drink dispenser had fallen over and been left. Other mech debris seemed to gather around it like driftwood. In the distance, a fox paused as it traversed the open plain, perked its ears at the new intruders, then hurried on its way.

Lena pulled the second cat up beside them. Everyone got out to stretch their legs except for Murdoch who slept on the last bench of Lena's cat.

"Rowan, you're with me." Conall beckoned her to follow. "Everyone else stay with the cats and stay vigilant. Just because it looks quiet, doesn't mean it is."

"Yes, boss." Clem leaned against the cat. She pulled one of the rods from her rail gun to inspect it for wear, then rammed it back into place and took her position on watch. Augie mimicked her, though he had trouble getting his rail back in the gun and he hummed while he did it.

Rowan called for Phalian who'd taken the opportunity to scout the area from above. The mech sent her calming vibes which meant he hadn't spotted any predators, or at least nothing big enough to worry them. He landed on her shoulder and she let him stay there. A second pair of eyes was welcome. They didn't know what they'd find inside the inn.

A wooden sign painted with a pair of crossed hammers and a mug of ale hung beside the door. A harsh wind blew off the Meadows and the sign creaked on its rusty chain. Rowan's tinker sensibility itched to stop and oil it, but Conall was already through the door and she followed him. Orson was tight on her heels.

Inside, the one large room was dim after the bright afternoon.

"We don't serve his kind." The voice came from the shadows at the far side of the big room.

Conall had frozen three steps inside the door, no doubt waiting for his eyes to adjust.

"What kind?" he asked. "We're rangers on a mission for the regent. The gates to Oxeye are closed. We were hoping to resupply here." He held his hands open in front of him to show he was unarmed.

Rowan's eyes were slowly adjusting to the gloom, and she spotted the man aiming a loaded crossbow at them.

"His kind." The man jerked the crossbow toward Orson. "He's an abomination."

Orson puffed out his chest and blustered. "I am a scribe from the Temple of the Word."

"I know what you are. Abomination."

"Scribes are welcomed everywhere. It is the law."

"Do you see any lawmen here?"

There was a tense moment while both aggrieved parties waited to see if Conall would force the issue.

Conall didn't even look back. "Orson, get out."

"But it is my duty…"

Rowan grabbed him by the arm and dragged him outside and all the way to the cats. She thrust him at Augie. "Hold him. Sit on him if you have to. Don't let him back inside."

"Yes, Striker!" Augie was flushed from the heat. He grinned and wrapped Orson in a bear hug. She left the scribe spitting like an angry meadow cat, but she was satisfied that he wouldn't cause trouble.

Back inside, Conall was seated on a stool by a long counter. The innkeeper gave her a big grin as she entered, then shook his head.

"Ah, so it's that time, is it?"

"What do you mean?" Conall's tone was a hair away from a growl.

"Nothing malicious, Commander. Nothing at all. Only that Mogra brings about change, as always." The innkeeper's voice boomed through the inn.

He served Conall a cup of ale and poured another for Rowan as she sat. She took a sip and considered the innkeeper's words. Mogra was the summer wind. Its winter counterpart, the Fanfara, brought cold but also stability. Mogra was known as a fickle wind that heralded change, and not always change for the better.

"Looks like Mogra brought a plague this year," Conall said. "Is that why you're all alone here?"

He held his arms wide. "Oh, I don't keep much staff normally. Just a cook and a kitchen boy, but yes, they're both gone home to care for sick family. It's just me."

Phalian chirped and flew to the innkeeper's shoulder.

"There's a good lad." He patted the bird, and Phalian settled on him.

Rowan eyed her normally capricious mech. It wasn't like him to take to strangers. She gave a short whistle and he flew back to her shoulder.

The innkeeper smiled.

Rowan sipped her ale again. It was warm and earthy and had a little tang as she swallowed. She put down the cup and grinned.

"You've got a mustache." Conall pointed at her mouth.

Rowan felt herself blush as she wiped foam off her lip.

"You missed some." His thumb wiped the corner of her mouth. She resisted the urge to turn into the touch. In the dim room, his eyes were nearly black, and she could read nothing in them.

The innkeeper cleared his throat. "A good ale leaves a mark. Can I offer you some food?"

Conall leaned away and Rowan was glad to put some air between them. Saints, the room was warm.

"A cold lunch would suffice," he said. "For us and our squad. And provisions for the road if you can spare them."

"Oh, I have plenty to spare. What with the gates shut and all." The innkeeper flapped the rag in his hand toward Oxeye. There was something in his tone that woke a memory in Rowan. Not a solid memory, but some gossamer image that evaporated before she could fully grasp it.

She studied the man while he set about filling two crates with fresh vegetables, cheeses and meats. He wasn't tall, but his barrel chest and thick arms suggested strength better fitting a blacksmith than an innkeeper. He walked with a slight limp as he moved between a pantry and the crates. Dark hair and a beard peppered with gray complemented his olive complexion. Large, round eyes fit into a wide, flat brow, giving him an owlish air. He whistled while he packed the crates and again, the tune woke something in her.

And just like that, she remembered the kind man she'd called Uncle Hermie. He'd been advisor to her father, and judging by the way Aunt Bella sighed whenever she mentioned his name, Rowan suspected they'd been lovers. He'd been a staple of her childhood, always there in the background at both ceremonial events and private family gatherings. He was also the one who'd gifted Rowan with her mech arm after the accident. She'd never had the chance to thank him because Uncle Hermie disappeared while she was still recovering from the incident.

The innkeeper turned to find her scrutinizing him. "Is there something wrong?" He glanced at the stripes on her sleeve and added, "Striker?"

Rowan quickly shook her head. "No. I'm sorry. It's just that you remind me of someone I once knew. Your name isn't Hermie, by chance? Or maybe Herman?"

The innkeeper frowned, then brightened. "Rude of me not to introduce myself. Most folks around here know me well enough. Name's Halstead." He held out a hand for Conall to shake. Conall's grip was firm but his eyes never left the old man's as if he expected a knife hid behind his back.

Halstead turned to Rowan and held out his hand. She hesitated for only a moment, then closed her mech fingers around his. He glanced at the black glove. His eyes rose to meet hers and he grinned. "That's a fine grip you have there." His fingers tightened and he leaned closer. Rowan tried to pull her hand away but he held on tight.

Conall was oblivious to her sudden struggle. In fact, he seemed excessively interested in his ale, as if he'd been frozen in time, staring into the depths of his cup.

Rowan pulled back her hand, but the strange man wouldn't release her.

"Hey! Let me go!" Her tone was sharp, and a flutter of panic was growing in her chest, but when she met the innkeeper's gaze, all fear and anger faded. His eyes were brilliant blue, like the wings of a blue jay, and framed by crinkles that spoke of a long life full of laughter. She felt herself getting lost in them, as if his eyes were growing big enough to swallow her.

"Who are you?" The words felt thick in her mouth.

He pulled on her mech, turned it over to examine the underside and smiled. He raised his other hand, and pointed at her forehead. Her eyes crossed as she tried to focus on his finger. It tapped her once, right between the eyes, and a zing like static electricity went through her.

He leaned in and pressed his lips to her ear. "Never mind who I am. It's time to remember who you are, Princess." He let her go and she nearly fell off her stool.

Phalian squawked and flew into the rafters.

By the time she'd righted herself and settled the bird, the old man was grinning at her while he wiped a glass with an old rag. She squinted, trying to see what she'd seen only a moment ago, but he was just an innkeeper again, slightly portly and disheveled.

"Who are you?"

"Name's Halstead." He pushed a crate of provisions across the bar. "Your order's all ready."

Rowan rubbed her brow, feeling lightheaded as if she'd drunk an entire pitcher of ale instead of one small mug. Conall paid Halstead and thanked him as if nothing had happened. They took their provisions out to the cats.

Murdoch inspected the crates and grunted his satisfaction. They moved some gear around to make room for the provisions.

Rowan took the driver's seat again with Conall beside her and they drove through the dusty expanse of the empty market square, away from Oxeye and the river.

"Did you find anything odd about that innkeeper?" she asked.

Conall kept his eyes focused on the road ahead. "What innkeeper?"

Rowan frowned. "The one back there. What was his name? Hampton? Holland? Whatever. He just served us ale."

"Didn't see him. What was so odd?"

"I don't know. Nothing, I guess." The memory of the owl-eyed innkeeper was already fading from Rowan's mind. She gripped the steering wheel as if it might spin away.

That night, while they slept on the road north, Rowan's nightmares returned.

INTERLUDE

"Come ON. DON'T BE A BABY." Ethan wiped hair from his eyes and looked past Dale at the shrubs that hid a secret tunnel under the city wall. He bounced on his toes, eager to find trouble.

"I'm not a baby." Dale wasn't even insulted. Ethan called him worse than that most days. He didn't really mean it. "But it's too early in the season, the water in the tunnel will be too high."

"So we get a little wet. So what?"

Dale didn't know why he bothered arguing. The prince never considered anyone else's opinion. Plus, the king had gifted Ethan with his first real sword for Founder's Day and he was dying to try it out.

Dale sighed and followed his friend around the shrubs. Strictly speaking Ethan's father had forbidden them to leave the city, and the guards at the gates would never let them through. That didn't stop Ethan. He prided himself on being sneaky, though he'd call it resourceful. He'd found this old tunnel that was once an access road used by keepers. In truth, it could barely be called a tunnel. It had collapsed a decade ago and now was more of a worm hole. The keepers didn't bother to guard it because no one could get through that opening.

No one but a couple of slender twelve-year-old boys.

Ethan pushed his sword through the hole, then lay down and slithered on his belly. They'd be filthy when they got back. Ethan's laundry maids wouldn't object, but Dale would be reprimanded for ruining his clothes. Again.

But he'd be in worse trouble if he let the prince leave the city alone. Dale heaved a dramatic sigh, hoping Ethan would note his objection. Then he crouched and squirmed through the muck. The opening seemed to get smaller every time they came this way. Maybe they were just getting bigger.

After the first section of fallen rock, the tunnel opened up and they could stand. In a foot of cold, murky water. Yuck. Ethan didn't seem to even notice the discomfort. He was already heading toward the grate at the far end where the tunnel emerged into the ruins of an old guard tower.

"I heard the guards talking about a nesting gaunt," he said. "We might even find the eggs."

"Gaunts don't lay eggs."

"How do you know?"

"Because I listen to Master Fry when he lectures."

Ethan made a *pfft* sound. He had no love for their old tutor.

The grate at the other end was rusted enough that the first time they'd come here, they'd been able to dislodge one of the bars to create a small gate.

Dale watched Ethan squeeze through the opening now. The metal grate grazed his shoulders and tore a hole in his shirt.

He won't fit much longer. That thought brought some comfort. Maybe these outlandish excursions would finally come to an end.

Yeah, right. And maybe Ethan will suddenly become a star student and I'll get home in time to finish my school work.

It wasn't that Dale disliked Ethan's games. Not exactly. It was simply that Ethan had no sense of self-preservation. And the first thing Chancellor Atherton had said to him when Dale came to live at the palace was, "Your secondary job is to keep the prince company. Your primary job is to keep him out of trouble." He'd said it with a stern look, but Dale soon discovered he was more afraid of losing Ethan's respect than he was of the chancellor.

And they didn't get into much trouble anyway, though that was mostly because they never got caught.

That was the other thing about Ethan. He was the luckiest son of a saint Dale had ever known. He could steal a cat from the keeper's garage, crash it, and walk away unscathed. And the shadow of blame would fall on someone else. Usually Dale.

"You're brooding again, my friend." Ethan shot him a brilliant grin. "What do I always say? Brooding is for…"

"Brooding is for losers not winners. Yeah, yeah. I know. Let's just get this over with. We still have a treatise on the first gaunt uprising to write for Master Fry."

"Old Fry won't mind if it's late."

Dale doubted that. Fry *would* mind. He just wouldn't punish the prince.

They crawled out of the tunnel. The ruins of the old guardhouse with its crumbling tower stood at their backs. Before them, the rocky remains of various other buildings made this the perfect place for two curious kids to find adventure. Dale shaded his eyes to gaze beyond the ruins.

"One day, I'm going to be a ranger and go out there." He pointed at the Meadows, a blank green slate full of possibilities.

"We already are rangers! Striker, take your position at the gate!" Ethan waved his sword in the air. It was only two-feet in length, more of a glorified dagger than a sword, but it caught the summer sun nicely. Dale had to admit it looked impressive in Ethan's hand. Regal even.

The prince pointed the sword toward the crumbling tower. "I'll survey the Meadows from up there. If the gaunts are on the move, we'll find them!"

Dale recognized the glint of determined mischief in the prince's eye.

"Yes, Commander!" He gave a little salute. Ethan started toward the tower, but a scraping sound made them both freeze.

A head poked up from the tunnel. A head full of ginger curls.

Ethan groaned. "What are you doing here?"

The princess squirmed through the grate. She wiped dirt off her pants and put two hands firmly on her hips.

"You're not supposed to go outside the wall."

"And you're not supposed to follow me," Ethan said.

The sun glinted off a sheen of sweat on Rowan's brow. She shook her head and sent the curls dancing.

"Well, I'm here now and unless you let me play too, I'm telling Father." She leaned forward and pointed a tiny pink finger at them. "Or worse. I'll tell Master Fry and he'll give you extra lessons as a punishment."

Ethan considered his little sister, then said. "Give us a minute." He put an arm around Dale's shoulder and pulled him aside. His blade scraped in the dirt.

"I'm tired of her following us everywhere."

"She's not so bad."

"She's worse than bad. She's annoying. If she wants to play, let's give her a scare she won't ever forget, yeah?"

Dale felt the heat of Ethan's breath in his ear. The arm around his shoulder weighed heavily.

"Yeah, okay. Whatever."

"Good." Ethan patted him on the back and turned to his sister.

"You can stay, but we're hunting gaunts. There's a nest around here somewhere. I heard about it in the barracks."

Rowan's eyes widened. They were already large and now they seemed to overwhelm her small face.

"And we're going to find the gaunt eggs," Ethan said with a grin. "I'll keep one as a pet. Maybe it will have to sleep in your bed."

Rowan frowned at him. "Gaunts don't lay eggs."

"Oh, does that mean you're too chicken to find one?"

"I'm not!"

"Good. Go with Dale. Find sticks and beat the bushes to flush out the gaunt. I'll go scout from above."

Ethan dashed off for the tower. It wasn't much of a tower, really. Most of it had fallen down, leaving a mountain of rubble at the base of a jagged round structure only one story high. Ethan leaped to the top of the rubble. One of the rocks was loose and it skidded down the slope. He stumbled and dropped to hands and knees. The sword clanged on stone, but he was up again without getting hurt.

Luck of the saints. Dale shook his head. If that had been him, he'd have tripped head-first down the rocks and knocked out a tooth.

Ethan climbed until he came to the tower proper. The mountain of rubble rose up high enough that he could feed his sword, then his feet and torso through a narrow window.

Concern lurched in Dale's chest. He'd been inside that tower. The floor wasn't stable. Neither were the stone walls for that matter. The whole thing could come crashing down, but there was no point in yelling after Ethan to be careful. He turned toward Rowan instead.

She looked small and uncertain.

Dale offered her his hand. "It's okay. You don't have to do anything he says."

She chewed on the end of a finger. "It's just a game, right?" Dale nodded. "Gaunts aren't real anyway, right?" Dale nodded again. This wasn't the time to tell her that gaunts *were* real, just very far away.

He pulled a stick from a tumble of deadwood and handed it to her. She held it like a sword and pretended to jab an invisible enemy.

"Cool." Her grin was infectious. Dale picked up his own stick and grinned back.

"Gaunts approaching fast!" Ethan called out. "Scout Andula and Striker Shannock make yourself ready!"

Rowan crossed her arms over her chest and frowned.

"I am not a scout! A princess would never be anything less than a maven."

"Fine." Dale tapped her shoulder. "I just promoted you to maven. Now are you coming?"

Rowan grinned, then she whooped out a triumphant call and ran through the ruins hollering for gaunts because she loved her brother and would do anything to make him happy. Dale waved his stick and followed because, at the end of the day, he loved Ethan too.

14

TARGET PRACTICE

Rowan WAS RUNNING DOWN THE DARK hallway that led to her bedroom in the palace. In the mercurial way of dreams, she rounded a corner and the palace walls morphed into the broken stone of a long tunnel. Something howled. She started toward the pinpoint of sunlight at the end of the tunnel. Black water sucked at her feet. No matter how fast she ran, the light never grew bigger. A hand yanked her arm.

She woke swallowing a scream in her throat. Sucking in a breath of cool morning air, she tried to calm her wildly beating heart.

Saints, that was one hell of a dream.

Except it wasn't a dream. Or it wasn't *just* a dream. It was a memory of the first time she ever went outside the city walls.

The night her brother was hurt and she lost her arm.

The night her father thought they were dead and had a heart attack.

And why now? The nightmares had plagued her as a child, but not in many years. Was it the titan attack that brought back the anxiety of those memories? Probably. That thought didn't reassure her. Facing titans was what rangers did. If she couldn't handle the stress, she had no right to be out here with the squad.

She glanced at the angle of the sun. It was light out, but with the short nights that didn't mean she'd slept long. She felt like she hadn't slept at all. Her hip was numb where it had pressed against the hard ground. Her head hurt as if her dreams had been laced with broken glass. She rubbed her mech arm. She knew it was impossible to feel pain in the mech, but sometimes it plagued her with a phantom ache.

She sat up feeling creaky and cranky.

A few hours before sunset, they'd stopped at yet another unmanned ranger outpost. It was little more than a slight rise in the plains that let whoever was on watch see for miles in any direction. Foresight was their best defense. A small stone building was kept stocked with provisions by the rangers and a well provided fresh water.

Other than Lena, who was on watch, everyone else slept.

Rowan rose and filled her canteen from the well. She used half the water to wash her face and filled it again. Breakfast would have to wait until Murdoch and Elias woke, but she wasn't hungry.

With no windbreaks for miles around, the wind pulled at her clothes and hair. She thought of the old myth about Mogra, the wind that brought change, and gave an inward laugh. Where had that thought come from?

She stepped around sleeping bodies and headed for the cats. Lena nodded at her, then turned her attention back to the vast grasslands.

Phalian let out a chirp and Rowan sent him a silent warning to be quiet and not wake the others. The mech's wings clacked as he circled her head then shot into the Meadows. As usual, he sent back his impressions—vast open spaces of glowing green and the hum of insects. No predators in sight.

With half her attention on Phalian, Rowan dug into the gear at the back of their cat until she found the antique mech valet. She dragged it to a small clearing away from the others and sat on the ground to begin cleaning off dirt and grime.

Phalian zoomed back to perch on her knee. He was very curious about the new mech and kept getting in the way as she tried to work. She finally coaxed him onto her shoulder and urged him to be still.

She sat back and studied the new valet. A vine was wrapped around its neck. She pulled that off and a thick layer of dead moss came with it. Underneath all that dirt an unusual design was revealed. It was definitely an antique, built in a style Rowan had never seen—vaguely humanoid with a boxy frame and an over-large rectangular head. Stubby arms protruded from its torso. She suspected they were meant for attaching extensions, but one had been broken off and replaced with a rusty bolt. Its legs were little more than metal sheaths for the wheels that were too clogged with gunk to turn well. Large copper eyes had oxidized and turned green. They were ringed in another metal that was chipped and rusting. Adjustment knobs were cleverly disguised as ears and antennae stuck up like horns from its head.

It was too cute for a mech, as if someone had built it to deliberately tap into the protective emotions one felt when confronted by a stray puppy.

She pulled off more moss. A dozen buttons ranged across its chest. Some were square, others round. One looked like a badge. She scraped away more dirt to reveal an etching of two hammers and an anvil. It looked like a maker's mark.

What if?

She sent a touch of magic to her finger, the same way she did when lighting a thera lamp and pressed it to the badge.

"Roger that!" The valet said in a high-pitched voice. It had been slightly bent over and now swiveled at the hips to stand straight. The antenna on its head waggled.

Phalian said, "SQUAWK!" and launched into the air to flap around the valet. Rowan touched the anvil again.

"Roger that!"

"Is that all you can say?"

His eyes shut and opened in an exaggerated blink. "Roger that."

Valets usually had a thera chip magicked with resonance to produce several useful phrases like, "How can I help?" and "Please move out of my way." Depending on the valet's duties, its vocabulary would vary. The postal mechs that delivered mail throughout the city had few words, but a private valet would have a broader range, especially one from a large noble house. Even though this mech seemed ancient, it was obviously finely crafted, and should have more phrases in its repertoire. Rowan wondered if its resonance chip was damaged, but with all the grime, she had yet to find any access port.

"Roger that!" His head swiveled to take in a new arrival.

Conall frowned down at them. "I see you got it working."

"Sort of. He seems stuck on that one phrase. But isn't he cute?" Rowan held him up like a prize. "I'm going to call him Roger."

"Of course." Conall grinned and shook his head.

"Roger that!"

Rowan pointed to the metal horns on his head. "These are some kind of receivers. Maybe. But what's really fascinating is this. Look." She turned it over to show the stylized anvil and crossed hammers. "What do you think that is?"

Conall leaned down and touched the etching. She waited for him to say she was wasting her time, wasting valuable mission time, but he just smiled and shook his head.

"I think it's really old. I can't even find a port for a thera chip," she said.

"You won't. That's a pneuma."

Rowan's head jerked back in surprise. "What? No way! Do you think it's a Harry Hightower?"

"Most likely. The mark is the same." He pointed to the anvil and crossed hammers. "You must recognize that from the Talos. Dale tells me you spend most of your days fixing that old hunk of junk."

Rowan bristled at the insult to Talos, but she knew most people thought of the giant mech as a relic.

"I've never seen this mark on Talos, but then, I never really looked for it."

"It's there somewhere. Hightower left it on all his creations. And this is definitely a Hightower mark."

"You're sure? Aren't there a lot of copycats?"

"Yeah, but I've dealt with black market mechs for long enough to recognize the real thing."

"In which case, I won't find a thera port."

"Probably not."

Thera had only come into general use in the last two decades when it was proven to be a renewable and inexhaustible source of energy. Thera was comparably cheap to produce and even a journeyman mage could work with it. And another bonus—the chips were replaceable. When one wore out, simply pop in another. It quickly became the power source of choice for all new mechs.

Before that, pneuma mechs were more rare and a lot more expensive because they were fueled by batteries that were charged with ley-line magic. Apart from the expense, it was finicky and dangerous magic to work with. Rowan didn't know of any modern mech mage who was still producing pneumas. Harry Hightower had certainly disappeared long ago, taking his secrets with him.

Rowan flexed her mech fingers. Could the same kind of glowing heart that was inside the Talos also be the power source in Roger?

If nothing else, dissecting the valet might give her some answers or a better understanding of the Talos. But she didn't have time or equipment to do that out here in the Meadows.

Conall was still frowning at the little valet.

"I suggest you don't tell anyone about that mark. Cover it back up with dirt and leave it until you're home in the palace. On the black market a mech like that would go for more than most of the rangers on this squad will make in a year."

"You don't trust our squad?"

"I don't know them. I'll trust them when we've been through fire together."

Rowan nodded. *I hope it doesn't come to that.*

She continued to clean the valet. Conall didn't leave. After several minutes, his looming presence became oppressive. She put down the cloth and shielded her eyes to look up at him.

"Did you want something else, Commander?"

"What are you doing awake? You're not on watch."

"I couldn't sleep. It's too hot." In fact, the cloying humidity of the previous day had let up and a breeze made the morning almost comfortable. Conall squinted as if he knew she was lying.

"Why are you up?" she asked, wondering if the reserved commander was actually lonely and just looking for someone to chat with.

He leaned on one foot, looking relaxed and boneless. "I'll tell you my secret anxieties if you tell me yours."

Yep, he was definitely chatty.

"Okay. If you must know…" She hesitated, not wanting to air all her laundry. Then Auntie Bella came to mind and she said, "Fuck it. I had a nightmare. About the day this happened." She held up her mech arm. Conall's eyebrows rose. Hah! Either the curse or the revelation had worked. She'd surprised him.

"Do you have nightmares a lot?"

"Not in years." She rubbed the back of her wrist over her forehead. Phalian took that as a signal to fly into the Meadows with a squawk. "I guess it's just the stress of this trip. Your turn. What's keeping you awake?"

Conall didn't hesitate. "Oxeye. And all those sick people. Feels wrong somehow to just drive away."

Rowan rose and took Conall's hand in hers. They stood there, mere inches apart. It could have been a ridiculously awkward moment between a commander and a striker, but she refused to see it that way. Conall was letting himself be vulnerable in front of her and she cherished that.

"We couldn't have done anything for them," she said. "We'd only have ended up sick too. Besides, I'm sure the regent is already sending help."

Conall let out a snort.

"You have a lot of faith in him."

"In Regent Atherton? Well, yeah. I mean, he's the regent."

"Right." Conall pulled away and turned to stare into the golden light that reflected off the endless grass.

Rowan knew she'd missed the mark somehow.

"And we have to keep to the mission, don't we?" she said.

Conall faced her again and smiled.

Saints. How could a smile be so sad and so damned attractive at the same time?

"I'm just wondering if this mission hasn't cost us too much already." He rubbed a hand over his whiskers as if they itched.

Rowan thought of Bretta's glass foot. Bretta had paid the price for all of them.

"Have you ever fired a rail gun?" he asked.

The swift change in the conversation's direction jarred her.

"Um…yes?" She said it like a question. In truth, Rowan had never even touched a rail gun before. New recruits got at least six weeks of basic training before being sent to the rangers or the keepers, but the council had skipped that requirement for Rowan. They'd given her a rank and an assignment and that was that.

"Good. Show me."

She was about to argue. They had enough snipers in the squad. But Bretta's sudden departure reminded her how easily their situation could change.

"Fine." She wiped her hands on the rag and called Phalian. He landed on her shoulder.

Conall pointed to the bird. "Can't you...you know, tuck him away or whatever you do?"

Phalian said, "SQUAWK!"

"Roger that!" The valet spun his wheels.

Rowan grinned. "I'm a package deal."

"Whatever. Grab a gun and ammo and meet me over there." He pointed to the north end of camp where the plateau was at its highest.

She packed away her tinker tools before hitting the stash of munitions. The guns looked all the same to her untrained eye, so she picked one at random, along with a box of bolts.

Roger trundled after her toward Conall's designated shooting range. She found the commander gazing over the Meadows and followed his line of sight. Not a mile away, the ground rose again and three mounted figures stood on that hill. The sun trickled along the eastern horizon and lit the group with harsh light.

"Who are they?" Rowan asked.

"Ebos. Dark elves."

"Really?" She'd only ever heard of the dark elves in stories. They were supposed to be distant cousins to the elves who lived in New Torwood. There were many old myths about Ebos stealing babies from their cradles to stew their bones. But Rowan had thought the Ebos were exactly that—a myth.

Elias chose that moment to bring them mugs of hot tea. "Breakfast will be in half an—" He froze as he saw the figures in the distance. Then he began to babble in the elvish tongue. Rowan, who'd had elvish maids all her life, recognized a few words. Elias was terrified. He dropped the mugs, fell to the ground and pressed his face to the earth. His eyes were closed and his lips repeated a prayer.

The Ebos slipped over the back side of the hill and disappeared.

Elias continued his manic supplication to whatever saints the elves' favored. Phalian had morphed into his mouse form and dodged into her pocket. Oblivious to any tension, Roger spun in a circle.

Rowan crouched beside Elias, not sure how to console him.

"Ranger, get a hold of yourself," Conall commanded. The words or the tone, snapped Elias out of his panic loop. He bolted upright, wiped his eyes and saluted with the same hand.

"Go tell Murdoch we'll be eating on the road. I want everyone up and ready to go in twenty minutes."

"Yes, sir." Elias's eyes were wide and wet, but he took his orders seriously and dashed off.

"Should we be worried about our friends out there?" Rowan asked.

"No. The Ebos won't bother us. They just like to keep tabs on what's happening in their territory."

Rowan lifted the gun. "I guess target practice is out for today." She felt relieved. That meant she could put off disappointing Conall with her obvious lack of expertise.

"Not so fast, Striker. We have twenty minutes and we're going to use them."

Rowan nodded and tried to hide her dismay.

"We'll start with something easy." Conall pointed to a boulder rising from the grass some two hundred yards away. "Aim for that."

Rowan lifted the rail gun. It was heavier than she expected. Two round barrels flanked an arrow shaped armature that held the projectile. The gun was powered by a thera chip that sent a strong current up one rail and down the other. When that current was broken, the gun fired. It held only two projectiles. Master snipers could reload in seconds, but after a full minute, Rowan still couldn't get the bolt to slide in.

Conall saw her look of panic and smiled. "It's all right. It won't bite you."

How did he see inside her head so easily? He showed her how to tilt the darts and line up the fletching. They slid in easily.

"After some practice, you'll be able to load it on the fly. But don't forget to check the rails often." He pointed to the double barrels that ran the current. "They can wear down quickly."

Rowan nodded. She'd seen Valko replace the rails while they fought the titan. He'd simply cranked the release shaft to pop them out, but after fiddling with the gun, she suspected that maneuver would take time to master.

Conall took the gun from her, opened one chamber to check the rail, then the other. He seemed satisfied with their wear and handed the weapon back to her.

"It's simple to use and almost no backlash on these newer models." He pointed to a switch on the side of the gun just above the trigger. "This is the lock. Keep it on until you're ready to shoot." He flicked the switch and the thera chip inside the gun whined. "Takes about two seconds to prime, just enough time for you to raise it and aim." He wrapped her fingers around the grip, not shying away from the mech arm. She liked that. Standing behind and beside her, he guided her hands as she raised the gun so she could look through the sight.

"Never point it at something you don't intend to shoot. Aim for that boulder." His words were quiet and the small space between his lips and her ear filled with heat.

The gun felt good in her hands. Her mech arm was already probing this new machine, assessing its balance and the power that flowed from the thera chip up one rail and down the other. She looked through the sight, but it was hard to concentrate on the target with Conall so close.

"Steady now. Don't yank the trigger. You want to squeeze it. Breathe first. In, out, then squeeze."

She took a steadying breath, let it out and pulled the trigger. The gun bucked as it fired the bolt, and she came up hard against Conall's chest.

"That's almost no backlash?" She instinctively jerked away from him. He was grinning.

"You should try shooting an old-school ballistics rifle. Those things will toss you on your ass if you're not steady."

"Have you shot a rifle?"

He nodded. "During the war. The council hadn't yet made its big push for thera. It was rarer then and we often ran out of chips. We used gunpowder rounds to kill gaunts, and knives when we ran out of those. A lot of rangers died. It gave the council ammunition to fight their detractors, and reason to build a second thera farm at Oxeye, despite…" He didn't finish that thought, but she knew what he'd been thinking.

Despite the king's protests. Before her father died, he'd been opposed to expanding thera production. Rowan didn't understand why and it no longer seemed important. The old king was dead and the city ran on thera.

"Never mind." Conall nodded toward the perfectly intact boulder she'd been aiming at.

"You missed."

"Thanks for the insight, Commander."

"That's perfectly normal. Keep practicing. We're heading out in fifteen minutes. I expect you to hit the target before then."

He left her to shoot. She sighted the boulder again. And missed. And again. The tiny sparks of energy lashing out from the gun's muzzle seemed to have a mind of their own. Her darts sailed into the empty Meadows or cut the ground ten feet in front of the target.

She wiped sweat from her face and looked up to find Orson standing nearby. He wore his usual frown. His eyes were locked on her with that creepy scribe intensity. No doubt her lack of shooting skill would be memorialized in the temple's archives.

She gritted her teeth, determined to ignore the scribe. She reloaded. Her mech fingers had learned the loading routine, and she snapped the darts into the chamber. Another shot went wide. Her shoulders began to ache, and just as she was about to give up, she finally hit the boulder. Once. And then Conall was calling for everyone to board the cat.

Rowan switched the safety lock on the gun and headed back to camp. Orson and Roger followed behind her while Phalian squawked and fluttered around her head. They made a bizarre parade through the Meadows.

At the cat, she was about to store the gun in its case when Conall stopped her.

"Keep it. You're on rear watch."

Rowan was about to protest, but something peered at her from Conall's eyes—something feral and determined—and she closed her teeth on her protest. He had better instincts for this environment, but even she could feel it.

They weren't alone out here. The sudden appearance and disappearance of the dark elves proved that anything could be hiding in that grass.

The others were already settled on the cat. Augie drove. Rowan took the last bench. There was barely enough room for her to sit with all their stored gear. She moved a crate onto the floor and perched on it, facing backwards, with her legs crossed on the bench. She rested the gun on the back of the seat, pointing it at the road behind them.

A minute later, the cat started to move. The sails unfurled and Rowan listened for any clanking or straining sounds that would indicate the sail mechs needed maintenance. She thought the right one opened a bit slowly. She'd grease the gears again when they stopped for the night.

Augie was a good driver. The cat's fat wheels plowed through the grass, and Rowan watched tracks lay out behind them. Even a blind gaunt would be able to follow that trail.

Phalian recharged on his cradle and she'd stowed Roger in a crate next to the guns. She couldn't find his off button though, and every once in a while she heard a quiet "Roger that" from the crate.

They traveled all afternoon and into the evening. The light never wavered. It was a constant golden glow along the southern horizon, slowly moving westward. At this time of year, it wouldn't set until well after midnight, and Conall seemed determined to use every bit of daylight.

At one point, they slowed to let the second cat come up beside them. Murdoch handed out food, and a small bundle wrapped in cloth was sent back to her. She unwrapped it to find some kind of flatbread sandwich. Rowan wasn't usually thrilled by wraps, but her stomach juices churned with hunger. She bit into it, expecting rubbery bread and bland filling and found instead, a delicately crisp bread around savory marinated vegetables, cheese and sausage. It was tastier than they had any right to expect on a military mission, tastier than most meals she'd eaten in the palace. She decided then that Murdoch was a genius and she'd learn to hit the target just so she could keep him alive to cook for them again.

She washed down her wrap with water from her canteen and watched the Meadows recede behind them. The empty plains stretched on forever and home seemed very far away.

Minutes or hours later, she realized that she'd been daydreaming and shirking her watch duty. She jerked the gun up and looked through the scope, scanning the horizon from left to right. Nothing. Just the endless shifting grass.

The wind that had been their constant companion died. The air grew heavy and oppressive. Distant clouds covered the sun, plunging them into an early twilight.

Augie slowed the cat to a stop.

"We're closing the sails," Conall called back. "Everybody off. You have five minutes to do whatever needs doing. No one wanders off alone."

15

NULL

They RESTED FOR NEARLY AN HOUR because Lena's cat refused to start under thera power. Rowan replaced the starter as fast as she could, aware of Conall pacing like a caged animal behind her. Finally, with her mech hand pressed against the engine, she called for Lena to start it again. The engine flared to life. Rowan closed her eyes and let her hand's knack search along the lines of power in the vehicle. Satisfied that all was in order, she shut the hood and stretched her back.

Orson stood one pace away. She nearly bumped into him.

"Seems the princess finally earns her keep." He smirked. She ignored him and went to find the others. They were gathered around the second cat. Conall had a map spread on the cat's hood.

"We should camp here tonight." Clem had no qualms about telling the commander what he should do. Conall wasn't looking at her as she spoke. Instead, he studied the map.

"We're heading here. It's the last unmanned outpost before we reach Eklridge Oasis." He pointed it out on the map, then slid his finger further south. "I think we're about here."

"The camp's too far," Clem said. "We won't make it before dark. Not without the sails."

"Maybe," Conall said. "But the sooner we find those saints-damned scientists, the sooner we can go home. So we're going to try. There's a lot of daylight ahead of us."

"I still think we should camp here." Clem stood with her arms crossed.

"Your protest is duly noted," Conall said. "Now get in the cat. You take rear watch. Rowan, you're driving."

Everyone got back on board. Rowan handed her gun to Clem, ignoring her scowl, and took the driver's seat. Without the constant wind and the long grass continually tugging at the cat, she found it easy to steer around the rocks that appeared in the path. Lena's cat followed close behind.

Conall grabbed the vox from the console and spoke into it for everyone to hear.

"We're driving until the light runs out. Everyone sleep except for those on watch—Clem and Noah."

Orson grumbled about the cramped conditions. Augie hummed.

Conall replaced the vox and tapped the compass on the console. "Just keep a steady northwest pace. Wake me in an hour." He propped his feet by the windscreen, crossed his arms and closed his eyes.

Rowan couldn't believe he was leaving her in charge just like that. Go northwest? Those were his orders?

An outcropping appeared in front of them like a beast suddenly rising from the sea, and she veered around it. Conall jerked in his seat, but he didn't open an eye or complain.

Damn him for trusting her. It was what she'd wanted from the beginning, but now this sudden bit of independence and authority unsettled her.

She glanced at the compass and realized she'd been going more north than west since that last detour. She corrected their course. The Ubruulen Mountains were straight ahead, an inky smear across a darkening sky.

The day became oppressively humid. Fat dark clouds seemed to weigh on them. Biting insects found every inch of bare, sticky skin. Rowan pulled a net over her cap and drove on.

A structure rose out of the shadows, the ruins of an ancient building. It was boxy and bone white with huge square windows that were deep with shadows like the eye sockets of a skull. She stared in awe as they drove past, wondering how the people from before could build something so huge and so perfectly square without the aid of mechs or magic.

The wind picked up but Rowan didn't dare open the cat's wings. The road ahead was barely detectable. It dipped and rose with big chunks of rock often blocking their way. Anything could be hiding behind those rocks.

It was time to stop for the night.

Rowan was about to wake Conall when the cat's thera engine stalled and it rolled to a stop.

Conall jerked awake at the sudden stillness.

"Why are we stopped?"

"I don't know. The cat stalled." She glanced back. The second cat rolled up beside them and stalled too. Lena sat in the driver seat, peering at the console in confusion.

Rowan hopped out to fetch her tools. Noah was alert and still on watch in the back seat. He moved out of the way to give her better access to the packed gear. Orson had fallen asleep with his head bent at a painful angle. No one bothered to wake him.

In the second cat, Murdoch slept on, snoring like a swarm of bees, but Elias jerked awake. He'd been sleeping with his head on Augie's shoulder. Augie smiled and patted the elf.

"Ten minutes to stretch folks," Conall said.

While she dug through the gear, Rowan's mech hand gripped the side of the cat. Its knack probed along the metal lines of the vehicle and sensed nothing. Worried now, Rowan found her tools and headed to the front of the cat. Phalian, who'd been quiet in his cradle for hours, decided to stretch his wings. He flew upward, then zoomed around the cat.

Rowan had no time for his fun and games. They were in the middle of nowhere, not a good place to get stuck without a vehicle.

She lifted the hood and studied the engine. It was a simple design—a battery to start the thera lighter that in turn ignited the ensorceled thera chip which generated a rotating magnetic field that caused the motor to turn. Thera burned efficiently and without residue. That meant the engine was clean except for some road dust.

She wiped the thera slot with a rag and pulled out the chip. It was bright cobalt blue. She wiped that too and reinserted it. Nothing. She laid her mech hand on the metal box that enclosed the engine's workings but detected no energy surging from the chip. That was odd. Even a burned out chip left some residual energy. Her black-gloved fingers caressed the engine box and trailed down to the wheels. Nothing. The whole cat was as silent as a corpse.

She straightened and found Conall standing beside her with his crossbow armed.

"The thera chip must be burned," she said.

"Didn't you replace it last night?"

"I did. It could be defective." A thera chip could power a cat for almost a week. There was no other reason it should have burned out so quickly.

"What are the odds that both cats burned through their chips at the same time?" Conall's eyes turned to the second cat.

"Not good," Rowan had to admit. "And it doesn't quite feel like a burn out."

"What do you mean?"

Rowan pulled off her cap and ran fingers through her hair. She'd been driving for hours and her eyes felt gluey with the need for sleep.

"I mean even with a chip burned out, there should be residual energy in the motor." She tapped the engine box again. "But there's nothing. I have no explanation for it."

Conall squinted. He was either thinking through the problem or wondering why he'd brought along a mechanic who couldn't even start a stalled cat. Then his gaze turned to the wall of darkness that surrounded them.

"Wake Murdoch. Change the chips just in case." His voice rose. "Everyone else is on alert. Arm yourselves."

Murdoch wasn't pleased about being woken up to hand out new chips. He grumbled as he got out of the cat to unpack his stores.

"I can't just pass 'em out like candy, you know."

"I know. I'm sorry." It wasn't Rowan's fault the cats had failed, but she felt the need to apologize anyway.

Everyone else had found rail guns or crossbows. The cats had stalled too far away from each other to make a defensible wall, so the squad had to cover all angles of attack.

"Are you expecting a fight?" Rowan whispered to Conall.

"Always."

Murdoch finally fished out the chips and handed them to Rowan. She squeezed them in her mech hand and frowned.

"These are dead too."

"Are not," Murdoch said. His black eyes shone through the fringe of black hair and beard. "I checked all the supplies before we left. You have a problem with my supplies?"

Conall ignored the cook and focused on Rowan.

"Are you sure?"

"I'm certain." She was starting to have a sneaking suspicion. She picked up the vox and turned it over in her mech fingers, looking for the tell-tale vibrations that any ensorceled mech with thera would have. The vox was dead too.

Phalian's metal feet scrabbled across the roof of the cat as he landed. "SQUAWK!"

Rowan's eyes narrowed on the mech bird.

Clem came around from the back of the cat.

"Commander, the guns aren't working." There was an edge of hysteria in her voice. She held up the rail gun and flicked off the safety. There was no whine of the thera chip priming.

Conall made a sound that was closer to a growl than a curse.

"Can you fire a crossbow?"

Clem nodded, her eyes wide.

"How about you?" he asked the others. Lena nodded but Noah and Augie shook their heads.

"Get out the crossbows," he said to Clem. "You two find knives. Everybody should be armed."

Rowan was still fiddling with the vox when an idea struck her. She found the mech valet riding in the crate at the back of the cat and touched his head. He came alive with a sharp "Roger that!" The sound seemed to bounce off the growing darkness around them.

Her eyes turned to Phalian on the roof of the cat.

"How come he works?" Conall asked.

And then at least part of the mystery became clear.

"Phalian doesn't run on thera," she said. "Neither does the valet. They're pneumas. Whatever is causing this affects thera, not just mechs." She made a fist with her mech arm as if to prove her point. Like Phalian, the arm was older than the rise of thera. It was something else entirely.

"What about him?" Conall nudged Orson who was still slumped in the middle seat of the cat. For the first time, Rowan realized he slept too deeply. All the noise should have woken him.

"Is he alive?" She reached out to test the pulse on his neck. Orson had been nothing but miserable on this mission. She hadn't wanted him along, but that didn't mean she wanted him dead.

A faint pulse thrummed against her fingers.

"He's alive."

"I don't know the specifics of scribe mechanics," Conall said, "but don't they work with thera too?"

"Yes." Rowan switched hands and let her mech fingers trail the wire that was plugged into the base of Orson's neck. It disappeared into the collar of his shirt and would be attached to a recording device on his hip. The scribes were very secretive about their mech. Rowan didn't have any experience with them, but whatever was affecting the thera was also affecting the scribe.

Elias jumped from his seat. His voice rose in a shrill squeak. "It's a null! We must leave. Now!"

It was an unusual outburst from the shy elf and everyone turned to look at him. A wolf howled in the distance. The call was answered by a second wolf.

"It's the dark ones! This is how they do it." Elias's eyes were wide and caught the last light. He took off his woolen hat and shook it at them.

"Do what?" Conall asked.

Elias was too agitated to answer. He jumped up and down, wringing the hat in his hands.

Conall gripped the elf's hands in his. "Settle down."

Elias swallowed hard and licked his lips.

"It's the dark ones," he whispered. "They eat children and make their bones dance like puppets."

Conall frowned. "There are no children here, Ranger."

Rowan returned to the front of the cat and stared at the engine. Her fingers itched to fix something, but without thera there was nothing she could do.

A sudden gust of wind slammed into them. Canvas flapped around the crates tied to the last car. The engine hood shook, straining the flimsy arm that held it open. Rowan lowered the hood.

"Can't fix it?" Conall asked. He kept his voice low, so the others couldn't hear. Rowan detected no hint of reproof in his tone, and his eyes continued to scan the swaying grasses. He just wanted all the facts before he made a decision.

"Without thera, we're stuck. Unless you want to sail out of here."

Another gust of wind battered them as if to remind them what a bad idea that would be in the dark.

"No. It's late anyway. We'll camp here. It'll be an uncomfortable night."

Rowan grinned. "If I'd wanted comfort, I would have stayed in the palace."

"Commander!" Lena yelled. "Something's moving out there!"

Rowan spun around. Dusk had fallen on the Meadows like a gray shroud.

"I see it too!" Clem's voice was shrill. Her crossbow fired with a crack.

Something screamed. Or someone.

Elias answered with a piercing cry and bolted into the night.

Figures appeared like wraiths from the shadows. Too many for a few crossbows to stop.

They were surrounded.

16

CHILDREN OF DARKNESS

Garou WAS STRANGELY QUIET IN THE back of Conall's mind. When trapped, the wolf usually lashed out, but he knew the scent that besieged them—horse and bone and a strange spice he didn't recognize, but would never forget.

They'd come across dark elves during the war, when a clan of bloodthirsty gaunts had trapped them in a mountain pass. Their squad had been out of ammunition, hungry, thirsty and sleep deprived. Conall had fully expected to die that day. Until the Ebos had materialized as if from the mountain rocks themselves. The elves rushed in on their odd little ponies, killing half the gaunts and scaring away the rest. They stayed long enough to share a meal, then the elves disappeared without a word, like ghosts misting into the darkness.

Conall studied the band that surrounded them now. Most were mounted on the same short, shaggy ponies with long manes that were braided and decorated with bones. The elves wore dun colored robes with elaborate chains of bones around their necks. More bones pierced their earlobes and nostrils.

They like bones. Garou made a snuffling, snorting sound in his mind, as if the wolf had just dug up something dead and didn't know if he should piss on it or roll in it.

An Ebos pushed through the crowd of ponies, shoving Elias before him. Elias had a wild-eyed look that was one shade away from catatonia. Two Ebos jumped down from their mounts to take custody of him. One of them ran their hand up his arm from finger tips to shoulder, then leaned in and sniffed him. Conall realized she was female. It was hard to tell under the sack-like robes. She ran a finger along Elias's cheek like he was a prize for her taking. It was all too much for the gentle elf. He crumpled to the ground and squeezed his eyes shut.

Conall felt for the little guy. Every culture had their bogeymen and for the Enos, those monsters were the dark elves—the Ebos. Elias had probably grown up on stories of Ebos stealing naughty children and now he was caught in one of those fireside tales.

Conall's knowledge of the elves wasn't much better than average. He knew that the Ebos and Elias's people were from the same home planet, Essa. The name Enos meant Child of Light in their language. And Ebos meant Child of Darkness. But the Ebos who stood guard over Elias could have been his siblings, they looked so similar—lean in body with long limbs and small delicate features, messy blond hair and amber eyes. Conall wondered what diverging roads in history had made the two races mortal enemies.

There had to be two dozen Ebos surrounding the cat, all pointing spears or nocked bows at his squad. Despite Garou's inexplicable silence, Conall's fingers itched to grab the air blades on his belt. Even if their thera magic was nullified, he felt the driving need to have blades in his hands. Or claws on his fingers.

Dark elves might have saved him once, but who could say these were the same elves, or even the same clan? An Ebos barked out an order, though in his high-pitched voice, it was more of a yip than a bark. Another Ebos jumped off his pony and stalked over to Rowan. His eyes were level with her elbow, but his spear was taller than him and tipped in sharpened bone. He pointed to Phalian who fluttered around her head with clacking wings.

"No…" The next word was lost on Conall. Rowan stared at the elf in confusion. He tried again.

"No…machine." He jabbed at the mech bird with his spear. Phalian squawked and dove to attack. The elf waved his hands like he was swatting a fly. "No machine! No machine!"

"Okay!" Rowan whistled. Phalian darted around the elf in one last rebellious loop then landed on her arm. The wings parted and folded into his back. He shrank until an inert mouse sat in Rowan's palm. She tucked it into her pocket and held her hands wide—one fully gloved, the other covered in a fingerless glove.

"See? No machine."

But the elf wasn't fooled. His eyes latched onto the black glove.

"No machine!" He gripped Rowan's arm.

Conall started forward and three elves leveled spears at his chest. He froze. Garou bristled. His complacency was shattered when they menaced Rowan.

Conall gauged the distance between him and the spears, how long it would take to let the wolf out, and how many he could take down before they killed him. Or Rowan. That possibility stalled him in his tracks. He glanced around. The others were also being held at spear point. Clem had thrown down her crossbow. Elias had definitely gone catatonic, and the female Ebos stroked him like a favored pet. Augie floated three feet in the air. A couple of elves clung to his feet. Only Orson was still knocked out in the cat.

Rowan pulled her arm away from the elf and rolled up her sleeve. Just below her elbow the merging of metal and flesh was almost seamless.

"It's not a machine. Look. I can't remove it."

The elf studied her arm. He pulled back on the black glove, then tugged on the arm too.

"Hey!" Rowan jerked it away from his grip. The elf came to some decision and pushed his way through the mounted elves again.

They waited.

Noah leaned over and spoke softly. "Commander, we should attack now. Before they summon more fighters. If we act as one, we can overpower them."

"Stand down, Maven. Let's find out what they want first."

The ponies parted and a tall Ebos strode forward—tall for an elf. He still didn't reach Conall's shoulder. He was older than the others, his face lined with fine wrinkles like cracks in antique crockery. Wisps of white hair fluttered around a crown that was studded with sharpened teeth like the pickets of a tiny fence. His dun-colored robe fell in loose folds to the ground. It shimmered in the fading light and made a faint tinkling sound as he moved. As he came closer, Conall realized it was covered in hundreds of polished bone discs. A necklace of more teeth and bones hung around his neck.

His shrewd gaze swept the scene, scrutinizing and assessing each squad member before landing on Rowan. Then the old elf smiled. He walked over and took her hands in his.

"Princess, I am pleased to meet you."

Conall wondered at his perfect diction before he registered that the elf knew Rowan. Or knew of her. He supposed the stories of the little princess with the mech arm had spread even outside the walls of New Torwood City.

Rowan inclined her head, but didn't try to pull her hands free. "Sir."

"Please, call me Omika."

"Omika, may I ask why you have detained us?"

Slender brows lowered over his eyes. "There has been violence in the north and sickness in the south. We reserve the right to make sure none of these troubles affect our territory." He spoke clearly but with an odd lilting tone. "And then, my scout told me of the unusual woman who is machine, but not machine and I knew I had to introduce myself."

"I am glad to know you."

"Good, good." He patted her hand. "I think it is time that our peoples become…friends."

"Of course. We always have room in New Torwood for friends."

Rowan's entire attention was focused on Omika. Conall felt as if he were witnessing a great moment in history—the formal greeting between two great peoples. And poor Orson was knocked out in the cat. He'd be spitting mad when he woke up.

The elf patted Rowan again and moved on to Clem. He scanned her from head to toe and nodded as if she'd confirmed some unspoken thought. He frowned at Lena after looking into her eyes. Noah got a smile, though the medic scowled. Omika stepped around Elias who was still cringing under the touch of the female Ebos. He touched Augie's foot and the ranger suddenly dropped to the ground. The elf squeezed his arm in a grandfatherly way. Finally, Murdoch gave the old elf a short salute.

And then Omika was standing before Conall.

"Striker West." He smiled. "You may not remember me, but we met once before, on a dark night in the mountains."

Conall nodded. "I remember your fighters. You came to our aid. I am glad to finally be able to thank you. But it's Commander West now."

"Of course. We have all moved on to bigger and better things."

Conall didn't know about better. He'd reserve that judgment until after this mission was completed. So far, an easy jaunt into the Meadows had turned into one problem after another.

"We won't detain you any longer, Commander. I only wished to meet the heir to House Andula." He smiled at Rowan, who stiffened at that title. "But this meeting has been fortuitous because I have a message for you too."

Conall squinted. The elf had to tip his head back to meet his eye, and yet Conall was the one who felt small in his presence.

"A message?" How could the elf have anything to say to him?

"Yes. A simple request. You might call it a prognostication."

Conall held his tongue. The elf could play his games but he wouldn't be goaded into reacting.

Omika leaned in and whispered, "One day you will come to me, Wolf. For Misha's sake."

Conall felt the words like a blade of ice spearing his heart.

The Ebos turned and limped off. Conall watched in frozen panic as the spears withdrew. Ponies turned and trotted into the night. The female Ebos gave Elias one lingering kiss on the lips, then followed the others.

The squad was left alone and confused.

For Misha's sake? How could the elf even know that name? It was impossible.

"Commander?" Clem drew his attention. She held a rail gun and the familiar whine of a thera chip being primed rang through the silence. The sound shook him back to reality.

Orson woke up. "What the saints did you do to me?" His voice rose like the squawk of an angry chicken. "The Abbott Archivist will hear about this! Scribes are—"

"Sacrosanct!" The shout came from Rowan, Clem and Noah at once.

"We know," Noah said. "Now shut up." Clem was grinning. Rowan refused to look at Orson who scowled at them all.

Conall shook his head. This night held many mysteries, but maybe it had revealed Orson's true purpose on this mission. Maybe he was meant to unite the squad against a common annoyance.

"Everyone on the cats," he said. "We're not stopping again until we reach the outpost."

17

STRANGE BEASTS IN THE MEADOWS

Everyone WAS GRUMPY. ORSON RETAINED HIS pissy mood after the Ebos left, as if his incapacitation had been the squad's doing. Elias took up the last seat in their cat and he was just plain freaked out. He sat with his knees drawn up to his chin, and his eyes unfocused. And Conall had taken brooding to a new level. Rowan really wanted to know what Omika had said to him. Whatever it was, it had shaken his foundations. He sat with rigid shoulders and stared at the unchanging landscape.

Despite Conall's insistence that they ride through the night, the terrain proved too unpredictable, and they stopped for a few hours, not bothering to make camp. Rowan didn't care. She was tired enough to sleep in the cat.

Morning met them with calm winds. They opened the sails and flew over flat ground. Without the thera engine, the chirp of crickets and the occasional yip of a coyote were the only sounds.

The short rest had barely taken the edge of her exhaustion and Rowan kept her eyes on the mountains. That was all she could focus on.

They drove all day.

The sun moved steadily toward the western horizon. A bank of dark clouds hovered over the mountains and they seemed to boil red, black and orange. The lowland Meadows stretched before them, miles of grass dotted with traps of marsh.

And thousands of caribou.

Rowan slowed the cat. She had never imagined anything this majestic could exist. Caribou covered the plains like a great, brown blanket. Males sported huge multi-pointed racks, getting ready for the fall rut. Smaller

156

females wore only budding antlers, many with young calves by their sides. Buntings, willets and geese fought for ground between the constantly shuffling hooves and feasted on the swarms of insects that followed the herd.

"We go around." It was the first thing Conall had said all afternoon.

"Do we have time?" Going around the herd would take hours, if not days. "They're just big deer. If we stay in the cat, surely we'll be fine."

"Those deer weigh over six-hundred pounds. And they've been known to stampede from warble fly bites. What do you think will happen if we're in the middle of that herd with nowhere to run when they panic?"

Conall picked up the vox and spoke one command. "Turn east."

Up ahead, Clem's cat turned away from the sun and skirted the edge of the herd. Every now and then, a stray buck would dart from the pack and challenge the cats, but mostly they were left alone. They were just another strange beast in the Meadows.

Hours later, they left the herd behind and turned north again. The sun was almost due west now. Soon it would dip below the mountains for the short night.

Animal sounds dimmed as the wind picked up. The cat had a windscreen, but no side windows on the passenger cars. They were open to the coming elements and the wind scoured them.

"We should find shelter." Conall scanned the ridge to their right.

A gust of wind snared their sails. The cat jerked sideways, and Rowan slowed down. Her mech arm had taken the full measure of the vehicle by now and it sent its knack deep into the cat's frame, always searching for loose bolts or worn gaskets that it could soothe before they caused trouble. Without it, she would have lost control of the cat already.

"I'm shutting the sails," she said.

Ahead, Clem had the same idea. She'd stopped her cat and was already furling up their wings. Rowan slowed and hit the button to retract the mechanical arms. She started the thera engine, ready to take off again as soon as the sails were stowed, but the left sail arm made a terrible grinding, stuttering noise and jammed. A gust of wind hooked the half-closed sail and the cat jumped. It teetered on two wheels before slamming back to the ground.

"Get that sail closed!" Conall shouted.

"I'm trying!" The wind was a screaming beast now. Rowan hopped out of the cat to inspect the problem. The sail arm was comprised of a series of interconnected metal bars that opened and closed like an accordion. She saw the problem right away. The sail had ripped and a piece of cloth was jammed in the accordion joint. When the retracting engine forced it, one of the metal bars had snapped. It swung loose in the wind. Rowan grabbed the bar and sensed how it was cut off from the rest of the arm.

"Roll it back!" she shouted over the growing wind. Thunder thrummed in the distance.

Conall reversed the sail arm engine. The snagged material was still caught.

"Stop!" She tugged at the snarl. A wind gust snatched the cap off her head and tossed it away into the Meadows.

Damn. She loved that cap.

"Okay, try it again," she shouted, then, "Stop!" as gears ground.

Conall turned off the thera engine and jumped out. Orson watched her from the relative safety of his seat and made no move to help. Elias rocked back and forth and seemed to be praying.

Clem was turning her cat around to see what the problem was. Conall walked out to meet them. The wind tore at his shirt and hair, making him look like a wild thing that belonged in the Meadows. He conferred with Clem, then the other cat rolled on into the darkening Meadows.

Conall returned just as Rowan finally wrenched out the snagged sail.

She wiped a grease covered hand across her forehead. "Okay, try it again."

Conall jumped into the front seat and hit the retract button.

"No! The other way!" The arm stopped, then began to open again. This time the gears didn't grind. "Okay, hold!"

With the accordion stretched wide, Rowan re-attached the loose metal bar. She primed her mech arm and touched her finger to the joint to solder the bar in place. The job was finished in seconds, leaving a whiff of hot metal in the air.

"Impressive," Conall said. Fat drops of rain were starting to fall. Phalian poked his head from her pocket, decided he didn't like the rain and ducked back inside.

Rowan guided the sail arm into its compartment. The door clicked shut and she leaned on it. There was something satisfying about mech that worked just right.

Conall returned to the passenger seat with his crossbow already pointing into the growing darkness. "Let's go."

Rowan hopped in beside him and started the engine. "Where did the others go?"

"To find shelter. We don't have a lot of time." He pointed northward. The storm was rushing toward them like a landslide. Gray streaks of rain made it seem like the mountains were melting. Lightning struck a scraggly tree not fifty feet away.

Rowan swerved.

"Fuckety-fuck-fuck!"

Conall slammed into her, but he was grinning.

"A princess with a potty mouth. I like it."

"You should meet my Auntie."

Another gust shook the cat. Even without the sails, they were taking a beating. She could barely see a dozen yards ahead. Thunder clouds blotted out the weak sun, making the sky as dark as the Meadows would be until winter.

Conall tapped her shoulder. "Over there." He pointed ahead and to the right. Rowan spotted a light. The other cat was stopped by a rocky outcropping and Clem had lit a thera lamp to guide them.

Rowan pulled up beside the other cat and Conall jumped out before they'd even stopped.

"Secure the cats. And put out that light before you bring a wrath of gaunts down on our heads!"

18

FACING THE STORM

He SHOULD HAVE LEFT ROWAN TO secure the cats while he saw the others safely into the shelter, but he couldn't abandon her outside with the growing storm. It wasn't that he didn't trust her to do her job, but she was a fucking princess, not some random mechanic, and it was his job to keep her alive.

Garou tutted in his mind.

You've been crabby as a hungry pup since the Ebos left. Shake it off.

Conall ignored the wolf and crouched in the rain and driving wind to help Rowan stake down the cats. Noah and Augie stayed to help, and it took all four of them to hold down the second cat when the wind menaced it. Augie hammered in the last stake. Conall lashed a rope to it, tugged twice to make sure it was secure, then shoved the boy toward the cave.

"Get inside!" His words were lost to the wind. Augie gaped at him until Noah grabbed his arm and hauled him away.

Conall turned to find Rowan fighting with the straps that tied a trunk to the back bench of their cat.

Lightning sizzled across the sky, followed a split second later by a crash of thunder.

Conall fought the wind until he was at her side.

"Leave it!"

She shook her head. She'd lost her cap, and rain plastered her hair to her head.

"I can get it!"

"Now!" The wolf snarled. Wolves didn't understand stubbornness. They faced every dilemma with reason. If it could kill you, get away from it. If not, eat it.

They couldn't eat the storm.

Lightning cut across the sky again.

He growled and yanked her left arm. Her other hand—the black gloved one—gripped his fingers like a vise and squeezed. The wolf yelped. His eyes met Rowan's through the downpour. He saw frustration there and a bit of desperation. Then she looked embarrassed when she realized she was pinching him, and her grip relaxed.

They ran for the shelter.

"I'm sorry." She was breathless and dripping with rain when they ducked into the cave. "I left Roger out there. I wanted to be sure he was secure." She glanced at the wall of water falling outside as if she might run back into it.

"You found that mech roaming the Meadows, right?"

She nodded.

"Then he's probably weathered worse storms. Come on. Let's see if Murdoch has anything hot to drink."

The cave wasn't one of the Meadows' finer accommodations. It was little more than a hole dug into the base of a rocky hill by some industrious creature and then abandoned. Probably because it flooded in the rainy season. Conall didn't like close, dark spaces, but Garou had no trouble with their den. He let the wolf take charge as they crept underground. The ceiling dipped and he had to bend almost in half. The rain had followed them in and flowed along the floor in a stream, looking for lower ground. Only a dim light from ahead urged him onward.

After a few steps, the ceiling rose again and Rowan was able to stand. Conall kept his neck bent so he didn't brain himself on the stone ceiling. Already, a puddle was forming in the middle of the open space. It would have been snug enough for a lone wolf on the prowl, but eight rangers and a scribe barely fit shoulder to shoulder along the cavern's walls. They couldn't stand up. They couldn't lie down. There was no room for a fire.

Noah stumbled over Lena and mumbled "Sorry," then bumped into Augie and apologized again.

Augie didn't seem to like the small space either. His humming had ratcheted up a notch.

"Ranger, cut out the singing," Conall snapped. Augie fell silent. A moment later, his feet left the ground and his back flattened against the roof of the low cave.

At least he's quiet.

Each ranger found a small bit of ground to claim. Sounds were amplified in the small space. The crackle of gravel underfoot and the rasp of uniforms against stone grated on his nerves.

Somehow, Murdoch had lugged the thera stove inside. It gave off enough light to see the outlines of huddled squad members. Elias had somewhat recovered from his ordeal with the Ebos and he handed out mugs of steaming tea.

Orson sat with his legs stretched out in front of him. They were in the way and Elias had to climb over him to reach the others. The scribe's eyes were open, but rolled back to show mostly white, and his eyelids fluttered. His jaw was slack, leaving his mouth to gape. His hands twitched in his lap.

"Why does he do that?" Clem nudged his legs away so she could sit against the wall. "Is he calling to his mother ship or something?"

"He's recording the day's events," Conall said.

"Recording? Like on a theragraph?" Clem cocked her head to get a better view of the scribe.

Conall wasn't sure exactly how scribe mechs worked, but he was pretty sure it wasn't like a theragraph, though that was as good a guess as any. The flat discs of a theragraph could be etched with sound waves and played back on a theraphone device. Good sized chips of thera were expensive though, so the devices were rare. The Temple of the Word that trained scribes and stored their data was rich, thanks to the regent's favor, but he didn't think they were rich enough to outfit every scribe with theragraph recorders. Besides they were too big to carry on a belt. Whatever mech Orson used was hidden in a pouch on his waist.

"Not a theragraph," Rowan said. Her teeth stuttered with cold, and Conall resisted the urge to warm her. "But something similar. They call it a cachet. The archivists at the temple are pretty secretive about their mech. No one really knows how they work."

"Well, whatever it is, it's super creepy." Clem turned her back to the scribe.

Conall was just glad that Orson was quiet for a change. Augie had settled on the ground, but the quiet hum of *Ode to Joy* rumbled from his chest again.

Suddenly the walls seemed to press down on Conall. The polite comments of strangers forced into close proximity, the nervous laughter, the humming… it all became oppressive. Even the wolf needed air.

He nudged Rowan. "You can listen to choir boy over there. I'm going to take first watch at the entrance. Keep the others in line, Striker."

Rowan gave him a half-hearted salute, then wrapped her hands around her mug of hot tea.

Conall rose, grabbed his crossbow, and lurched over feet and legs toward the narrow corridor. His breath came in rough gasps by the time he reached the outer cavern. He crouched by the entrance and gulped in the blessedly fresh air, not caring that rain splashed over his boots.

The thunder and lightning had moved off, but rain continued to fall in straight sheets that pounded the grass flat. This was the worst kind of storm. Gaunts and titans would take shelter from lightning, but rain didn't bother them.

He backed up to stay dry, but kept a close eye on the cave entrance, scanning the dark Meadows for the shining eyes of gaunts on the hunt.

They'd be slaughtered if the creatures found them. There was no escaping this bolt hole. And they wouldn't be able to wait them out. Gaunts didn't play subtle games like that with their prey. They would rush the cave, getting in each other's way in their mania to kill and eat the crunchy humans. Conall could probably shoot a couple, but that wouldn't stop them. Even if he managed to get a lucky head shot—because that was the only thing that could take out a gaunt—the others would simply climb over the body of their fallen comrade to finish the job.

Why are you worrying about monsters? Garou asked.

It was a good question. They hadn't seen any evidence of gaunts yet. Perhaps the Ebos had stirred up too many memories. Omika's words came back to him.

One day you will come to me, Wolf. For Misha's sake.

It hadn't surprised him that the Ebos had known he was a wolf. Omika commanded deep magic. Even Conall's human nose could smell it on him.

No, it wasn't the strong magic coming off the elf that bothered him. It was that name. Misha. Omika shouldn't know it. *Couldn't* know it.

A bird flew into the rain. It took a moment for Conall to register the mech. Then it let out a piercing "SQUAWK!" The thing sounded ridiculous, like it had once heard a human imitating a bird and chose to mimic that call.

Phalian squawked again and bolted back inside, to flutter around the small cave. Conall turned to find Rowan crawling through the tunnel.

"Food's ready. I brought you this." She held up a small bundle.

"Thanks. You'd better settle your mech down. You'd be surprised the way sound carries in a storm."

Rowan whistled and the mech bird landed on her arm. Its wings clicked and a tiny motor whirred as they slid into its back. In a moment, a mouse sat on her wrist. Rowan opened a flap on her glove. The mouse attached itself to a cradle and stilled. Conall had seen the mech transform a dozen times but it never failed to fascinate him. He couldn't resist the urge to take her hand and study it. His finger ran along the glove to the sleeping mouse. He felt her shiver.

"It's weird, I know," Rowan said. He couldn't read her expression in the dim light. "Phalian came with the arm."

"He's an interesting bit of mech. Is he charging?"

"Yeah. Most people think it's creepy that I have a rodent attached to me at all times."

"Not creepy. Just..." He searched for the right word. "Quirky?"

"My dressmaker in the palace would have another description for it." She gave a small laugh that hit Conall right in the heart. It wasn't a happy laugh. His thumb traced a line across her mech palm and their eyes met above this connection.

"Are you flirting with me, Commander?" Her voice was barely a whisper and yet it filled the small space. "Isn't there something in the rule book about fraternizing with a subordinate?"

"Yes, there is. But let's not pretend that I have any authority over you, Princess."

"Hmmm. That's not what you said the day we left the city. You were quite explicit about how I ranked less than a slug."

"I was...grumpy. The council had just coerced me into taking command of a bunch of greens. I don't like being forced into anything. It's why I live my life alone in the Meadows."

He let go of her and she leaned against the stone wall. The cave entrance sat between them, glowing faintly like a portal to another world.

"Besides, I remember you putting me in my place like a naughty pup."

"You *were* naughty."

She handed him the bundle of food. He opened it to find cold rations—travel bread, jerky and some kind of dried fruit. He wasn't hungry, but the wolf urged him to eat anyway.

Rowan lowered herself to the ground and crossed her legs.

"If you don't mind, I'll sit with you for a while. It's very tight back there."

Conall nodded and chewed the tough jerky. They sat like that until he finished the meal. His eyes grew hot and heavy. The rain was a constant tattoo that soothed and lulled. He stood and poked his head outside, peering eastward. The sky was still dark. They had at least another two hours before sunrise.

The cold rain revived him, and he scrubbed hands over his face to wake himself up before settling back against the wall again.

Rowan's dark eyes watched him. Her wet hair was drying in curlicues.

She looks like a flower, Garou said. Conall scowled. The wolf was constantly trying to shape his opinion of the princess. But she *did* look like a flower. A black-eyed Susan, he decided. The kind that grow untamed along the roadsides.

"You're frowning." Her voice came out of darkness.

"I'm sorry?"

"I said, you're frowning. You haven't stopped since we left those elves. Can I ask what Omika said? It seemed to upset you."

Conall made a noise deep in his throat, but didn't answer.

"Was it something about your wolf?"

He turned to stare at her. "What do you know about my wolf?"

She held up her hands as if to fend him off.

"Not much. Only what Dale Shannock told me. You're the Wolf of Algid Pass."

"Dale should keep their mouth shut."

"Maybe. But they're a good friend. Since we were children. They wanted to be sure I had all the facts. Dale also told me you were a great commander, before…you know."

"Before I killed my general, you mean." Conall grunted. "Does everyone else know?"

"Not from me."

He thought about that. Bretta knew, of course. And Clem. That probably meant they all knew.

"Omika surprised me. He mentioned Misha. It's a name few people know." He paused. Rowan didn't prod him on, and he liked that about her. She would keep his secrets. "In my clan…our wolves are part of us but separate." He ran a hand over his beard. He was making a hash of this. "What I mean is that they are a distinct spirit inside here." He tapped his head. "And when in wolf form, they take control. As such we give them names—names that we only tell to friends and family. Misha was the name of my brother's wolf. He's been dead for nine years and there's no reason an elf lord should know that name."

"I see."

They sat in silence for a while. He faced the driving rain, but he could feel her presence beside him, like the glow of a fire nearby.

"Did you really kill that general?"

He nodded and let out a harsh laugh at the sudden detour of her thoughts.

"I'm surprised it took this long for someone to ask."

"It's not the sort of thing that comes up in conversation."

"No, I guess not."

"Why did the regent make you commander of this mission then?"

He paused for a moment.

She should hear the worst of it, Garou said. *She can handle it.*

"Because he expects us to fail."

Rowan stared at him for a moment, then her shoulders sagged. "I kind of figured that. We're the misfits. The shifter, the princess no one wants, an elf, an embittered scribe and a medic who can only heal in a fit of rage. And let's not even talk about Lena. She's broken."

"Don't forget the floater."

Rowan huffed out a laugh and started to hum Augie's signature piece.

Conall grabbed her hand. The mech fingers curled around his grip. "We're only misfits if we let them label us. I don't plan on sticking around long enough for that."

"Lucky you." Rowan's eyes locked on his. She swallowed hard. Then she scooted back. The cool wind blew between them. Rowan shivered. She was still damp from the rain.

"Come here." He pulled her over to his side of the entrance, putting himself between her and the storm. He tucked his arm around her. She stiffened.

"Don't get any ideas, Princess. This is all about conserving heat. Unless you want to go back into that storm for blankets."

"N—no, sir."

"Good." He put his crossbow on the ground within easy reach and pulled her close against him. After a moment, her shivering slowed.

"Why do they think we'll fail?" she asked. "It's pretty straight forward isn't it? Find the science camp. Report back."

Conall was silent for a long moment.

"I'm not sure, but one thing misfits generally have in common is that they're expendable. Only this time…"

"This time, there's a princess in the mix," she finished for him.

"Exactly." He didn't like the treachery that hinted at, but he'd let her come to her own conclusions.

They listened to the storm for a while. The wind was ramping up again for round two.

He couldn't ignore the weight of her body against his. She was warm. And she fit into the crook of his shoulder like a puzzle piece he'd never known he was missing.

"Are you really posting watch out here," she asked, "or are you just too claustrophobic to go inside?"

"The last time I waited out a storm like this, I woke up to a pack of gaunts prowling around my camp."

"What did you do?"

"I hid until the fuckers left. But there's no escape from this cave if the gaunts find us. We'll be slaughtered before the others even wake up."

She was quiet for a long moment before she said, "Good pep talk, Commander."

His wolf snorted. He liked her. Even wet, she didn't reek of rage like the medic or fear like Augie.

She smelled like mate.

Not gonna happen, buddy. I don't do princess stuff.

What is princess stuff? the wolf asked.

I dunno. Cupcakes, probably. And frilly dresses. Parties with cupcakes and frilly dresses. And boring music and endless, meaningless chatter.

She's not frilly now.

Yeah, well…just shut up.

It wasn't his best come back, and he could feel the wolf smirking. He could also feel the weight of Rowan's body as she relaxed against him. He stayed awake, watching the storm lash the sky.

"Conall?" Her voice was soft as if it came from her dreams.

"Hmmm."

"Can you tell me your wolf's name?"

Garou was close to the surface. He reached a hand to stroke her hair and Conall didn't know if the gesture came from him or the wolf.

"One day, when he's ready."

"Tell him…" Her words slurred as sleep came for her. "Tell him, I'll be very glad to meet him."

INTERLUDE

They DIDN'T FIND ANY GAUNT NESTS or eggs, but only a rotting weasel carcass.

"Look, it's a titan!" Dale was getting into the game now, more for Rowan's benefit than his own. Ethan had wanted to scare the princess with their talk of gaunts, but she was an Andula as much as her brother. It would take more than a few pretend gaunts to scare her.

She peered into the shadow where the dead weasel lay.

"It's not. Titans are huge." She extended her arms as wide as they could go.

"It *is* huge, if it's a mouse titan."

"Oh!"

Rowan crouched to examine the dead thing. She poked it with her pretend sword, but it continued to be a dead weasel, so she moved on.

The ruins were littered with fallen walls and crumbling foundations. They cast deep shadows, and Rowan seemed determined to investigate each one. She jumped onto the next rock pile, brandishing her stick.

"Where to now, Commander?" Dale called up to the tower. Ethan's ginger head poked out the window.

"East, Striker! I see a wave of beasts coming right at you! I'll give cover fire!" He pointed his sword into the sky and made gunfire sounds, quicker than any real ranger could fire and reload.

"Quick, duck in here!" Dale jumped into the shadow of a crumbling foundation. Rowan turned and pretended to fight off a horde of snarling gaunts with her stick blade. Dale had brought his slingshot and he launched stones at the invading army.

"I got you! And you! And you!" Rowan stabbed at the invisible gaunts.

"Good job, Maven!" Dale said. "There's more coming in from the east!"

Rowan paused and brushed hair from her sweaty face.

"Which way is east?"

Dale peered at the sky. The dim light seemed to come from every direction. How long had they been out here? Too long, he decided.

He took Rowan's hand. "Come on. We should get back."

A scream tore through the day.

Rowan's eyes widened. "Was that a gaunt?"

Another shout, deeper this time. A man's voice.

And a boy's furious yell.

Ethan!

"Wait here. Don't move!" Dale shoved the princess behind him. He ran toward the tunnel. A cat was parked beside the tower. A man stood on the mountain of rubble. A second man dragged Ethan out of the tower by one arm. The prince bled from a cut on his face. He shouted and the man backhanded him. Ethan's head snapped back, and he collapsed in the stranger's grip.

Dale didn't understand what he was seeing. It was so…wrong. No one hit the prince. No one. It was impossible!

One of the men ripped Ethan's shirt, exposing a bony chest. Ethan's head hung forward. Blood dripped from his nose. The other man took something from the cat. It looked like a garden rake with three tines. His hand rose and came down, embedding the tines in Ethan's chest. He scored downward, leaving three jagged, bloody lines.

Ethan bucked and shrieked.

Dale wanted to help his friend, but his feet were frozen to the ground.

The man lifted the rake again and slammed it into Ethan's stomach.

"Dale?" The little voice came to him from seemingly far away. He swallowed down the gorge that rose in his throat, and fisted his shaking hands.

Rowan. He had to get her away. He ran to the princess and grabbed her hand. He yanked so hard, she lost her footing. She cried out as her knee hit stone.

"*Quiet!*" Dale hissed. He covered her mouth with one hand and dragged her into the cover of the ruins. He found a small alcove, little more than the corner of a foundation where a wall had fallen to make a recess. He scrambled into the hole and pulled Rowan in after him.

"You have to be quiet. They're out there." His whispered words came between ragged breaths.

"Who? The gaunts?"

"Yes!"

Rowan stared at him. He could smell fear oozing from her pores.

"For real?"

"For real." Dale pulled her against his chest and tried to make them as small as possible. She hadn't seen the men or the horrible things they'd done to Ethan. Better that she believe in gaunts, instead of having that nightmare chase her for the rest of her life.

No sound came from outside. That meant the killers were still out there. He would hear the cat engine if they left. Or would he? Dale hadn't heard them drive up, but they'd been deep in the ruins, and deep in their game of pretend.

Stupid, stupid! How could they have been so reckless? Everyone knew raiders lived outside the walls, men and women who would kill for the shoes off your feet. The stories said they even ate children.

Dale shivered and pressed Rowan close. She was trembling now.

But raiders wouldn't drive a cat.

That thought stuck out. And why would raiders stab Ethan with a big fork?

The low rumble of voices scared any other rational thought from his mind. A crunch of gravel told him the men were only yards away. He squeezed Rowan tighter. The footsteps receded, but still they didn't move.

Minutes went by that felt like hours. How long would it be before someone at the palace realized they were missing?

It didn't matter. They'd never come searching here. No one knew they came to play in the old ruins, no one except…

Dale *had* told someone.

Chancellor Atherton's secretary, Flora Bosman. She'd promised that Ethan wouldn't get in trouble. She'd made it sound like it was Dale's duty to keep the prince safe, and that meant telling an adult where they liked to play. Just in case.

In case of what? In case raiders that weren't raiders tried to kill the prince?

Assassinate, not kill. Master Fry had made that distinction. When royalty was murdered, it was called an assassination.

Someone had assassinated the prince.

Oh, saints, oh saints, oh saints. Dale didn't know what to do. He was just a kid, how was he supposed to keep the prince out of trouble? That was like trying to hold off the spring melt in the Ikon.

He'd known he'd failed as soon as Ethan had got that glint in his eye this afternoon. He'd failed Ethan. But he wouldn't fail Rowan too.

He squeezed her tight, wishing he could squash her down to something that would fit in his pocket. Instead, he shielded her trembling body with his own.

And he waited.

19

STALKING NIGHTMARES

The DREAMS PLAGUED HER AGAIN. SHE ran through a maze of broken stone walls. A scream chased her. The gaunts had come in from the east to attack them…

Rowan woke with a moment of disconnect.

A sandhill crane let out a garbled caw in the distance.

The Meadows.

She was far from home and far from her nightmares that were already misting away in the sunlight that warmed her legs.

Her face was pressed against…a shoulder? It was possible she snorted as she jerked away from Conall in horror. There might have been drool involved.

Had she slept on him all night? The poor man probably didn't get a wink.

"Sorry," she mumbled and wiped her mouth. Definitely, drool was involved.

It was hard to tell behind his scruffy beard, but the commander was grinning at her.

"It's okay. You only snored a bit."

Wonderful.

She glanced outside. The morning was bright with no trace of the storm.

"Is anyone else awake?"

"No. It's dark in the cave. I figured I'd let them sleep."

That was fine but her bladder was about to burst and she needed to go outside.

Except, in the cramped space, that meant crawling over Conall. Her hand landed on his thigh and slipped down…Jupiter and Jocasta, it wasn't even her mech hand. Bare fingers felt every twitch of his hard muscle clamp down as she groped her way past him. Her only thought now was to get her butt out of his face and into the open air.

Who ever said princesses were graceful?

With many mumbled apologies she finally fumbled her way outside and away from the cave. Away from the sound of his deep, rumbling laugh.

Phalian launched from her pocket and shifted in mid air.

"TWEET!" His metal wings shot straight out and he wheeled around in the sun. Rowan had once seen a picture of an airplane in the palace archives. When Phalian soared with wings outstretched, she could almost imagine how such a massive machine could fly.

She didn't want to hike too far on her own, so she found a private spot and quickly did her morning business, then stretched and studied the weather.

Clouds still blanketed the sky to the north, but it was clear overhead. The day wouldn't get any brighter. Might as well get to work and assess the damage to the cats.

She'd lost her cap, so she tamed her tangled hair with a tie as she rounded the outcropping of boulders that hid the cave entrance.

Then she stopped. Only one cat remained where they'd staked them down. She turned in a circle. The storm had torn out the stakes, lifted the other cat and dropped it five-hundred feet away.

Phalian let out a squawk and returned to her shoulder.

Conall appeared at her side and she heard the others emerging from the cave behind them. No one spoke. The wind whistled through the grass like a mournful song.

Finally Conall said, "This is why we have redundancies, folks. The Meadows are harsh. We'll be getting to know each other a little more intimately now."

"You can't mean we're all going to fit onto one cat?" Noah said.

"We sure are. The elf can sit in your lap, Maven."

Noah reddened but didn't protest.

"Maybe it's not so bad," Rowan said. "Maybe I can fix it."

Conall considered the sun as if it might charge over the horizon and eat them.

"You have ten minutes."

Rowan turned to Augie. "Can you help?" The young ranger nodded. She hoped he was as strong as he looked. She grabbed her tools from the back of the other cat and they ran into the Meadows. Orson was right behind them.

"You don't need to document this. It's just a repair."

"Council's orders, Princess." He always made her title sound like an insult. "To you it's just a repair. To the council, it's history in the making."

Rowan sighed and reminded herself that she'd begged for this commission.

The cat was more mangled than she'd feared. The engine car teetered precariously on two wheels. With Augie's strength, they were able to tip it upright. It landed with a thud and a screech of metal as the passenger door broke away. The sail was a write-off. The storm had torn open the latch to the sail compartment and the retractable arm was bent and broken in several places.

She'd hoped the damage was cosmetic, but there was no fixing the sail in just a few minutes. They'd have to burn thera until she had time to repair it.

She sat in the driver's seat and tried the engine. It stuttered but wouldn't start.

She got out and lifted the front hood.

Orson stood nearby, his gaze fixed in that zoned-out expression he wore when committing an event to memory.

"If you're going to just stand there, you can at least help. Pass me my wrench."

Orson blinked and smiled. It wasn't an encouraging smile.

"I'm not your flunky, Princess."

Why do his lips always look disgustingly wet? Hers were dry and cracked from the constant wind.

Augie stepped forward with the wrench.

"Thank you." He gave her a big—dry—grin as if he were pleased to be included.

She unbolted and re-bolted the battery connections, hoping that fixed the problem.

"Augie, try the engine again."

She listened to it whir, then shouted, "Okay. Stop."

The battery wasn't the problem. The thera wasn't lit.

Thera was an amazing fuel. It burned with clean magical energy for weeks or months before it needed replacing, but if it went out, it required a spark of magic to ignite it. It seemed the cat's thera lighter was the issue. Rowan's mech arm could do the trick, but that meant crawling under the cat to relight it.

She straightened and stretched her back.

"What's the verdict?" Conall had snuck up on her.

"The sail is broken. But I think I can get the thera engine going."

"There's no time." He turned and waved over the others. "Take any supplies we need from cargo. We're leaving in five minutes."

"But I can fix it!" Rowan protested.

"I told you, there's no time."

"It won't take more than a minute." She glanced at Orson who still watched with that awful half grin. She didn't like to argue with the commander on the record. She grabbed his arm and pulled him aside, turning away from Orson so he wouldn't be able to read their lips.

"You brought me out here to be a mechanic. Let me do my job."

Conall stared at her. Rowan could see he was deciding if he should just dismiss her or actually use his words and explain. Words won out.

He nodded toward the open sail compartment where the accordion arm hung in pieces.

"See that? The storm didn't do that. Look at the scratches."

Rowan looked closer at the marks. She'd assumed they'd been made by the broken sail arm when the wind battered it against the cat. Now she realized they were score marks. Something with incredibly powerful claws had wrenched open the compartment.

The image of Ethan's chest with three long red scars flashed in her mind. Gaunts did this.

"And do you hear that?" Conall cocked his head.

"I don't hear anything."

"Exactly. Where are the bird sounds? And the cicadas? Have you heard any animal calls since we've been out this morning?"

"Just a crane, but it was miles away." Rowan was starting to feel stupid. And afraid. Neither feeling sat well with her.

She looked around. They were near the foothills of the Ubruulens. The grass was as tall as her knees, and it went on for miles in undulating knolls. Anything could be hiding in that grass.

"You think gaunts wrecked our cat?"

"I think something is out there watching us, and I won't wait around to find out what."

Rowan gripped the cat's damaged door with her mech hand. It went against everything she loved about mechs and machines to leave it out here to rot.

"It's just a cat, Striker. It doesn't matter. Only the mission matters."

Rowan nodded.

"At least let me connect the cargo car to the other cat." Roger was in that car. She wouldn't lose him too.

"Make it fast." He turned to Lena and Clem. "You two keep watch. Anything comes out of the grass, shoot it."

20

SHIFTING WINDS

Lena DROVE. WITH THE EXTRA CAR attached, the thera engine struggled and she opened the sails. The storm had left a decent wind in its wake and they made good time.

Conall and Rowan sat in the last car of the train, their feet propped on crates of gear and weapons pointing into the Meadows.

Clem rode beside Lena with Noah and Orson on the bench behind them. The second car had one bench packed with gear and Elias sandwiched between Augie and Murdoch. The elf climbed over the seat to sprawl across the gear. He'd found an extra rail gun and he lay on his stomach, looking through the sight.

"You know how to use that?" Conall asked. Elias gave him a toothy grin and a thumbs up.

Conall leaned toward Rowan. "How about you? Feeling confident that you can fire that thing?"

"Sure." Her mech hand tightened on the gun's grip. He tried to smile reassuringly, but since they'd spotted signs of gaunts, the wolf was close to the surface and his grin might have had a predatory edge.

"If something comes for us, fire your bolts, then stay out of this fight. Gaunts are hard to kill and they rarely let you get in more than one shot."

"You really think we'll be attacked?" Her eyes never left the unending vista of swaying grasses. Conall grunted. He probably seemed overcautious to the squadlings. The grass was pretty. Calming even. He'd thought so too on his first mission. It wasn't long before he discovered what could jump out of that grass.

"I think we need to be ready for anything."

They drove on, leaving their dead cat, but not the feeling of an impending attack. The meadows were empty of wildlife except for a couple of hawks circling high overhead. The cat's fat wheels flattened a trail behind them. Sunlight glittered on the grass, making individual stalks sparkle. It was beautiful and mesmerizing. Conall could see his squadlings becoming complacent, their eyes glazing over at the unending vista of shimmering green.

"Stay alert!" he growled more than once, but it was like poking at a banked fire. The flame of attention sparked up and quickly died. Halfway through the morning, they stopped so Murdoch could hand out rations.

"No one leaves my sight," Conall said, as everyone tumbled from the cat. "You have to piss, you do it in front of your squad. There is no privacy in the rangers."

There were a few grumbles at that, but nature called, shyness be damned.

They made it through lunch without an incident.

"You think we outran it?" Rowan asked, as they reloaded the cat.

"Maybe." But Conall didn't believe it. Garou was still on high alert and Conall couldn't shake the feeling that something stalked them.

They drove north. The wind kept them on a steady pace. They passed a sinkhole, easily fifty feet in diameter. Terns perched on its edge, pecking the dirt for night crawlers. Lena slowed the cat and everyone peered into the massive hole. Darkness swallowed the bottom.

The wolf's hackles rose.

"Get us out of here, Tracker!" Conall didn't shout, but his tone was clear. Lena let her foot off the brake and they sailed away from the menacing hole.

They drove without stopping for hours. Eventually, even Conall felt like they'd outrun whatever had destroyed their cat.

Until Rowan grabbed his arm.

"Did you see that?"

She lifted the gun and pointed it toward a stand of scrubby bushes. The sun had swung around the horizon and was making steady progress westward. Shadows from bushes and rocks snaked along the ground. They had another few hours of weak light before they'd be plunged into darkness again.

"There!" Rowan pointed with the gun.

He saw it.

Something black broke from one shadow to leap into another not fifty yards from the cat. No normal animal moved with such cunning.

Just as he was about to call a halt, Lena slowed the cat to a stop. She knew what she was about. That's why he'd wanted her to stay on this mission. She'd seen the creature too and knew the sails would be a hindrance if they had to jump from the cat in a hurry.

"Why are we stopping?" Clem couldn't resist filling the quiet with her voice. It was a habit Conall would have to break or it would get her killed.

"Shhh!" Lena hissed. "Eyes on the Meadows." Clem straightened her back and adjusted her gun.

Conall listened. No cicadas, no grunting of bison that normally carried across great distances in the plains. Garou was a tense, growling presence in the back of his mind. If he'd been wearing his fur right now, it would have been standing on end.

Monsters were out there. The only question was, would they be facing one or a whole pack?

Lena caught his eye and nodded. She retracted the cat's sails and started the thera engine. It would be slower going, but more predictable and easier to maneuver. And even with the speed of the wind power, they wouldn't outrun a pack of gaunts.

They rolled on through the Meadows.

"Everyone stay focused," Conall barked. Noah straightened and gripped his blade more firmly. At least he was holding it right. Augie rose a few inches off the bench and began to hum. The elf joined in. Conall was about to snap at them to be silent, but the elf's voice seemed to soothe Augie and he settled on the bench.

Conall let them sing. If it kept the kid centered, he'd put up with it. And whatever was out there already had them in its sights.

At least Clem and Rowan stayed vigilant. He couldn't see Murdoch, but the old cook could hold his own. The damned scribe was lost in his reporting trance again. What a useless waste of space and resources.

Shove him off the vehicle, Garou urged. *He is a burden that weakens the pack. Leave him for the monster that hunts us and maybe we can get away.*

As always, the wolf was practical and made good points. Conall also noted that he considered the squad pack. That was interesting.

A streak of movement on the left caught his eye. He leaned forward. Rowan leaned with him.

"Did you see that?" She shielded her eyes with a hand as she stared into the Meadows.

"Uh-huh."

Wind gusts made the grass dance, tricking his eyes into seeing things that weren't there. But he *had* seen something. The wolf was silent, a sure sign that he was getting ready to fight.

"Eyes out, everyone!"

A black figure shot up from behind a hill, appearing as if from nowhere. It sprang at the cat. Someone screamed. Conall got off a shot, but the figure jumped onto the roof and leaped away. His second arrow disappeared into the grass.

Lena slammed on the brakes and Conall pitched into the seat in front of him.

"Everyone out!" He jumped to the ground. The grass reached his knees. "Spread out. Keep the cat at your back. It's a lone gaunt, but don't underestimate it. Head shots are the only way to kill it."

Conall reloaded his bow and swept it across the field. The sun glinted off grass and made judging distances difficult.

Clem had jumped from the first car's passenger side and stood a dozen feet away. The whine of her gun seemed over-loud in the quiet. Murdoch stood beside her, brandishing a butcher knife. Elias leaned against the back end of the cat, pointing his gun at every shadow. Lena, Augie and Rowan were on the far side. Too far for Conall to protect.

Damn the saints! They should have had protocols in place for this sort of thing. And yet, what else could they do? They were rangers. They would fight.

Someone was groaning. Garou scented blood in the air.

"The scribe's been slashed," Noah said. "He's bleeding." Orson took that as his cue to start screaming.

The wolf snorted. *Like a pup looking for attention.*

Conall spared precious seconds to lean into the cat and inspect the situation. The medic was trying to stanch bleeding from a gash across the scribe's shoulder. It didn't look too serious but Orson's flailing made Noah's job more difficult.

"Do what you can," Conall said. "But keep him quiet. Sedate him if you have to." Orson protested even louder. Conall turned back to the Meadows and shouted, "Everyone else, eyes on the grass!"

They waited. Even the wind died. The Meadows were utterly silent except for the scribe's whimpering.

"Are you sure it's a loner?" Clem whispered.

"A pack would have swarmed us by now."

"You know a lot about gaunts."

"Too much. Now be quiet and listen. You'll hear the swish of grass against its plating before you see it."

Clem's eyes got even bigger and she focused on the shadows ahead.

The sizzling snap of a rail gun broke the silence.

"Sorry!" Augie called from the other side of the cat. "False alarm."

Conall ground his teeth. They were so green. He couldn't keep them all alive. No one could. The council had tasked him with a superhuman feat.

It's not up to you to keep them alive. They are pack. The pack will survive even if every wolf doesn't.

Conall ignored the inner wolf monologue.

The gaunt rose from the grass and stalked down the flattened trail left in the cat's wake. Elias fired. The bolt clattered off the beast's armor-like skin. It was seven feet tall with shoulders as wide as the cat. Black eyes glittered with red, like chips of ember. Saliva dangled from jaws studded with finger-long teeth. It raised an arm that bulged with muscle and pounded at the sky in a simian rage.

The fist came down on the roof like a battering ram.

Elias squeaked and fell backward into the cat. Conall loosed his arrow. The beast stumbled when it slammed into its shoulder, but the metal tip didn't break skin.

Conall locked in another bolt. The gaunt leaped, impossibly high. Conall fired as it sailed over the cat to land between Rowan and Augie.

The beast turned toward Rowan, reared back and bellowed. Spittle flecked her face. Rowan was frozen to the spot. Her arms fell slack and she gaped into the maw of death. Phalian launched from her shoulder and dove straight for the gaunt's eye, pecking like a rabid bee.

Augie hovered three feet off the ground. His gun was empty. He'd tried to reload it and failed. One of the rails stuck out from a shaft at a bad angle. He turned the gun around and held it like a club, battering at the gaunt while Phalian attacked.

All this happened in a fraction of a moment. Conall could see the gaunt raise its hand, claws bared and ready to strike at Rowan.

Garou's howl tore through him. Conall retained enough awareness to shirk off his coat and quiver. The rest of his clothes shredded as his body morphed from man to wolf.

Then he had no thought for anything but pain.

Joints stretched and popped. Muscles tore and bulged. Nerve endings burned as fur overcame flesh.

The world shifted. Colors muted but shadows lightened. Scents sharpened. Blood was in the air. And fear too. The musky stench of gaunt hung over it all.

Garou shook the last shreds of humanity from his coat.

Rowan screamed.

Fear for his mate-who-was-not-mate filled his entire being and he leaped. His paws found the gaunt's back as Rowan punched its muzzle.

The scream had not been in fear or pain. It was primal rage. A sizzling crack like lightning came from her mech fist and the gaunt's face exploded in fire. It shrieked and fell back. Garou used the gaunt's momentum to drive it to the ground. The stench of burning flesh filled his nostrils.

His teeth glanced off bony plating. Claws grappled for the soft flesh under the beast's chin. He found it and bit deep. The beast thrashed, tearing open punctures made by the wolf's fangs. Garou's stomach revolted. *Bad meat.* But he wasn't only a wolf. The tiny human voice in the back of his mind urged him to ignore the poison and hang on.

A silver glint whipped by his nose. The pack's youngest brandished a blade. He sang his battle call as his fist plunged down, piercing the gaunt's eye.

Good pup.

Garou tightened his grip on the throat. Blood gurgled around his fangs, hot and rancid.

He hung on until the beast finally lay still.

Garou released its throat and spat blood into the grass. He snorted and swiped a paw across his muzzle but there was no wiping away the foul taste.

The day had fallen silent.

The gaunt twitched like a dog infested with fleas as it fought at the gates of death.

Garou turned. The pack pup stood over the dead gaunt, holding his blade in front of him now as if the wolf might attack. He floated. Garou looked at the rest of his pack. They were wary.

Of him.

He backed away, snorting blood from his nostrils and banged into mate-who-was-not-mate. Her eyes were moon-round as she took in the sight of the wolf. Garou cocked his head to the side and let her look. *He* was not ashamed. And she had to know. She had to see him as he really was.

She reached out and stroked his fur with her human hand. Fingers ran down his ear, across his shoulder. Garou leaned into the touch. No human had ever touched him. Only the wolves in his pack had been so free with their affection, and that was so long ago, it felt like another lifetime.

Her eyes met his. Human to wolf. And she smiled.

Garou's sensitive nose noticed the shift of body scents—from fear to relief. The other humans relaxed now that the threat had passed.

You did well, brother, Conall said. *Let me finish the job.*

The wolf heaved a sigh and gave control back to the human.

Fur misted away into the night. Bones crunched and shrank. This change was always faster, but no less painful. Within moments, Conall stood naked in the grass.

His squad stared at him. Some faces were marked in horror for witnessing the startling change, others reflected pity.

He reached for Augie, who for once had his feet firmly planted on the ground, and took the blade from his hand.

"You have good aim, Ranger."

"Head shots only, Commander." The boy's voice was shrill and it petered out to a hum.

Conall bent, not caring about his nudity, and examined the gaunt. Their blood was laced in magic, and he'd seen the creatures revive from worse wounds.

He dug the blade into the gaunt's throat, finishing the job the wolf's teeth had started. Blood poured over his hand, but he kept sawing through bone and cartilage. When the head separated from the body, he fell back on his heels and handed the knife back to Augie.

"Good blade. See that it gets a cleaning."

Augie grinned and gripped the bloody knife.

Conall stood to find Rowan and Clem right behind him. Rowan handed him fresh pants and a shirt.

"That was something to see, boss," Clem said. She held out his boots and the shreds of his old clothes. Conall took them and walked back to the cat. He drained his canteen over his head and used the rags to clean blood off his hands. He would stink of gaunt for days.

When he returned, the others had gathered around the carcass. No one spoke. He knew what they were feeling. You never forgot your first gaunt.

The creature was vaguely humanoid, with a muscular frame and long ropey arms that it used to propel itself across the Meadows. Black scaly skin covered arms, chest and legs like armor. A prominent brow with a bony ridge down the middle overshadowed sunken eyes. Eyes that were nearly obliterated by Augie's knife. Its nose was like an open sore, wet and dripping with mucus. It was an adaptation that allowed them to scent prey from miles away. A wide mouth with a square jaw hung open to reveal jagged teeth meant to tear meat.

They were alien, but also strangely human, and it was that similarity that made them so much more frightening. And disgusting.

Noah crouched in the grass to vomit. Lena patted his back with a grim smile on her face.

Conall wanted to say something inspiring, something that a true leader would say, but he remembered the look in their eyes when they'd watched him shift. And he wasn't ready to confront that.

"We make camp here for the night," he said. "The smell of the gaunt will keep other predators away."

They had several hours of daylight left, but Conall wouldn't push them. Not today.

Murdoch was already setting out the camp stove to make dinner.

"Clem, see if there's wood around for a fire," Conall ordered.

"I'll go with her," Rowan said.

Conall hesitated only a moment before nodding.

He'd told them the other gaunts would stay away, and it was true. Mostly. But he and the wolf would stay vigilant anyway.

21

Triumphant Failures and the Smell of Dead Gaunt

A NEARBY STREAM BED PROVIDED A tangle of driftwood for a fire. Rowan and Clem gathered what they could and dumped it in a pile near Murdoch's makeshift kitchen. He already had the thera stove going and a pot boiling when they returned with a second load of wood. The campfire would be more for comfort than for cooking. Rowan felt the need for a bit of light and warmth that night and she suspected the others felt the same.

Augie hummed and floated nearby while Noah treated a gash from the gaunt claws on his arm. Orson sat on the ground beside them. He was lost in his scribe trance, no doubt recording the eventful night for posterity. That was just great. Everyone from the regent down to the lowliest scribe acolyte would know the princess had panicked on her first mission.

Rowan frowned. "Is he okay?"

"Not sure," Noah said, not looking up from his task. "He seems stuck." He touched a sore spot and Augie lurched upward like a loose balloon. Noah tethered him with one arm while he bandaged the wound.

Rowan knelt and studied Orson. His eyes were rolled back in his head and his mouth hung slack. It was an off-putting expression, but she'd seen him like this many times. Still, his trances didn't usually last this long.

His shirt was open from the collar down to his navel, and Noah's handiwork was evident by the bandage on his shoulder. So were the silver scars that covered his entire torso. They were intricate lines, almost like tattoos drawn with a knife.

Noah finished with Augie and turned to examine Orson.

"Was he badly wounded?" Rowan asked.

"Not really. A superficial scratch. I don't know why he hasn't come out of it."

"Maybe it's some kind of self-preservation?"

"Maybe. I did what I could for him. There's something odd about his… essence."

"What do you mean?"

Noah ran a hand over his short hair. "I mean, his blood is odd. I can usually feel the flow. It's hard to explain. But that's how my knack works. I can send it through the network of veins and arteries to soothe pain. With him?" Noah shrugged. "It doesn't work."

Rowan noted the lines around Noah's mouth as he held his jaw clenched. Even Augie's simple healing took a toll from him.

"Are you okay?" She laid her mech arm on his, wishing that it had the same ability to assess humans as it did machines.

"I'm fine. Don't fuss." Noah snatched his arm away and stalked off.

"He doesn't mean to be mean," Augie said.

"I know. I just wish I could help him in some way."

"Who heals the healer?"

"Who indeed." Rowan smiled at Augie. The boy had more depth than they gave him credit for.

Noah wasn't the only one feeling bruised in spirit. Clem had started the campfire and the others gathered around its glow, but no one spoke. Elias handed out bowls of stew that Murdoch had hastily put together from dried rations. The meal was hot and savory but it did little to comfort Rowan's jittery stomach.

She'd let her team down today. She knew it. They knew it. Thanks to the scribe, the whole city would know it.

Firelight ringed them like a dome of protection. It was an illusion, of course. Outside the light, monsters prowled. When the wind shifted, she still got a whiff of the one they'd killed. Memories of that battle and the childhood fear it overshadowed dropped a cloud over Rowan.

The gaunt had been the stuff of her night terrors for years, but today it had jumped from her nightmares into reality like a demon springing from a hole in hell. It had been so close, she'd smelled its fetid breath. Its face was the face of death. Her death.

It was the eyes that had truly terrified her. That thing had wanted to slaughter them, but unlike a grizzly or a wolf that killed for meat, the gaunt *hated* them—hated them to the point of frenzy.

In that moment, fear had stolen her breath, and she had reverted to a little girl, hiding in the ruins with Dale while the gaunts hunted them.

Her mech hand still tingled with that tell-tale buzz that meant she'd lashed out with a bolt of galvanic magic, but she didn't remember doing it. All she could remember was those eyes, black as coal and rimmed in red. And that gaping, oozing hole of a nose.

Then a wolf had slammed into the monster and Augie was stabbing it and Phalian was shrieking and the world had seemed full of blood and chaos.

Oddly, she hadn't been afraid of the wolf, even with his muzzle covered in gore. Maybe she'd passed through fear by that point, but she wanted to believe she'd recognized Conall the moment he leapt on the gaunt. Recognized him in a way that went deeper than skin and fur.

She glanced at him. Conall ate standing up, leaning against the cat. His crossbow was loaded and hung over his shoulder. It seemed impossible that this man was also the wolf, but she'd seen a lot of impossible things in the last few days.

Conall caught her eye and smiled. She ducked her head. The memory of her failure resounded like a bell in her thoughts.

"I have something to say." Lena's voice was soft but steady. All eyes flicked toward her. "I…um." Her lips pursed as if the words fought to get out. "I'm sorry for my actions during the fight, or rather my non-actions. I let you all down."

There was a murmur of dissent, but Lena held up her hand. "My knack has always been too wild. And so I ignored it. I even actively repressed it for years. After my wife died, I joined the rangers again because…well, because I'm good with guns and tracking and I thought I could be useful without needing my knack. And then, Bretta."

"That wasn't your fault," Clem said. "You saved her."

Lena gave her a sad smile. "Maybe. But it rattled me. Badly. And when the gaunt attacked. I froze. Even the thought of dying at the beast's hands was less frightening than the idea of letting my knack free again." She turned to Conall. "I told you I should have gone home with Bretta."

Before Conall could respond, Clem said, "I froze too. My gun jammed and it was like every target practice vanished from my head. I couldn't load a dart to save myself. Or any of you. I'm also sorry."

Rowan felt tears heating her eyes. "Me too. I froze too. And I've been sitting here thinking how ashamed I am for it." Her throat felt raw with unshed emotion, but finally speaking those words felt like a cool shower.

"But you were amazing!" Clem said. "You blasted that gaunt. I saw it."

Rowan shook her head. "I don't remember that. I only remember seeing it loom up from the shadows and…and it brought back…" She gulped down hot tears that blurred her vision, took a deep breath and tried again. She held up her mech arm. Phalian, in his mouse form, ran up it to perch on her shoulder.

"Few people know this, but the night I lost my arm, my brother and I were attacked by a gaunt." There was a soft gasp, probably from Clem. "I'd blocked those memories, but this mission has brought them all back to the surface. And when I saw that gaunt, I was suddenly nine years old again. I'm sorry. I'll do better next time."

Conall pushed away from the cat and stepped into the ring of firelight.

"Let's face it, you all screwed up." He glared at each member of the squad. Rowan felt her stomach turn over, then Conall smiled. "And I couldn't be prouder."

"What for?" Clem asked.

"You're alive. You kept each other alive. That's better than ninety-nine percent of rangers on their first gaunt fight. We survived. That's all that matters. We're a team. No one is solely responsible for this mission, not even me. You were tested today. You won't ever forget it. Next time will be easier." Grumbles met that statement, but Rowan felt the tension in her ease. She might have failed in the moment, but they *were* a team and she *would* do better next time.

"Tomorrow we'll reach the oasis," Conall continued. "Only the saints know what we'll find there, but tonight I think we should congratulate the one ranger who didn't freeze in the face of the gaunt. Augie."

Augie looked up in surprise. "Me?"

"Yes, you. It's amazing what you can do when you stop singing for a minute. You took on that gaunt with nothing but a hunting knife and your damned *Ode to Joy*. You gave Rowan a chance. You gave *me* a chance to get in and kill it." Conall leaned down and squeezed Augie's shoulder. "I'm proud of you. We'll make a ranger out of you yet."

Augie beamed and sat taller like he was blossoming under the praise.

Good for him. Rowan was glad the boy had found his place in the squad.

Orson made a gurgling noise. The smile on Rowan's lips died as she turned to him. His back was arched, legs splayed and rigid. Noah rushed to his side and shook him gently.

"Orson, can you hear me?"

The scribe didn't react. His mouth opened and lips stuttered but he made no sound.

"He's having a seizure!" Noah flung his shirt open and laid hands on his chest. Orson bucked and fell sideways, and Rowan barely caught him before his head hit the ground. She staggered and then Conall was there, taking half the weight.

"Bring something to put under his head," Conall shouted. Elias rushed in with a rolled blanket. They lowered Orson onto it. His convulsions slowed to twitches.

Noah pressed his hands to Orson's chest and bowed his head as if in prayer. After a moment, he sighed and sat back on his heels. The lines around his mouth had deepened.

"He's coming out of it now, but I can't find the cause of the seizure. His blood is too strange."

Everyone clustered around. Augie floated, making squeaking noises like a frightened puppy. Phalian fluttered around his head.

Orson finally stopped twitching and lay still. Drool and blood covered his chin. He'd bitten his tongue.

"Will he be all right?" Rowan asked.

Noah laid a hand on Orson's chest. "I think he's sleeping now. But I still can't tell what's going on in there. His insides are all wrong. I really don't understand it."

"Scribe magic," Conall said. They all turned to look at him. "I saw it during the wars. The scribes were there to report back to the Temple of the Word. Only the Temple. It costs a lot to raise a scribe from childhood, train him, feed him, house him. The Temple needs assurance that their investments don't go astray. See those marks?" He pointed to the silver scars on Orson's chest that glinted in the firelight. "They're like the etchings on a mech. Deep magic made those. Not sure how it works, but it alters them. Keeps them from divulging their secrets to anyone else." He looked down at Orson, "And sometimes it backfires."

"What do you mean by backfires?" Noah asked.

"I mean, sometimes the magic is too much for the flesh and blood that contains it. I saw one scribe go crazy and kill himself in front of an entire squad when the magic inside him went bad. Another one imploded."

"Imploded like how?"

"Like blood sprayed from his pores."

"Oh, like that." Noah made a good attempt at sarcasm, but Rowan was feeling sick to her stomach.

"Will he come out of it?" she asked.

Conall nudged Orson with a toe. "I hope so. I don't relish carting his unconscious ass all over the Meadows." He stepped back and addressed them all "There's nothing we can do for him. Clem, you're on watch. The rest of you need to sleep early. There'll be no celebrating tonight. We're moving out at first light."

"Sure thing, Commander." Clem flung him a very non-regulation salute and went to find her rail gun.

Elias brought out a small flute. It had a low, lilting tone. Augie hummed in accompaniment. Despite Conall's admonishment, Murdoch passed around his water-into-wine flask. Everyone took a sip, but no one over-indulged, not with the smell of dead gaunt still hanging in the air.

It was a quiet, comfortable night. Rowan left the ring of firelight and walked over to the body of the beast that had almost ended her life. Phalian was perched on her shoulder, but as soon as she approached the carcass, he hid in her pocket.

Her little mech was brave, but even he'd had enough of gaunts for one day.

She crouched and examined the corpse. It was frighteningly human-looking but also monstrous. And yet, it was nothing like the beast that had haunted her dreams.

Because I never really saw the beast.

In her dreams it was just a shadow that chased her. A scream in the darkness. Dale had shielded her from the worst of the gaunt's attack. What she remembered most of that day was the pinch of his hands holding her and…something. A sound that wasn't right. A feeling of wrongness.

Her mech fingers closed over the gaunt's hand. Her knack didn't work on organic tissue. It felt only rough-skinned and cold. She tried to turn its wrist, but stiffness had already set in. She leaned in closer for a better look and counted. Four fingers and a thumb. Like all primates. Like a human.

She thought of Ethan and the three red scars that scored his chest. Why only three?

A small noise startled her. She fell back on her butt in the dewy grass.

"Something wrong?" Conall asked. He was silhouetted by the campfire and the light ringed him like a halo.

"No. I just wanted a better look." She shifted to kneel, and he crouched beside her.

"You'll never forget your first gaunt kill."

"But I didn't kill it. You forgot to praise the real champion of the day." She leaned her head on his shoulder. She didn't care who was watching. "Your wolf saved me. I will never forget it."

Conall turned and she felt his lips press against her hair.

His voice came out low and deep. "His name is Garou. He would like you to know that."

She laid a hand on his chest. Her sensitive mech fingers picked up the beat of his heart. His gaze held hers.

"Garou. I like that. Thank you, Garou."

22

HEAVES

Eklridge Oasis was a tiny forest in the middle of the vast Meadows that gave researchers protection from the wind. It had no protection from the constant threat of titans and gaunts, of course. The trees didn't make it defensible, but the grass was low and scrubby around the oasis. With a good ward and a few guards on watch, they would see any attack coming long before it became a threat.

All these thoughts ran through Conall's mind as he lay flat on a low rise to study their target. Garou mostly agreed with his assessment, but added his distaste for camps in general.

One doesn't shit where one eats. That was his reaction to any human settlement, but his disapproval made Conall's lip quiver into a snarl.

Clem lay on her stomach on the same hill with a scope pressed to her eye. She was a good scout, calm and focused. She'd been a fidgety child, always needing to be the center of attention, and he'd worried that her natural cheerfulness would work against her in the Meadows, but she had a way of calming herself to the point of invisibility. It wasn't on the level of his own obfuscation knack, but it would serve her well as a tracker, if she chose to take that route.

She methodically scanned the oasis from one end to the other. Conall estimated its size at twenty acres, big enough to hide in, but not big enough to get lost in. The trees were a mix of alder, pine, and juniper with nothing taller than a two-story house, except for a few titan pines. Like the beasts that grew to monstrous proportions in the river, titan pines were mutated progeny of the Scots Pine. They towered above their normally stunted cousins. It was odd to find them so far from the Ikon, but the oasis brought animals from all around and it wasn't impossible that the seeds had migrated with them.

"Anything?" Conall asked.

"No movement. Except for the ground. It seems to be breathing." Clem handed him the scope.

He put it to his eye and focused on the nearest point of entry into the oasis. A gust of wind ruffled the hair on the back of his head. A moment later the ground just outside the trees rose and fell. Then again, as if a giant slumbered under the grass.

Curious.

They lay quietly for another ten minutes while Conall studied the trees through the scope and listened for the sounds of human activity among the buzzing of cicadas.

The wolf grew bored of this hunt. He'd determined in the first minutes of their scouting mission that the camp was abandoned.

Smells like death.

There's nothing wrong with verifying a hypothesis.

Garou harrumphed.

Conall didn't want to just walk up to the stand of trees. If there were any rangers left on guard, they might panic at the sudden invasion. Panic made fingers trigger happy.

He lowered the scope. Something wasn't right, and not only the oddly pulsating ground. The forest around the oasis was too quiet. Where were the birds and other animals? An oasis in the Meadows should have been teeming with life.

"I have a bad feeling about this."

"We could send in Rowan's valet first," Clem suggested. "If someone's trigger happy in there, better they use him for target practice than us."

"Maybe, but that would let them know we're coming."

"You make them sound like enemy soldiers. They're just science geeks."

Everyone is an enemy until they prove themself, Garou said and Conall agreed.

"They have rangers with them for protection. I don't want to set off any alarms. If they're alive and hiding, they're scared of something." Conall had a pretty good idea what that something would be.

But Clem was right. They were just scientists. And they had to know someone would come to investigate their silence. The best way to avoid being shot by panicked guards would be to walk into the camp in the full light of day, giving them plenty of time to recognize them as friendlies.

"We'll wait for Lena's report before we move."

Clem nodded and took the scope to continue surveying the oasis. He'd sent Lena in a counter-clockwise trek around the trees. A quick calculation told him it would take thirty minutes to walk that distance, but Lena was careful. The effort to stay hidden would double that time. She'd been gone for nearly an hour now. He waited another five minutes, and just as he was starting to worry about her safety, she appeared like a raindrop from mist. Even the wolf had to admit she was stealthy.

She crouched beside them.

"There are tracks leaving the trees, heading northwest."

"Human?"

"Cat tracks. Heavy cats. Carrying a dozen people at least or a lot of cargo. And…" She paused and squinted at the stand of trees as if they might pull up roots and charge across the grass. The sun chose that moment to hide behind a cloud and the light went cold.

Conall resisted the urge to prod Lena.

"…and non-human tracks running alongside the cats. Gaunts, actually."

"You're sure?"

"Very. I tracked a clan of gaunts for a week during my first tour of duty."

Conall grabbed the vox on his belt and held down the talk switch. "Striker, can you hear me?" Nothing. "Striker Andula?" Nothing. Not even static. He flipped the device over. It was a flattened egg made of silver with elaborate scrolls etched all over it. The designs on this vox matched exactly the one that Rowan held in camp. That precision detail caused the thera in each vox pair to resonate on the same magical frequency. The beauty of the mech was part of its power. Mages devoted hours of intense creativity into each design. It was the only way to create resonance.

Conall didn't care about aesthetics of mech. In the field, it just had to work. He pounded the vox against his palm until a small door popped open, then he shook it until the thera chip fell out. The chip had lost its normal cobalt blue luster. It was lifeless gray against his palm.

"Saints. The chip's burned. Anyone have a spare?"

Clem shook her head. "Murdoch keeps those under lock and key."

It was true. Their quartermaster ran a tight ship, something he usually appreciated.

"Run back to the others. Bring Rowan and Noah. We're going into those trees. Tell Augie I want him to stay back with the cooks and the scribe until we give the all clear."

"Orson will probably follow us, no matter what I say. Posterity and all that."

Conall ground his teeth and considered leaving Rowan behind so the scribe wouldn't get in the way, but they might need a mechanic, and damn the saints, he wouldn't let the council's intrusion stop him from doing the job properly.

"Orson is not our concern. Go."

Clem scrambled backward on her belly, rising only once she was several yards away and below the small rise they'd been scouting from.

Conall waited until he heard the others coming before turning to Lena.

"Take Rowan and Clem and come in from there." He pointed to the west side of the oasis where a clear trail led into the trees. "Tell Noah to catch up with me." Then he rose and checked the bolt in his crossbow.

He held the bow low to appear non-threatening as he walked toward the oasis and stopped a hundred yards from the trees where the ground heaved in rhythmic breaths. Now that he was closer, he saw the cause. The titan pines had shallow root systems but they shot far into the Meadows. A heavy layer of grass had formed a skin over the roots, but wind tossed the trees with unrelenting regularity. As the tall pines swayed, the roots rose, then settled, making the ground seem to breathe.

The earth heaves and there is blood on the wind.

With the wolf's heightened senses, Conall could smell it too.

It could be just a kill. There must be wolves or prairie cats here.

Garou snorted and Conall could almost feel him shaking out his ruff.

This is not an oasis. Listen. There are no voices bigger than a squirrel. These hunting grounds are dead. We should avoid them.

We cannot avoid them. This is the mission, Conall said.

Human missions are foolish. The wolf grumped and went silent.

Conall heard footsteps and turned to see Noah striding toward him.

"What in the saints is that?" Noah pointed to the heaving ground.

"Just some over-active roots and wind. Be careful where you step though. There may be hollow pockets."

Lena waved as she led Rowan and Clem in the other direction. He gave her the signal to halt. Then he turned to the trees and called out, "Commander West here! This is my squad. The Regent's Council sent us. We're coming in. Hold your fire!"

Only the wind answered.

Conall waved the others onward.

They spread out, Lena in the middle, Clem and Rowan on either side. The scribe followed a few steps behind. They walked in slow formation, keeping each other in sight.

There's hope for these misfits yet.

He shouldn't take pride in their accomplishments. That way led to misery. The council would never let him keep this commission after the mission ended. Squad 54 would be passed off to another commander. A *human* commander.

Still, they'd left the gates of New Torwood greener than spring grass and he'd taught them at least to be cautious. That might keep them alive a little longer, and he could be proud of that.

Despite the saints' teachings, Conall didn't believe pride was a sin. Pride was sustenance, like food and water. It was the rations that kept soldiers going in the face of great adversity. It was the protein that built heroes. And it was damned necessary to surviving in the Meadows.

He crept past the heaving ground and entered the trees along a well-worn path. This far north, the shadows were long and sharp even at midday. As he moved deeper into the woods the alternating gloom and sunlight confused his eyes and he relied on Garou's senses.

Noah didn't have Lena's stealth, and he blundered down the path like a titan bull. Conall motioned for a halt. He picked up the scent of old woodsmoke and something astringent that made Garou shake his head and snort again.

They'd made it all the way to the camp's first sentry point without being stopped. A simple metal gate blocked the path.

"Why put a gate here?" Noah asked.

"It's a ward. Look." Conall pointed to the ground where a wire lay nearly hidden in the dirt. It was attached to the gate posts and stretched in either direction. Conall tossed a stick onto the wire to confirm his suspicions. It was dead. He motioned Noah to follow as he stepped over the ward and around the gate.

The first body they found was a woman in a ranger uniform lying face down in the dirt. Noah bent to inspect her, but Conall didn't need the medic's confirmation to know she was dead. Her body was bloated and black. It was an old kill, seven days at least.

"Those are bite marks." Noah pointed to her shoulder where the uniform was torn to expose desiccating flesh blackened with blood. He rolled her over and Conall bit down a gag. Dirt and maggots fell away from her mangled face.

"Her throat's been torn out," Noah said. "An animal did this."

Or a gaunt.

Neither of them needed to voice that last part.

Conall used the tip of his bow to flip over the dead ranger's rail gun. It was still loaded.

They moved on. Noah took care to tread quietly now. Garou approved.

The next bodies were a mother and infant lying just off the path. The mother's body had fallen over the infant as if her last thought had been to protect it.

Noah gaped at the pair.

"What in the saints were these scientists studying?"

"I don't know, but I think we have to find out." Conall took in the scene—churned up dirt, broken branches, blood dried to black blight on the leaves. This hadn't been an easy kill. The mother had fought back.

In his mind, Garou howled. From the very beginning Conall had felt the wrongness of this mission, and now he knew for certain that the regent had never meant for any of them to return home.

The mother and infant staring at him with lifeless eyes confirmed it.

They weren't human. They were gaunts.

23

POSTMORTEMS

The SCIENCE CAMP WAS SET UP with more than a dozen tents in a ring around one large clearing. Conall stood on the path with the forest at his back and studied the layout of the site. A screened-in mess hall had been constructed at the far end. Large tents were clustered near this hall. Smaller tents—probably sleep quarters—were scattered among the trees. The scientists hadn't expected to stay for the winter or they'd have built sturdier structures.

He raised his nose to the wind and let Garou come to the forefront of his mind.

Blood. Rotting food. Death. Garou would be able to pinpoint these scents better in his wolf form, but Conall needed to keep control for now. At least until they'd secured the camp.

Lena and her crew had just arrived from the other path and stood near the mess hall. He waved at them to spread out and check the tents.

Noah headed for the closest and listened for movement inside. Conall trained his arrow on the dark slit of the tent flap and nodded. The medic parted the canvas. Nothing moved. Conall lowered his bow. The heavy canvas shaded the interior, but he could just make out two tables turned on their sides with instruments scattered and broken. The place reeked of some chemical that made Garou huff in annoyance and Conall spied smashed bottles in the debris.

Noah stepped inside and picked up a fallen piece of mech. "It's a lab of some sort. Looks like it's been ransacked."

"Or searched." Conall noted movement on his flanks. Lena and her team were steadily progressing around the camp.

"Should we document this?" Noah waved a hand at the destroyed lab.

"Leave it for now," he said. "We have to secure the site, then we'll figure out what the saints happened here."

On the way to the next tent, they passed a fire pit with two charred logs piled in the center. Conall bent to touch them. His fingers came away blackened by soot. The logs were cold. That wasn't surprising. The council had received the last communication from the camp nearly two weeks ago. And the bodies they'd found were in an advanced state of decay. Whoever—whatever—had attacked this camp, they were long gone.

The stench of rotting food grew stronger as they approached the mess hall. Conall peered through its mesh walls. Trays of food lay abandoned on flimsy tables. Benches were overturned. A body lay in the dirt between tables.

Noah went inside to inspect the corpse then turned to Conall and shook his head.

They moved onto the next tent. And the next one.

They found another body. A woman lay in her bunk. Dried blood covered her neck and chest. The wound on her throat had blackened as the skin dried, but it was clearly made by a blade.

The stench was overpowering and Conall let the tent flap drop back in place, trapping the flies that swarmed the body.

Garou's nose was ten times more sensitive than Conall's but conversely, strong organic smells didn't bother him. *That meat is no longer good to eat,* was all he said.

He found Rowan in the next tent, holding two broken pieces of mech as if she were trying to put together a puzzle.

Orson stood by the door, watching. Always watching. Conall pushed past him, but the scribe didn't yield the space willingly, and he gave him a shove with his elbow. Orson grunted and retreated to the open doorway.

Rowan ignored the exchange, just as she always ignored the scribe. She had the patience of a saint.

"This is the communications center," she said. "But the graphium's been smashed." She held up the tablet. Other mech was strewn around the room—several vox, thera lamps, and a wave booster.

Phalian pecked at the broken graphium as if it threatened them.

"Think you can fix it?" Conall asked.

She cocked her head and studied the design of the broken mech. It was a flat piece of silver about the size of a notebook with a single sheet of thera embedded into it. The etchings on the silver matched in resonance with another graphium, probably at Oxeye Outpost. Using a metal stylus one could write a note on the thera screen and its duplicate would appear on the matched graphium. But cracking the screen broke that resonance.

Rowan sighed and dropped the graphium to the table. "It needs a new screen. Even if we had a chip that big, which we don't, it wouldn't match the resonance."

Thera chips big enough to make a screen were rare and expensive. Graphiums weren't standard issue for a single squad. The nearest one would be back at Oxeye.

"It's not a priority right now," Conall said. "When Augie gets here, take him with you to find the ward generator. See if you can get that up and running. We'll all sleep better tonight with some protection at our backs."

The ward hadn't helped the scientists, but Conall was starting to think that whoever had attacked the camp had help from the inside. Most of the bodies they'd found so far had been at rest, with no sign of a struggle. Garou scented no blood in the communications tent either. There had been no fighting here, just meticulous destruction.

He glanced at Orson. There was no way to stop him from reporting everything he saw, but Conall could keep his suspicions to himself.

They met Noah outside.

"We cleared all the tents," he said. "No one is left alive."

Conall nodded. Clem and Lena met them in the middle of the camp, near the fire pit.

"Clem, did you bring a new vox?" he asked.

She nodded and handed over the device. Conall called Augie and ordered him to bring the cat into the oasis.

"Yes, Commander." Augie's voice sounded tinny and far away.

He turned to Noah. "Report."

The medic stood a little taller as if acknowledging the importance of what he was about to say. "We found eleven bodies…plus the other two." His gaze met Conall's. They hadn't told the others about the dead gaunts yet. Noah cleared his throat and continued. "All were in advanced states of decay. At least one died by a knife wound. The others seem to be victims of a wild animal attack. Perhaps gaunts."

"Of course it's gaunts," Clem said. "What else would it be?"

Conall held up a hand to stop any further outbursts.

"There are two dead gaunts in the woods." Conall didn't mention that they were a female with her offspring. He was very conscious of Orson watching. And until he knew exactly what was going on, he would leave the scribe guessing.

"Do we think they did this?" Rowan asked.

"Probably not. Their throats were slit. And, as Noah said, at least one of the scientists died from a knife wound. Also someone trashed the labs and communications."

He let that sink in. Gaunts didn't wield knives. And they didn't destroy mech. Someone human had done those things.

But gaunts had also attacked. It didn't make sense. Gaunts didn't work with humans.

Gaunts ate humans.

"So who did this?" Lena asked quietly.

"I don't know."

The sound of a thera engine announced that Augie and the others had arrived. As soon as they parked, Conall started giving orders.

"Augie, go with Rowan to find the ward generator. Lena and Clem, start bringing out the bodies. There were eight scientists, five support staff and four rangers here. That means we are missing five bodies. Find them." He pointed to the end of the camp, far from the mess tent. "Put them over there."

Lena's expression was locked down tight. Clem scrunched up her face in disgust, but she didn't argue.

"Noah, you will document the victims. Every wound. I have the manifest of who was meant to be here. I need you to try and identify the dead and match them to that list. Then we'll bury them."

Noah just nodded, his eyes on the ground.

Conall turned to Murdoch. "You and Elias clean out that mess hall. Burn the rotting food before we get vermin. I want it clean enough to sleep in there tonight. Let's go, people. We have eight hours of daylight left. Let's use them!"

The squadlings scattered.

Conall stood beside the fire pit. Turning in a circle, he tried to imagine what had happened here. Did the gaunts attack first? Had the scientists defended themselves and been weakened? Could raiders have attacked them afterward when they were recovering from the first fight? It was possible, just not plausible. The ghost raiders from Taiga had been known to come over the Ubruulan Mountain Range, but only after particularly harsh winters when they had little to eat. And they wouldn't smash the graphium. Any mech they found was prized since they had little opportunity to trade for it.

No, someone other than raiders had killed those people.

Squad 54 had come here to find the scientists. Now they would stay to learn what had killed them.

Elias returned carrying trays loaded with spoiled food and dumped them on the cold fire. If he'd been in his wolf form, Conall would have put a paw over his nose. Instead, he sent Elias back for more, then tossed kindling over the remains of the scientists' last meal. He nestled a fire-starter among the sticks and lit it with a flick of his thera lighter. The fire starter was standard ranger issue. It was an oblong bit of steel with a thera core. Once lit, it would burn hot enough to kindle wood. If they stayed long enough for the fire to cool, he could recover the starter to use again.

By the time Elias returned with more trays, he had a decent bonfire going.

Lena and Clem arrived, carrying a body between them, an older man this time. The bottom half of his jaw was missing. His shirt was torn to shreds and blackened claw marks covered his chest.

Clem shielded her nose with a scarf, but Conall doubted that did anything to mask the stench of death.

Augie had been hanging around while Rowan unloaded her tools from the cat. He gaped at the body and looked a little green as if he might throw up. He rose a few inches off the ground and hovered there.

Conall gave him a gentle shove and he floated toward the cat like a parade balloon.

"Go help Rowan."

"Hmmmm. Yes, Commander."

Conall didn't care if he hummed through the task. They weren't hiding. Smoke from the fire would give them away to anyone approaching from the Meadows.

Rowan arrived and handed Augie a bag with her tools. The weight settled him on the ground again.

"Come on," she said. "Let's find that generator."

Conall watched them walk away. Or at least Rowan walked. Augie skipped along on light feet as if he might launch himself into the sky.

"You should let them pick up bodies," Orson said. "The princess should get her hands bloody. And the kid's gotta learn about death sometime. All that bloating and farting. And maggots. Saints, I hate maggots." The scribe sneered at the growing pile of bodies.

He smells like fear, Garou said. *That's why he babbles. Like a pup before his first hunt.*

The scribe turned to follow Rowan, and Conall stepped into his path. Orson tried to step around and Conall grabbed his arm.

"I know you have a job to do, but so do my rangers. Stay out of the way."

Orson turned his head and looked at Conall. His gaze was strangely dead, like the eyes of a mech. "That's not how this works, Commander." He puffed up his chest. "A scribe goes where the story is. My right to interfere is inviolable. Regent's law states…"

Conall squeezed his arm tight enough that he squeaked off his words.

"If you don't stay out of the way, I will chain you to the cat. And if you continue to piss me off, I might make you run behind it on the way home. There are a hundred ways to die in the Meadows. For you, make that a hundred and one."

Orson narrowed his eyes. "The regent will hear about this."

"That's fine. He doesn't like me much anyway."

Orson opened his wet lips to make some asinine comment. Conall let the wolf glint in his irises, and Orson slammed his mouth shut. Conall gave his arm another squeeze. There was a lot of flesh to work with. Orson's face reddened as he tried to hold in a squeal of pain.

"Good. Just so we understand each other. Let the striker do her job." Conall let him go.

He watched Orson scuttle off like a crab without a shell.

Murdoch stuck a scone slathered in jam under his nose.

"Eat. A hungry commander is a cranky commander."

He left the sticky mess in Conall's hand and went back to preparing dinner for the squad.

Conall was licking jam off his fingers when Noah called to him.

"Commander, you'd better come see this."

Noah led him out of the camp to a tent they'd overlooked in their initial search. It had been trampled, the poles broken. The canvas was torn and bloody. A dead gaunt lay partially buried by mud beside it. Noah stepped over the body to pull back the canvas and reveal a human man dead underneath.

"That's scientist number twelve" Conall said.

"Yes, but that's not what I wanted to show you. Look at the gaunt." He nudged the beast with his boot.

Conall stepped closer for a better look. It was another female. She was curled into a fetal position. A blade had nearly severed her head from her body.

"There are more," Noah said. His arms were crossed tightly as if he were trying to hold in his guts.

"Where?"

Noah pointed behind the tent.

Conall stepped over the corpse. The ground fell away to a small ravine where bodies lay in a tumble with their heads separated and piled nearby.

"Do you notice anything odd?" Noah asked.

Conall shut his eyes for a moment, then opened them. He took in the scene again. Five heads. Five bodies. Five pairs of legs, arms and breasts.

"They're all female."

"Yup."

"Any more infants?"

"Nope. Unless they're under that mess. You want us to pull them up?"

It didn't seem likely that the infants would all be hidden under the bodies. And even if they were, what could it mean?

"No." He tapped the tent with the dead man lying inside. "Help me carry him back to camp so you can do a proper postmortem. Document the gaunts as best you can and we'll burn them here. For now I don't want the others to know about this."

Noah scratched the short hair at his nape. "You mean you don't want the scribe to know. You think the council had something to do with this, don't you."

"At this point, I think anything is possible."

"Commander!" Augie's sing-song voice came from the camp. A moment later, the ranger came bouncing through the trees.

"Commander, Striker says to come quick. We found a survivor!"

24.
WARD WORK

The AIR SMELLED OF HOT METAL and ash, but it wasn't coming from the generator. That was cold and silent. Rowan knelt beside the machine to inspect it. She pried open a small door on the side and plucked out the thera chip, happy to see that it was still a nice deep blue. Murdoch was getting a little sour about the way they'd been burning through chips.

She brushed it off and inserted it back into the slot, then flicked the on switch. The generator hummed to life.

Behind her, Augie changed his pitch to match the generator's hum. Phalian fluttered around his head. The clack of his wings added to their little symphony.

Rowan rose and dusted off her pants. She pressed her mech hand against the machine and listened to its many vibrations. It wasn't a happy machine. It would prefer not to run. Its cogs and gears needed oil and they grated against each other. The engine belt was worn but not enough to need replacing. She ran her hand along the generator's casing until she found one of the wires that made up the ward. It should have been a live wire of angry energy, hot enough to kill, but even with the generator humming, the ward was still down. That could only mean one thing. For the ward to work, the wire had to be grounded back to the generator. It had to be a complete loop.

Somewhere, the wire was broken.

She sighed, shut off the generator and motioned for Augie to follow her. "Come on, we need to find the break in the wire." She didn't worry about Orson. He would follow her or not. She didn't care.

She picked up the wire and ran it through her mech fingers. "Follow me. Watch the forest."

Augie nodded, his eyes wide and his gun pointing at her. Gently, Rowan reached out and tipped the barrel down.

Had the kid not taken gun safety in training? Even she knew never to direct a weapon at someone unless you meant to shoot them.

"Point it out there." She nodded towards the shadows between trees. "Anything coming at us from outside the camp isn't a friend."

Augie nodded vigorously. Phalian chirped and flew on ahead.

They crept forward. The wire slipped through her fingers. Sometimes she had to tug on it where dirt or rocks held it down, but then it fell away behind her as they moved farther into the trees. Her path disturbed a squirrel and it chittered angrily from a branch overhead.

They stepped out of shadow into bright sunlight only to plunge back into shadow. Her eyes wouldn't adjust to the constantly changing light.

So she didn't see the body until she nearly tripped over it.

The gaunt lay face down across the ward. The entire creature and three feet of wire in each direction were burned to a blackened crisp.

Augie stopped humming. Behind them, Orson made a gagging noise.

"Well, at least we know why the ward went down," Rowan said. "Augie, help me move it."

Augie's complexion paled by three shades.

"It can't hurt you. It's dead. But I need to see the wire underneath."

Augie gulped and nodded. Together they rolled the body. It was stiff as charred wood.

"That's enough. Let it go." Rowan had seen all she needed. The wire was burned through. Eight feet of it was probably unusable. She sat back on her heels and wiped her hands on the ground as she considered her options. She'd brought a roll of wire with her, but it had been left behind on the ruined cat. Unless the scientists had spare wire in their stores, she wouldn't be able to fix it.

A moan startled her. Augie whirled and fired his gun into the trees.

"Augie! Stand down!"

A man lay in the dirt. He moaned again and lifted a feeble hand.

Augie's eyes were wild, and he floated high enough that his head scraped at lower branches.

"Go get the commander. And Noah. Tell them we have a survivor."

Augie gaped at her, his fists clutching the gun to his chest like a favorite toy.

"Go! Hurry!" She made a shooing motion and understanding finally broke through fear. He dropped to the ground and loped off.

Rowan rushed to the man's side.

He lay on his back with his face turned away and nearly hidden by a mass of dark curls that stuck to his cheek. One leg was awkwardly bent under him. Blood had dried and caked on the other pant leg.

Her hands hovered. She didn't want to move him for fear of making his injuries worse.

With grim resolution, she reached for his shoulder and gently squeezed.

"Are you okay?" Stupid question. Of course, he wasn't okay. He twitched under her touch. His eyes opened—huge and dark brown—and a wave of sharp fear washed over Rowan. She jerked backward and fell on her butt.

The sensation faded quickly as the man lapsed back into unconsciousness.

She had only a moment to wonder at its origin because that's when she noticed a second body, its legs sticking out from the underbrush. She parted the branches and one glance was enough to confirm this woman had been dead for a while. Her skin was black and shrunken, making her sightless eyes prominent and ghoulish.

With the advanced state of decay, it was hard to tell her age, but her hair was dark, without any gray and cut in the scribe's style—short on the sides and shaved at the back.

Phalian was pecking at something shiny and partially buried near her outstretched hand. Rowan brushed away the dirt and uncovered a small silver box. It was round and flat and fit into her palm. She recognized it immediately. It was a scribe's cachet, the repository for their observations.

She glanced back at Orson, but he was standing over the unconscious man, taking in every detail.

She didn't know what made her do it. Maybe it was Orson's contrary nature, maybe it was the mystery surrounding their discovery at the oasis, but instead of alerting Orson to the cachet, she tucked it into her pocket.

Noah and Conall arrived. The medic knelt by the unconscious man and examined him. Rowan touched Conall's arm and pointed to the dead woman.

"There's another one."

Conall knelt by the woman. His gaze scanned her from head to toe, taking in details. When his nose twitched, Rowan wondered if the wolf was cataloging scents. He gently turned her head to the side. The port for the scribe's recording wire was torn. Blood had caked around it. He lifted the wire that lay on the dirt and showed it to Rowan.

"Someone tore out her wire?" she asked.

"Violently."

"Would that have killed her?"

"Possibly. It's connected right to the central nervous system." Conall shook his head. "Barbaric."

"Does she have other wounds?"

Conall tried to lift the hem of her shirt. It was stiff with dried blood. Black, putrefying marks covered her stomach.

"A gaunt did this." Conall lowered the shirt.

"It must have caught her wire in its claw."

"Maybe."

"A scribe?" Orson had wandered over to document the second body. "How dare they kill a scribe!"

Conall rolled his eyes.

Rowan ignored the scribe's posturing. "Do you know her?"

Orson scoffed. "There are over a thousand scribes working at the Temple of the Word. How could I possibly know every one?"

Rowan spread her hands wide. "It was just a question."

Orson shoved Conall aside and began rifling through the woman's belt pouch. When he found nothing, he roughly searched her pockets, then flipped her over to run his hands down her back.

"It's not here! Where is it?"

"Where's what?" Conall asked.

He was too smooth. He knew exactly what was missing.

"The cachet! I must return it to the Abbott Archivist."

"Let me guess. It's sacrosanct."

"Don't mock me, Commander. Help me find it. It is a matter of national safety!" He started turning over leaves near the corpse, muttering, "Losing one's cachet is a fate worse than death. It has to be here."

Neither Rowan nor Conall made any move to help him.

"Maybe whoever killed her took it," Rowan said.

Orson stared at her. His eyes were glassy as if he neared tears. "We must find whoever did this and get it back!"

"That's not the mission." Conall turned his back on the scribe as if to dismiss him. Orson made a motion to grab the commander, but Rowan stepped between them and gave Orson a scathing look. He sneered, but backed off.

Noah had finished his scan of the patient. He stood with his hands fiercely gripping his bag. His lips were pressed flat and eyes hard. His knack was getting to him again.

"Will he survive?" Conall asked.

Noah heaved a sigh. "He's alive. That's all I can say for now. He has some old wounds, cuts and a broken rib, but this one," he pointed to a bloody lump on the man's forehead, "this looks fresh. Maybe in the last day. Let's get him back to camp. I can't do much more here." He turned without a word and stalked into the bush.

Instead of taking offense at being ordered around, Conall lifted the patient into his arms like he was carrying a child, and followed Noah.

Phalian fluttered after him.

Rowan held Orson back.

"If you ever lay a hand on the commander, or any squad member, I will have you banned from the Temple of the Word. You will be stripped of your vestments and thrown into the street to live like a beggar, because I assume you have no other talents. You might like to mock my title, but if you push me, I will show you just how much power a princess really has. Do you understand?"

Orson nodded.

"Say it."

His eyes were lifeless black pools. "I understand, *Princess*."

25

ALL ROADS LEAD HOME

Rowan WOULD BE SPENDING THE REST of the day trying to make sense of the records in the communications tent, so they set up a cot inside for their patient. She watched as Noah stripped off his shirt to look for other wounds.

The man turned and groaned. His eyes opened and focused on Rowan. She felt a splash of his raw pain and fear before he reined it in.

"Did they kill them?"

"Who's they?" Rowan stepped forward and took his hand. She assumed he was talking about the dead scientists but she was more interested in the "they" who did the killing, until he spoke again.

"The babies. Are they dead?" Then he gasped as Noah hit a tender spot on his hip and he passed out again.

Babies? What babies? Rowan glanced at Conall and beyond him to Orson, who watched. Conall shook his head, then nodded toward the tent's doorway.

Noah was deep in concentration, assessing the patient's internal wounds. Without disturbing him, she followed Conall outside.

"Striker, can you report on the state of the generator?"

She scrunched up her face, confused by his sudden formality.

"The wire is burned out where that gaunt fell on it. I suspect it was a deliberate act of sabotage."

"Can you fix it?" Conall's eyes followed Orson as he left the communications tent and sat by the fire pit.

"Not unless there's more wire in the camp's storeroom." Her gaze followed his. Orson sat with a straight back. His eyes rolled to white, and his jaw went slack. He was deep in recording mode.

Conall pulled her around the side of the tent.

"We have only a few minutes while he's off in scribe la-la land. Our patient wasn't just rambling. Noah and I found another six female gaunts, all dead, but no infants."

Rowan put a hand to her mouth as if to hold in a gasp.

"You think those are the babies he's talking about?"

"Seems likely, unless there was a daycare out here."

Conall continued, "We need to find out what these scientists were studying. Go over that communications equipment carefully. If there are any log books, they'll be in there."

"Or here." She reached into her pocket and pulled out the cachet.

Conall's eyes narrowed. "Where did you find that?"

"Next to the dead scribe. I think she tried to bury it."

He took the silver disc and turned it over in his hand as if weighing its heft and its significance.

"Can you access the information on it?"

Rowan shook her head. "No, but he could." She nodded toward Orson.

"But you don't want him to have access to it. Why?"

Rowan dragged her tongue across the back of her teeth. The sharp bite on flesh helped her focus as she considered his question.

"Maybe it's just to spite him," she said. "He's such a shit." Conall grinned at that. "But something's not right...hasn't been right all along." She smoothed back her messy hair and sighed. "I'm not sure why I feel that way. But this whole thing seems like a set up. Why send us..."

She lowered her gaze.

"Go on."

"I mean no offense, but why you as commander? And why me? They denied my request to serve in the keepers for years. They were ready to hang you. So why let us out into the Meadows? Why now?" She waved her mech hand in a circle as if to encompass the entire camp. "Then we arrive to this cluster-fuck. Sorry, this disaster."

Conall grinned. "It's okay. I kind of like your potty mouth." His thumb brushed aside a stray lock of hair that clung to her cheek. It was such a small thing, almost a non-thing, but the connection felt vital.

"It seems to me the council didn't give us all the information. It's like they don't want us to succeed," she said.

"I agree. We're running blind here. That cachet might provide the answers, and so yeah, I also think we need to keep it from the scribe. For now. Find out what you can from in there. Quietly." He nodded toward the communications tent. "And then we'll decide what to do with this." He handed the cachet back to Rowan and she tucked it into her belt pouch. He squeezed her hand again.

"There's one more thing." Her eyes went to the tent where, through the open flap, she could just see Noah beside his patient.

"I think the scientist is an empath or something."

Conall frowned and it made the crease between his brows deepen.

"Are you sure?"

"No. I don't think I'm sure of anything anymore. But twice now, I felt something when he woke up. Fear and pain and confusion. It felt like someone else's emotions. Empaths can do that right? Push their feelings outward?"

Conall nodded. "Some of them."

Noah stormed out of the tent. His lips were pulled back in an angry sneer and thunder boiled in his eyes. He picked up the first weapon he saw—a shovel beside the fire pit—and started beating a nearby boulder with it.

Everyone in camp stopped what they were doing to watch the medic work out his knack's revenge.

A primal cry of rage burst from Noah's chest as he slammed the shovel against the rock. Sparks flew off the metal head. The shaft finally broke and Noah whipped it into the trees with a last furious shout. He doubled over, hands on knees, and vomited into the bushes.

Eventually, he raised his head and wiped his mouth on the back of his sleeve.

"Feel better?" Conall asked.

"Yes, sir."

"How's our patient?"

"Stable for now." Noah's voice rasped. "He's taken a blow to the head, but there's no internal bleeding that I can sense. A concussion for sure."

"Good. Get back to documenting the dead. I want them identified by sundown."

"Yes, sir." Noah lurched off like a drunkard on the verge of passing out.

"Everyone else, back to work. Until the ward is fixed, I want two of you on watch at all times. Clem and Lena, you're it. Augie, you're on grave digging duty." Conall gave him a small smile. "You'll have to find a new shovel."

Dinner HAD BEEN QUICK WITH EVERYONE eating when they found a few spare minutes. Murdoch and Elias spent the evening cleaning up the stores, but didn't find any spare wire. They would have to spend the night without the protection of a ward.

Even though the evening was muggy, Rowan wrapped her arms around herself as she left the stores tent. Fireflies sparkled in the shadows between trees, tempting her eyes to see monsters hiding behind every bush.

For years, she'd begged Regent Atherton to let her serve her city in the military. Now she wondered why she'd been so eager to leave the comfort and safety of home. A small but growing part of her also wondered if this mission truly served New Torwood City. The only way to find out was to understand what the scientists had been studying and why they'd been murdered.

She returned to the communications tent. Their patient was still sleeping on a cot in the corner, but his breathing seemed easier. She looked at the mess of mech scattered around the tent, then back at the sleeping man with envy. She wouldn't be getting any rest this night.

When Orson saw that she meant to keep working, he gave a disgusted sigh and left. A few minutes later, he returned with a camp chair, set it up beside the cot and slumped down on it.

"If you're going to stay, you could at least help me straighten this place up," Rowan said. Orson crossed his arms over his chest and glared. She didn't know why she even tried to connect with him. His heart was as dead as his eyes.

She returned to her task sorting through the debris. A few minutes later, she was excited to find the logbook of graphium messages to and from New

Torwood. She flipped to the last entry. It was sent from the oasis ten days ago. The others were regular check-ins every morning and evening. That gave her a general timeline for the attack. It had to have happened sometime during the night after that last message was sent.

She picked up all the scattered mech. Most of it was broken and useless, but she found one vox set still working and a valet that might give her some useful parts for Roger.

While she worked, the patient slept like he was dead in the cot beside her. She paused every few minutes to be sure he was still breathing. Once, he gasped and flailed an arm. She tried to get him to drink but he only managed one sip before he fell unconscious again.

Phalian didn't like this place. Not just the tent, the whole camp. He kept shifting from bird to mouse and back again as if neither form felt safe. Now he poked the tip of his brass nose from her shirt pocket.

"SQUEAK!"

"Inside voices please."

"SQUEAK."

"That's better. Now shush while I work."

But the little mech wouldn't settle. He shifted into bird form and battered the tent roof with his wings like a wild bird caught unexpectedly inside a house.

Finally, she called him down and commanded him to sleep. He shifted back to mouse and crawled into the recharging port on her arm.

Rowan stretched and the chair under her creaked. It was an awful chair and her lower back would be feeling its abuse in the morning. What she really needed was a few hours sleep.

Other than the graphium log, the search had yielded few clues. She'd been hoping for some kind of journal that would detail what these scientists had been studying. They must have kept notes, but if so, they weren't here. She was just about to get up and search one of the labs when she spied something lodged under a pile of debris. Pushing broken mech aside, she revealed a journal bound in brown leather. She opened it and read:

The Nursery - Planning and Implementation - Year One - Dr. Sonny Banerjee

The first entry was dated March 18, 589—over two years ago.

Finally. She'd found something to shed light on the work these scientists were undertaking. Rowan settled back in the uncomfortable chair and began to read.

From his perch beside the cot, the scribe's eyes were black lenses, recording every expression that passed over his subject's face.

26

FOR POSTERITY

Dr. Banerjee's journal began before the scientists journeyed to Eklridge Oasis and detailed the preparations and finances needed to undertake such a huge enterprise. Rowan was disappointed that it had little detail about the actual lab work, but she started to get a sense of the scope of the research. It was amazing, mind-blowing really, but she had no idea why people would be murdered for it.

She closed the journal and drummed her mech fingers on it. The diary ended only a few days after the scientists had set up shop that first summer in the oasis. There had to be more of them. Dr. Banerjee struck her as a meticulous man. He wouldn't have stopped writing once he arrived. So where were the other journals?

A light breeze blew in through the open tent flap. She pulled her short hair into a ponytail to let the air cool her neck. The sky outside was brightening. Rowan had read all through the short night.

She glanced at their patient asleep on the cot. His breathing was deep and even. Noah had been by to see him before he took his turn on watch. He felt sure the young scientist would wake soon. Maybe then, he would fill in some answers to her many questions.

Orson had also fallen asleep. His bulk seemed to melt over the edges of the small chair. She had no desire to wake him, but if he slept with his head bent like that, he'd be grumpy in the morning. The scribe was already as nasty as a pissed off fisher rat. She didn't relish dealing with him after a cranky night.

She was about to gently shake him awake when the patient groaned,

219

rolled and threw up on himself, the cot and Orson's boots.

Orson woke with a start and jumped to his feet.

"Damn the saints! Those are my only boots." He shook his foot, spraying the pile of mech debris with vomit.

Just perfect. Rowan hadn't sorted through that pile yet.

"Go clean up," she said. "Then go to bed. I'll take care of him, then I'm done for the night too."

Orson's reply was a grunt of displeasure.

"Right back at you," Rowan said as he left.

She found a shovel, scooped up the vomit on the ground along with a chunk of dirt, and tossed it all outside. Then, not wanting to disturb Murdoch, she found a small bowl in the mess tent and used her scarf and the water from her canteen to wash the patient. She dunked her cloth in the bowl and wiped his face. As the dirt and blood came off, she realized he was much younger than she'd first guessed. Younger than herself by a few years. His skin was clammy and an unhealthy gray. She dabbed gently at the knot above his ear. His black hair was thick and wavy and she took some time to free it from the mat of blood and dirt.

She worked quickly, moving on to his hands. His nails were broken and crusted with dirt as if he'd clawed at the ground.

Why? The only answer she had was that he'd been crawling, desperate to get away from the monsters that had overrun the camp.

"You're good at that," Conall said. He stood in the doorway with dawn's shadows hugging his frame.

"Thanks. I've had practice bathing unconscious patients."

"You volunteer at King's Cross?" He meant the hospital that catered to residents of Hightown.

"No. I suppose a princess should take on charitable work, but I meant my brother."

"Oh. Of course. I'm sorry. I should have known."

An awkward silence blushed between them. Everyone in New Torwood knew the prince and heir to the throne had mysteriously survived in a coma for nearly two decades.

"In the early years, after the incident, it was all anyone could talk about.

Now it's like Ethan is a myth." Rowan rinsed her cloth and wiped it across the patient's forehead.

Conall sat in Orson's chair and scooted it closer to her side. "Tell me about him."

Rowan looked up, trying to decide if he really wanted to know, or if he was just filling the fiddly silence with chatter. He watched her with a steady gaze. An inviting gaze.

Rowan sighed and set the cloth aside. "There's not much to tell, really. Ethan sleeps. No one knows why. He's like that princess in the old fairy tale, except there's no one to come wake him with a kiss."

Conall took her human hand in his. He turned it over and kissed the middle of her palm. Her fingers flexed involuntarily.

From outside, she heard Lena challenge someone and Orson respond with his usual gruffness.

Rowan groaned. "Saints sinner, he's coming back."

She tried to pull her hand away, but Conall hung on to it. His grin was just a bit wolfish.

"Let's get rid of him." And just as the scribe threw open the tent flap, Conall leaned in and kissed her. His lips parted hers and his tongue teased the soft inner flesh. His arm circled her shoulder, and he deepened the kiss before pulling away to face the scribe.

Rowan didn't know who was more surprised, her or Orson.

"Have some decency," Conall snarled. "Or do you want to document the exact moment I bed her too?"

Orson's nose twitched like he smelled something foul.

"I'll just make a footnote." He turned and stalked out, letting the tent flap close behind him.

Rowan's hand had strayed to Conall's chest, and she felt the rumble of his laugh.

"I'm sorry if I offended you, but the look on his face!" He sat back, giving her space. Rowan felt herself sway toward him as if caught in a vortex, and she pulled her hand from his to brace herself.

"No offense taken." Her lips still tingled from the kiss. "In fact…"

She tucked her hand around his neck and pulled him in again. His eyes widened when their lips touched, but he relaxed into it. The week-old beard was less rough than she'd expected and it added a certain spice to the softer sensation of his tongue on hers.

He made an animal noise in his throat, and even though she wanted to take things further—much further—she put her hand on his chest and gently pushed him away.

He looked like she'd sucker-punched him.

"What did you do that for?"

"Do what? Kiss you or push you away?"

"Both."

"For the same reason, I suppose. To let you know that in matters of the heart, this princess is always in charge. Unlike those old fairy tales."

"Message received." He leaned back in the chair, his eyes unreadable.

Rowan wished she felt as confident as her words sounded. Her stomach roiled with unspent desire and uncertainty. Better to get on with business as usual.

"Also, as much as I'd like to, um, continue, I need to tell you what I found out while we have a few scribe-free minutes."

Conall licked his lips. The crush of their kiss had darkened them. "Go on."

Rowan's thoughts were scattered now as if the encounter had blasted all reason from her head.

"I found this." She grabbed the journal from the desk and handed it to him, amazed that her hand trembled only slightly.

"What is it?"

"A journal from the lead scientist, a Dr. Banerjee. It's from two years ago, but it gives a rough outline of the camp's scope."

Conall flipped through the first pages, then put it down and focused on Rowan.

"Tell me."

She took a deep breath and laid it all out.

"They were studying a group of female gaunts that had taken up residence in this oasis. It seems that communal living is very unusual for gaunts."

Conall's brows furrowed. "But they often live in clans."

"Not nursing mothers. The females go off alone to give birth, then they remain alone until the offspring are old enough to fend for themselves."

"Makes sense. Male gaunts are known to eat their young."

"Exactly. Anyway, there was a similar community of females down south, near Dowchester. Dr. Banerjee was studying them. The females lived in harmony together, raising their young as a group, until another gaunt clan found them and killed them all. That's why these southern scientists were excited about this new community, and why they petitioned the regent for the right to set up camp here."

"I still don't understand. Gaunts have been studied before. Why does a bunch of nursing mothers suddenly spark so much attention?"

It was a good question. The resurgence happened nearly six-hundred years ago. The titans and gaunts had been studied since then, exhaustively, if only to find ways to kill them. What more could they learn?

Rowan tilted her head from side to side. It had been a long day and the adrenaline rush of the kiss was wearing off.

"I don't understand it either. Dr. Banerjee talks briefly about the evolution of a species, but I'm not sure they even knew what they were looking for. At least not when they first arrived. And I haven't found any other journals. I think they were taken. Also," she looked at their sleeping patient, "Dr. Banerjee clearly mentions multiple gaunts with infants. But you didn't find the infants, did you?"

"No. Just the one when we first arrived."

"So the others were killed elsewhere?"

"Or taken. But let's not make any assumptions right now." Conall rubbed his eyes. If she was tired, he must be doubly so. She wondered when was the last time he'd slept. "All we know is that sometime in the last two years while studying a bunch of gaunt babies, they discovered something alarming enough that it had them killed."

"You don't think this was a random attack either," she said.

"No. It was too well coordinated."

"There's something else. Dr. Banerjee mentions Myron Wrede several times in the journal. He made the initial journey with them."

"What's odd about that? I'd expect the Minister of Science and Mech to be part of this group. In fact, I asked Dale about that before we left."

"His interest in the project isn't odd, but it could be a disaster if he's out there among the dead."

Rowan let that little bomb explode between them. If one of the palace's highest ranking nobles was dead along with an international group of scientists, that would turn this obscure little rescue mission into a conspiracy. Or possibly a crime with far-reaching repercussions.

"And there's a satellite site," Rowan said.

"What do you mean?"

"I'm not sure, but Dr. Banerjee mentioned it several times. He called it the Academy. I thought it was an odd name, considering he called this place the Nursery."

"Sounds like the next phase of the project."

Rowan nodded. "That's what I thought."

"And was Wrede involved with both projects?"

"Apparently Wrede split his time between here and the Academy. Banerjee doesn't say why, but he clearly disliked Wrede."

"So he might still be alive. Wrede, I mean. Would you recognize him?"

"Yes, we've dined together many times."

"Good. It's been too many years since I met him. Augie and Noah haven't buried the bodies yet. If Wrede is among the dead, you need to identify him. If not…"

He let that idea fade because their patient suddenly groaned. His eyelids fluttered and opened. Surprise came to him at the same time as consciousness and he shrank from the sight of two strangers looming over his bed.

Rowan reached for him and he let out a cry. She had the sudden urge to jump up and run into the night. Fear cramped her hand into a fist.

Conall felt it too. His face had gone pale and he took a step toward the door before he steadied himself.

"Shit, he *is* an empath."

The emotion drained away as suddenly as it had appeared.

"Sorry." The patient mumbled and turned his face away.

"It's okay. You're safe." Rowan let her hand drop, and glanced at the tent flap, hoping Orson had truly gone to bed.

"Let me help you up." She hesitantly reached for his shoulder to prop him up, wary of being blasted by his rogue emotions again. The man's cracked lips opened but no sound came out. Conall opened his canteen and held it to his lips.

"Not too much," Conall cautioned. "You'll be nauseous from the head wound."

The man raised a trembling hand to his head but let it drop before his fingers found the bloody knot. Rowan bolstered a pillow against the cot so he could sit more easily.

"Who are you?" His eyes were unfocused as they tried to fix on their faces.

"Rangers," Conall said. "Sent to find out what happened here."

"Are they gone?" His voice quavered.

"Who?" Conall leaned in closer, his face hovering at Rowan's shoulder.

"The gaunts…"

Those few words seemed to exhaust him and his eyes fluttered closed again. Rowan thought that was all they were going to get out of him, but he opened his eyes again.

"What…what happened?"

"That's what we're trying to figure out," Rowan said. His eyes were rimmed in bruises, making them seem bigger. She revised his age again. He was probably at least her age, since he was part of the science team, but the contrast of his dark curls and pale face made him look younger. Now that he was awake, she realized he was startlingly handsome. Wide set, dark brown eyes, almost painfully thin nose and high cheeks, with only a shadow of whiskers above his lip.

"More…water."

"Go easy on it." Conall handed him the canteen and he took it with trembling hands. After a couple of sips, the canteen slipped from his grasp and Conall caught it.

He blinked like they'd suddenly appeared before him.

"What's your name?" Conall asked.

"Denny…Denlyn Feist." He was shivering. A blanket lay folded at the end of the cot. Conall handed it to Rowan, and she wrapped it around his shoulders.

"You're an empath?"

"Y…yes. Sorry about…I'm so tired…hard to control it."

His eyes closed again.

"Are you part of the science team?" Conall asked.

Denny didn't open his eyes, but his lips moved. They leaned in closer to hear the words that were barely above a whisper.

"Junior tech."

"Can you tell us what happened?"

Denny opened his eyes and clutched the blanket at his throat.

"Are they gone?" His sunken eyes were pleading.

Rowan patted his free hand. "The gaunts are all dead or fled."

This confirmation didn't soothe him. Denny shook his head. The movement must have hurt. He groaned and dropped back onto the pillow.

"It's okay. You're safe now," Conall said.

"We're not safe," he whispered. "Not out here. They broke the wards. They killed Susan…and…and Brent." A sob hitched in his throat.

This wasn't the time to tell him the gaunts had killed many more.

"Did you see the attack?" Conall asked. "How many gaunts were there? How many men?"

Denny's eyes were huge and dark, nearly all pupil in the low light.

"Too many." His voice had lowered to a bare whisper. "I could hear them, howling like a pack of wolves. But I saw only one. They were controlling it like a dog on an invisible leash." The last word came out in a sob.

"Who?"

"I don't know." Denny shook his head, then groaned again. "Soldiers." He had a sudden thought and gripped Rowan's hand. "Did they get them all? Did they get the babies?"

Rowan glanced at Conall, who spoke. "We found one gaunt mother and an infant dead. And six more females. No babies. If there were others, they're gone."

Denny sank into himself, the blanket clutched like a shield against the world. His gaze went from Conall to Rowan and his hand reached for her as if begging to be understood. Then he looked around the tent at the piles of destroyed mech.

"They took everything." He shook his head again, and this time the motion turned his stomach. He leaned over to vomit and Rowan stuck the bowl under him.

Movement outside caught her eye. Orson was standing in the shadows watching, listening, recording. For posterity.

27

GOOD RECORDS

Conall GOT LITTLE ELSE FROM DENNY. He'd seen the gaunts attack, but been knocked out early in the fight. When he came to, everyone was dead. He hid for days, fading in and out of consciousness, awake only long enough to drink some water and eat whatever he could scavenge in the destroyed stores. In his weakened state, he'd finally tried to flee, but only made it as far as the burned out ward when he'd collapsed and hit his head.

Conall tried to question him about the work going on at the oasis and about Dr. Banerjee and Minister Wrede, but the questions seemed to panic Denny. He curled into a ball on the cot and squeezed his eyes shut, refusing to speak more.

"Let him sleep," Rowan said. "We can try again in a few hours."

After breakfast, Conall and Rowan joined Noah where the bodies had been laid out. Thirteen humans in all with the addition of the dead scribe and the other scientist Noah had found, along with the pile of dead gaunts.

Conall decided hiding information from Orson was pointless. If he worked for the council, they already knew what was going on here. Now Conall needed to figure it out. So he'd brought the dead gaunt mother and infant back to camp too, and had them laid out beside the others. They were a part of this puzzle and he was slowly putting all the pieces together.

Orson had leaned over each body with his creepy stare, recording their deaths for the Temple. Now he watched while Noah laid out his findings.

"I was able to identify the rangers because of their ranks." Noah pointed to the insignia on the shoulder of the closest corpse. "And the scribe's name was Sandra Kane, according to the manifest. The others, I can only guess at."

Rowan stood before the first corpse, a young ranger. She studied the woman's face as if committing it to memory. Before she moved on, she closed her eyes and pressed her fisted right hand against her heart while her lips silently spoke Jocasta's prayer. The saint of healers couldn't heal the dead, but it was tradition to invoke Jocasta's help for an easy passing into the afterlife.

She repeated the scrutiny and the prayer for each body, including the dead gaunt mother and infant. When she finished, she turned to Conall.

"He's not here."

"Who?" Noah asked.

"Myron Wrede."

"Wait, why's that name familiar?" Noah removed the folded personnel manifest from his pocket and scanned it. "It's not on the manifest. Was he a scientist here?"

"He's more of a liaison, I would think. He's the regent's Minister of Science and Mech," Rowan said.

"What would a minister be doing out here?"

"That's a very good question. But Denny says he often visited this site."

Noah rubbed his chin where several days of stubble grew. "We haven't found all the bodies yet. The manifest says there should be seventeen. Now you say there may be more. Should we continue the search?"

Conall turned to stare at the shadows under the trees. He didn't want to let on, but he had no idea what they should do next. Their mission, as it had been outlined, was essentially over. They'd come, they'd seen, they would bury the dead. They *should* return to the city and report their findings, but he couldn't help feeling that he was missing something vital, like some gigantic beast was stalking them just outside his peripheral vision, and no matter which way he turned, he couldn't catch a glimpse of it.

"We should try to find the other bodies," he said finally. "If only to give their families closure." That would give him a few more hours to figure out their next steps.

Rowan nodded. "Clem's on watch. I'll take Lena with me. We'll walk the entire ward line and see what we find."

Conall didn't like sending her out there and was glad he had a solid reason to make her stay in camp.

"I'll go with Lena," he said. "There's a garage behind the mess hall with at least a half dozen cats. They're probably all trashed, but you need to get one working. I don't want to hit the Meadows again with only one vehicle."

Rowan hesitated. He could see she was trying to decide if he was coddling her or not. But she was the mechanic, and she would do her job.

A figure came toward them from the other side of camp. Noah ran toward Denny, who was stumbling along, blinking at the weak sunlight and clutching the blanket around his shoulders. Denny yanked his arm away when Noah tried to steady him. He stopped at the first body. The scribe. Sandra Kane. He made a fist and pounded it against his heart. Then he moved onto the next body and repeated the gesture just as Rowan had.

When he got to the gaunt with her infant, he fell to his knees and bowed his head. Sobs shook his shoulders.

Interesting. Denny was more upset by the dead gaunts than any of the human corpses. Conall gave the kid a moment for his grief, then laid a hand on his shoulder.

"Can you tell us who's missing?"

Denny wiped his eyes on his bare arm and looked back at the line of bodies.

"Dr. Banerjee. He's not here. And…and Elsie Myer. She was his assistant. And Jake. He was staff. Worked with the cook. And…" He looked around. Tears welled in his bruised eyes. "And Susan. I saw a gaunt drag her off. That way." He pointed to trees beyond the mess tent and covered his face in his hands.

A wall of sadness slammed into Conall. Someone in the squad gasped. Denny was losing control of his empath knack again.

Garou growled. He didn't like having his emotions manipulated.

Conall reached out to Denny. "Reel it back, kid. You're projecting again."

"Sorry. I'm usually better at controlling it." Denny sniffled and wiped his nose on his sleeve. The crushing weight of sadness lifted.

"What in the saints was that?" Clem asked. Conall ignored her for now. He didn't want to spook Denny again.

"Is that everyone?" Conall took Denny's arm gently and turned him back to face the bodies. The numbers matched up with the manifest. Thirteen bodies and four missing. But that didn't account for Minister Wrede. "Is there anyone else who should have been here, but isn't?"

Denny scanned the bodies again.

"No. No one."

The boy is lying. Garou was always better at sensing deceit. He said it smelled like rot.

"Okay. Tell me about your research here," Conall prodded. The kid started to look panicked again. Noah intervened.

"Commander, I think questions should wait until after he eats."

It was a request. Noah was only a maven, but as a medic, he could command even the commander. That he didn't, showed he had diplomatic skills that would take him far with the rangers.

"Fine, but after he eats, I want answers."

Denny LATCHED ONTO ROWAN LIKE SHE was his lifesaver. He wouldn't let anyone else help him settle at a table in the mess tent.

Garou grumbled at this manhandling of his mate-who-was-not-mate.

He's just a boy. Relax.

He's closer to her age than you are, old man.

They sat at a rickety table. Conall made sure to keep his distance from the twitchy scientist. Elias brought him a bowl of porridge with some dried fruit. At first Denny only picked at the food, but once the first spoonful hit his stomach he devoured it.

When he finished, Conall said, "Tell me about the attack. Everything you can remember."

Denny fiddled with his spoon and wouldn't look up. "It was like they were controlling the gaunts."

"You said that before. Controlling them how?"

Denny looked up and found Orson watching with his dark stare and he seemed to shrink into himself.

Rowan touched his shoulder and made him turn so he looked only at her. "It's okay, Denny. Just tell us what you remember."

Denny smiled a bit, then he pulled an old knotted piece of string from his pocket and started fidgeting with it. His eyes never left the string as he spoke.

"I don't know how the gaunts were controlled. There were men with them. Maybe soldiers. They weren't in uniform, but they had guns. Didn't use them though. The gaunts did all the killing, like…like hunting dogs that were pointed at prey."

"Why would these men attack the camp?" Conall tried not to let frustration creep into his tone.

Denny shook his head.

"I don't know." His voice was barely above a whisper.

"What were you studying here?"

Denny's eyes were fixed on the string. He looked sullen. "It's complicated."

"Explain it to me like I'm a child."

Denny's lips were pressed flat. Slowly, one of the knots on the string began to unravel without any help from Denny's fingers.

Interesting. He smells like earth magic, Garou said. Conall was more impressed by the fact that the kid had two knacks. Most people had only one. Conall had two, but he didn't really consider shifting a knack. It was just who he was.

Rowan squeezed Denny's arm, bringing the kid's attention back to them. "I read some of Dr. Banerjee's journal. So how about if I tell you what I know and you can correct me if I'm wrong?"

Denny nodded.

"It seems that this one clan of gaunts is unusual in that they are all nursing mothers. Am I right so far?"

Denny nodded again. The knots unfurled and re-knotted. It was a fidget tool, Conall realized, something to keep fingers occupied and mind soothed.

Rowan continued slowly. "The males can get aggressive during mating season, I understand. Fights to the death among young males are common. And sometimes this aggression leaks over to the young."

"They eat their own babies." Denny's voice sounded hollow.

"Yes. They eat their young, so the females leave. But usually they go off alone. Raise the pup until it's mature enough to survive on its own, then return to their clan. But these females stuck together to raise their young as a group."

"I still don't understand why that's significant enough to warrant a whole operation set up around them," Conall said.

Denny sat up, his expression now animated. "This is only the second time in recorded history that female gaunts have lived together. And our studies show it's for more than just protection. They're raising their young together like in a commune."

Conall gave him a flat stare.

"Don't you see? This is a prime moment in their evolution. This is *the* moment. When the mindless beast becomes something else…a thinking being with compassion for others."

"A compassionate gaunt." Conall didn't believe it for a minute. "And you think this is why the others were murdered? To keep this secret?"

The string exploded with activity.

"I don't know why they were killed," Denny said.

Lying.

Conall agreed with Garou. He changed the direction of his questions.

"What was your position here? What were your duties, exactly?"

Denny licked his cracked lips and glanced at Orson. Conall had to remind himself that he had no authority over the young scientist, but Denny was acting like a sullen teenager, and he wanted to shake him. Conall pushed the canteen toward him, then crossed his arms and waited while Denny drank. His hands shook as he lifted the canteen to his mouth.

"Answer the question."

Denny looked at Orson again and shook his head.

Rowan spoke over her shoulder. "Orson leave us alone, please. Go download your findings, or whatever it is you do."

"No." The scribe's tone was as flat as his expression. Rowan's gloved hand pounded the table lightly, as if she wanted to pound Orson's head.

Conall rose and was about to tackle the scribe. Orson could see it in his face. He held up his hands and backed up a pace. "Hey, man, you can't—"

Phalian launched from Rowan's shoulder and flapped around Orson's head, yelling "TWEET!" Metal wings sliced a red line down his cheek.

The scribe shrieked and tried to swat him, but Phalian was as fast as a hummingbird. Orson covered his head with his hands and ran into the woods with the mech bird in pursuit.

Conall sat down again.

"Thanks for that."

Rowan held up her mech hand. "Wasn't me. Phalian does his own thing. Mostly."

Conall wondered just how true that was. Rowan and Phalian seemed to act in unison, like her thoughts propelled him, and sometimes it was the other way around.

Denny watched the altercation with wide eyes. Rowan cleared her throat and patted his hand. "It's just us. You can talk now. Tell us what you were doing here."

Denny held his head like it still pained him, but after more reassurances from Rowan, he started to speak.

"I'm a field tech. I helped Dr. Banerjee in the lab too. He and Elsie were studying the blood of different generations of gaunts. Thera is present in all gaunt blood, and they were looking into the concentration of thera and its significance on their behavior. I don't really understand the science behind it. Like I said, I'm a field tech."

"What does that mean exactly?"

"I…study the behavior of the gaunts. I live among them for days at a time."

"How is that possible? Why didn't they attack you?"

"Because of my knack."

"You're an empath." Conall sat back in his chair. At least something in this mess finally made sense.

Denny nodded. "It's why I was chosen for this study."

"So you can sense what the gaunts are feeling?"

"I can influence their emotions too. They trusted me. After a few months, they were almost like family."

Anger and sadness crept around them again like an oily shadow. Garou's hackles rose. Conall crossed his arms over his chest and gave Denny a moment to get his feelings under control.

Empath knacks were rare. Impact empaths—the kind that could push out emotions—were even rarer. Conall didn't like having someone around who could influence his rangers in such a way.

Denny wiped tears from his eyes and gave a harsh laugh.

"I can see the idea of my knack horrifies you, like it does most people, which is why I was lucky to get this job. And now it's all gone."

"Tell me about the Academy." Conall didn't change his stance. He threw the question out to unbalance Denny and was pleased to see his expression stiffen like lightning had hit the seat beside him. His gaze met Conall's and his pupils dilated for a split second.

"I don't know…I mean what is that?"

Conall didn't need Garou to tell him Denny was lying.

"It's a satellite site. Dr. Banerjee mentioned it in his journal. In conjunction with Minister Wrede."

Denny looked away. "I know Minister Wrede is working on several projects. He often consulted with Dr. Banerjee. I don't know any more about it."

"I don't believe you."

Denny shrugged. He balled up the string and gripped it in one fist.

"If they took the other infant gaunts, would they take them to this Academy?" Conall asked.

"I don't know. Maybe."

"Where is it?"

"I don't know."

"You must have some idea." Conall let a growl into his tone.

Denny shrank back. "I don't. I swear."

"I think that's enough for now," Rowan said. Her eyes told him to lay off.

"I think you're lying." Conall let Garou peek through his eyes. "I think you know a lot more than you're letting on."

Denny looked down at his fist. "I don't know anything."

INTERLUDE

Something MOANED OUT IN THE RUINS.

"Is that a gaunt?" Rowan whispered.

Dale held his fingers to his lips and listened to the terrible sound. After a moment, he nodded. He would not be the one to tell her that was the sound of her brother dying. Let her think it was a monster.

She started to cry.

He grabbed her face, cupping her pudgy cheeks in both hands.

"Listen to me. There *are* monsters out there. They want to kill us." He gulped. "And eat us. You have to keep silent. Do you understand?"

Rowan nodded. He slowly let her go. She sat frozen in the grip of fear, her eyes wide and glistening with tears. Snot ran from her nose. She began to tremble violently, and her leg kicked out involuntarily, sending a rock flying.

The sound of the stone hitting the ground seemed as loud as gunfire.

Saints help him, his next thought was to smother her. The Princess. There was no way a child of nine could cope with the magnitude of the situation. No way she could sit silently while those men hunted them. His hands were reaching for her nose and mouth when he heard the distinct sound of a cat driving away. Relief washed over him, cold and hard as ice-water.

He waited another five minutes before taking her hand.

"Come on. It's time to go home."

"Are the gaunts gone?" She rubbed her eyes, smearing dirt with tears.

"I think so, but let's be super quiet anyway."

"I'm thirsty."

"Me too, but we'll get something to drink at home."

"What about Ethan?"

"He got tired and went home already."

"He's such a jerk. He could have told us!" Her voice rose and he shushed her.

"Let's hurry and be quiet. Pretend the gaunts are still around."

Rowan sniffled. "I don't want to pretend anymore."

Dale pulled her along, not bothering to argue. When they got to the tower, he was relieved that the mountain of rocks blocked the view. The men might have taken Ethan or not. Either way, he didn't want Rowan to see the scene of his murder.

Assassination. A prince was assassinated.

His only purpose now was to get the princess to safety. They were just about to the tunnel entrance when Rowan stopped, jerking on his hand.

"Look! Ethan forgot his sword. He's so stupid!" Her little hand slipped out of Dale's. "Father will kill him if he loses that sword."

She ran toward the pile of rubble where a glint of silver caught the fading light.

"Rowan, no!" Dale ran after her. She scampered up the precarious pile of stones.

And froze.

He caught up to her as she stared down on the bloody, broken body.

"Is he—"

Her foot slipped. It knocked a stone loose. Her arms windmilled. Dale tried to grab her, but the stone pile seemed to melt under his feet.

Rowan screamed as she skidded down the slope. Rocks tumbled after her. The last thing Dale saw before the avalanche took out his feet was Rowan being buried next to the body of her brother.

28

A KNACK FOR QUESTIONS WITHOUT ANSWERS

"Rowan, hurry!" Dale's voice. Something howled. The sky pressed down on them. There would be no escaping. Her feet knew this and wouldn't move even as Dale tugged and begged.

Her legs moved. Finally. She stumbled over rock, but now a cat's engine revved as it made ready to run her down.

And another howl. They were all around her.

Rowan opened her eyes and blinked in the darkness. She lay on her bedroll in the mess tent.

The dream wasn't real.

Dale was home, far away in New Torwood.

But the howl was real.

She listened to it again. A wolf. She turned to find Conall watching her.

"It's far away," he said. "Probably out in the Meadows."

That gave her some comfort, but she felt unsettled from the dreams.

"You were having a nightmare again."

"Yes." She reached across the darkness for his hand. Instead of taking it, Conall lifted his blanket and invited her to join him. She turned and scooted her back against his chest. He let the blanket and his arm fall over her.

"Go back to sleep," he said. "You're safe."

And for the first time since they'd left the city, she *did* feel safe. She slept with the heat of his body warming her.

Rowan SPENT THE NEXT MORNING AND most of the afternoon going over every cat in the camp, looking for one that would run. So far, they'd all been disabled on purpose—thera cells missing, battery lines cut, wings broken. Someone wanted to be sure that if anyone survived the attack, they had no way to leave.

The steady work gave her time to think, and the saints knew, she had enough mysteries to ponder. There was the big question mark about what happened to the scientists, of course, but she was starting to believe that they might never know the full truth.

Another mystery nagged at her today. Her nightmares.

Those dreams always ended the same way—with her being chased by the gaunt until she stumbled over the bloody and broken body of her brother.

And yet…

Last night's dream had been different. The monster chasing her had been a cat. The sound was unmistakable to her now. The howl that had plagued her dreams for years, the one she had always thought was a gaunt, had actually been the scream of an over-taxed thera engine.

Was that a memory or was she simply projecting impressions from her current situation into her dreams?

The accepted story about that night was that a gaunt attacked Ethan. Rowan was lost under a pile of debris when she found his body. Her arm had been crushed beyond repair and her father had been forced to order its amputation. That, along with the news that his son was in a coma and likely brain dead, had been too much for the old king. His heart had given out. He was dead before he hit the floor.

Or so the story went.

But Rowan was starting to question the story. Where did the cat fit in? And why did Ethan have only three scars on his chest? Was there a gaunt running around the Meadows missing a finger? Or had something else made those scars?

These questions tugged at her all morning as she worked, but she had no answers. If there were answers, they'd be back in New Torwood. And the only way to get there was to fix the saints' damned cat.

She sighed and placed her mech hand on the cat's engine. It was the last one in the garage. If she couldn't get it working, they'd be heading into the Meadows with only one vehicle again.

She sent her arm's knack through the metal workings to find the fault.

There it was.

The wire leading to the battery had been cut.

"Find it." She let Phalian out to scamper along the underside of the cat's carriage.

His nimble feet and sensitive nose would find the break and then she'd decide if she could fix it.

"SQUEAK!"

"Okay! I'm coming." Lying on her back, she dragged herself under the cat. Phalian perched on a metal bracket where the wire disappeared into the engine box. Its black casing was torn in several places and the threads stuck out in silver sprays. Someone hadn't just cut the wire, they'd shredded it.

She sighed. She'd have to replace it, and they had no wire to spare. Maybe she could cut a piece from another cat and splice it in? It would be a tricky job, but she had to try. Their journey from New Torwood had proven that traveling with only one vehicle could be suicidal.

"Come on." They'd been working on these cats for hours, and she sensed that Phalian was near depletion. She tapped her gloved arm. He twitched his metal whiskers and clamped into his recharging cradle. She pulled herself back into the sunshine, then took the dirty rag from her back pocket and wiped her face.

Denny sat in a camp chair nearby. He hadn't left her side all day. His fingers fussed with his knotted string while his gaze followed her everywhere as if she were his guardian angel, just because she'd found him knocked out and bleeding in the woods.

Perhaps she was. Perhaps he wouldn't have survived if she hadn't found him. There were other monsters out there besides gaunts, monsters that would make an easy meal from an unconscious man.

But Rowan didn't want to be a guardian angel any more than she wanted to be a princess.

Beside Denny, Orson also sat in his regular vigil. Augie had finished burying the bodies, and she'd set him to cleaning her tools. That hadn't been done since they'd left the city, and she didn't want to pull out a wrench in an emergency and find it gummed up with ash from the ward generator or grime from the valet mech.

Denny held out a hand. She grasped it and he pulled her up.

"Shouldn't you be resting?" she asked.

He touched the bandage on his head. "I feel a lot better. Your medic worked wonders. He's got an amazing knack."

Rowan wiped her hands on a rag. "And you should thank him. It takes a steep toll."

Denny nodded. "I will. Any luck with the cat?"

"Wire to the battery is cut."

"At least the wings on this one aren't broken," he said. "If we can get it into the Meadows, it'll run with the wind."

Rowan nodded. "I'm thinking of splicing a piece of wire from one of the other cats."

"Would that work?"

"It might last long enough to get us out of the forest. Augie, can you cut a piece of battery wire from that one?" She pointed to the last vehicle they'd worked on. Its wings had been snapped, and its thera cell taken, but the rest of it was intact. "Cut as long a piece as you can so we have some extra to play with."

"Sure." Augie hummed as he picked up wire cutters.

Half an hour later, she had spliced in the new wire, and Rowan pushed herself out from under the cat.

"Start it now," she called to Augie. The engine caught. She laid her mech hand on the cat and listened. It all sounded good. Relief washed through her. They'd have a second cat when they left this saints cursed oasis.

"Okay, turn it off." Rowan stood up and wiped her hands. *Ode to Joy* floated back to her as Augie packed away the tools. She reached her arms overhead and stretched out her lower back. She'd been scuttling about underneath the cats all day. Add in nights sleeping on the hard ground and she was starting to feel ancient.

When the humming stopped, it took her a moment to realize that something had changed. Augie was floating, his eyes fixed on the shadows between trees.

"Augie?" She tucked the greasy cloth in her back pocket and reached for him at the same moment as Denny said, "They're here."

His face had gone ashen.

"Who?"

Frozen in fear, Denny could only shake his head and clutch his string.

29

RELEASE

After LUNCH, CONALL SAT AT A mess table, looking through the screened walls at the camp and the rangers busy with their jobs. Rowan and Augie were fixing the cats with Denny and Orson as their audience. Murdoch and Elias pulled everything out of the storeroom to catalogue it. Lena and Clem were on watch, hidden in the trees, and Noah sat on a stump by the fire, scribbling in a logbook, no doubt filling in the details of his postmortems.

All the squadlings were accounted for.

Conall had his own logbook open on the table in front of him. He was supposed to be writing a report, but found that his thoughts were too jumbled.

Yesterday, they'd buried the dead and rested. Tomorrow they would leave Eklridge Oasis and Conall had to decide which direction they would go. North, into the Meadows—a life of hiding and running. Or south to the city, and the dubious reception of the Regent's Council.

The day was overcast and the light inside the mess tent poor. He made a few notes in his logbook, then shoved it away in frustration.

He still didn't have enough information to make the right decision. His gaze locked on Denny, who was watching Rowan as she glided underneath a cat. Maybe if he hung the kid up by the ankles and shook him, the answers would fall out. If not, it would still make Conall feel better.

He watches her too much, Garou said.

Conall agreed, though he didn't think there was anything sexual in Denny's desire to be close to Rowan. He seemed to worship her like she was a saint. Maybe that's how saints became saints. They found lost souls in the woods and saved them. It was as good a first step to canonization as any other.

Garou grumbled something about staking his claim with his mate, which Conall ignored.

Rowan had cleaned up the little valet mech, and Roger trundled around the tables, trying to pick up garbage, but mostly bumping into benches. His one good arm reached out like the beak of a bird to pick up a mug that had been left on a bench, but it couldn't get a solid grip, and the mug slipped to the ground with a thud. The mech spun in a circle and rammed itself into the bench again. And again.

Conall shook his head. It was one thing to be obsessed with mechs in the city, but they had no place in the wild.

"Roger, come here." The mech whirled and rolled over to him. He placed it on the bench, and it immediately tried to roll off.

"Lock your wheels."

The mech lurched as it complied with the voice command.

"Do you have a light function?"

"Roger that!"

"Good. Light this logbook."

The mech's eyes warmed from green to red, then to bright white as light burst from them. Conall adjusted the angle of the mech's head until his logbook was well lit.

Rowan was right; Roger was a most unusual mech. Despite his almost comically antiquated look, he had advanced voice command function. Just another mystery in a long line of mysteries they'd encountered during this mission.

Conall turned back to his journal and tried to pick up his thoughts where he'd left off. He was reporting on the interview with Denny. Orson had recorded the whole event, but like mechs, the scribe couldn't be trusted. He clearly had his own agenda, one that aligned with the regent. No, the only ones Conall trusted out here were himself and his wolf. And possibly Rowan. At least he wanted to trust her.

He glanced up again to watch her lean over the open engine of a cat.

Jupiter and Jocasta, he was no better than the scribe or the science kid, watching her like some stalker. But he couldn't take his eyes off her.

Rowan stood up and stretched. Her hair had come loose from its ponytail again and it framed her face like a rusty halo. She said something to Augie, and he dug into the box of tools. He wasn't even floating. She kept him grounded. She kept them all grounded.

She'd blown the top off all his expectations. He'd assumed she would be a pampered, flighty princess who would need to be catered to at every step. Instead, she was hard-working and determined. He'd set her a monumental task—to fix one of the cats before they headed home—but she never complained even when he could see exhaustion in the droop of her shoulders. She was also capable and took initiative, like finding Dr. Banerjee's notes. It was only because of Rowan that they had even the smallest clue about what happened here.

And she'd seen his wolf and not run away screaming.

Saints. He needed to keep his focus on the mission.

The mission is dead, Garou said.

The mission is dead when I say it is.

He looked down at the logbook. So far all he'd written were questions that nagged at him.

Who killed the scientists and why?

Why would someone take their research records?

Why kill the gaunt females?

Where are the baby gaunts?

He thought about Denny lying in the woods, the dead scribe not far away.

Was the camp's scribe trying to hide her recordings?

The answer to that last question was probably yes. Someone didn't want anyone to find out about the research going on here. They would have taken the scribe's recordings, but she managed to hide them.

From whom?

His suspicions went right to the regent, of course. Atherton was corrupt, Conall had no doubt. But he wasn't stupid. If he'd ordered the hit on the camp, it was for some reason that benefited him. But if he did order the hit, why send Squad 54 out to find the dead scientists? Unless the regent was innocent and there was a third party at work here.

He tapped his pen on the logbook. His questions were just circling now and he was back to the beginning with, who attacked the oasis? What were the scientists hiding?

Denny knew. He was certain of it. The kid knew and he was too stubborn or too afraid to speak.

Conall tucked the pen inside the journal.

He watched Rowan wipe her hands on a filthy cloth. There was a smear of grease across her face, but somehow it only seemed to highlight her beauty.

She doesn't mind getting dirty, Garou added.

No she doesn't.

A blur of motion startled him. The shadows under the trees tricked his eyes, but Garou let out a howl in his mind as a gaunt leapt into the clearing. Conall jumped to his feet, knocking over the bench and the valet that shouted, "Roger that!"

Augie screamed. Others were shouting, but it was all a background haze to Conall as adrenaline spiked in him.

The gaunt lurched to his feet and sighted Denny. He was already running, but he didn't get far. He tripped and went flying as the gaunt attacked. If he hadn't fallen, the beast would have taken his head off. Instead, the gaunt soared over him, landed in a roll and turned to face Denny with a snarl.

The next minutes happened blindingly fast, and yet they also took an eternity. Garou was howling in his mind, begging to be let off leash. The gaunt turned to face Rowan. They both seemed to move in slow motion like flies caught in honey. Slowly, but still too fast for Conall to get there in time.

To save her.

The gaunt reared up. Massive fists thumped the bone plating on its chest and a roar blasted from gaping jaws.

It leapt.

At Rowan.

Garou screamed.

And Conall let go.

Fur burst from his pores. Muscle rippled. Bone cracked and shifted. Clothing tore. Never had the change taken him so quickly or so violently. Pain seared him like a flash fire, leaving his nerve endings raw. He panted and staggered to his feet—four feet.

Garou ran. He burst through the mess tent. The mesh wall clung to him, slowing him down.

He'd never make it in time. The gaunt would rip her apart.

He bounded across the clearing, his paws barely touching dirt, and he rammed the beast. His shoulder took it out at the knees. They landed in a heap of limbs and gnashing teeth. His jaws clamped onto the beast's calf as it tried to drag itself away.

Rowan shoved her black-gloved hand into the gaunt's face. Blue energy sizzled across her fingers, searing the creature. The gaunt screamed and the night filled with the stench of burning flesh. It flailed, trying to get away from the fire in its eyes, but Rowan hung on. Its claw raked her arm. Garou switched the grip of his jaws, sinking teeth into the ligaments behind the creature's knee. He twisted until he heard the joint pop.

Augie fell from the trees and hammered the creature with a wrench. The metal broke the beast's bone plating, shattering its skull. Augie hit it again. Blood splattered across Rowan's face as she fell back.

The gaunt shuddered and lay still.

Garou let go. He tasted blood as the last of his shocking change rippled over him.

The day was utterly silent. Then a howl broke the stillness. Too close to be out in the Meadows.

Rowan stood over the dead gaunt. Her mech fingers smoked. She smiled at him.

"Hello, Garou."

Denny gripped her shoulder, shaking her. Stealing her attention.

Garou growled.

"We have to go," Denny said.

Garou pricked his ears. In the distance, he heard a shout. The other humans were on watch. And the gaunts had found them too.

30

A FULL SQUAD

When Rowan looked into the wolf's eyes, she saw Conall staring back. Except it wasn't Conall. If she understood correctly, Garou had taken over, and Conall was only a dim voice in the wolf's mind.

That left her in charge of the squad.

She searched Garou's eyes again as if seeking his permission. He licked his lips and nuzzled her hand.

She turned to Augie. "Take Denny and find Murdoch and Elias. Hide. Protect him. This is your only job. Understood?"

The young ranger squeaked out an affirmative noise. He grabbed Denny's hand and pulled him toward the mess tent. For once, Augie wasn't humming or floating. His feet were firmly on the ground.

Rowan spotted Noah standing near the fire. He'd been too late to help with this fight, but he gripped a knife in his hand with grim determination.

"Maven, you're in charge of the camp. If we don't come back. Take the cat and get the others to safety." Noah nodded even though it was an impossible task. Nowhere was safe.

"Good. Let's go."

Garou took off into the trees, toward the sounds of fighting. Rowan followed, barely able to keep up. He ran swiftly and nimbly. His feet made no sound in the underbrush. Next to that stealth, she felt like an ogre blundering around the bush. She stopped to pinch the stitch at her side and the wolf paused, turning his head to watch her.

Saints, he was beautiful. Nearly all black, with a mane of bronze and ears tipped in red. When the light caught them, they looked like flames rising from his head.

He paused halfway up a small incline, waiting for her even though they could hear screaming ahead.

"Go on!" She waved at him. "I'll catch up."

The wolf took off. Rowan stumbled up the hill, ignoring the pain in her side.

At least she ran faster than Orson. She'd left him behind in the camp. He was probably shouting about the sanctity of scribes and her need to protect him. To saints with that. He could protect himself or hide.

Clem and Lena were under attack. Orson wasn't going to hold her back. Neither was a cramp in her side.

She stumbled over the top of the hill and heard a yelp. A gaunt dropped from the tree overhead and landed on Garou. They grappled. The wolf snarled and kicked up dirt and leaves. The gaunt seemed to be all long limbs and claws as it tried to pin the wolf.

Rowan didn't think. She didn't even pull out her knife. She threw herself onto the beast's back. Bone plating smacked her chest and scraped her face. The wolf had it by the throat, but the gaunt thrashed, keeping him from the killing bite.

Blue energy laced her fingers. It crackled and smoked.

"Jump away!" she yelled. The wolf let go and scrambled out from under the beast. The gaunt swiped at his feet. Garou fell and Rowan couldn't see if he got up. She smashed her hand to the gaunt's back and poured every ounce of energy she had into it. The day turned black around the edges as lightning streamed from her fingertips.

The gaunt reared up. An unholy scream ripped from its throat and it fell backward. Right on Rowan. Her back crashed into solid ground, driving the breath from her lungs. Her muscles seized until her diaphragm remembered how to contract, and she sucked in a gulp of air. Pain lanced up her jaw into her eye. She tasted blood. An armored shoulder had smashed her lip.

She lay still. The beast's stink clogged her nose. Its massive body pressed on her chest making each breath an agony. A cold black nose snuffled her forehead. Garou used his head to push the gaunt while Rowan struggled to pull herself free. Finally she was able to roll away, and she lay on the ground, panting. Every muscle in her body trembled. She raised a hand to her face and felt the tender spot under her eye that would blossom into a bruise.

Garou whined and shook his mane, spraying blood from his muzzle.

The dead gaunt lay across the path. Even in the deep shadows under the trees, Rowan saw that it was just a juvenile, only a youth and already a killing machine.

She looked away. Her vision was still blurred, and the silence was ominous. Something dark flitted through the trees and she braced herself for another attack.

She couldn't fight another gaunt, not fight and win. Never had she used so much of her arm's magic at once. It seemed to pull energy right from her heart, and she felt like a wind-up toy whose string was about to run out.

Garou grounded himself in front of her, legs taut and ready to spring at whatever leapt from the trees next. A low growl rumbled from his chest. She laid her human hand on his back, feeling his muscles ripple with each growl.

A sound echoed through the trees. A howl or maybe a horn. A call that rang through the oasis and went on and on until the noise crept under her skin to shiver along her nerves.

And then everything fell silent again. Nothing moved in the trees.

Rowan stood on trembling legs. Garou dashed toward the last sounds of fighting. Rowan limped after him, bracing herself for the worst. Clem and Lena had been alone on watch. How many more gaunts were there?

She jumped over the burned out ward wire and skidded to a stop. Lena lay bleeding in a tumble of branches and leaves. A dead gaunt sprawled in a twisted heap beside her, an arrow shaft sticking out of its eye.

Clem held a crossbow.

"It's a good knack right? I found its eye." Her grin was fierce but she was trembling.

"It's a great knack." Rowan could feel her own guts trying to shake themselves loose.

It's shock. I have no time for it now. None of us do.

Garou loped over to Lena and sniffed her wounds. Mercifully, she was unconscious. Her shirt was torn and bloody. And a gash cut across one eye and down her cheek.

"Hey, boss," Clem said. "It's good to see you in fighting form."

Garou snorted, then slunk into the trees. Rowan made a move to follow him, but Clem stopped her.

"He's shifting. Leave him alone. He doesn't usually like people to see it."

Rowan nodded.

How lonely that must be. To keep the most basic part of yourself hidden from everyone.

For the first time, Rowan noticed other bodies lying in the shadows under the trees. Half a dozen more gaunts with arrows protruding from throats and eyes. Each one a kill shot.

She turned to Clem in wonder. "Did you?" She waved a hand at the destruction. Clem shook her head and pointed. Two Ebos stepped into the light. They wore brown and green leathers that blended seamlessly with the forest. A male and a female. She wore bones, sharpened to spikes to hold back her long blond hair. His hair was shorter, but he also wore a headband of leather and bone. More bones were sewn in patterns across their chests and backs. Short bows were slung over their shoulders.

They bowed in unison and the female spoke. "Good evening, *Evani*. We bring greetings from the Evafara."

"Who?"

"From Omika. He is our…you would say elder. He was very…ah… influenced by you when we last met."

"Influenced?" Rowan's head pounded and she didn't have the energy to decipher the elf's meaning.

"I think she means impressed," Clem said. "You impressed the old guy." Clem's crossbow was loaded, but she kept it pointed to the ground.

"Yes! Omika sent us to keep watch over our new friends. I see our arrival was perfection." The elf beamed at the bodies lying all around.

"I don't understand." Rowan's voice was thick like she spoke through a mouthful of syrup. She swayed on her feet and the elf ran to prop her up.

"My name is Minna." She smiled and tucked her shoulder under Rowan's arm. "This is my mother-sister spawn, Ferlan. We come to serve the Evani."

Rowan didn't have the brain power to follow mother sister spawn to its conclusion. Instead, she latched onto the other unfamiliar word.

"Evani. What does that mean?"

Minna pursed her lips. "You would say, princess, Evani."

"I'm not a princess out here. Please call me Rowan or Striker, if you must."

Minna gave a hesitant nod. "Yes, Evani. We were sent to protect you."

"But I don't need protection." Rowan paused. "Or rather I don't need it more than any of the others here. But thank you."

Minna nodded and stood back as if waiting for instructions. Rowan was at a loss. Clem stood over Lena. Her eyes never stopped scanning the trees.

Minna smiled. "The *magridons* are gone, Evani. There is no more need for vigilance tonight."

Rowan rubbed a shaky hand over her face.

"Magridons. You mean the gaunts?"

"Yes, Evani, the creatures of false bone. And their human handlers too," Minna said. "You can rest now."

"Um, okay." Rowan didn't feel like resting. She was still in fight or flight mode. Her mech fingers tingled with the recent release of magic.

Clem had lowered her bow to examine Lena and Rowan joined her. Lena's face was covered in blood. There was no telling how much of it was hers.

"She held back," Clem said with a pinched expression.

"What do you mean?"

"When the gaunt first attacked. She shot it instead of using her knack. It almost killed her."

Rowan understood. The memory of lightning pouring from her fingers was still fresh. It had scared her. She could even smell the tang of burned flesh on herself. Lena didn't trust her knack. It was too wild. Rowan pitied her for having to live in fear of the power inside her.

"Help me get her back to camp." Clem lifted Lena by the shoulders. The adrenaline was wearing off and pain lanced Rowan's shoulder as she hefted Lena's feet and then instinctively let them drop. She was surprised to find her shirt hanging in shreds and blood leaking down to her wrist.

"Let me take her." Conall's voice was raspy and harsh. He stood naked in the sunlight dappling through the canopy. Rowan let her eyes drop for only a second.

Don't be juvenile. The man just saved you. Don't look a gift wolf in the...

Saints, there wasn't an ounce of unnecessary flesh on him. Blond hair fuzzed his solid legs, lending a softness to their hard toning. She skipped the next part and planted her eyes firmly on his bare chest. He was sculpted, all hard angles shaded with rippled muscle.

He caught her gaze and quirked a grin. "Like what you see, Princess?"

She lifted her chin, then lowered her gaze pointedly. "I just didn't realize how cold it was out here."

Conall flexed his shoulders like a man with nothing to be ashamed of and winked. Clem stifled a laugh against her shoulder. They were all a bit giddy. Rowan had never guessed how exhilarating and conversely how emotionally draining a fight to the death could be.

She brought herself under control. The fight might be over, but they weren't safe yet. She reached for Lena's legs again, but Conall was suddenly there, taking the burden from her. He seemed completely unconcerned by his nakedness.

Rowan stepped back and watched them carry Lena away.

Minna cleared her throat.

"Evani, should we follow them?"

Rowan dragged her attention back to the elves. Ferlan was crouched next to a dead gaunt to retrieve his arrows.

"Yes," Rowan said. "But I want to examine the gaunts first. You said there were human handlers. What did you mean?"

Minna shifted, hitching her quill of arrows higher on her shoulder. "Men, Evani. We have heard rumors."

"Rumors of what?"

"Of magridons who run with men in the north."

"Do you know where, exactly?"

"No, Evani. Rumors are like the wind. They shift too often to hold onto."

"Right. Well, I guess we should take note of these anyway."

Orson caught up with them at that moment. As he stepped from the shadowed path, Rowan was actually glad to see him. The Ebos were not. Minna jumped away from the scribe and pulled her bone knife. Ferlan actually hissed.

Rowan remembered the Ebos's dislike of all things mech and wondered how they sensed it in Orson. But those were questions for later. She wanted to get back to camp and find out how Lena fared.

"Orson, please record these deaths, but hurry. We need to get back to camp."

"I am not yours to command, Princess. I take my orders from the Abbott Archivist only."

"Fine. Then I'll leave you here, since you have no need of me." She motioned for the Ebos to follow her and turned for the path. The light was starting to fade and the shadows hiding dead gaunts seemed full of menace.

"Wait!" Orson called. "I believe, that is…the Abbott would want a full report of these creatures. If you will wait, I will walk back with you."

Rowan stopped. "Of course." Her face was too sore to smile, but she gave him an encouraging nod. Maybe, just maybe, she and the scribe could learn to work together.

They CAUGHT UP TO CONALL AND Clem just as they reached the camp. Rowan jogged on ahead to alert Noah. He came out of the mess tent, his hands covered in blood and a haunted look in his eyes. When he saw Conall and Clem carrying Lena, he snapped out orders.

"Get me a blanket or a tarp, something to put her on. Quickly." Rowan stepped around him to comply. "Not you!" Noah pointed to the ground. "Sit. I'll see to you next."

Rowan's legs crumpled under her.

Elias arrived with a canvas tarp and laid in on the dirt.

"Put her down." Noah barked the order. Conall carefully laid Lena on the tarp. His bare chest was streaked with her blood. He watched Noah tear away Lena's shirt, then headed over to the pump to clean up.

Murdoch showed up with a water bucket and cups for everyone. The cool drink soothed Rowan's aching throat. She'd burned too much energy and it left her feeling raw and hollowed out.

"Was anyone else hurt?" Rowan was worried. Noah had already been covered in blood when they arrived. She glanced around to see who was missing. "Augie?"

Noah nodded but didn't look away from his work. Lena was a mess of scratches. Most were superficial, but the one across her shoulder and collar bone was deep and oozing blood. And her stomach was already turning purple. Something had hit her there. Hard. Noah splashed some kind of tonic over the wounds. Lena groaned but didn't wake. He prepared a needle and thread for stitching.

He'd be at it for a while, Rowan realized. She pushed herself to stand. She needed food now, before she passed out. And she needed to find Augie, to assess his injuries for herself.

Someone had rolled down the flaps on the mess tent and hung a tarp across the screen that Garou had burst through. It was a futile attempt to keep out the bugs. The day was hot and the evening mosquitoes were already out and biting. She swatted one as she entered the mess hall.

Conall was standing next to a table. He wore a clean uniform and his hair was wet. He stared down at Augie's still form.

"Is he all right?" Rowan came up beside him, and she saw. Augie was not all right. Augie would never be all right again. No more humming. No more floating.

Phalian sensed her agitation and crawled out of his cradle. He leapt down to Augie's chest, laid his head flat and bowed like he was praying. Rowan had never seen him react like that before.

Phalian is part of the squad too, as much as the others.

And he was mourning one of their own.

Rowan laid her hand on Augie's shoulder, feeling the utter lifelessness under her fingers.

"He saved me," she said. "For once his knack for floating actually helped. He brought that damned wrench down on its head…" Her voice caught and she sucked back a sob.

Conall squeezed her arm. She thought the action was one of sympathy, but when she looked at his face, she saw nothing but rage.

"He saved everyone," Murdoch said from behind them. "After you left to find the others, another gaunt came into the camp. Augie fought it off. Alone. Giving us time to hide."

"He wanted to be a hero," Rowan said.

They stood in silence over the body, then Conall growled, "Where's Denny?"

"I don't know. Why?" Rowan reached for him, but he shrugged off her touch.

"Because he's got Augie's blood on his hands. And Lena's."

He stormed through the flimsy door, nearly taking it off the hinges.

31

WIND OF CHANGE

The WOLF MIGHT HAVE LET HIM back into his human skin, but he lingered close to the surface. Conall stormed across the camp to where Denny was hovering over Noah as he finished Lena's stitches. Only the saints knew what it cost him to hold back his fury. He almost grabbed the kid by the throat. Instead, he shoved down the wolf with a growl, hauled Denny to his feet by the collar and shook him. Hard.

"Wha—?"

"Tell me. What were those soldiers looking for?"

"Soldiers?" Denny's face was slack. Conall shook him again until Noah grabbed his arm.

"You'll hurt him! He's not over his concussion."

"What are you protecting?" Conall let the wolf peer through his eyes. Denny went slack in his grip and he let the kid drop.

Rowan arrived. She steadied Denny before he fell. She turned him away from the scary wolf and said, "You'd better tell us, Denny. It's important."

"Wh…what are you talking about? What soldiers?" Denny was close to blubbering.

"In the forest," Conall growled. "I could smell them. Close enough to shoot, but they chose not to. They let the gaunts attack and take the damage."

"He speaks truth," said the dark elf. Conall vaguely remembered her introducing herself when they'd returned to camp. Minna.

"The men fled when we killed their pets," she said.

"How many?" Conall asked.

"Six men. In two of your moving machines. They left no one behind."

"No one but the dead gaunts," Rowan said.

The science kid seemed to have gone catatonic, but Conall wasn't ready to let him off the hook yet. Rowan had other ideas. She grabbed his arm and pulled him away.

"We have no time for interrogations," she said.

"He knows something."

"Yes. And we'll figure it out. But not here. Those men will be back with more gaunts."

Conall nodded. She was right and he felt ashamed that he'd let his anger blind him to his duty. The mission was over. His only job now was to keep everyone left alive.

He took a deep breath and let it out. "Thank you, Striker. How many cats do we have?

"Two. But one is untested in the field."

"Load everyone onto them. We stay together, but we're leaving now."

Denny finally came out of his reverie and said, "I will tell you what you want to know."

Orson stepped forward as if he were the Abbott Archivist himself ready to accept a confession. Conall shoved him away, ignoring the scribe's squeal of indignation. Denny stared up at him calmly. The kid's face was colorless, except for the haunted circles around his eyes. To Conall, he looked like someone who'd come to an important decision. The wolf saw only a broken man. Weakness. Prey that was ready to be taken down.

"I will tell you," Denny said.

"You will." Conall didn't bother to hide the growl in his voice. "But not now. Get on the cat and stay alive long enough to tell me later."

He turned around and bumped into Orson. Again. He pushed past him and headed for the cats. Elias was tying crates of supplies onto the last car.

Orson trailed after him.

"I will be party to that interrogation, of course." His fingers grasped at Conall's arm.

Conall snapped.

He grabbed the rope from Elias, spun Orson around and roughly tied his hands together.

"Hey! What the saints?" Orson squirmed but Conall only wound the rope tighter. "What are you doing? You can't detain me! This is an egregious offense! I'll see you all arrested for this!"

Conall jerked the rope tight to secure the knot and Orson let out a shrill cry. Conall picked up a greasy rag that Rowan or Augie had discarded.

"My mission…" Orson panted. Sweat poured off his brow. "My mission is sanctioned by the regent and the Temple of the—"

Conall balled the rag and jammed it into his mouth. He shoved him backward. Orson's knees buckled when they hit the side of the cat and he toppled onto the bench. Conall grabbed him by the shirt and hauled him upright. The scribe's eyes bulged with fury and his cheeks puffed in and out as he tried to breathe with a mouth full of rag.

Conall patted Orson's cheek.

"Sit tight, buttercup."

Rowan was making her inspection of the cats. Her brows rose when she spotted the bound and fuming scribe.

"Is he a prisoner? Why?"

He pulled her aside and lowered his voice.

"The gaunt that attacked Augie and the others must have run right past him. If humans really are controlling the gaunts, ask yourself why they didn't attack the scribe."

"Because he's a scribe. They're sacrosanct in war."

"This isn't war. This is murder. They killed the scribe with the science team. Why not Orson?"

He saw the moment she made the connection. Her eyes widened, and fear replaced curiosity.

"He works for the council. You still think they did this."

"I think the regent is the only one with the power and the resources to build an army of gaunts."

"But why?"

"Why do megalomaniacs do anything? For power. For money. Just because they can."

Rowan shook her head. "No, it doesn't make sense. Why would Atherton send us to find the science team then. He must have known they were already dead."

"Yes." Conall filled that word with all the weight of his rage and frustration.

Rowan covered her mouth with her hand as if she didn't want to let the next words out. "They wanted to kill us too."

"Yes." Of course the Regent's Council would send him on a suicide mission, but even Conall was disgusted that they would involve the princess. Not surprised, but sickened by the underhandedness, the cowardice. They clearly wanted the princess out of the picture, even though she'd never made any claim to the throne of New Torwood.

He saw all that understanding flash through her mind. The woman should never play cards. She let every emotion animate her features, from confusion to understanding, then fear.

"What are we going to do?" She glanced back at Orson. He knew exactly what she was thinking. They would never outrun their problem if they brought the regent's spy with them.

"We're going to get away from here first. Then we'll decide. All of us, together." He took her hands in his and squeezed.

She nodded even as she held back tears. He watched her walk away, wishing she was far from this mess. All he wanted to do was keep her alive, to keep all of them alive, and so far, he was failing at that mission too.

Murdoch and Elias came out of the mess tent carrying Augie between them. Elias saw the two Ebos standing quietly beside Noah. He yelped, dropped Augie's legs, and ducked behind Murdoch, leaving the cook to stagger under the weight.

Minna smirked. "Hello, handsome. You remember me." She waggled long elegant fingers at Elias. He staggered backward until his back pressed against the cat.

Murdoch threw his hands in the air. "Oh, bugger the saints, man! She isn't going to bite you." He leaned toward the dark elf. "You won't, will you?"

She grinned. "Not right now. Here, let me help you with that." She picked up Augie's legs.

"We can't take him with us," Conall said. "There's no room."

Gently, Murdoch propped Augie beside the cat. He pulled two duffel bags off the back seat and dumped them beside the fire pit.

"Now there's room."

Conall just nodded. A good commander didn't pick a fight he couldn't win. "Fine. Go help Noah with Lena. We're leaving in five."

With eight rangers, dead or alive, the bound scribe, the scientist and now two Ebos, Conall was thankful that Rowan had got the second cat running. They loaded Lena onto a bench. She came into awareness long enough to let out a moan, then her head drooped and she leaned limply against Noah. He propped her up with a gentleness that was at odds with the fury in his eyes. He needed to let off steam and they had no time for it.

Rowan drove the second cat with Orson, Murdoch and Elias. And Augie, wrapped in a white sheet on the last bench. Clem and Lena would go with Conall, along with Noah so he could keep an eye on his patient. Minna and Ferlan refused to get on the cats.

"Our mounts wait for us in the meadows," Minna said. "We will catch up."

Conall nodded. He was grateful to the Ebos for their intervention, but their safety was not his concern.

He made sure everyone had a weapon.

"Stay alert. Keep those guns primed and ready." He jumped into the driver's seat and flicked off the safety on his own rail gun. He preferred a bow, but not if he had to drive. With the lurching cat, the gun was a better weapon.

He started the engine and the cats rolled out of the camp. The wolf was riding his hind-brain, a sharp pressure that threatened to propel him into a shift. But Garou agreed that they needed to stay human. The pack couldn't run and so someone needed to drive. Besides, with the dead and wounded, they needed all the trigger fingers they had left.

For now.

It wasn't a fast trip. Until they cleared the oasis, they couldn't open the wings to take advantage of the stiff wind that turned leaves on their backs. The Mogra. The wind of change.

The thera engine whined as they rolled up a small hill. He risked a glance backward and saw Rowan gripping the steering wheel as if she could push the cat forward by sheer will.

He breathed easier when they burst through the last line of trees into the

Meadows. They were alone except for two shaggy ponies that looked up from grazing as the cats appeared.

He stopped and jumped out to deploy the wings. Rowan was fighting with a jammed hatch on her cat. Her hair had come loose and it tossed around her head like flames. She finally got the hatch closed and jumped back into her cat.

The Ebos sprinted from the trees and leapt onto their ponies.

The wings on Conall's cat snapped into place, and as soon as he released the brake, they shot forward. He turned them east and let the wind take them. The short night was coming fast and the Ubruulens were haloed by the setting sun.

Spook-lights danced on a rise ahead. They were translucent sprays of golden light that shifted and swirled, sometimes forming shapes that looked vaguely human before dissolving into amorphous clouds again. Spook-lights were rare, but they appeared in many legends because it was said they only came out to watch events that changed the world.

Garou howled in his mind. He knew what the lights meant too.

First Mogra. Now spooks. Conall gripped the steering wheel hard enough to make it creak and prayed to Mogra. If the wind couldn't be merciful at least it could push their cat faster.

The Ebos fell in line behind them, letting the cat do all the work of flattening the grass.

We leave a trail a pup could follow, grumbled Garou.

Conall gritted his teeth. The wolf was right, but they had no choice.

He shifted their route southward. Whoever was coming would expect them to go east and south toward the safety of the city. But as soon as they found hard ground that could mask their trail, they'd head north.

"Commander, we can't be out here long," Noah said from behind him. "I need to stabilize her."

Conall glanced back. Noah had laid Lena across the entire second seat, and he crouched beside her.

"We can't stop now. Do what you can."

Conall slowed the cat and waved for the Ebos to ride forward. Minna came up alongside, but not too close to the mech. He had to shout to be heard over the wind.

"We need shelter. To the north, if possible, but where no one can follow."

"Yes, Commander. I will take you there." She kicked her pony into a trot. The little beast didn't seem bothered by the grasses that tugged and slashed its legs.

He motioned for Rowan to follow the elves, then he brought up the rear.

Half an hour later, they left the plains for the rocky lowlands of the Ubruulen Mountains. For another long, bumpy hour, they twisted back and forth, into gullies and around steep switchbacks. It was slow going, but each seemingly arbitrary turn protected them from pursuit.

Finally Minna signaled a halt. They'd been driving for hours. The sun would rise soon, but the road ahead was still lost in shadow.

"There is cover ahead," she said. "Only a small cave, but many rocks that will provide shelter too. If you store the wings on your machines, we can hide them. I will stand first watch." She turned her pony's back to the mountain and stared into the darkness.

They drove the cats into a narrow channel between two rocky outcroppings. The wings scraped against stone. They could go no further. Conall parked his cat and left Rowan to stow the wings. He helped Noah carry Lena up the trail and into a cave, then returned to find Rowan struggling with Orson. The scribe jumped from the cat and tangled his feet. Rowan was trying to help him sit up, but he thrashed against his bindings

Conall hauled him to his feet. He leaned down until their faces were inches apart and let the wolf shine in his eyes.

Orson stilled. His cheeks were red from struggling to breathe against the gag. Conall removed it.

Orson stretched his jaw and licked his lips.

"You'll be…"

Conall slapped him. "Shut up. You should be dead. Augie's dead. The others only survived because they hid. You didn't."

Orson stood taller. His eyes flashed with hate. "I was in no danger. A scribe's life is sacrosanct."

"You keep using that word. Gaunts don't care about words. But men do. And you knew there were soldiers behind this attack, didn't you?"

Orson's eyes darted to Rowan and then Murdoch and found no allies there.

"Didn't you?" Conall slapped him again.

Orson shut his eyes and slumped. "I don't have to answer to you. I answer only to the council."

"So you do. Funny thing about that. Scribes are supposed to answer only to the Abbott Archivist. Isn't that why they're sacrosanct? They're outside the normal workings of law and politics. Or at least they're supposed to be." Orson turned his head away. Conall let him go. "Put him down beside Augie. Let him contemplate the result of his council's work while we prepare to bury a good man."

Conall turned away.

You should not turn your back on such a man, Garou said.

He is of no use and no consequence.

Useless men can still throw knives.

Conall huffed. He didn't see Orson as a threat, but he wouldn't be unbinding him any time soon.

Once he made sure they were all safely camped down for the night and Murdoch was preparing a cold supper, he found Denny sitting with his knees tucked under his chin and his arms wrapped around them. The knotted string was wound tightly around his fingers and the loose ends waggled like tentacles. He rocked gently and stared into nothing.

Conall was worn out. Tired of acting the bully to get answers. He sat beside Denny with a heavy sigh.

"Now, you're going to tell me what the hell is going on."

32

A WORLD UPSIDE DOWN

With Clem's help, Rowan camouflaged the cats using the few leafy branches they could find. The cave was on a trail that wound into the Ubruulen foothills. It had a clear view of the Meadows and anyone coming from the south.

Minna and Ferlan sat on their ponies, watching the plains below. Even from up close, Rowan had to train her eye to see them properly. The shaggy coats of the ponies and the elves' green and brown clothing let them blend seamlessly with the backdrop of rocks and shrubs.

"I'll stand watch too." Clem nodded pointedly toward the Ebos.

"You don't trust them?"

"The only person I trust out here is Conall." She smiled. "And maybe you."

Rowan bowed her head. "Glad to be among the worthy."

Clem grunted and pulled the rails from her gun, checking them for wear, then locking them into place again.

"You'd better get inside," she nodded toward the cave, "before Conall takes a strip off that scribe."

Rowan called Phalian. He settled on her shoulder but let out a squawk when she ducked into the cave. He didn't like closed spaces anymore than she did.

"Shush," she admonished. His tiny claws pricked her as he pranced.

Near the entrance, the cave was too small to stand. Stooped over, she let her eyes adjust before moving inward. The first thing she saw was Augie's wrapped body laying against the stone wall. Her heart lurched at the sight.

Beside him, Orson glared daggers at her. She noted that his hands were still bound.

As she moved deeper into the mountain, the cave opened up. Someone had lit several thera lamps and the light reached to a rough-hewn ceiling high overhead. Square wooden beams crossed the expanse and buttressed the walls. Her toe caught on a metal rail embedded in the stone floor.

She was still gazing around in wonder when Murdoch shoved a warm mug into her hands.

"This isn't a natural cave," she said. "Did the Ebos build it?"

"Doubtful. It looks like an old mine from before."

"Before the Resurgence?"

"Probably." He sniffed. "It smells like coal. No need for mines like this anymore." Murdoch tapped a wood buttress before returning to his camp kitchen. Rowan's gaze followed the beam to where it met the cave's ceiling. She felt a shudder go through her. She longed for the endless expanse of the Meadows. Out there, she felt like she expanded to fill that space. Under the mountain she felt small and vulnerable and easy to squash.

"TWEET!" Phalian fluttered on her shoulder and she wondered how much of that unease came from him.

She leaned against the stone wall, trying to still her wildly beating heart. Noah found her like that and insisted that he examine her injuries. They'd left the oasis too quickly for him to do a proper assessment, and in the long drive, she'd almost forgotten about them, though her lip felt fat and tender when she ran her tongue over it.

Noah prodded her cheek and pain flared through her skull.

"Does that hurt?" he asked.

"A little. But don't use your knack. I'll be fine."

Noah's lips pressed thin. "You're not supposed to worry about the medic. I'm supposed to worry about you."

Rowan smiled and felt the scab on her lip pull. Noah sighed and pronounced her free of broken bones.

"I'll have Murdoch prepare some willow bark tea for the pain."

She thanked him, then sought out Conall. He was sitting beside Denny at the far end of the cave where the metal rails on the ground fell away into a black tunnel. Light from the thera lamps barely reached them.

Denny's expression was sullen. His fingers moved obsessively over his piece of string. It was tattered and filthy, but he held it like a prized treasure. It was fascinating to watch the knots unfurl and reform, spurred on by the force of his knack.

Conall gave her an encouraging nod as she sat.

"If someone had told me last month that I'd be spending this much time in caves, I'd have thought them mad." She tried to catch Denny's eye, but he ignored her. His gaze was focused on a particularly nasty knot. The string loosened and he gave a satisfied smile.

Conall's hand closed over Denny's, pushing them down to his lap.

"Denny is about to tell us everything," Conall said.

"Not everything." Denny gave a feeble laugh. "I don't know everything."

"Tell us what you know."

Conall looked like a predator ready to tear out Denny's throat. He was holding himself back by sheer willpower. Denny licked his lips and turned to Rowan. His eyes pleaded for understanding. She clamped down her pity for him. He would find no help from her. Just as Augie had found no help.

"It's…proprietary work. You won't understand most of it." Denny's eyes were huge and nearly black in the dim light. Dark curls had fallen over the bruises on his forehead.

Conall dug into a pouch on his belt and pulled out the dead scribe's cachet. He held it between two fingers in front of Denny's nose. The silver disk caught the light like a jewel.

"Do you know what this is?" he asked. Denny nodded. "It belonged to Sandra Kane. We found it near her body. I suspect it has all that proprietary work recorded. So you might as well tell us."

Denny still hesitated.

Noah was suddenly there. He grabbed Denny by the collar, lifted and shoved him against the stones.

"SQUAWK!" Phalian launched from Rowan's shoulder and flapped around the wall above Denny's head. His metal wings sparked on stone and Rowan called him back.

Noah ground Denny's back against the wall. Denny winced.

Wow. Rowan hadn't expected such power from Noah's lanky form.

"I have one dead ranger, and another clinging to life because of what's on that cachet. So you're going to tell us right now, or I'm tossing you outside for the gaunts to find. Understood?"

Denny swallowed hard and tried to nod against Noah's grip.

"That's enough," Conall said.

Noah shook Denny once more, then let him go.

"Go burn off that knack, Maven," Conall said. Noah stood fuming, with fists clenched at his sides.

"Go." Conall pointed to the cave entrance.

Noah nodded once and left. Some bush was going to get beaten to a pulp outside. But better that than Noah hurt himself by punching stone walls.

Denny sucked in a ragged breath. His eyes flicked from Rowan to the commander, and he seemed to shrink inside himself.

"Look at me." Rowan touched his shoulder and he flinched. "It's okay. Nobody's going to hurt you." Conall made a dismissive noise and she ignored him. "You can't help those scientists anymore. They're all dead. Killed by someone who wanted that cachet, right?"

Denny hesitated, then nodded. That was good. At this point, she would take any response.

"They won't stop looking for it. They'll assume we have it and hunt us down. The only way to stop them is to make their secrets public. So you have to tell us. What were the scientists studying."

"I told you. The gaunts." Denny closed his eyes as if he could hide from the truth. "They were studying the gaunts."

"I need more than that, Denny." She squeezed his shoulder, not hard, but enough to make a connection. "We'll help you. I promise. We'll keep you safe, but we can't do that unless you're honest."

There was a long moment of silence. Then Denny seemed to come to a decision. He sucked in a breath and opened his eyes.

With only the thera lamps lighting the deep cave, his face was like a harlequin's—half bone white and half black shadow. His eyes locked onto Rowan's and he spoke in a clear voice that resonated through the cave for everyone to hear.

"The titans didn't come from another world like the histories tell us. They were once creatures of earth. Changed into monsters by magic during the Resurgence. And we found the link. It's thera. Thera ingested in large quantities can alter the DNA. The titans were once sea creatures that ingested thera and the magic wave boosted it in their systems. They mutated almost immediately. Studies of their bones going back six hundred years prove this. The changes were sudden and profound. We think of the Resurgence as a long period of time, but really it was a short wave. A tsunami of magic that drowned our world. And when the wave of magic receded, there was no going back."

Denny paused to gulp air. His string was dancing as if delighted by his words.

"Thanks for the history lesson," Conall said "but what does it mean. Why would anyone kill for this information?"

"Because gaunts are native creatures too. They were mutated by a massive dose of thera, just like the titans. Dr. Banerjee's research proves it." His voice dropped to a whisper. "They were once human."

Rowan gaped at him. And she was gratified to see her stupefaction reflected on Conall's face.

"There's more." Denny sat straighter. "The gaunts are evolving at an exponential rate because of their continuous diet of thera. The implications for humanity are enormous. Thera is all around us. We burn it in every mech we use. It's in our air, our water and our food. Dr. Banerjee believes…believed that if we continue to ingest thera, within a hundred years, maybe less, the changes will be irreversible."

"And what kind of changes are we talking about?" Conall asked.

Denny shivered. "You have only to look at the gaunts to see it."

Rowan felt his words like a punch to the throat.

Gaunts were once human. And humans could be—would be—gaunts.

"Saints save us," Conall said, but she could see by his expression that he didn't hold out much hope for saintly intervention.

Rowan TURNED THE CACHET OVER IN her hand. Conall had given it to her for safe-keeping. She wished she could access it and read the data that would prove Denny's extraordinary claim.

Gaunts were human. Or had once been human. How could that be?

Every child in New Torwood was taught the history of the Resurgence, so called because it described the tumultuous time when magic blossomed in the world. Priests, scientists, and story-tellers all had their theories about why this happened, but the cause was less important than the effect—monsters.

And now Denny and the dead scientists had proven that titans were products of thera ingestion. The sea serpents were just eels that chowed down on nacara mussels. The carnivorous bison were once buffalo that came to drink at the edge of the Ikon River and took in the thera that flowed freely in the waters at that time.

And humans? Well, they'd done what they always did when they found a new substance. They tried to eat it and many died of gangra. Then they snorted it up their noses for a great high, and more died. Later, they cultivated the giant clams and farmed the thera as a fuel source. Thera farmers still died in that process.

But somewhere along the way, the thera hadn't only killed humans. It had mutated them. And those changed beings had bred and grown into the wickedly smart monsters that stalked the nightmares of Rowan and her people.

Lena woke up and cried out in pain, dragging Rowan back from her thoughts. She watched as Noah laid his hands on her, taking more of her pain into himself. His face twisted into a mask of rage, but Lena relaxed and slept again. Noah rose and stumbled outside to work off his knack-induced rage. Again.

He was going to kill himself if he didn't go mad first.

Everyone else rested. Denny had curled into a ball, clutching his string full of knots. Conall dozed, sitting upright with his back against the wall. Orson had finally stopped fighting his bonds, but his eyes were open and watching. Always watching. Murdoch and Elias were asleep. And, of course, Augie would never wake. Rowan's eyes kept drifting to the lifeless bundle.

"We'll bury him tomorrow before we leave," Conall said.

His voice startled Phalian and he pranced on Rowan's shoulder before settling again.

She nodded. Augie deserved at least that much, but Conall's words brought up another problem that had been nagging at her.

"Where will we go?"

Conall grunted. It was a question that had no obvious answer.

"Do you really think the council is behind this?" she asked.

"Yes."

It was one simple word that turned Rowan's world upside down. The regent had ruled in New Torwood since the old king died. He hadn't replaced her father in her affections—no one could do that—but he had been a stable, comforting presence in her life. The council ministers were like a bunch of aunts and uncles who looked out for her welfare.

Her life had been simple. Easy. Safe.

Now it was none of those things. But if she was honest with herself, she had never been safe.

"I think they tried to kill me once. And Ethan too. It was the day of the accident…the day I lost my arm." She held up her mech. "I thought we'd been attacked by gaunts, that Ethan had…" The words were choking. Conall scooted closer and put his arm around her. She laid her head on his chest and found the courage to say the words aloud. "It wasn't a gaunt. It was men. They drove a cat. I remember now." She laughed. "Funny how being attacked by a real gaunt made me realize. Someone tried to kill my brother, and my father…"

Conall rubbed her back. He didn't speak. He'd probably figured it out long ago. Everyone probably had. Her father hadn't died of a heart attack. It wasn't grief that had killed him.

"He was assassinated."

Conall made a rough noise, somewhere between affirmation and comfort. He kissed the top of her head and leaned his cheek against her hair.

Rowan let grief wash over her. It was like her father had died all over again. Minutes passed while she fought with it and Conall simply held her. Finally, she wiped tears from her face and sat up.

Crying wouldn't help them now. They needed a plan.

"We could seek refuge with the Ebos." Her voice was rough from the tears. She sniffled and tried again. "They would take us in."

Conall nodded his agreement, but they both knew that was a stopgap plan. They couldn't hide with the Ebos forever.

The truth came to her slowly but with immutable certainty. She had to return to the den of snakes that destroyed her family.

"We have to go back. We have to make sure they know about the dangers of thera."

"They know," Conall said. "The council knows all about thera and they don't care."

"What do you mean?"

"I mean they won't stop producing it and pushing it on people as long as they're making a profit."

"You can't believe that!"

"It's true. Have you ever seen a working thera farm? People die every month there. It's brutal, dangerous work. And the council deems the loss of life acceptable as long as their profit margins are made."

Rowan had toured a thera farm once. The farm had seemed quaint, like a fishing village on the edge of the river. Until she'd slipped away from her escorts to see the parts of the town they didn't want her to see.

Hollow-eyed workers watched her from alleys and taverns that didn't even have doors to keep out the cold. Their arms and hands were covered in thick red scars from years of handling the sharp mussels that produced thera. They were all too thin, and too quiet, and too suspicious of strangers to talk to her, but she'd left there thinking the farms weren't the happy, prosperous places the council made them out to be.

And then, she went back to her life and rarely thought of those faces again. She'd been sixteen at the time and caught up in the excitement of being allowed to attend adult galas and parties for the first time. She'd also been undecided about the role she wanted to take in government and visiting the thera farm had frightened her into avoiding future engagements.

Selfish. She'd been selfish and blind. And now, looking back, that time in the thera farm seemed like a dream that she'd forgotten upon waking.

Could Conall be right? Was the council suppressing the scientists' findings in order to protect their thera trade?

"It doesn't matter." She shook her head. "That's all the more reason we have to go back. We have to tell everyone—all the people of New Torwood."

"Atherton will kill us."

"No he won't. Not outright. That would be too public. And he can't be sure we know the truth anyway. We'll go back and report that we found the scientists all dead. We'll hide Denny. They won't know what we found. Not until we crack the cachet. Once the truth is made public, they will have no reason to silence us."

"That might work," Conall said. "But you forgot one thing." He nodded toward Orson who sat bound and gagged. His eyes were open and hateful and watching them.

"I think we have to enlist his help," Rowan said. "He's the only one who can read the cachet."

"He won't help us."

Rowan sighed and pushed away from the wall. "We have to try. We have to make him understand how important this is." She crouched in front of Orson and pulled the cachet from her pocket.

"Can you access this information?"

His eyes narrowed.

"Can you?" she prodded.

"Water first."

Conall growled a protest, but then took out his canteen and dribbled water into Orson's mouth.

He can't be too dehydrated. His lips still look wet. Ugh.

Finally, Orson turned his head. Conall spilled water down his shirt before pulling the canteen away.

"Now talk." Rowan held up the cachet. His eyes trained on it like a starving man fixed on a loaf of bread.

"You have to untie me." Orson held up his bound hands.

Conall glared at him. "If you make any attempt to escape, I will shoot you and bury you next to Augie in the morning. Understood?"

Orson's lips curled in a sneer. "Of course."

Conall pulled a knife and cut away the ropes. Orson rubbed his wrists before reaching for another cachet tucked into his belt pouch. He unplugged the wire connected to it, a wire that snaked up his shirt and came out at his collar to plug into the access port at the base of his skull.

He reached for the new cachet. Rowan reluctantly handed it over. She wasn't sure this was a good idea, but she was all out of better ones.

Orson plugged in the new cachet. His head fell back and his eyes rolled up so she could barely see the irises. They flickered from side to side like someone caught in a bad dream. He stayed like that for several minutes.

Conall took Rowan's hand and squeezed. She gave him a grateful look. Like Clem, he was the one she trusted to see them out of this mess.

After several minutes, Orson lowered his head. A bit of drool had slipped from his lips and he wiped in on the back of his hand.

"So?" Conall demanded.

"It's garbage." Orson unplugged the cachet.

"What do you mean?"

"I mean the scribe scrambled her brains before she was killed. Probably to protect the information on the cachet."

"You can do that?" Rowan asked.

Orson nodded. "It's a kill switch, programmed right in here." He tapped the side of his head. "If we're taken by the enemy we can scramble our memories and all records on the disks. Everyone knows this. It's why we're never attacked, never taken in battle. Scribes are…"

"Sacrosanct, I know," Rowan said. It didn't make sense. Why would Sandra Kane try to hide the cachet if it was useless. She took it from him. "I'll hold onto this just in case."

She turned to Conall. "So we have no proof."

"Do you believe Denny?"

Rowan thought about it. "He has no reason to lie."

"Unlike this piece of shit." Conall kicked Orson's leg.

"Ow! Scribes don't lie! My words are endorsed by the Temple of the…"

Conall kicked him again and held up the rag. "Do I have to use this again or are you going to behave?"

Orson smiled. It wasn't pretty. "Oh, I'll behave if only so I have a front seat to your execution."

"Leave him be," Rowan said. "He's useless." She rose. The cave was suddenly too small, and darkness was creeping into her lungs. She couldn't breathe.

Stumbling over the uneven ground and banging her head on the low ceiling, she staggered outside, ignoring Conall's worried call.

33

PNEUMA

Standing ON THE TRAIL HEAD, ROWAN couldn't see the Ebos, but Clem's silhouette stood out against the sky. Phalian flew away from the mountain into the Meadows. The ground was mostly bare, with low, patchy grass and a few hardy shrubs. Watching him flit around a bush and land on a branch, she remembered a story Auntie Bella used to tell her about a puppet who dreamed about being a real boy and wondered if Phalian ever had such dreams.

Saints, she missed Auntie. She even missed her quiet moments with Ethan. The palace seemed a world away and a lifetime ago. She wasn't sure she could ever go back to that life, not fully. Something had changed in her, and thoughts of home no longer brought peace.

Denny's revelations had rattled her. Every time she got a new piece of information, she only realized how big the scope of her ignorance was.

The gaunts were human. Humans were potential gaunts.

And her father had been assassinated.

None of it got better, no matter how many times the words echoed in her head.

And Regent Atherton knew about the gaunts. He had to. How many of the other ministers were aware of this...this bombshell?

How many of them had been involved in her father's murder? She felt as if she'd been living with a titan in the palace all her life—a mysterious titan that lived just on the edge of her awareness, waiting to pounce.

Of one thing she was certain: she couldn't go back to being a princess in name only—a princess who ignored her family's right to rule. A princess who hid from her duties in her tinker's lab. She didn't know how or when, but she would expose the council's schemes and make them pay for the deaths they'd caused.

Phalian shifted into his mouse form and hopped across the ground. He rose up on back legs, his metal whiskers twitching, then he scampered around the base of a bush.

The ground erupted in a shower of dirt. A tentacle emerged, flailed, then smacked the ground inches from Phalian.

"SQUEAK!" The mech dashed up the hill. The burrowing creature lunged, and Phalian barely escaped its grasping tentacles. He shifted in mid-leap and landed on her shoulder in a ruffle of metal feathers.

"SQUAWK!"

"That'll teach you to wander." Rowan patted him with her mech fingers and felt agitation trembling through his gears.

"There are worse things out there than burrowing slugs." Conall approached, carrying two mugs. "I thought you could use something hot in your stomach."

"Thanks." Rowan took a mug and sipped, expecting tea and happy to find broth instead. The savory steam coming off it reminded her that she hadn't eaten in nearly twelve hours. She chugged the rest down in a most unprincess-like manner.

"To be fair to poor Phalian, that slug was the size of a cat. And it had arms," she said.

They watched him fly off again, the light catching his metal wings.

"I saw the way he shifted in the air," Conall said. "He's not a normal mech is he?"

Rowan was silent for a long moment, pretending to enjoy her drink so she wouldn't have to answer. Finally, she said. "He was a gift from my Uncle Hermie, well not really an Uncle, but he was in love with my Auntie Bella for years and a good family friend. He gave me this too." She held up her mech arm. "It's linked to Phalian, and in a way, so am I."

"What do you mean linked?"

Rowan rubbed the seam just below her elbow where flesh met mech.

"It's hard to explain. You saw Phalian recharging?" She pointed to the covered port and Conall nodded. "Well, that's only part of the connection.

Even when Phalian is away, flying or scampering, I sense…impressions from him."

Conall took her arm gently in his hands, holding it like it was a precious thing. Rowan flinched. She couldn't help it. In twenty years, no one had willingly touched her mech arm. Until Conall.

"Are you okay?" he asked. "You ran out of there pretty fast."

"I'm fine. It just became too much all of a sudden."

Conall nodded. He got it. She didn't have to explain to him.

"We're going to fix this…this mess, right?" She waved her other hand at the cave where their squad was resting and licking their wounds.

"We will. I promise. Tomorrow, we'll figure it out."

And now? she almost asked, but she wasn't sure she was ready for the answer.

His eyes were soft. His fingers kneaded the flesh above her elbow while the other hand held the mech. "Is this okay?"

Rowan swallowed, her mouth suddenly dry. "Yes."

"So what kind of impressions do you get from him?" He didn't look at her, but continued to caress her skin and mech. Rowan closed her eyes and the sensations of his touch rippled through her.

"Sensory things, mostly. Light and dark, heat and cold. But also…" She hesitated and opened one eye. She'd never told anyone this. "You're going to think I'm crazy, but sometimes I can sense emotions from him—fear, excitement and even affection."

"I'm not one to call anybody crazy." He tapped a finger to his temple. "I have a wolf living in here." He smiled, then turned his attention back to her arm. The heat from his hands warmed her right through the glove.

"What ever happened to Uncle Hermie?"

"I…I don't know. I was just a child. It was shortly after the accident. He gave me my arm and found a doctor to attach it, I guess. Then he just left the palace and New Torwood as far as I know. I never saw him again. He was old then. He's probably dead by now."

Conall nodded as if that explained the mystery.

"Do you mind?" He tucked a finger under the lip of her black glove and pulled it away from the mech. He waited with one eyebrow raised until she nodded, then peeled back the glove. His fingers trailed over the intricate mage etchings that covered the silver arm.

"It's beautiful. You shouldn't hide it under a glove."

His words and his touch woke an alien emotion in her—something warm and curious and thrilling. It had been a long time since she had truly looked at her mech arm. Now she saw it through Conall's eyes—a new perspective, fresh with curiosity and something more. Affection. And reverence even. That thought almost made her pull her hand away. She'd had enough romantic encounters ruined because of her status. But Conall didn't care about that. She felt it in the deepest part of her heart. The reverence she saw in his gaze was solely for her, for the core that made up Rowan. Not the princess, not the royal, not even the striker.

His fingers traced the etchings. An organic vine-like pattern gave the metal texture. He slipped the glove further down her arm. Rowan tried and failed to suppress a groan. The etchings made the silver skin hypersensitive. Even through the special glove, she could feel minute vibrations, heat, and cold that her flesh hand would be blind to. Without the glove, she felt naked and exposed. If the mech arm had hair, it would be standing on end.

He tugged the glove further down. Phalian's cradle was revealed along with two other ports at her wrist. His fingers trailed over them.

"How do these work?"

She pointed to the first one.

"That's for Phalian. The others…I don't know. I've never used them." Her voice was raspy and her throat raw. She felt worn out and abraded like she'd been forcing down tears.

"You're not curious?"

"Are you curious about your kidneys or liver?" she snapped. Phalian squawked and pranced on her shoulder.

His gaze flicked to the mech then locked onto hers again. Strong and steady. A wolf's gaze. His touch and his scrutiny left her feeling raw. But he wouldn't be put off by her knee-jerk reaction.

She sighed. "I guess I was curious once. But I have nobody to ask about it."

Conall made a noise deep in his throat and continued to peel off the glove, revealing her palm and fingers. This is where the appendage looked most mech-like. The fingers were articulated with rotational joints that allowed for maximum flexibility. Etchings continued up the palm and fingers, mimicking the lines and swirls of a human print. The resonance imbued in those etchings allowed for sensitivity well above that of human flesh.

She sucked in a breath when his fingers closed over hers. He turned her hand one way, then the other. He spread her fingers and ran his index finger up each of hers from base to tip.

"Can you feel that?" His voice was low. She nodded and closed her eyes. She could barely form coherent thoughts around the sensation of his touch. It was so alien and yet so intimate.

He twisted her hand and trailed fingers across her palm and up her forearm, sending shudders down her spine. She didn't think she could stand it much longer, when he sucked in a breath.

"There. I knew it."

She opened her eyes. He'd turned her arm to reveal a mark on the silver just below her elbow.

"Have you seen this before?" he asked.

"I guess. I thought it was just part of the etchings."

"It's a mage mark. The same one we found on your lost valet."

"Harry Hightower?" Rowan's heart pounded. She twisted her arm and bent her neck to get a better look.

"Yes. I suspected as much from watching Phalian. He's a pneuma too. He wasn't affected by the Ebos null trap. Neither was your hand because they don't use thera. It all fits."

"But how can that be? Harry Hightower built the Talos almost three hundred years ago. He couldn't have been alive to make my arm."

"Your uncle probably bought it off the black market. Saints know there's a booming trade in antique mech, especially pneumas. I've been making a living off it for years. Maybe when you get home you can ask your aunt about it."

Conall let her arm drop and she felt the lack of his touch keenly. He stepped back and there was a sudden chill in the air as if invoking the word "home" had opened a rift between them.

Rowan put on her glove and took the time to adjust each finger. Her thoughts turned round and round in her head, but kept coming back to one place.

Home.

"What's the matter?" Conall asked.

Rowan looked up and found him watching her with a mixture of curiosity and concern.

"We have answers, but they only seem to raise more questions and I find…" She sucked in a breath. "I feel like we're standing on the edge of a precipice, staring into darkness. And I don't like it. I don't like being ignorant."

Conall frowned. "Nobody likes feeling ignorant."

"You don't understand. I spent my whole life being willfully ignorant. With my father gone and my brother…gone, I'm the only one left who can answer for my family, but I let the regent make all the decisions."

"You were just a child."

"But I'm not anymore. I haven't been a child for a long time, and still I let the council rule in my brother's name. I let them meet behind closed doors and build an empire while I did what? Tinker in my shop? Run away from my responsibilities by fixing mechs? I've been so stupid."

"Not stupid. Young."

Rowan snorted. "I feel like I've aged a lifetime on this mission."

"We all have." Conall ran a hand over his beard, then he stepped forward, close enough to kiss. "But we gained a lifetime of wisdom too. Now we have to use it."

"We have to go home." She stared up at him. He nodded and his nose brushed against hers.

"We have to go home. Together."

Whatever intrigues and danger they found at the regent's court, they would face them together.

Rowan shivered despite the warm wind coming off the Meadows. Conall wrapped his arms around her and pulled her against his chest.

"I guess we've seen each other's spirits now." His breath was warm in her ear as he spoke.

Rowan let out a laugh. "What does it say about me that my spirit is a metal hummingbird?"

"It says you're the most unique person on the planet."

He fell quiet and they watched the light play off the plains below. It was truly beautiful, like a great, green ocean that never sat still. Rowan turned just enough to rub her cheek against the stubble on his chin.

She settled back against him, knowing they'd just crossed some new boundary of intimacy.

"So what do we do now?" she asked.

"I'm not sure, but there's one piece to this puzzle that doesn't fit." His words were muffled as his lips pressed against the hollow beneath her ear.

"The dead mother gaunts at the oasis."

"And the missing babies," he confirmed. His lips blazed a line down her neck. It was wildly inappropriate to talk about death and betrayal while his hands were doing the things they did to her. But somehow that only quickened her desire. She closed her eyes and let the sensation fill her.

"Dr. Banerjee mentioned a satellite lab. We should go there." Her voice was breathless now.

"We should. Tomorrow." His words confirmed the danger they were in, but it all seemed so far away now. His lips told another story as they continued to nip and kiss her throat. "Right now I want to do something I've been resisting since the moment I saw you in the mess hall with your badly fitting uniform and your firecracker hair." His hands slid under the hem of her shirt, finding skin. She turned and his mouth closed over hers. His tongue teased her until she fell limp against him. It was a kiss she felt down to her toes.

"Get a room!" Clem shouted. Rowan's head jerked up. Clem's back was still to them as she scanned the pass through the lowlands. Phalian fluttered over to land on her shoulder.

Rowan put a hand on Conall's chest. "Maybe we should go somewhere more private, Commander."

"Yes." He kissed her again. "Got any suggestions?"

She pulled away until only the tips of her mech fingers held onto his. Conall's eyes were thunder dark and his smile held traces of a wild beast.

"It's not like I'm a princess who needs a bed of lace." She fluttered her eyelashes at him. "A bit of soft grass will do me just fine. But first you have to catch me." She dropped his hand and took off. He growled and lunged for her, his hands closing on air. She let out a mock yelp and tore up the path into the mountains with her wolf in close pursuit.

On watch at the trail head, Clem let out an exaggerated sigh, but she couldn't hide her grin. She petted the odd little mech bird, and whispered, "You go, Princess."

34

EXHALE AND INHALE

The NEXT MORNING THEY LEFT THE cave and rode back into the lowlands of the Ubruulens. At the first protected valley they found, Conall halted the cat. The ground here was soft enough for a burial, and he ordered Noah and Clem to start digging.

Minna approached him.

"Commander West, I would not impose our beliefs on you, but it is custom for us to take a remembrance from the dead."

"What kind of remembrance?"

"A…hmmmm…memento. A bone. It can be a small one, a finger even." She touched the bones sewn into her tunic, and Conall realized they weren't animal bones. "A hand is better."

"I'm not sure that's appropriate."

Minna smiled. "Your wolf would understand."

"Maybe. But the other rangers won't."

"If I explain it to them and they agree, may I have your permission?"

Conall hesitated. It seemed like a big imposition and unnecessary.

"Please, Commander. It is important."

"Fine. But if they disagree, you will leave off."

"Thank you." She bowed her head.

They approached the site of the grave together. Clem was trying to etch Augie's name onto a large boulder, but Conall stopped her.

"Leave no sign," he said. Clem glanced upward as if the mystery men with their pet gaunts might be falling from the sky. She let her blade drop and scowled.

Conall didn't like it either. Augie would rest forever in an unmarked grave, but they would remember him and that was all Conall could do for the kid.

They'd dug down six feet so scavengers wouldn't disturb him. The ground was sandy, but it was hard work and everyone had taken a turn with the shovels except for Lena who was still too weak to stand and Orson who sat in the cat, watching with his usual bland expression.

Noah and Elias carried Augie's body over to the hole, but Minna stopped them before they laid him down. Elias no longer reacted with terror at the sight of the Ebos, but he still flinched when Minna came near enough to place a hand on Augie.

"Before you mourn for your lost comrade, I have a request. We wish to take a part of your friend with us to our city at the end of the mountains, so that we may remember his bravery always."

Elias let go of Augie's feet and jumped in front of Minna brandishing a knife. "My mother's mother says your kind eat children and make puppets out of their bones. You won't make a puppet out of Augie."

Minna let out a long suffering sigh. "We don't eat children. And we don't play with bones. We cheer for them. No…" She searched for the right word. "We honor them. We collect sun-whitened bones in the Meadows, so even those who die alone may be remembered. When we kill for food, we ask for…consent from caribou and rabbit. We eat the flesh and honor the bones. We…care for the memory of one who gave so we might live. When one of ours dies, we boil the body and preserve the bones. For all time."

Someone made a gagging noise and Minna held up her hand. "We won't boil Augie. But he will have no place of memory here." She pointed to the stone with the few scrapings that Clem had attempted. "I offer the chance to have his life sung about in our halls, where we revere bones and all the spirits they represent."

The elf smiled and lifted the bone necklace that hung around her neck. "We keep them close. Forever. It may seem cruel to you, or…repellent. It certainly does to our brothers the Enos." She nodded toward Elias who'd lowered his knife. "But we do it out of love. Love for the *coho-ne-teno*." She paused with a frown. "There is no one word in your language to translate that. You would call it the exhale and inhale. A dual spirit perhaps. Or the essence of body and mind. To us, they are two separate entities. After death, the *coho* goes onward. *Teno* stays here, to guide its ancestors." She rubbed the bone disk at the center of her necklace.

"That is the great division between my people and the so-called 'elves of the light.' We don't cause death. We don't revel in it. We understand it, cherish it. While the Enos only fear it." She shook her head as if she spoke about a disappointing child.

"What exactly do you want?" Rowan asked.

"I want to take Augie's finger. To preserve it and his coho-ne-teno with it."

"Just a finger?"

Minna nodded.

Conall looked to Elias. The elf seemed uncertain now.

"Will you swear that Augie won't be forgotten?" he asked.

"I swear it."

Elias backed away and nodded.

Conall spoke up. "I'm not sure I believe in your coho-ne-teno, but Augie won't be needing his fingers now, and on the off chance you're right and his spirit needs the help…"

"On the off chance." Minna smiled. It seemed a genuine smile, without guile or hidden malice. Conall nodded for her to proceed. She unraveled the sheet. Elias looked away as her knife flashed out. She took her memento quickly and hid it in the folds of her robes. As if recognizing that her audience would not stand up to anything more, she nodded and backed away.

Noah and Elias picked Augie up again and settled him in the grave.

Rowan stepped up beside Conall and spoke quietly. "That was a little odd. Do you thinks she's legit?"

"I think there are more mysteries in this world than we can ever know. And if even one voice raising the name of Ranger Augustus Paddon makes his passage easier, then I have no regrets."

She squeezed his hand. "You're a fair man, Commander."

"Thank you." The memory of their night together was still fresh in his mind. Even the awful job of burying one of their own couldn't quench the fire he felt for her. Quite the opposite. His newfound passion seemed to color every thought, every word he spoke, every interaction.

His wolf rumbled happily.

That is what mates do. Everything is different now. You will see.

Conall pushed the wolf to the back of his mind. Now was not the time to ponder over the intricacies of matehood.

He stepped forward and gazed at the sheet-bundled package in the hole. It seemed cold and hard to leave the boy out here alone.

"Does anyone want to speak?"

Elias stepped forward. "Augie was kind." His voice was pitched high and he reddened as he stepped back. Conall nodded. It wasn't much, but in a harsh world, kindness was worth more than thera or gold.

Noah spoke next.

"You all know about my knack. I can take away pain, but not this kind of pain. And even if I could, I wouldn't. Sometimes you just need to feel. Augie's life was too short. His death sits here," he tapped his chest, "like a rough piece of ice. As it should. We will never forget him. And I, for one, won't rest until the people who did this are brought to justice."

He stepped back. No one contradicted him.

Conall could feel the mood of the squad turn. Sadness was morphing into rage, into the need to take action. He felt it too. His wolf wanted to run, not flee, but to flex his muscles to prove that he was still alive and capable of taking down the enemy.

But first they needed to find the enemy.

Someone started humming. Conall thought it was Rowan, but other voices took up the song—Augie's song. And suddenly the little valley was filled with the ringing joy of an eight-hundred-year-old symphony. Murdoch surprised them all by voicing the original German lyrics in his deep baritone. As the song came to a crescendo, he switched to English for the finale and his words rang out:.

> *"Do you sense the creator, world?*
> *Seek him above the starry sky!*
> *Above the stars must He dwell."*

The song ended, but its echo carried on. Clem wiped tears from her cheeks. Rowan looked shell-shocked. Noah's jaw was clamped down hard. Murdoch stepped back to his usual place behind the scenes as if he hadn't just stirred their emotions like one of his famous stews.

Clem and Noah filled in the hole and they rolled back the layer of grass, tamping it down. The disturbed ground was obvious, but it would pass a brief inspection.

When they were done, all eyes turned to their commander for their next orders. Conall could lead these people through the Meadows, and even through battle if need be, but he had no idea how to lead them through sorrow. It was better that he turn their attention to finding Augie's killer.

He cleared his throat, surprised to find it a little raw from unshed tears.

"I believe that the men who killed Augie were sent by the Regent's Council." He paused to give the squad members a chance to disagree, but met only silence. "We have Denny's admission that gaunts were once human and more importantly that thera is responsible for turning them into titans. The science team at the oasis was murdered to keep this secret. Those soldiers would have murdered us too. And they will keep trying."

"But why?" Clem asked. "I don't get it. Who cares how titans were made?"

Rowan answered before he could.

"Because the Council has invested heavily in thera. And they want to open up exports to the south. New Torwood already relies almost exclusively on thera. If they can get the big cities in the south to adopt it as their primary energy source, they will control the biggest thera market in the world."

"So this is about money? Augie was killed so a bunch of old guys can make a buck?" Clem's expression was hard.

"A lot of bucks," Rowan said.

"There's not enough money in the world to pay for a life." Clem pointed to the grave at their feet.

"No, there's not." Conall took the reins of the conversation again before emotions got out of hand. "And like Noah, I plan to make those responsible for this murder accountable for their crimes. But that means going home to New Torwood. We can't do that without all the facts. And we won't make it home with soldiers trying to kill us." He let that sink in.

"How do we stop them?" This was from Lena. Her voice was shaky, but grim with determination.

"We stop them by finding proof and making it public. Once that happens, the council will have no reason to pursue us. So I'm looking for options. How do we prove it?"

This question was met with silence. Then Denny raised his hand. Conall frowned. He didn't trust Denny, but he waved at him to speak.

"I know where the remote lab is. The one they call the Academy. If they're controlling those gaunts, that's where they're training them. That's where they took the babies." He paused and scrunched his lips together, then he took a deep breath and let it out. "We might also find Minister Wrede there."

Conall's nose twitched and he ground his jaws together. The kid continued to hide the truth. Rowan touched his arm as if to hold him back.

"Can you bring us there?" she asked.

Denny looked scared now. "I'm…I'm not sure. I know where it is. At least I have the coordinates. But I visited only a few times, I don't know that I could find it again."

"And you think there will be proof of Dr. Banerjee's research at this Academy?"

Denny nodded.

Conall had already been considering the idea. It meant more time traveling the Meadows, more time looking over their shoulders for the gaunts and soldiers that hunted them.

"Commander?" Murdoch stepped forward. "There's another option." The old cook lifted his cap to show his eyes. "Those soldiers don't know we saw them. In fact, they made sure we didn't. We have only the word of the scientist and those elves," he nodded toward the Ebos, "that there were soldiers involved."

"Are you suggesting that we're wrong?" Conall asked. "That no one is hunting us?"

"Nay, not that. But they don't know Denny is even alive, do they? And they don't know the elves spotted them. We could go home and tell the council that we found everyone dead. End of story. Let their secret lie, and we'll be in the clear."

Conall had also considered that idea. It had some merit. The council had sent them out here to be killed, but they wouldn't attack them outright inside the city.

But they'd tried to kill the princess.

He glanced at Rowan. He couldn't get over that idea any time soon. Then his gaze fell on Orson. He was the council's creature. Even if he wanted to, he couldn't keep his records from the Abbot Archivist. And then they'd be shown to the regent.

"What about him?" Conall asked.

Murdoch waved at the scribe. "Oh, we'd have to kill him."

Orson bolted upright in his seat.

"I will see you all on the gallows for this! You're all dead!"

"Someone gag him again," Conall said.

Murdoch and Elias cornered Orson and his protests quieted when Elias stuffed a rag into his mouth. In minutes, Murdoch had him trussed up like a newly gutted boar.

Conall considered the scribe. He didn't like the idea of carting him all over the Meadows, but at least they didn't have to listen to his whining.

He turned to Denny. "Come with me. You're going to tell me everything you know about the Academy."

They CAMPED FOR A NIGHT IN the valley where they'd laid Augie to rest. Grief, fear and anger had taken a toll on the squad. Conall didn't want to push them. Murdoch set up a camp table and three chairs. Rowan and Denny took the first two. The kid looked like a thera addict about to crack. Conall stood behind the last chair, gripping it until it creaked.

"You're looming, Commander. Sit down." Rowan nodded toward the seat. Phalian fluttered from her shoulder to Denny's and shifted into a mouse. Denny smiled and opened his hand. Phalian jumped to his palm and nibbled the old piece of cord that Denny carried everywhere like a security blanket.

Conall sat. He leaned in and skewered the kid with his best wolf stare.

"SQUEAK!" The mech leapt onto Rowan's shoulder and hid in her pocket. Conall ignored it. His attention was focused solely on Denny.

"I've had just about enough of your lies. You need to give us something to work with. Something we can hurt them with, and you need to give it now. No more half-truths, no more holding back. Everything. Now."

Denny's lips worked at an answer, but words seemed to strangle him. He was turning red and his eyes bulged.

Conall's hand reached for his throat. He was out of patience. The kid promised to talk, but still he hedged.

Rowan intervened.

"Denny, look at me." Her calm voice reached something inside the nervous scientist. He gazed at Rowan with adoration shining from his eyes.

She'd saved him and now he thought she was sent by the saints. Conall hoped Denny's feelings didn't complicate an already complicated situation.

Like your feelings have?

Mind your own business, Conall snapped, but the wolf only let out a laughing huff.

"Why don't you just tell us about your research?" Rowan's tone was light, as if they chatted about the weather. "What did you like about it?"

That made Denny pause, then a small smile crept across his lips.

"They were like a family, you know?"

"Who? The scientists?"

Denny shook his head. "The gaunts. It was the first time we'd seen them doing something other that fighting or mating. We'd never been able to observe a clan at close range before. But those females, the mothers—they seemed to understand that we wouldn't hurt them, that we would protect them even. That's all they wanted. A chance to raise their young in safety. They worked together, raising their babies like in a commune."

"That's really interesting. So how many mothers were there?" Rowan kept her voice soothing.

"At the oasis? Seven. And eight babies because Frieda had twins." He smiled up at her. His fingers were tangled in the cord, but one end wormed its way out of a knot. Watching it made Conall's stomach queasy.

"You named them?" he asked.

Denny startled as if he'd forgotten the others were there. Rowan nudged Conall. He leaned back and let her take the lead.

"Denny, why don't you tell us their names?" Rowan said. He could see what she was doing. Every time she spoke his name, Denny's attention swung back to her. She'd make an impressive commander one day, but he suspected she was bound for greater things.

Denny smiled. "Frieda with her twins, then Betty, Sara, Candy, Fay, Kami and Marta. They let us watch them because of my knack. I soothed them." His hands tangled in the knotted string again.

Before he could drift into self recriminations, Rowan changed direction. "And that was at the oasis?"

Denny nodded.

"What about the Academy? You said you were there. Are they keeping mothers and babies there too?"

Denny shook his head and he seemed to shrink into himself. "That place is different."

"Different how?"

Denny shrugged. His fingers gripped the string. The ends looped around in a knot that Conall recognized. A sheep shank, used to shorten a rope. His grandfather had taught it to him. It was mostly a useless knot. Then the string unfurled and twisted around in the heart pattern of a half hitch. Then a bowline. The kid was going to go through every knot in his repertoire. Conall wanted to grab the string and toss it away, but Rowan laid her hand over Denny's and gently forced him to look at her.

"Can you tell us how the Academy is different, Denny?"

"I...I don't know. Dr. Banerjee kept that research locked away. But it's not like the Nursery. We were only watching the gaunts. At the Academy..." His voice fizzled out.

"Here's what I think." Conall leaned in, but Denny wouldn't look at him. "I think that Minister Wrede and Dr. Banerjee found a way to control the gaunts. And they've been breeding them for that purpose in this Academy. It's probably where your missing babies were taken to. Am I wrong?"

Denny shook his head. Conall didn't trust a man who wouldn't look him in the eye. Garou growled. The sound came out of Conall's throat and Denny jumped. Rowan shot him a stern look.

"There can only be one reason to breed monsters that you can control,"

Conall continued. "Do you know what that reason is?"

Denny shook his head.

"War. They're building an army. I don't know who their perceived enemy is, but I can guess. Anyone who comes from the southern cities to take their thera trade away from them. The council has poised themselves to be the leader in thera production. But Dowchester has an army three times the size of New Torwood's. If they join with Shythe, they'd have twice that number. How long do you think the council can control the most potent magical power source the world has ever seen before a bigger dog comes and takes it away?"

"I'm just a scientist," Denny mumbled. "I don't know about all that stuff."

Conall sat back in his seat and crossed his arms.

"Well, tell me one thing. Are you loyal to Minister Wrede?"

That got a reaction from Denny. The knots on his fiddle string suddenly sprang loose.

"Why?"

"Because if we go back to New Torwood, our every move will be scrutinized. If the council learns that you're alive, we'll all be dead. We will hide you, but first we need to know. Are you loyal to Wrede?"

Denny lifted his chin. For once, the kid met his eye. "I was. But not anymore. Not if he's responsible for killing all those people and the babies. They didn't deserve that."

"Good. Now tell me everything you remember about the Academy and what kind of reception we can expect when we get there. Because we're going to find proof of what these bastards have planned. And failing that, we're going to capture one of their pet gaunts and bring it back for the council to choke on."

35

SQUAD 54

They'd come a long way north to hide, recuperate and bury Augie, and now they had to turn south again. Wrede's Academy was only a few miles from Eklridge Oasis in a place Denny called the Warren. On the map, it was just a rocky section in the Meadows, but when Denny described it as a maze of stone formations, the Ebos knew exactly where to go. They proved to be excellent guides again. Conall would have found the Warren eventually with Garou's help, but the elves seemed to know every hidden path through gullies and rocky passes.

Eventually, they left the Ubruulen lowlands for the vast plains again. The day was one of those rare still days in the Meadows. Black clouds churned over the mountains behind them. The air felt heavy and Mogra had turned sulky as the wind barely stirred the grass. They ran on thera fuel. The engines weren't especially loud, but in the quiet of the plains, they resonated like a stampede of bison.

There was no hiding now. They had to get into the Warren, search the satellite lab and get out before the mystery soldiers found them. Wrede's soldiers. Conall was convinced the minister was behind all these murders, and he was connected to the regent, most likely acting on the regent's orders.

But there were other questions to be answered. Would they find Dr. Banerjee and his assistant at the Warren too, or were their corpses lost in the woods of the oasis? And how deeply was Regent Atherton and the rest of the council mixed up in all this? Conall's talk about war with the southern cities had only been a theory, but the more he thought about it, the more it made sense. The Theracine Corporation, the entity that owned the thera farms and harvested the precious mineral, was poised to make a fortune if they could export to the south. And how many of the Regent's Council members were shareholders of Theracine? At least half. Probably more. It was something to look into when they returned to the city.

Rowan drove the cat with a grim expression, her lips pressed flat as she navigated the bumpy path behind the Ebos ponies.

Conall turned in his seat to study his squad. No one spoke, as if the heavy air weighed them down. Lena was sitting up, though her face was pale as bone with an unhealthy sheen. The jostling ride had to be excruciating on her wounds. Noah kept trying to siphon off her pain and his rage-inducing knack had finally worn him out. He slept on the back bench.

Denny sat beside Lena, propping her up when she began to slide sideways. His face was almost as pinched and white as hers. He had to be absorbing every jolt of emotion coming off Lena, not to mention the fear and anxiety streaming from the rest of them. Conall didn't envy him. He couldn't think of a knack that would be more terrible than extreme empathy. A small part of him thought he should cut the kid some slack for it. A bigger part of him knew that he would use every weapon in his arsenal to find the truth and bring the squad home safely. And if that meant leaning hard on Denny, he would do it.

In the cat behind them, Clem drove with Elias riding shotgun. The elf had proved himself on this mission. If Conall's word meant anything when they returned, he'd request the promotion to tracker that Elias wanted so badly. But that was wishful thinking, of course. If they returned to New Torwood, the regent would find some reason to hang him.

They passed north of Eklridge Oasis, too far to spot the dark blotch of green among the paler grass that marked the twenty-acre stand of trees. Conall kept watch for any movement in that direction, but no one came storming across the plains to intercept them. It seemed their attackers had retreated, maybe waiting for new orders. He hoped they were calculating their losses and would decide that another attack wasn't worth the risk. Or maybe they'd regrouped at the Warren and were waiting for Squad 54 to drive right into their trap.

They navigated through a waveless sea of green. The landscape never changed. Time seemed to stand still and he imagined that the hand of some great and vindictive god pulled the carpet of grass backward so that even though their engines propelled them forward, they never gained any ground.

And then, the Warren appeared ahead so suddenly, Conall wondered if he'd dozed off. At first it seemed like a boulder on the horizon, but it grew as they closed on it. Soon it appeared as big as Eklridge Oasis, only instead of trees, the Warren was a vast field of stone spurs jutting from the Meadows.

He motioned for Rowan to stop the cat. Clem rolled hers to a halt behind them. Conall leaned on the dashboard and stared at the maze of rock blocking their path.

"What are we doing?" Rowan asked.

"Waiting to see if there's a welcome party." But nothing moved ahead.

The outer edge of the Warren was made of impossibly smooth rock. It was more of a wall than a slope, and Conall could make out no way inside.

Denny leaned forward and spoke quietly.

"It's not a natural phenomenon, you know. The Warren. People think it is because man could never build something so huge, but it didn't exist before the Resurgence. Historians have proven it. Dr. Banerjee was fascinated by it and he used to go on about all the theories of how it was formed. The most popular one is that a ley-line burst and the excess magic formed the Warren. Or pulled it, fully formed from another world. It looks solid from here, but it's really a labyrinth inside."

Conall nodded to show he'd heard. He appreciated the information, but right now, all his attention was focused on the half-mile of empty plains between the cats and the Warren.

If Wrede's soldiers were waiting for them, this is when they'd attack.

Silence crept over him like a thousand stinging ants.

They'd been driving most of the day, and color was slowly leaching from the world. Conall estimated they had less than an hour of light left. A hot wind blew and a small cyclone popped up in front of the cat. It flew apart as quickly as it formed, spraying them with dust and rock.

When Mogra blows from the east, she chases trouble.

Conall turned his face east and felt Mogra bite his cheeks. He didn't need Garou's wolf wisdom or the weather to tell him that they were on the edge of a precipice and about to leap.

"How do we get in?"

"That way." Denny pointed over Conall's shoulder at the sheer rock face. "There's an entrance."

Conall squinted into the growing darkness and he could just make out a shadow that marked a split in the rocks. "It's easy to get lost inside," Denny said, "but there are many natural staircases that take you to the top of the stones. From there you have a good overview and can navigate the maze."

They'd waited long enough. If Wrede's soldiers were inside, they'd have to chase them out, like rat-terriers in a ferret's den.

He reached for the vox and opened the channel to Clem. Her cat waited only twenty yards behind them, but he didn't want to shout across the Meadows.

"This is it, folks." His voice was clear and calm. "The moment you hear about sometimes if you hang around the barracks long enough. Old soldiers talk about it. That moment when you go from being an individual to being a squad. Look to the people beside you. You traveled hundreds of miles together. Survived storms and monsters. You had their backs and they had yours. Trust in that now. Whatever we find behind those stones, we'll face it together." He clicked the vox back to the console. A quiet murmur of "Saints, yeah!" and "Squad 54!" rose up behind him.

He motioned for Rowan to drive on. They drew up to the rock wall, as tall and solid as any man-made fortification, and parked. Clem's cat followed while the Ebos kept to their ponies and turned them to face the Meadows.

The wind was growing and without the hum of the thera engines, it seemed to howl through the plains and crash against the stones.

Conall stepped from the cat and turned to gaze up at the Warren. The stones rose at least three stories high. He was still nervous about the lack of a welcoming party. Anyone could crawl along the top of that wall and fire down on them. He rubbed the back of his neck, feeling like a rail gun's scope was sighted on him.

Garou prowled around his mind like a caged beast. He yearned to be let out, but Conall needed to keep his human skin for a bit longer. Rowan jumped from the cat and he felt better with her at his side. Even Garou stopped his psychic pacing, like they could face anything that came out of that stone maze so long as she was beside him.

He turned to Denny who had tucked his knees and wrapped his arms around them as if trying to make himself small and unnoticeable. He'd already given them the rundown of what they'd find inside. A dozen gaunts in cages. These were the juveniles that Wrede's team was trying to turn into tractable soldiers. Denny hadn't been sure about the number of guards because they worked in rotations, but he'd never seen more than six on duty at a time. And ten scientists. But he'd also emphasized that it had been over a year since he'd visited the Academy. Wrede could have doubled or tripled those numbers by now.

Conall laid a hand on Denny's shoulder and squeezed. It wasn't a gesture of comfort. "If you're hiding anything more, now is the time to tell me. Not after we go in there."

"I don't know anything more. Truly!"

He speaks the truth.

Rowan put her hand on Conall's arm and pulled it away from Denny. He wondered if her mech had some kind of knack other than zapping things because every time she touched him, he felt calmer. Even now when his stomach churned with so much uncertainty, her touch soothed away the rough edge of fear.

That is matehood, old man.

Conall ignored the wolf.

Rowan nodded toward the open plains and they walked away from the others. "So what's our plan?"

He ran a hand over his beard. It had grown too long and it itched.

"We can't go in there blind. Clem and I will scout first. If all is clear, we'll come back and get you."

"I'm coming with you."

"You're not."

"Saints, Conall. Stop treating me like a princess. You'll need a mechanic in there if you find the lab. And I think I've proven that I can hold my own as much as anyone else on the squad."

Conall ground his teeth.

She challenges you. The wolf seemed pleased by that.

"I'm not treating you like a princess. I'm treating you like a striker."

She'd opened her mouth to protest again, but shut it. He wanted to smooth away the little crease between her brows. He wanted to kiss her. But the whole squad was pretending very hard not to eavesdrop. Instead, he pulled her farther into the Meadows, until the howling wind masked his words.

"Listen to me. I trust you to see them safe." He clutched her hands in his. His gaze took in every detail of her face—the dance of freckles across her nose the wisps of hair that curled around her ears. "That's the only mission now. Stay alive. Keep Orson gagged and bound and watch Denny. He's unstable. I saw empaths in the war. He's got not only his fear to deal with, but all the fear leaking from the rest of us. It might tip him over the edge."

Rowan nodded. Her eyes were shining with unshed tears.

He ran his thumb down the side of her jaw. Her gaze locked on his and he willed her to see the depth of his feeling because his heart was hammering in his chest and he couldn't bring himself to speak the words he really wanted to say. Not now. Not when they were about to be separated.

"If Clem and I don't come back, don't go home. Go with the Ebos. If we survive, I'll find you there."

Rowan licked her lips and his gaze snagged on the tip of her tongue. Then she nodded.

"I'll keep them safe."

36

The Academy

Conall and Clem slipped through the small breach in the rock wall. It was just wide enough for his shoulders to scrape stone. He didn't like the idea of having to retreat in haste through that gap. He wore his air knives on his belt and a rail gun over his left shoulder along with his quiver of arrows. His crossbow was armed and ready to shoot, but in the small tunnel, he wouldn't be able to maneuver it. He was cursing himself for not switching to the gun when the tunnel opened up. He jumped into the open space and quickly put his back to the wall, scanning the shadows for an attacker. Clem emerged and did the same on the other side.

The wind howled overhead but didn't touch them inside the maze. They waited a full minute for an attack that didn't come.

There was only one way to go from here and Conall waved his crossbow forward. Clem stepped up, but he held her back. He would go first and face whatever was ahead. Clem scowled, but nodded.

They headed down a narrow passage. Stone walls rose on either side, close enough to touch. Overhead, the light was fading and already the passage was deep in shadow. It ended abruptly, and they had the choice to turn left or right. Conall scanned each direction for movement, then chose left because he felt it would lead them deeper into the maze. They wandered like this for some time, choosing turns at random, sometimes backtracking when they came to a dead end. Neither spoke, using hand gestures that were increasingly difficult to see in the deepening dark.

Garou's grumbling unease grew and Conall was having trouble ignoring him.

At yet another juncture, Conall knew they were lost. He chose a direction at random and started down it. Clem tapped his shoulder. He turned and she pointed at the wall, then upward. At the corner of two passages, the rocks sloped. He stepped closer and ran his hands over the stone. Slight indents could be footholds. His gaze followed them to the top of the wall. It wouldn't be an easy climb, but if Denny was right, they'd be able to navigate the maze from above.

Conall started to climb. A few feet up, the footholds became actual stairs. They might have been a natural formation, but chisel marks proved they'd been recently enhanced. He pulled himself up by hand as much as by foot and rested on the last step to peer over the edge. The Warren seemed to go on forever. The shadows between the walls were deep and impenetrable, but the tops of the stone walls shone in the pale light of the midnight sun.

Clem finished the climb and crouched on the stair beside him. The wind lashed at them.

"How far is the lab?" she asked.

"Denny said it's near the center of the maze."

"We'll be spotted way before then."

"Maybe."

Garou smelled smoke, but with the erratic wind he couldn't sense the direction of its source.

They watched the falling night for several long minutes until Conall was satisfied that nothing moved on the stones above the labyrinth.

"Come on."

They crept across the tops of stone walls that were mostly flat and three to four feet thick. Conall felt exposed. Below him the ground was lost in shadows. Anyone could be hiding down there. Anything. And they would travel past dozens of such black pockets before they found the lab. If they found the lab.

With the maze laid out for them, it was easy to plan a route that led them inward. They hopped over a few small gaps and had to backtrack once when they hit a breach too wide to jump. As they neared the center of the labyrinth, the walls became shorter and Conall could see the ground. Signs of recent habitation were evident. They stopped to study a group of rough structures that had been built in one of the larger open spaces. Conall was reluctant to jump down and inspect them because he worried he wouldn't be able to climb back onto the wall.

"It looks abandoned," Clem whispered. "Could it be the lab?"

"I don't think so. Look." He pointed to the remains of a campfire and a makeshift table. "I think this is housing, maybe for the guards or the scientists."

Garou marked the spot. The smell of every human habitation was unique and he'd be able to find it again.

Conall indicated that they should keep moving. They passed a group of larger gaps that had been closed off like prison cells, but peering into the shadows, they found them empty. Except for the bones. They littered the floor of every cell—bones that had been stripped bare and gleamed whitely in the shadows.

Elk or bison bones. Meat for a large predator, Garou confirmed.

Clem pointed her gun into a cell as if she expected something to jump out of it. "This must be where they kept the gaunts."

Conall nodded. His lip curled at the strong stench. Definitely gaunt.

They kept moving. Smoke rose from a gap in the stones ahead, adding to the reek with a sharper smell of burned flesh. They stopped to gaze down on the remains of a pyre.

"Those are bodies." Conall pointed to a charred mass on the edge of the fire where a leg stuck out of the mass.

"Human or gaunt?"

"Can't tell from here, but I suspect gaunt. I think whoever was here panicked when their last posse of murderers didn't return from the oasis. I think they bugged out and burned all the evidence of whatever was going on here." It was what he would have done.

"Is there any point in continuing then?" Clem asked.

"We're here. We might as well look around."

The lab was only a short distance ahead. Another natural staircase led back to ground level. Here, the maze opened into several small gaps that acted as rooms. Someone had been living and working here, and recently.

"Looks like they left in a hurry." Conall's eyes swept across the area. A tent had been left behind. Clem used her rail gun to prop open the tent flap and peer inside.

"Empty."

Conall stepped over to look for himself. Equipment was strewn across the ground. A table lay on its side. Tangled cables led to various broken machines. He could only guess at their functions. The place looked ransacked.

"Is there anything useful?" Clem asked.

"I doubt it, but I'll look. Stand watch."

Clem turned her back to the tent while Conall lit a small thera lamp and hung it from a hook dangling from the ridge pole. It gave off just enough light to fill the small space. Methodically, he scanned the mess from one end to another. Something shiny was hidden under a knot of cables. He tugged them aside to reveal a metal tray with some medical implements on it. That was it. No records. No vox or graphium. No scribe's cachet. Nothing that would even hint at what kind of experiments were going on here.

He remembered the bodies at the oasis. Someone had been directing the gaunts to kill. How? How did you control an uncontrollable monster?

And what about Dr. Banerjee's discovery? So there was a link between gaunts and humans. So what? There had to be more to it. Why were his people killed? Why was he missing? And how did that research connect with whatever Wrede's people were doing here?

He turned in a circle, willing the destroyed lab to shed light on the mystery. Maybe Rowan would find something of use here, but he doubted it. Wrede and his team had left in a hurry, but they'd covered their tracks.

"Commander, you should come and see this." Clem's voice broke the stillness of the night. He took the lamp and left the tent with its unspoken secrets.

Clem stood on the far side of the clearing. Her gun was primed and pointing into a shadow at her feet. As Conall approached with the lamp, the light revealed a staircase leading to an underground tunnel.

"Should we go down?" Clem's impassive expression revealed no fear, but Garou could smell it on her. Conall didn't want to go down a dark hole either.

"I think we're going to have to, but not yet. Let's secure the site first. Make sure we're alone."

Clem relaxed her stance. "I think it's deserted."

"Probably, but let's be sure and then we'll go back for the others. I want Rowan to look at the equipment in that tent."

They'd been gone for over an hour already. Rowan would be worrying.

They inspected every tent and wooden shack and found no humans or gaunts, only a few meadow rats pilfering crumbs from discarded stores.

Conall doused the thera lamp. The sky was never truly dark this far north and it provided enough light to see by. The lamp would only alert others to their presence and ruin their night eyes.

Clem leaned against the wall and sipped from her canteen. She was calm, almost relaxed. A mind couldn't keep up vigilance and fear forever. It would crack under pressure. And Conall knew that smart commanders relied on that fact. It was exactly that moment of complacency—that hour of darkness before dawn—when the best offensives were launched. Squad 54 didn't have the luxury of complacency.

"Drink up," he said. "We're heading back."

Clem swallowed another gulp and stowed the canteen.

"Keep your gun loaded."

"You think they're still here?" Clem's gaze tried to pierce the shadows.

"I think we're still alive because we're vigilant. Let's not stop now."

They climbed back onto the top of the wall and started walking. His legs felt weak. He could see that Clem was tired too. They'd been on the move for nearly half an hour when she almost missed a leap over a short gap. Her arms pinwheeled and he grabbed her collar, hauling her forward. Her feet skidded on the stone and she crashed to one knee.

"Thanks, boss." She stood and shook out the damaged leg.

"You okay?"

"I'll live."

Garou had been unusually quiet, but suddenly Conall felt like he wore wolf ears, and they were pricking upward, listening to the empty night.

Only it wasn't empty. Somewhere out in the Meadows a cat was running on thera power.

And it was heading toward the Warren.

37

A Thousand Miles of Worry

The wind was picking up. It lashed Rowan's hair, pulling it from her tie. It tossed sand into her eyes so they felt gritty every time she blinked. And it masked any sounds on the plains.

Staring into the vast tract of grass lit only by the midnight sun, Rowan felt defenseless and decided to move the squad inside the Warren. They left the cats at the entrance with the Ebos standing watch. Murdoch grumbled about having to leave their gear behind to fit through the tight tunnel, and insisted on lugging the thera stove inside.

Rowan felt more secure with the stone walls at her back and only one passage leading into the maze to guard. And as soon as they were away from the wind, she realized how much it had been irritating her all day. She set Elias on watch with his rail gun pointing down the dark passageway, then removed Orson's gag long enough to dribble water into his mouth.

"Isn't this a privilege," he sneered. "To be served by the great Princess Andula herself."

"Why do you hate me so much? What have I ever done to you?"

"Why shouldn't I hate you? Fat nobles living on the profits of hard working citizens."

She poked his prominent gut.

"Doesn't look like they starve you at the Temple of the Word."

"You know nothing of my life, of the hardships I endured just so I could document the sordid lives of spoiled noble bitches."

That was about enough of that. Rowan stuffed the gag back in his mouth. Orson thrashed and tried to grab her with his bound hands.

"Don't try it." She waggled a finger at him. "I'll remove the gag when food is ready, but only if you promise to behave."

Ooh, if eyes could shoot daggers, I'd be dead.

Rowan sighed and turned away. She didn't understand Orson. All her life, she'd been dogged by scribes. At every public event, they followed her around, documenting her actions and words. Some of those records would be shared with the rag newspapers for public consumption, but most would be filed away in the archives of the Temple of the Word. For posterity. So that one day, future citizens of New Torwood could read the biography of Princess Rowan Andula. It seemed like such a waste of time and effort.

But that's not what bothered her. Orson's outright animosity was abnormal. Scribes were supposed to be neutral. In all her years, she remembered speaking to only one other scribe, and that was because she found him in her personal quarters which were supposed to be off-limits. After filing a complaint with the Temple, she'd never seen him again. One word of reprimand from Rowan could see Orson's career ended. And yet he had no qualms about insulting her at every turn.

They don't expect us to return.

The thought hit her like a crossbow bolt. Conall had known it since they drove out of North Gate. In their conversations, he'd been steering her toward that conclusion, but he'd wanted her to make up her own mind. Now she understood.

Regent Atherton wanted her dead. He wasn't the bumbling, kindly uncle she'd thought him to be. He was a politician who needed to solidify his seat of power.

The thought chilled her. Ethan and Auntie Bella were in the palace at his mercy. She had no doubt Bella could take care of herself, but Ethan? He was the definition of vulnerable.

And she was a thousand miles from his bedside.

Putting her back to a stone wall, she slid down it until she sat with her arms wrapped around her knees. She heard the metal tinkle of feathers as Phalian landed on the wall. His tension rippled through her. She'd been expecting an attack all day and the constant vigilance was exhausting. Every muscle in her body felt bruised with strain.

Murdoch brought her a cup of broth. "A little something hot in the belly drives away the worry."

She thanked him and wrapped her fingers around the warm mug. If there was a knack for soothing emotion with food, Murdoch had it.

While she sipped the drink, she kept her sore and tired eyes fixed on that passage into the maze, the one where Conall and Clem would appear.

She'd told the others to rest, but she couldn't sleep. Her mind turned to events of the past few hours. Had it been hours? It felt like days.

Burying Augie had left a scar across her heart. And then Conall…Just thinking about the night they'd spent together, tucked away in a rocky alcove in the mountains, made her toes curl inside her boots. It's not like she'd been without romance in her life. Saints and sinners, she was twenty-eight. Even princesses didn't make it to that age without a few romantic entanglements. But those earlier encounters had only proven that everybody wanted something from her. Because she was royal, and they believed she had the ear of the regent.

Her last lover had been the son of a wealthy wool merchant. When he'd asked her to intervene with the guilds on his father's behalf, she'd broken off the relationship. There hadn't been anyone to warm her bed since.

But Conall didn't want anything from her, or at least anything beyond her help in keeping their squad alive—help she would give willingly. That and more.

She glanced overhead. The sun would rise in a few hours, but she didn't expect it to chase away all the shadows inside this maze of stone.

Murdoch was awake, preparing a meal. He nodded to her when she rose and picked up the vox.

"He hasn't called?" she asked.

Murdoch shook his head. "Been silent as a tomb."

Not the best analogy.

She checked in on the others. Noah had finally fallen asleep beside his patient. Denny too. Elias slept with his head on a sack of oats. With his expression slack and hands tucked under his chin, he looked like a child, not like the fierce fighter he'd proven himself to be.

A smile ghosted across her lips. Somewhere in the last thousand miles, Squad 54 had become a unit. A family. Not Orson, of course. And maybe not

Denny. Not yet, at least, but she was willing to give him the benefit of doubt.

Grabbing the vox and a rail gun, she squeezed through the gap that led to the Meadows. Minna was sitting on her pony near the entrance. The Ebos seemed to spend more time on horseback than on the ground. As she approached, Minna turned and watched her with a half-amused expression. Except for when they'd buried Augie, Rowan hadn't seen Minna without that wry smile. She seemed to find the whole world amusing.

"Evani," she said with a nod.

Rowan had given up trying to talk her out of using that title. She wasn't even sure what it meant.

"Why don't you go in and get something to eat. I'll stand watch. And when you're done, Ferlan can take a break too."

"Yes, Evani."

Minna was about to dismount when she suddenly went rigid. The sound of hooves on stone came from up the escarpment. Ferlan was coming fast.

"Mech!" he yelled, pointing into the Meadows. Ferlan's English wasn't as good as Minna's and that was all he could muster, but Rowan had heard it too. A thera engine. For a second, she was tossed back into her nightmare, hiding from the gaunts with Dale. As a child, she hadn't understood that sound. She'd never heard a thera engine on the open plains. Now, she knew exactly what it meant. Someone was coming to kill them.

The vox in her hand squeaked and Conall's tinny voice said, "Striker, are you there?"

Rowan clicked it on. "I'm here."

"Someone's coming in a cat. You need to move out now."

"I just heard. We could take the cats and run."

"No, they'll catch you. Leave everything and go into the Warren. Ask Denny if he knows a place to hide."

"How will you find us?"

There was a short silence, then, "We're almost back to you. Start moving out and I'll find you. Tell the elves to go around the Warren to the east side and wait for us there. You hide. If the sun comes up and we haven't found you, go to the Ebos."

Fear nearly stopped the next words in Rowan's throat. "Okay. Be careful."

But she was talking to empty air. Conall had already clicked off. She sucked in a breath.

"You heard him. You'd better move out now."

Minna leaned down from her pony and laid a hand on Rowan's head like a benediction. "May the coho-ne-teno of your ancestors fill your lungs and guide your feet."

Rowan nodded her thanks. It was a good prayer. Better to pray to ancestors than some misty saints.

The thunder of pony feet added to the sound of thera engines as the Ebos galloped away.

Rowan found the others alert when she squeezed through the gap. They'd heard the cat too.

"We're leaving now," she said.

Lena stood with her back against the stone wall and her eyes closed.

Rowan turned to Noah. "Can she walk?"

"She'll have to." Noah glanced at his patient, then pointed to Orson who was still bound and gagged and staring daggers at them. "What about him?"

"Untie his feet, but leave the gag in and his hands tied." Rowan raised her voice to be sure the scribe heard her. "If he tries to run, shoot him. If he makes a sound, shoot him. If he drags his feet…"

"Got it. Shoot him."

Sweat ran down Orson's cheeks, and Rowan could see her death being planned in his busy little mind.

Murdoch took her aside. "You should just kill him now. At best he'll slow us down. At worst he'll give us away."

"We might need the data in his head," Rowan said. But she wouldn't risk the rest of the squad for the scribe. "If we have to, I'll smash his cachet and put a bolt through his brain too."

Murdoch grinned. "Just say the word and I'll do the honors."

The others stood in a semi-circle around her. Their faces were dirty and sweaty and scared. She suddenly appreciated the monumental task Conall had faced bringing them all out here. A week ago, they'd mostly been greens. But they weren't green anymore. And she wasn't a princess. She was a striker, and she'd better start acting like one.

She took a deep breath. "Your only purpose for the next few hours is to stay alive. Denny, you're in the lead."

"Me?" His voice squeaked.

"You. Find us a place to hide. Can you do that?"

His eyes were wide, but he nodded.

"Good. Let's move."

The squad filed into the Warren. When they came to the first crossroads, Denny seemed uncertain.

"Time's short," Murdoch grumbled.

Denny swallowed hard, making his Adam's apple bob. Then he wiped his eyes and pointed down the left passage.

"This way."

Noah followed him, propping up Lena with one shoulder. Orson, Murdoch and Elias were next. They were moving slowly, too slowly. A figure dropped from the wall and landed in the passageway only feet from Rowan. She whipped up her rail gun and pointed it into the darkness.

"You should really prime that thing if you plan to shoot me." Conall stepped forward and tipped the barrel of her gun down. Phalian squawked and circled his head. Clem dropped to the ground behind him.

"Oh, thank the saints." Rowan wanted to hug them both, but there was no time.

From somewhere on the plains, a gaunt howled.

The soldiers were coming and they were bringing their hunting dogs.

38

OBFUSCATION AND EMPATHY

Conall TOOK IN THEIR STATUS IMMEDIATELY. Lena was the biggest concern. Noah practically carried her. Elias tried to help, but he was too short to take much of her weight.

"Denny has a place for us to hide," Rowan said.

Conall nodded and stepped aside so they could lead. He motioned for Clem to fall back with him. If they were going to be attacked, it would come from behind.

Orson waddled. Conall was glad that Rowan hadn't gone soft and let him go free, but with his hands bound, he moved too slowly. Conall jabbed him in the back with his crossbow.

"Faster or I'll put a bolt in your head."

Orson grunted an angry response but picked up his pace.

We should kill him and leave him for the scavengers. Garou wasn't a fan of prisoners. People were either friends or prey. There was no in-between.

Half an hour later, Conall was seriously considering Garou's option. The scribe seemed to drag his feet at every turn and Conall was tired of prodding him on.

Rowan had stopped the group to give Lena a moment to rest. Conall drank from his canteen. It was almost empty. Suddenly the silence felt like a crushing weight. The soldiers had to be at the stone warren already, probably going through their vehicles. They'd know their prey was on foot and had minimal supplies.

What would he do in their place?

If I had enough soldiers, I'd surround the Warren, make sure the enemy couldn't escape, then pick them off at our leisure.

But they'll see the hoof prints, and know the Ebos help us, Garou reminded him.

Then I'd send the gaunts in to kill as many as possible before entering the maze.

A gaunt howled. The sound bounced around the stones so it seemed to come from every direction.

They are foul beasts, Garou said. *Bigger and stronger than humans, but with no stealth. Easy to ambush.*

Easy for you, maybe. But there is no place to hide in these rocks.

Only up.

Conall glanced up. The wolf was right. They had to get on top of the stone walls. It was the only way to outrun the monsters and men who were probably already inside the Warren.

"Watch my back."

Clem nodded and took point at the rear. Conall jogged to catch up to the others.

Noah was almost carrying Lena now. Denny had stopped them at an intersecting passageway, uncertain about which path to take.

"How far is that cave?" Conall asked.

A gaunt howled, closer this time.

"I…I don't know. Twenty minutes maybe, if we're not lost."

"What about stairs." He pointed up. "Can we get up there?"

Denny looked around nervously. "Yes. We just passed a way up."

"Turn around. Now!"

Everyone turned and shuffled back the way they'd come. They met Clem. Her gun pointed into the darkness.

"This way." Denny led them down another passage and under a stone bridge that plunged them into darkness. Emerging on the other side, the night seemed suddenly brighter. "Here." He pointed to the wall beside the entrance to the tunnel.

"Those aren't stairs," Noah said. The rock wall rose nearly six feet vertically before it became a more gentle slope.

"There are footholds," Denny said. "Watch. I'll go first." He scampered up the wall like a monkey. Noah went next, then Rowan helped Lena up the steep incline until Noah could safely pull her up. They untied Orson's hands for the trip, but he refused to move. His cheeks puffed out as he tried to suck in breath around the gag.

Rowan removed it, but pressed a knife to his back.

"Climb and be quiet or I'll end you here. No one will miss you."

In Conall's mind, Garou gave an approving yip for their fierce mate.

Orson cursed but he started to climb. Rowan followed. Conall kept his gun trained on the black hole of the tunnel behind them. He was the last to climb. He stood on top of the rocks, looking down. A gaunt could easily climb that.

"This isn't high enough. We need to hurry."

Denny led them across the stones. It was treacherous terrain in the dark. Twice they had to hop small gaps. Lena collapsed after the second hop. Noah opened her shirt to assess her wounds.

"She's torn her stitches." He was already pulling bandages from his pack. "We can't move her now. She'll bleed out."

"Leave me here." Lena's voice was barely above a whisper. Give me a gun. I'll…hold them."

"We're not leaving anyone behind," Conall snarled. The wolf was close to the surface. The need to shift prickled over his scalp.

They were crammed onto a stone plateau, no more than twenty feet wide. He assessed the drop to the ground.

At least fifteen feet. Maybe higher. And a sheer drop. The gaunts won't be able to climb it.

The wind whipped them, but that would work in their favor too, taking their scent away.

Now if only the humans could stay quiet, Garou sniffed. He didn't have much faith in the stealth of clumsy humans. And he was right. Lena murmured to Noah. He could also hear feet scraping across stone, and Clem nervously fidgeting with her crossbow.

"What are we doing here?" Orson's voice rang like a temple bell in the quiet. Conall walked over, grabbed one of Noah's bandages, and stuffed it in his mouth. Orson immediately reached for it.

Conall jabbed the crossbow into his gut. "Don't touch it."

Orson's hand fell away.

"Quiet yourselves," he said to the others. "Lie down. Flat on the rocks. Make no shadows. Make no noise." He looked around the group and could see fear in their eyes. This wasn't a plan for escape. This was barely a plan at all. Rowan was the first to drop to her knees. She pulled Orson down beside her. When he resisted, she punched the back of his knees and he collapsed.

Mate. Garou whispered with pride.

Conall lay on his stomach and didn't bother to push his obfuscation outward. The knack would only cover him and leave the rest of the squad exposed. But years of hiding from predators in the Meadows had taught him stillness. It was as simple as breathing in and out. What did the Ebos call it? The coho-ne-teno. Exhale. Inhale. Calm the heart. Relax the muscles. Keep the mind sharp for when the monsters came.

The others weren't so good at true stillness. Garou could hear breathing and twitching. Conall willed them to be quiet. It would only take one scraping of boot on rock for the gaunts or their soldier handlers to look up.

The anticipation and dread were almost unbearable—not because of coming monsters, but because someone might panic and give them away. And just when he thought Garou would explode through his skin, a wave of warm calm washed over him. The sound of blood thumping in his head dimmed. The rock beneath him suddenly felt comforting, like a favorite bed. He turned his head and found Denny watching.

Denny, the empath. He'd cocooned them in a bubble of warmth and comfort. Suddenly the night seemed brighter. Kinder. Softer. His fingers relaxed on his gun. Even the wind felt like a caress.

Keep your wits! The wolf bit into his mind and magic slid off them. Conall felt Garou shake like he'd just come out of water.

Better. Magic will blind you. Distract you.

Not all magic.

Yes. All magic. It is the refuge of the weak.

Like the magic that lets you speak inside my head?

The wolf huffed.

See? Already you've become stupid.

With Garou's intervention, Conall hardened his mind against the empath's knack. He would remain vigilant, but he was grateful to Denny for calming the others. They might actually pull this off. He glanced at Clem. She was deep under the empath's influence. Her head drooped to the side and she wore a dumb grin on her face. He'd get no help there.

Garou heard them coming first. Conall felt the wolf bristle.

The gaunt was nearly silent when it loped down the passageway. It paused at a diverging path to scratch the ground with dagger-like claws. Had it scented them? Or had it found a mole hole?

A soldier came around a bend and spotted the gaunt crouched and digging frantically in the dirt. He watched for a moment, then raised some kind of mech and clicked it with his thumb.

The gaunt jerked backward, but it was still focused on whatever scent attracted it in the dirt. The soldier clicked again and the gaunt shrieked. It jumped backward, clawing the air, barely three feet from the soldier. He held his ground, sure in his mastery over the beast. Eventually, the gaunt calmed and moved along the passageway, right under Conall's nose. It didn't walk in a straight line, but lurched from side to side with its long arms dragging against the stone walls.

The soldier came into view again. He carried a gun in one hand and his gaunt-controlling mech in the other.

He needed to get his hands on that mech.

The soldier stopped and swung his gun around, pointing into the darkness behind him, before moving again. Had he heard something? Conall prayed that Denny's soothing knack would hold and the others would remain silent.

Not fifty feet up the passage, the gaunt paused. The soldier paused. Conall held his breath.

"Over here!" Orson jumped up. He'd spit out his gag and he leaned over the edge of the plateau, yelling and waving his arms.

The soldier shot him. Orson shrieked and fell backward.

Conall jumped twenty feet to the ground below. His first shot struck the soldier in the chest and he staggered back. The second took him down.

The gaunt leapt over the fallen soldier, no longer restrained, and his prey now in sight.

Conall barely had time to reload. He let loose one more bolt that struck the bone plating on the creature's chest before the gaunt tackled him. He struggled to keep the beast's teeth from his throat. His crossbow was pinned between them. He kicked out and struck bone. Pain lanced up his leg. He tried to roll, and it was like moving a mountain. The air knife on his belt might have been miles away. He couldn't let go of the beast's throat to reach it.

Fangs dripped saliva on his face and he stared into a nightmare of rage and insanity.

A bolt appeared in the gaunt's throat. Blood sprayed Conall's face. The bolt pierced it from back to front, a clean shot that left the arrow head quivering inches from Conall's nose.

He shoved with every bit of his strength and the beast fell away. Conall saw Clem standing over him, holding her crossbow and grinning.

"It's a good knack," she said.

Conall grunted and she held out a hand to haul him up.

Everything hurt. His ribs ached from being crushed by the three-hundred pound beast. His ankle was most likely sprained from the jump off the stones. And his head pounded from excess adrenaline.

Saints, I'm too old for this shit. I should find myself a nice crossroads and become an innkeeper.

You'd be bored in a week, Garou said.

That sounds good, right about now.

Rowan peered over the edge of the plateau.

"Orson's been shot."

"Tell the doc not to waste any bandages on him," Conall said.

Another gaunt howled. It was far away, but they were hunting inside the Warren. This night wasn't over yet.

"Get to the cave. Stay up top as long as you can, then barricade yourself in. Clem and I are going hunting."

Rowan hesitated only a moment. Then she nodded and backed up out of sight.

Clem stared into the darkness behind him. Her stance was poised for flight, but her crossbow was steady.

Conall leaned over the fallen soldier and plucked the mech device from his hand, then he turned to Clem.

"Are you ready for a fight?"

"I'm just getting started." Her grin was a little maniacal, but they would need that ferocity tonight.

39

FLIGHT AND FIGHT

Rowan STOOD OVER ORSON. NOAH WAS already wrapping his bloody arm in a bandage.

"You heard the Commander. Don't waste your time with him."

Noah ignored her and kept winding the bandage. She crouched and forced him to look at her.

"Work fast and don't use your knack. I don't care if he's in pain. I need your focus."

Noah scowled and she softened her tone. "Noah, I can't do this alone. I need you."

He met her gaze and she tried to fill it with earnest desperation. Noah nodded. He tied off the bandage and pulled Orson to his feet. The scribe whimpered.

"He shot me." His lips trembled. "He can…can't do that. Scribes are sacrosanct."

"I don't think he got the memo." Rowan grabbed his arm and pulled him along the stone wall, not bothering to gag him again. He'd learned his lesson.

Behind her, Noah and Denny helped Lena stand. She was barely conscious. Murdoch and Elias brought up the rear.

Squad 54 limped along the top of the walls. Rowan felt exposed, but at least this route gave them an advantage. Instead of running through the gaunt-infested maze, they hopped across the rocks as the crow flies. When they came to gaps in the walls, Elias's uncommon strength became a gift from the saints. Between him and Noah, they managed to pass Lena from one wall to another. Until they came to a gap that was too wide. Alone either one could jump it, but it was too far to pass Lena across.

Noah studied the problem. "I could maybe piggyback her."

"You'll never make it," Rowan said. "We have to climb down or go back." She scanned the edge of the wall for a trail, but it was hard to see past a few dozen feet and the shadows played games with her vision.

Phalian looped down from above and tugged at her sleeve with his beak before flying off again. She sensed urgency vibrating in him.

"Wait here," she said, then followed the bird to where the stone wall had collapsed, leaving a slope of tumbled rock with a ten-foot drop at the end. It was hidden in shadow and without Phalian, she would have never seen it. She waved Noah and the others over.

"We go quickly and quietly." Rowan pointed to the lower ledge. "Denny first to keep watch. Then you, Noah. Elias will help Lena from here and you catch her. The rest of us will follow. As soon as we're all down, we move. Denny, do you have our position? Can you find the cave from here?"

Denny nodded. He was scared. She could see it in the whites of his eyes and the slight tremble of his upper lip. He was also exhausted. Using his knack on the entire squad had probably depleted him. Who soothed the empath when the empath panicked? That thought reminded her of Augie and she pushed it firmly from her mind. She hoped Denny could handle the stress. He had just proven himself a valuable part of the team, and she needed all the help she could get.

She squeezed his arm and tried to convey as much with her touch. He met her eyes and nodded, then slid down the slope.

Elias helped her carry Lena to the ledge and gently lower her into Noah's waiting arms. They were all aware of the seconds ticking away. How long before more soldiers and their gaunts found this section of stone passages?

Murdoch followed Lena, then Orson. He limped even though he'd been shot in the shoulder. Rowan couldn't find it in herself to care. He stopped at the edge and she pointed down.

"Just sit down and slide."

The scribe's eyes flared with murder. He was going to be difficult. Again.

"You either jump or I push you."

Before she could react, Elias swiped Orson's legs out from under him with a kick. He shoved the scribe off the ledge and caught him by the collar. Orson squirmed and a scream gurgled in his throat.

Elias lowered him a couple of feet, then let him drop. Orson landed hard and fell over. Elias beamed at her.

"Are all elves that strong?" she asked.

"You would call it a knack." He cocked his head, reminding her of Phalian, then hopped off the ledge and landed with a soft thud.

Rowan scrambled down after him. As soon as her feet hit gravel, she urged, "Go!"

Noah had slung Lena across his shoulder. The sound of gunfire echoed through the Warren, followed by screams. Conall and Clem were cleaning house. It was impossible to tell how far away they were, but the squad needed no more encouragement to run.

Conall HIT THE SOLDIER IN THE chest, but it wasn't a kill shot. Too far to the right. The man screamed and fell. Conall threw down his crossbow. He was out of arrows. He leapt across the stones and silenced the fallen soldier with a knife to his throat. He turned to help Clem. The soldier's pet gaunt had her pinned against a wall. He unslung his rail gun. The two seconds it took to prime seemed like an eternity. He fired. The blast ricocheted off the gaunt's thick hide.

Conall was already running when Garou took over. The shift ripped through him—sharp and searing like a bolt of lightning through his soul.

Conall left the ground in a leap and Garou landed awkwardly on four paws.

He ignored the pain and shook his thick pelt to settle muscle and bone. Another agonizing bound and he tackled the gaunt. The beast was made of armored plating like it wore its bones on the outside. But the wolf had fought gaunts before. He knew where to find the chewy bits. The neck. Under the arms. Behind the knees.

They fell to the ground and the gaunt flailed, lifting its leg helpfully so Garou could sink fangs into flesh. The beast howled and gnashed its teeth, finding only a mouthful of fur. Garou slashed a tendon behind the knee with his claws and pinned the gaunt.

The human pup leapt into the fight. She had no teeth, but she had a blade, and she sank it deep between shoulder and jaw. The beast thrashed. Garou hung on until it stilled.

He jumped back and shook blood from his muzzle.

"Thanks, boss."

Garou whined and licked her hand. Clem was pack. He'd thought of her as just a pup, but tonight she'd proven herself to be a fierce fighter. He was happy to continue the hunt by her side.

"How many do you think there are?" She cocked her head. "I guess you can't answer that. I'd bet there aren't more than six soldiers with their pets. They think those beasts are inescapable. But we'll show them, right?"

Garou leaned against her knee to show his support.

"Right. So I vote we head back to the cats, take out anyone we find along the way. Once they realize they are the hunted and not the hunters, they'll regroup. And we'll finish them off."

Garou growled, a deep, low rumble like a coming storm. It was a good plan—the plan of an alpha hunter.

Clem retrieved Conall's gun but left his bow, and they stalked through the dark, looking for prey.

By the time Denny found the cave, Lena was unconscious. Noah carried her into the dark hollow. It wasn't really a cave, just a covered dead end in the twisted maze of rock, but it suited their purposes. It had been used for storage and several crates were still piled at one end. Murdoch and Elias were already moving those forward to create a barricade.

Rowan stood at the entrance, pointing her gun at the stone spire that marked the end of the narrow passage. It was the only approach and she'd shoot anything that came around that bend.

Noah crept up beside her and whispered, "I'm not sure this is a good idea. We're trapped here if those soldiers find us."

A gaunt screamed in the night, followed by the sound of gunfire. Clem and Conall had taken out another foe. She had to think of it that way. The reverse was unacceptable. She would imagine Clem fighting like a true warrior, hair flying and every shot hitting its mark, with Conall laying out bolt fire beside her. Or better yet, running as the wolf to take down the enemy. She would imagine this scenario until someone proved otherwise.

"We hold our position," she said. "We might be trapped, but they have to come at us one at a time." She motioned with her gun at the narrow passage. "I like those odds better. Just see to the wounded."

Noah paused like he wanted to say more, but then nodded and ducked back inside.

Elias appeared beside her. He primed his rail gun and leaned against the dead-end rock wall.

Two against one. She liked their odds better and better.

Behind her, Orson's shrill voice shredded the silence.

"I can't believe they shot—" The words were cut off. Noah must have gagged him again.

Orson was a problem with no good solution. Part of her wanted to abandon him to the gaunts. It wasn't the risk to his life that stopped her from ordering that. It was the chance that he would escape alive—that the soldiers would realize at the last moment he *was* a scribe and call off their dogs. And if the soldiers caught Orson any hope of ever going home would be shattered.

A shadow fell from the sky and landed thirty feet in front of them.

The gaunt hit the ground and reared up, fists raised to the sky. It howled.

Sins of the saints! She should have expected them to use the upper roadway. A soldier jumped down behind the gaunt. A rail gun was slung over his shoulder, but it wasn't primed. He relied on the brutality of the gaunt to do the job. He raised a fist. Something was in his hand. She couldn't make it out. His fist jerked and the gaunt charged.

Rowan fired. Elias too. Bolts ricocheted off the gaunt. The soldier screamed but she didn't know if it was a scream of rage or pain. The beast prowled forward. She fired again. Her hands shook as she tried to reload. The gun wouldn't prime. Damned rails were burned and she had no time to swap them out.

Now she understood why Conall preferred the bow.

Elias threw down his gun too. He pulled blades from his boots and let out a shrill cry as he ran at the gaunt. The beast swiped claws, and Elias ducked under them. Sliding through the gaunt's legs, he came up and slashed the tendons at the back of its knees.

The gaunt bellowed and fell to one knee. It grabbed Elias by the arm. The elf shrieked as his arm was wrenched from its socket. He'd taken down the beast, but it wouldn't be enough.

Rowan ran. Her mech fingers sizzled. Phalian squawked and tore through the night like a bullet to hit the gaunt in the eye. It was all the diversion she needed. The gaunt dropped Elias and swung a fist, trying to swat the tiny metal dagger that assaulted it. Rowan ducked under its reach and pressed her hand to its chest.

She let go a blast of galvanic magic. It sizzled across the beast's plating, a crackle of blue fire. The gaunt seized. Lips spread in a rictus of pain and surprise. Its back arched and its disabled legs could no longer hold. It crumpled to the ground, lifeless.

Rowan collapsed. The surge of magic felt like it had come from her toes and ripped her veins out as it passed through her. She turned her head in time to see Elias, his left arm hanging useless, swipe his knife across the gaunt's throat. Just in case. Then she lay panting, feeling raw and oddly sensitized. She could count every tiny stone digging into her back.

She pulled herself up on one elbow, then to her knees. One look at the soldier told her he was dead. A lucky ricochet had hit him in the throat.

Elias made a gurgling sound and stumbled backward, clutching at his arm that hung too far from his shoulder.

Rowan swallowed down the gorge that rose in her throat.

"Noah! I need you!"

Noah bolted from the cave and caught Elias before he collapsed.

Rowan was shaking. On her shoulder, Phalian trembled too. She opened his port on her arm and urged him to rest. Her feet felt leaden as she approached the gaunt. It had bitten its tongue and blood soaked its lips and chin. More blood leaked from the gaping hole that was its nose.

She turned her attention to the dead soldier and suppressed a gasp.

She knew him.

His name was Striker Nestor Lukko. She'd been seated next to him at the All Saints feast last fall. He was a rising star in the ranger ranks, and he was also assigned to Minister Wrede as his personal bodyguard.

She inspected his uniform. It wasn't ranger attire. As a striker he should have worn three stripes on his shoulder, but the uniform was devoid of all insignias.

They don't want to be recognized.

She glanced at his hand that lay open against the stones. A mech device had rolled from his open grip. She picked it up. It was a four-inch long cylinder etched with mage scroll work. Indentations on one side let it fit nicely in her grip. One large button topped the cylinder and two others were on the upper end of the shaft. Gripping it in her mech hand, she could feel its resonance.

This device controlled the gaunt somehow. She clicked the large button on top. Nothing happened. The other two buttons also produced no effect. She peered at the mech, looking for a mage mark, but like the soldier's uniform it was anonymous. But her close inspection revealed a cap on the bottom of the cylinder. She flicked it open to reveal a fourth button. She pressed it.

The gaunt's head exploded, spraying bone and blood across ten feet of rock.

"Well, fuckety-fuck."

Before her sluggish thoughts could work through all the implications, more gunfire echoed through the night. The stone maze tossed sound around, making it impossible to tell its origin, but the shots seemed far away. This time, there was no beastly gaunt scream following the gunfire. Only silence. After several minutes dragged by, that silence became unbearable. Rowan felt blind and hobbled. She spread her fingers and pressed her mech arm to the stones behind her, hoping the maze would act like a giant machine so she could read it. But the maze wasn't mage-made and it didn't conduct magic. It was dead under her touch.

She came back to the present to find Noah standing over her, frowning at the mess on the stones. She tucked the cylinder into her pocket.

"Elias?" she asked.

"He's fine. Just a dislocation. It'll be tender for a while, but he's mobile."

"And the others?"

Noah shook his head. "Orson will live, unfortunately. Lena lost a lot of blood. She needs rest and fluids."

They both knew they were in short supply of both.

"I'm giving us until dawn and then we're moving out." Dawn was less than an hour away.

"They won't be ready."

"None of us will be."

Garou AND Clem WORKED THEIR WAY south. The human wisely let the wolf take the lead. The passages doubled back with hairpin turns. They crossed other trails and hit dead-ends, but the wolf's nose easily picked up the rank scent of gaunt, and they followed it back to its origin.

Twice they stopped to fight. Once, they rounded a bend right into the back of a soldier. He let out a shout even as Clem cut his throat. With his handler dead, the gaunt went berserk. Garou had seen rabid wolves with more sense. The creature raged and pounded its fists on rocks.

The deranged were easy prey. Garou took its legs out, cracking its head against stone. Clem finished it with a swipe of her blade.

"We make a good team." She wiped blood from her face. Her teeth shone in the pale light, her expression only slightly less demented than the dead beast's.

They moved on.

The next fight was brutal and seemed to take forever. Clem shot the soldier, and even though her knack hit the target, he didn't go down. The gaunt pounced. The following moments became a frenzy of fangs, claws and screams of rage. He tore out the creature's throat, as he'd known he would, but it cost him. A bite to his right hind leg left it hanging useless. He cut off the pathway of pain from hip to knee, but it wouldn't support his weight. He limped on three legs to Clem. She stood over the dead soldier, a bloody knife gripped in an unsteady hand.

Garou whined.

"Come on." She didn't bother to stop and wipe off blood anymore.

They made it to the entrance of the Warren without encountering more of the enemy. The sky was already brightening. They'd taken most of the short night to get there.

A strange cat was parked next to theirs. Garou panted as he hopped toward the vehicles. Wolves had a much higher tolerance for pain than humans, but his leg was broken and even he could no longer ignore it.

He needed to change. The shift broke all his bones. Every time. It was horrific and beyond excruciating, but on the other side, he'd be whole again.

He let out a whine, half from the pain, but also to alert the human to his needs.

"Go ahead. I've got your back." He licked her hand, glad that it was Clem beside him and not someone who wouldn't understand the ways of the wolf. He'd known Clem since she was a newborn. She'd played with him in his wolf form as a pup. And now she'd kill anything that came out of that warren while he lay vulnerable during the shift.

Might as well get it over with, Conall said. It was the first time he'd intruded on their thoughts since the shift. They had an unspoken agreement that when they ran on four legs, Garou was in charge. And the human had honored that agreement. Now it was his turn to fight.

The shift was agonizing this time. On a good day, he could change between breaths. But he couldn't do that again, not without food and rest. And not with pain flooding his veins.

He flopped on the ground in the shadow of the cats, tendons popped. Muscle screamed. When he was finally done, he lay naked and panting from exertion. And human. And whole. His back leg flexed without pain, or at least with little pain. He'd abused his body this night and he would pay for it.

He gave himself a moment to let the world stop spinning before standing and rifling through his pack for clothes. And food. Two shifts without rest was only bearable if he had fuel. He shoved one of Murdoch's high protein travel cakes in his mouth. It was dry and he had no saliva to break it down. He gulped water from an extra canteen.

Then he found the spare vox. He'd dropped his inside the Warren when he'd shifted. Along with the mech device the soldier had been carrying.

Saints sinner, there was no going back for it now.

He clicked the vox. "Striker Andula. Do you read me?"

Static answered him. He'd told her to wait until sunrise. He glanced at the sky. They were minutes away from the sun. She'd be moving toward the other side of the Warren soon.

The vox crackled. "I'm here. We're safe. Found the haven."

"Stay there. The enemy are dead, but be vigilant. There may be more. We're at the cats. Wait an hour, then send Elias back to get us." If the elf wanted to be a tracker, now was his chance.

"Elias is hurt."

"Is he okay?"

"Yes, but we're all tired. I don't think he can make it back on his own right now."

"Understood. Sit tight." Conall turned the volume down, but he didn't sign off. "And Rowan?"

"Yes."

He rubbed his thick and very itchy beard. "Stay safe."

There was a dark pause, then, "Yes, Commander."

He flipped the vox shut. Thunder rumbled in the distance. The storm brewing over the mountains was finally making itself known.

"Commander!" Clem's shout brought him round. She had her rail gun primed and pointing into the Meadows.

That wasn't thunder.

Conall grabbed a gun from the back of the cat and turned to face whatever beast was racing across the open ground toward them.

40

FATAL OBLIGATIONS

Rowan PUT DOWN THE RADIO AND a sense of relief washed over her. A part of her had thought Conall and Clem dead. She'd been subconsciously preparing to accept that reality.

"They're alive," she said to the rest of the squad, as if they hadn't heard the vox transmission too. Noah nodded with a weary smile. Murdoch grunted and raised his water-into-wine flask in salute. Denny and Elias slept curled up like a couple of kittens.

Orson, of course, didn't care. His hate-filled eyes still followed Rowan's every move, slight as they were in the cramped space.

Until he choked.

His face turned red and his eyes goggled. Rowan's first instinct was to ignore him. It was just Orson acting out. Again. But then his eyes rolled back in his head.

"He can't breathe!" Rowan rushed forward, but Noah was already there, pulling out the matted gag. Orson sucked in a great breath, but that only made him choke again. His body stiffened and convulsed.

"He's having a seizure." Noah's hands were quick and sure as he unbound the scribe's arms, freeing his chest so it could rise and fall unhindered. He pulled him away from the wall and laid him flat.

Orson seized once more, then went slack.

They waited. Noah pressed fingers to the pulse on his throat.

"Is he dead?" Rowan leaned in. Was his chest expanding?

Orson's eyes shot open. They were red-rimmed, irises nearly taken over by black. Spittle foamed at the corners of his gaping mouth.

He lunged.

Fingers clamped on Rowan's throat. Orson's face turned red as he strained to squeeze. She choked and tried to drag air into her lungs. Her mech arm flailed as she willed galvanic magic to flow from her fingertips. He shrieked as she zapped him, but it wasn't enough. Not nearly enough. She was too depleted from fighting the gaunt. All she could do now was batter uselessly at the hands that were stealing her life. She was barely aware of Noah grappling with Orson. Her heart thudded. Her lungs begged for air, and still the fingers squeezed.

She heard Phalian's desperate cry like a distant echo. Her world shrank to the sight of Orson's rage-filled eyes. She clawed at the hands gripping her throat. A metallic tang filled her mouth as she bit her tongue. The edges of her vision blackened. Lungs burned. Death rumbled in her ears.

And then, when pain and fear and loss of oxygen nearly drowned her, the clamp released. She sucked in air through a bruised throat. She coughed and swayed. Someone caught her before she hit the wall. Seconds passed, minutes maybe, before her body was convinced that it wasn't going to die. Her vision cleared and she saw Denny standing over Orson. With a rock. The scribe bled from a head wound. Dead or unconscious. She didn't care.

Phalian was dive-bombing the fallen scribe, stinging him over and over with his beak like a vengeful wasp. She called him back with a cluck of her bloody tongue and he settled on her shoulder.

"I thought…I thought he was going to kill you," Denny said.

"He certainly tried." Noah was bent over Orson. He listened for a moment then stood up. "Too bad. He's not dead."

Denny dropped the rock like it was suddenly on fire. He studied the unconscious scribe with a deep frown, his other hand clutching his knotted string.

"What's the matter?" Rowan asked.

"I don't know. There's something odd about his mind."

"I felt it too," Noah said. "But scribes are all bonkers. It's the training. They're taken as children and brainwashed. And worse." He tilted Orson's head to the side to reveal a metal implant like a plug. The curl of his lip revealed his disgust. "They're butchered in order to jack into this thing."

"It's more than that." Denny sighed and let his string drop, as if when confronted by a real problem, he no longer needed the comfort of his talisman. "There's something inorganic, some kind of obstruction in his head, or…I don't know. It blocks my empath knack." Denny took Rowan's mech hand. "May I?"

Rowan almost jerked out of his grasp, but she saw the question in his eyes; not "May I," but "Do you trust me?"

She knew Conall didn't trust the young scientist because he'd held back information. But where Conall saw connivance, Rowan saw fear. Denny had suffered and that suffering led to caution. He hadn't held back information from spite, but from wariness. And why should he trust them?

She held out her hand.

He pressed her black-gloved fingers against Orson's temple. Millions of sensors in her fingertips came alive. Normally, her mech didn't respond to flesh and blood, but Orson wasn't wholly human. She felt the inorganic bits in him. They weren't just in his head. They coursed through his veins. They were embedded in every muscle and bone. Like infinitesimally small mechs living in his body. And the mechs were laced with thera. It was all through his system. Resonance from the magic matter flooded him.

Denny gripped her hand and smiled. He felt it too.

Scribes weren't wholly human, but some kind of human-mech-magic hybrid.

"Did you know about this?" she asked.

Denny shook his head. "I suspected. I was friends with the scribe in our camp. I knew Sandra was different, but we never talked about it. Scribes are trained to keep the secrets of others, but they keep their own too. Now, if you don't mind. I want to listen."

His grip on her hand tightened and she held very still. His other hand gripped her shoulder. She felt like a conduit. His empath knack tingled through her mech fingers and into Orson. The scribe's eyes rolled side to side beneath closed lids.

Denny listened to a song that only he could interpret, but Rowan felt like she could almost hear it too, like the song was being sung far, far away, during a thunder storm and every once in a while, the wind would shift enough for her to make out a few notes.

Then Denny sighed and let go. He slumped backward and Noah caught him before he fell.

"Just as I thought. He has a geas on him."

"A what?"

"Maybe geas isn't exactly right," Denny explained. "It implies magic, and this is more like…programming."

"I don't understand. What is a geas?"

"It's a compulsion. Usually with some kind of trigger. When Orson had that seizure, I felt…well, it's hard to describe. But it wasn't natural, no more natural than an exploding rail gun." He could see that she still didn't understand, and he shook his head.

"I'm sorry. I'm making a muddle of this. Orson had a compulsion put on him to kill you and something triggered it."

"The vox," Noah said. "Right before his seizure, Conall made contact."

Rowan shook her head, not wanting to believe. "But we've always used the vox. It never triggered him before."

"Not the vox itself. The message. Conall told us the enemy was dead. And that set him off."

The gears clicked into place in Rowan's mind. "If the soldiers and their gaunts failed to end us, Orson was primed to kill me."

"Yes." Denny met her gaze and held it.

The council wanted her dead. It was true. It was irrefutable.

And she still had to go home to face them.

41

ONE JOB

"Stand down." Conall relaxed his grip on the gun. Clem gave him a worried glance. Whatever was heading their way was fast. And big. It sounded like a stampede of mad bison, but Garou had already caught the scent of horse and bone and that strange but familiar spice.

The Ebos were coming.

They waited in the frail morning light for the troop of dark elves to cross the Meadows. Before long, he could make out individual ponies, then faces under dun colored cowls. He estimated forty Ebos thundered over the plains to surround them. Riled up from the long run, the ponies pranced and stirred up dust.

Clem gripped her rail gun, but kept the muzzle lowered.

"Easy, Ranger," Conall said, not taking his eyes off the lead Ebos who, in a show of dominance, forced his pony to dance a sharp circle only a few feet away. Conall refused to be intimidated and stood his ground.

The elf seemed young, but elves lived longer than humans and their age wasn't always obvious. This one had a certain arrogance that spoke of youth. His blond hair was long and loose around his shoulders. It came to a widow's peak on his brow above piercing blue eyes. He didn't speak, but only glared at the humans while yanking on his mount's reins.

Minna's pony inserted itself between the newcomer and Conall. Even after the hard ride, she looked composed.

"Commander West, I present Dalkyn, my brother and *cohenne* to Omika, the Evafara."

"Cohenne?" Conall flicked his eyes from one to the other. He saw the resemblance now. Minna's hair was darker blond, almost brassy, but they had the same eyes and mouth, though Dalkyn's was more suited to derision and Minna's to laughter.

Her eyes sparkled. "It means heir or perhaps you would say apprentice. One who will take over the title of Evafara when the day comes for Omika to lay down his bones. If my brother lives long enough." She leaned in as if to impart a secret, but didn't bother to lower her voice. "He likes to race the ponies, you see. Mother always swore he would break his neck and leave his bones for the scavengers."

"The human is not interested in your kitchen tales, sister." Dalkyn's expression was devoid of humor and completely focused on Conall. "Omika has sent us to aid you in whatever way we can." A slight sneer curled his upper lip.

Conall glanced at Clem. She was swaying on her feet and covered in blood and dirt. He probably didn't look much better after a night of shifting and fighting. He smothered a laugh that could be taken for insult. The need for help had come and gone.

Or had it?

They were still exposed. Minister Wrede could send more soldiers and gaunts at any time. They were tired, hungry and carried wounded. And if they had any chance of returning home, they needed to hide all evidence that they'd been here.

The Ebos had miraculously appeared twice now to aid them. Not that he wasn't grateful, but Conall's mother had a saying too: a suspicious wolf might eat last, but he will live long enough to find another meal.

"Why are you helping us?" His gaze locked on Dalkyn, but Minna answered.

"I have already explained. Omika and our elders wish us to…how do you say…make relations with your princess."

Clem snorted.

"I think you mean you want to build a relationship with Rowan." Conall rubbed his temple. He was so very tired and these elves were about as transparent as obsidian. "Why do you want to be friends with her? Because she is this Evani you mentioned? What does that mean?"

Minna glanced at her brother but Dalkyn looked away.

"Evani means…prized one, as does princess, yes?"

They were going in circles. He would sort out their true motivations later.

"Fine. I accept your help. My people are wounded. They're holed up inside the Warren." He pointed toward the immense stone maze. "I need you to get them out. Then we need to clean up the bodies inside. Leave no trace behind. Can you do all that?"

Dalkyn seemed affronted by the question. "Of course, Wolf."

Conall chose to hear that name as a title rather than a slur. The Ebos were big on titles.

Dalkyn whirled around and started issuing orders in the Ebos tongue.

Minna dismounted and handed her reins to another elf. Feeling lost and utterly exhausted, Conall stood beside the cat and watched the Ebos slip into the Warren. One advantage to the smaller mounts was that ponies easily fit through the tight gap that led into the maze of stone.

"I should go with them. I can find the others."

Minna took a small water pouch from the folds of her robe and handed it to him.

"Rest, Commander. We will find your people. You did your part on this turn of the bones."

Conall didn't quite get the analogy, but he was too tired to argue. He took the water skin and drank. It wasn't water, but some fermented drink like wine. It went straight to his head.

How long had he been awake? He couldn't remember. And other than the travel cake, he couldn't remember his last meal either. Add two shifts on top and a slight buzz from the Ebos's alarmingly strong drink…

Minna took his arm as his knees buckled.

"I sssshould go with them." Even he could hear the slur in his words now. His legs folded under him and he sat where he'd stood, right beside the cats. He had the presence of mind not to sleep, at least until he saw the ponies return carrying his squad.

His EYES OPENED WHEN THE HEAT of the afternoon became too much. He stared at the blue sky as he took an inventory of every muscle that ached in his body. He sat up slowly. Denny and Clem were sleeping on blankets in the shade of a cat. The Ebos had retreated to their own camp, far from the mech vehicles. He spotted two mounted ponies among the rocks—the elves on watch—and suspected there were others he couldn't see.

Minna sat beside him, calmly skinning a hare.

"What was in that water skin?" Conall rubbed his head. "Did you drug me?"

She smiled. "Nonsense. You were simply exhausted. I had no idea you would react to our wine in such a way."

"Wine? You call that wine?"

"No, you would call it wine. We call it *yenni*. Fermented caribou milk mixed with elderberries."

He rubbed his head as if that could brush the clouds from his mind. Maybe he had simply overdone it, but he'd be careful about accepting food from the elves again.

"Where are the others?"

Minna tipped her head toward a cluster of people standing near the farthest cat.

Rowan. Just the sight of her sent a jolt through him that left Garou snort-laughing in his mind.

Her body was rigid and slightly bent forward as she argued with Dalkyn. Conall rose and walked over to them. Dalkyn was listening to Rowan's pleas with an impassive expression on his face. When she saw Conall, the storm in her eyes softened. He wanted to take her in his arms and he saw the desire reflected in her, but, of course, he did no such thing. He was Commander. She was Striker, and they had business at hand.

"What's the problem?" he asked.

Rowan waved a hand at Dalkyn. "He won't let us take the cats. And Lena can't walk or ride."

Conall turned to Dalkyn. The Ebos crossed his arms. "No mech."

Of course.

"We need to leave here," Conall said. "Soon. If we walk into the Meadows, we won't make it out."

"Omika has gifted you with mounts." Dalkyn wasn't giving an inch.

"Lena won't make it on horseback." Rowan's voice was growing strident.

Noah appeared, looking as haggard as the rest of them. "Lena is awake," he said softly. "She insists that she can ride."

Rowan spun around and they all looked at Lena's pale form, sitting on the last bench in the cat.

She lifted a trembling hand and waved. "I'll be okay Commander. If we have to ride, I'll ride."

Noah's lips were pinched into a hard, flat line. "I gave her everything I could," he said. "She'll make it."

Conall nodded. "Walk it off, Maven."

Noah stalked away with a stiff-legged gait. After only a few paces, he stopped and let out a primal bellow of rage. His fists rose and he shook them. Lines of tension ran from his hands down his neck and shoulders as he worked out his fury.

Rowan watched with one hand pressed to her lips and tears shining in her eyes. Conall reached for her, and she leaned into his touch. He circled his arms around her, not giving a damn about protocol or who was watching. Noah continued to scream and it felt like he was vomiting out the anger and stress of the entire squad.

"I don't know how to help him," Rowan said quietly.

Conall kissed her hair. It smelled like blood and sweat and hot metal. He whispered into her ear. "You did good. You kept them safe. We'll help Noah, I promise."

Noah turned. His eyes were rimmed in red. "My knack is disgusting." He raked his hands over his chest as if he wanted to claw out his heart. "It takes and takes and…" His voice faded to a sob that hitched in his throat.

Conall gently pushed Rowan away and gripped Noah's shoulder. "You helped Lena," he said. "Keep that as your center."

Noah held his face in his hands. "I didn't help Augie." Noah's words were muffled.

"You helped Elias," Rowan said. "And Orson. And…and me." She touched her throat and Conall notice red marks that looked suspiciously like finger prints. His eyes narrowed, but now wasn't the time for a full accounting.

"I failed." Noah's words were haunting.

Conall looked around at the tired and sore faces. Murdoch and Elias stood nearby. Noah's outburst had woken Clem and Denny too. They sat up to watch. Clem hugged her knees. Denny watched with wide eyes. The Ebos were standing vigil too, but Conall had eyes only for his squad.

"Listen to me, all of you. Nobody failed. Not even me. It was my job to keep you all alive, but it was an impossible task, one we were never meant to accomplish. Someone wants us dead. The council, the ministers, I don't know who. But they're the ones who failed. Not us. We slipped through their snare. *We* are alive. And we will stay alive. For Augie, and to prove to those bastards who want us dead that they don't get to win. I couldn't be prouder to be part of this team. "

"We win!" Clem said with a fist bump to the sky.

"We win." Conall nodded. "Now we have some decisions to make. But first we need to hide all proof that we were here. And we need to get somewhere safe. Then, together as a squad we will decide how to move forward. Agreed?"

There were grunts and nods all around before the group dispersed. Rowan wiped her nose and eyes on her sleeve.

Conall pointed to the red marks on her throat.

"Now you're going to tell me what in the saints made those."

42

RANKING OFFICERS

In the end, Dalkyn relented about the mech vehicles, if only because they needed to hide them. Rowan was relieved. Despite Lena's assertions, she didn't think the scout could ride for long even with the Ebos's sturdy little ponies.

Clem and Conall had killed four soldiers and gaunts. They piled those bodies onto the third cat and added Nestor Lukko and the gaunt Elias and Rowan had killed.

Conall searched their pockets but didn't find the key to the cat, so Rowan jump-started it with a magic flare directly from her mech arm to the open engine. It was only a tiny spark, something she'd done a hundred times before while fixing the Talos or working in her shop. But her body was tired and abused. She'd overused her magic, and even that tiny effort left her insides feeling scoured and raw. Conall saw her sway on her feet and bundled her into the passenger seat.

"I'll drive."

"I can drive," Rowan said. "You're better as a look out anyway."

His eyes found the bruises on her neck and his mouth pressed into a tight line. He hadn't been pleased when she'd told him about Orson and the geas. The only reason the scribe was still alive was because he was unconscious. Conall wouldn't kill a defenseless man.

"The elves are our lookouts. I can drive." He jumped into the driver's seat and they were off before she could protest further.

The caravan of cats traveled with their escort of Ebos for three hours, driving away from the Warren and New Torwood City, into land no one had inhabited in over six hundred years—no one but the Ebos and the few ghost raiders who sometimes came over the mountains during harsh winters.

They'd been traveling through the Meadows long enough for Rowan to realize there were trails hidden in the grass, tracks worn down by elk and smaller animals. The Ebos followed these as easily as Rowan would have followed the cobbled roads of New Torwood.

Noah drove the second cat and Clem had the third. All three vehicles were heavy with bodies and the cats lumbered through the grass.

In deference to the Ebos and their dislike of mech, Clem had switched her rail gun for a crossbow. Rowan also had a bow resting on her lap, but she had no idea how to fire it if the need arose.

There was no need for guns or bows. When Dalkyn finally called a halt, they seemed to be…nowhere. At least this place looked no different than any of the other thousands of acres they'd passed through. But as she stepped from the cat, Rowan saw it *was* different. They'd parked the cats beside a small depression in the vast plains. The grass was thinner here, little more than scraggly bunches of short stalks. A few bushes took advantage of the bare earth to cluster around the depression. A mass of broken metal lay nearby. It looked like a vehicle of some sort, but time and rust had ground it down to an unrecognizable heap.

"We leave mech here." Dalkyn pointed. "And you may bury the dead."

Conall didn't hesitate. He put their crew to work digging and laying out the bodies. The Ebos pitched in, and the job went quickly. Rowan helped Murdoch and Elias strip the cats of any gear they could pack into the saddle bags on the little ponies. The Ebos insisted they leave everything behind—vox, cats, scopes and all her tools. She'd be saints-damned if she'd leave Roger though. She was trying to figure out how to fit him onto the back of her pony when Minna approached.

"I don't care what you say, he's coming with me." Rowan's tone was harsh, but she meant it.

Minna held up one hand as if to fend off an attack. The other held a crumpled leather sack.

"Please, Evani. I help you. Look, see. Straps fit into here." Minna tucked the straps from the sack into loops on the saddle pad. "Later you wear them across your shoulders like a...how do you say?"

"Like a backpack?"

"Yes, a backpack."

"Roger that!" said the valet.

"Shush. Sleep now." Rowan tucked him into the pack and secured it before turning back to Minna.

"Thank you, but can I ask, why are you allowing this mech and not the others?"

Minna smiled and patted Roger's head that was poking from the pack. "This mech has coho-ne-teno."

Rowan still didn't grasp the Ebos idea of dual spirit, but before she could ask, she heard a whistle from across the field.

Shielding her eyes against the sun, she spotted Noah and Conall crouched beside the dead gaunts. Conall raised a hand and waved her over. The men stood. Conall looked wan in the bright sunlight. There were charcoal circles around his eyes. Noah, with his darker skin, still looked gray around the edges.

They all needed sleep, but she didn't expect them to find any rest, not until they were home in New Torwood, and maybe not even then.

"What's up?" She pulled her scarf over her nose. The stench of dead gaunt was enough to gag her.

"Noah is worried that they might have a tracking mech in them."

"It occurred to me after Denny described the set up at the Warren. They were testing the gaunts. They would have to track them if they escaped, but I can't sense anything once they're dead," Noah looked at her. "I was wondering if you might…I mean, after Orson…" He pointed to her neck where she wore the evidence of the scribe's attack like a badge. Conall scowled.

"You want me to find the tracker?"

Noah nodded.

"I can try." She didn't mention that her magic was sorely depleted because Conall would refuse to let her help. Instead, she laid her hand on the chest of the wrapped body before her, glad that she couldn't see its monstrous face. She didn't really expect to feel anything, and at first she didn't. Then, like when she touched Orson, her fingers tingled. Just a bit. She moved her hand up the chest. The tingling intensified. She gasped and pulled away as if she'd been stung.

"What is it?" Conall's tone was sharp.

Rowan shook her head and placed her hand back on the gaunt. Yes, there it was again. Thera. In the creature's veins. In its bones and skin. She moved her hand back and forth, ran it up and down the gaunt's limbs. It was everywhere. Did that confirm Denny's theory that gaunts and titans were simply earth creatures, mutated by thera? She couldn't be sure, but it was one more piece in the puzzle.

And yet…she'd felt thera in Orson too, except his thera had seemed alive, like millions of tiny organisms carried it around his body. The thera in the gaunt just tingled. She could sense it for sure, but it was inert. Was that because the gaunt was dead? Or was this something else entirely?

One spot on the gaunt's neck was so hot with thera, it seemed to burn. She jerked her hand away and rested back on her heels.

"What is it?" Conall gripped her hand before she fell backward.

"I…I'm not sure. But if there is a tracker, it's probably there." She pointed to the creature's neck.

Noah took a scalpel from his bag and sliced through skin. He dug around in the wound until he pulled out a small piece of mech covered in clotted blood. It was about the size and shape of a bee.

"Damn the Saints." Conall rubbed a hand through his hair. "Check the others."

Twenty minutes later, Noah had found four more trackers. He tried to crush them under his boot, but the trackers were solid silver.

Conall took the trackers to Dalkyn.

"If we bury the dead with these, they will be found." He held the tiny metal bees on his open palm. Dalkyn stared down at them with utter disgust, then he nodded toward another Ebos.

"Take these and ride west and north. Do not stop for a day and a night. Throw them into the River Sienni." Rowan didn't recognize the name of the river, but the Ebos seemed to. He nodded. Minna appeared as if out of nowhere and produced a leather bag. Conall dropped the trackers into it and she handed the bag to the waiting elf who looked horrified to be holding mech, even if it was bundled in leather. Dalkyn spoke sharply to him. The elf straightened and bowed. Then he leapt onto his pony and rode off at a gallop.

They LEFT THE CATS IN THE depression over the filled-in grave of the gaunts and soldiers. Then they stripped off their clothes and put on elf robes. Elves were generally shorter and slimmer than humans, but the robes were loose and they covered the rangers well enough.

Minna insisted they each wear a necklace of bone beads to complete the disguise. Up close they would never pass for Ebos. Conall was much too tall. Noah was too dark. The squad men all wore beards from days of living rough, and even mature elves were beardless. But from far, with their cowls over their heads, they looked like a tribe of nomadic Ebos traveling the plains.

When they were ready, Dalkyn rode up to address them. His pony was anxious to be away from the smell of death and it pranced in place. "Omika offers the hospitality of *Benni* to the Evani and her friends. It is a great honor to be asked to visit our city." Dalkyn bent his head in something close to a bow, but his tone suggested that he didn't agree with the offer. He stared at Rowan when he spoke and not Conall. She glanced at the commander, who simply shrugged.

Fine. He was going to let her sort this one out herself. She straightened her back and conjured up all the etiquette and diplomacy lessons her tutors had drilled into her. "We are fortunate to have found such good allies in the Ebos, but our squad is tired in body and spirit. We need a few hours to rest and discuss our options." She held his gaze, hoping she didn't insult him.

Dalkyn frowned, but Minna winked. Rowan didn't understand the dynamics between these siblings.

Finally, Dalkyn said, "We will bring you to a place of rest." He turned his pony and trotted off.

"Evani, this way please." Minna led her to the group of ponies that had been set aside for them. "I chose Hessa for you. She is a kind-hearted mare with good bones. She will run for as long as you ask her."

"Thank you, Minna. For this and everything you've done to help us."

"Evani." Minna nodded, then cupped her hands to give Rowan a leg up onto her mount. Instead of a saddle, the pony wore a thick pad made of sheep or goat skin. Hessa was a sturdy little thing, and even without the comfort of a saddle, Rowan felt secure. It helped that the pony was only about twelve hands high. She glanced at the other squad members who were mounting up with varying degrees of success. Lena looked like a ghost, she was so pale, but she sat her mount with the confidence of an experienced rider. Conall and Noah had the most trouble. Their legs nearly touched the ground and they looked like they were riding a child's carousel. Surprisingly, Denny also seemed comfortable on horseback. Clem had a look of grim determination on her face, while Elias looked terrified and Murdoch resigned. Two Ebos carried Orson in a large sling that hung between their mounts. They rode with such precision that the sling swayed in an even rhythm.

Rowan settled on her pony. Its gait was smooth, but she hadn't been on horseback in years. She knew she'd feel the strain on unaccustomed muscles soon. When they'd been traveling for only a few minutes, she glanced back, but already the cats were hidden by the rise of land beside the shallow depression. Dalkyn had brought them here for precisely that reason. How well these Ebos knew the land of her ancestors. It truly belonged to them now.

After an hour on the dusty road, her throat ached from Orson's attack and the dry wind. Rowan sipped continually at her canteen even though she had no idea how long it would be before they found fresh water again.

Conall spied her and kicked his heels into his pony until they rode side-by-side.

"We still have to talk about that." He pointed to her neck, where Rowan suspected the bruises were turning a spectacular shade of purple.

She lifted her hand to prod at the tender flesh.

"It's fine, really."

"Is that why you sucked back your entire water ration in an hour?"

"My throat's just a little raw. It'll be fine in a day or two."

Conall made an animal noise that sounded like it came from Garou.

"What we really need is proof that Minister Wrede is involved in this," Rowan said. "I recognized one of the soldiers that we buried back there, you know. I've dined with him at the palace. He was Wrede's personal guard."

Conall made that noise again.

"So we know the truth. Now we need to prove it. I had one of their mechs that controlled the gaunts, but I lost it when I shifted."

Rowan smiled and fished the mech from her belt pouch.

"This mech, you mean?"

Conall's mouth relaxed into a grin. "Princess, have I ever told you that I adore you?"

"Nope, but now's a good time."

"I adore you. And as soon as they let us off these goats they pass off as horses, I'm going to show you exactly how much."

It TURNED OUT THEY HAD NO time to be alone and together that night. The Ebos rode until late afternoon and chose a seemingly random patch of grass to camp on. But Rowan had learned that nothing the Ebos did was random, and while the Meadows spread to the horizon in every direction, this patch of grass was just a little greener. And she soon saw why when the elves turned over a rock to reveal a well dug into a natural spring. They filled their empty water skins and ate a cold meal. Then the Ebos retreated again, leaving Squad 54 to decide their future.

Orson lay bundled in his sling not far away. He mumbled and stirred, but so far he hadn't woken. Noah refused to sedate him because of his head wound and Conall refused to let Noah take his pain away because they needed the medic focused and not overcome by a knack-induced rage.

They took a vote and everyone but Denny wanted to return to New Torwood.

"I can't go back." Denny clutched his talisman. His fingers were white where the cord dug into skin. "They will kill me."

"Not if they don't know you're there," Rowan said. "We can hide you. Not forever, but we're all agreed that the truth needs to come out, right?" She looked around the group and everyone nodded.

"Roger that!" said the valet. He spun once as if to punctuate his outburst.

No one laughed. The little mech was just another part of their quirky squad now.

Squad 54 had left the gates of New Torwood as strangers, but this harsh landscape had forged them into something else, in the way wind shaped rock. They were harder now, but honed into a unit. Their knacks were shared. Denny's empath knack had kept them hidden from the enemy. Noah's temperamental magic treated their wounds. Clem kept them alive by never missing a shot.

And what is my contribution?

Rowan's talent for mechs hadn't proven its worth on the trip. But maybe, just maybe, she could keep them alive when they went home. She touched Roger's head. The storage compartment in his belly now hid the scribe's cachet and the odd mech she'd taken off the dead soldier. The answers they sought were tied to those bits of metal and thera. Orson had said the data on the cachet was scrambled, but she didn't believe him. She'd find a way to access it. Only the truth could keep them alive now.

"Once the people of New Torwood know what really happened out here and what the regent is doing to gaunts, the council will have no reason to hurt any of us," she said.

"They might just throw us all in prison though," Murdoch said. No one disagreed.

"The plan isn't without risk," Conall said. "It all hinges on us finding proof that at least one minister plotted to kill seventeen scientists. Then they came after a group of rangers that included the heir to House Andula. We find that proof and it won't be us spending the rest of our days in prison."

"What about him?" Noah nodded toward Orson.

"We have to kill him," Conall said.

"We can't." Rowan crossed her arms over her chest as if to hold back some undefined emotion that was trying to take over. It was fear and anger with just a little bit of resignation.

Since that first attack in the oasis, a plan had been tickling her subconscious. A plan that would let them all go home. And now that she'd been attacked by his personal guard, she could definitively link Minister Wrede to these murders. But would it be enough to force the council to act?

No.

She needed more. And that meant they had to go home and pretend ignorance. It would be their only defense while they worked toward uncovering the truth. Surely the council wouldn't attack her publicly. If they thought they could get away with that, they wouldn't have gone through this elaborate charade of sending her on a ranger mission.

They had to unravel the council's schemes and let the public decide their fate. It was the only way. But that plan relied on the fact that no one in New Torwood expected them to come home. And no one in their squad would reveal what they'd learned.

Orson was the weak link in that scenario. Which brought her back to an angry Conall who was ready to kill the scribe.

They'd been skirting this argument all evening while the sun flirted with the edge of the Ubruulens.

Rowan folded her arms over her chest. "We can't kill him.

"I expected that from him." Conall nodded toward Noah. "Doctor's oath and all, but he tried to *strangle* you."

"I'm well aware." Her throat still hurt when she swallowed. And every time she closed her eyes, she saw Orson's eyes bulging with crazed hate as he tried to choke the life from her.

Phalian said, "SQUEAK!" She petted him absently. Since her ordeal with the scribe, he'd stayed in mouse form in her pocket, as if he needed to be closer to her.

Conall pounded a fist on his thigh. "If we let him live, that…thing in his brain will give us all away. The council will know what we discovered and we won't last a day in the city."

"We still can't kill him."

"It's not your decision to make. I'm commander. I'll do it myself." He unsheathed the knife at his belt. Rowan stepped between him and the unconscious scribe. She touched his chest and felt a little shock go through her mech arm. Conall stopped. She forced him to look at her. And he scowled.

He doesn't like what he sees. He's going to like what comes out of my mouth even less.

But she'd known it would come to this since the minute he'd confronted her in the hall in New Torwood City. Back then, Conall had been just some cocky commander whose authority she took pleasure in tweaking. In the days since, he'd grown into something more. Much more.

She took a deep breath and willed her voice to stay calm.

"You may be Commander, but I am Princess, heir to the House of Andula. I outrank you. And I say we don't kill him."

Conall's mouth dropped open. Then he cursed the saints and threw down the knife. He stalked away with one hand fisted at his side and the other dragging fingers through his hair.

Without facing her, he said, "So tell us, *Princess*, why should we keep him alive?"

"Because they expect us to kill him. That's the easy answer, but there's more." She looked around at the squad. Her squad. Their faces were highlighted in gold from the flickering fire. They were waiting for her to speak, eager to hear what she had to say. Somewhere along their journey, she'd earned that respect. It was an odd and humbling feeling. No one in her twenty-eight years had ever respected her. Not really. They deferred to her because she was a princess, but no one thought anything she had to say was worth listening to. Certainly not the regent nor his council who now ran her father's kingdom like it was their own. It was time to change that.

"You all thought I would be a dimwit at best, a burden at worst. I don't blame you, but I hope I proved you wrong. I hope to continue to prove myself. I haven't always been a good princess, but I can do better. I should know what the council's planning because I'm on the council. Right? Except that's an honorary appointment, one that I never actually fulfilled." She thought of the empty seat in the council chamber, the one reserved for the reigning Andula. It had been her father's seat and should have been her brother's, but Rowan had never presumed to take it for herself.

"When we go home, I want things to be different and I'll need your help. I want to get to the bottom of the council's plotting. I want to be the kind of princess who makes a difference, the kind of princess who stands up to the regent." Her voice faltered.

"Maybe one day we won't need a regent," Clem said. "Maybe we'll have a queen."

Rowan looked at her friend. Hope shone from Clem's eyes like unshed tears.

"Maybe you're right." Rowan's heart pounded. These thoughts of rebellion shouldn't have come as a surprise. They'd been whispering to her on the wind and in the shadows. They'd come from the Meadows, around the campfire and on the road. In the dark while she waited for gaunts to kill them.

The squad watched her. Clem grinned. So did Denny, though he hid it by ducking his head. Noah's handsome face was stern, but he was nodding. Conall had turned around. His expression was unreadable.

She reached for his hand and gripped it.

"I'll have to decide what kind of leader I want to be. But I already know I don't want to be the kind who kills an innocent man."

"He's not innocent." Conall's tone was no longer sharp, but he would make her chase the logic right to the end of her argument.

"He was following orders."

"Some orders shouldn't be followed."

"Agreed. But I don't think he had a choice. The geas made sure of that."

Conall wasn't ready to relent. "He is a product of the council. Their weapon."

"Yes, he is. And we should pity him for that. He's been under their control since he was a boy. Maybe he's unlikable, and maybe that makes it easier to condemn him, but if the council had put a geas on one of us, wouldn't you at least consider an alternative to murder?"

Conall glared at her. She glared right back. There was no easy answer here.

"We can't let him go," Conall said softly.

"I know. But we shouldn't kill him either."

"Fine. What do you suggest?"

The anger and resentment were gone from his eyes. She saw something else shimmering there. She dared to hope it was admiration.

Noah cleared his throat. "Denny and I may have come up with a solution to the Orson problem." He turned to Rowan. "We would need your help."

"Of course. You have it."

"You might want to hear our plan before you agree." Noah looked at Denny. The scientist blushed. It was painfully obvious that he didn't like being the center of attention. The knots on his talisman suddenly unfurled like blossoms. He tucked the string away and looked up shyly.

"I think, if we work together, we can wipe his memories."

43

NO PLACE LIKE HOME

Rowan SHIELDED HER EYES TO SCAN the horizon for the great stone walls of New Torwood, or better yet, her beloved Talos, but found only the endless swaying grass and a dark blotch that could have been a herd of bison or gaunts. She prayed it was bison.

Conall gave her a small smile. He was anxious to get back to the city too, but for different reasons. He pushed his pony into a trot and caught up to Dalkyn in the lead. Despite the fact that the mount was much too small for him, Rowan couldn't help admiring the easy way he moved on horseback. She felt like every bone in her body had been rattled to pieces, but Conall swayed in time to the pony's gait in a way that suggested he'd been riding all his life.

Dalkyn had taken them along a circuitous route that avoided the Kanta Highway. They'd had no indication that anyone followed them from the Warren, but he'd ordered a group of elves to ride behind and mask their trail.

Her pony climbed a small rise and Rowan lifted her hand to shield her eyes from the afternoon sun.

There it was. New Torwood City shone like a diamond in a crown of emerald Meadows.

It was time to say goodbye to the elves.

The squad dismounted and returned the ponies and dun robes to their rescuers. Rowan slung Roger's pack over one shoulder. They would walk the rest of the way.

Dalkyn sat on his pony, looking stern and regal.

"Commander West," his tone was oddly formal, "Omika asked that I remind you of his invitation."

"I wasn't aware it was an invitation. It sounded more like a threat."

Dalkyn lifted his chin. His lip curled. "Because you are a wolf. You see the very wind and sky as a threat." With that, he turned his pony and rode off.

Rowan sought out Minna and Ferlan to thank them for all their help.

"We couldn't have come this far without you. And please thank Omika for us too." She held out her hand to grip Minna's. The dark elf looked down from pony-back with a grin. She dismounted and handed the pony to one of her clan.

"You misunderstand, Evani. Our task is not over. Ferlan and I will walk to the walled city with you. We are your servants, for now and for always."

"That's not possible."

"It is, Evani. Omika has charged us with your safety."

Rowan shook her head, at a loss for words. There had never been an Ebos inside the walls of New Torwood. The Enos who lived in the city were terrified of their nomadic cousins. That terror had blossomed into myth, and even the human population believed the stories about Ebos eating children. If Elias's initial reaction to them had been any marker of this disparity between the races, then bringing two Ebos into the palace would cause havoc.

Rowan looked to Conall for backup.

"It's a great idea," he said.

So, no backup there.

"Think about it. You're heading home to a palace full of snipers. Is there anybody you can trust?"

Rowan considered. "My aunt. And Dale." The regent's secretary couldn't be part of the plot that had almost seen her killed. She would never believe that. And yet…they had kept the truth of her brother's attackers from her. She would make sure they explained their motivation for that.

"Not a lot of allies," Conall said. "Take the elves with you as a personal honor guard. No one would deny you such a right. I know I'll feel better with them at your back."

Because you can't be there. That was the unspoken truth. A shapeshifter would never be allowed a position within the keepers, and so he'd be denied access to the palace.

Unless I married him.

Wow. That thought came like a sucker punch. She shoved it away just as quickly. A dalliance in the Meadows did not equate to a lifelong commitment. No matter how much fun that dalliance had been. And saints' sinners, it had been fun.

Minna cocked her head and a small smile played around the edges of her lips. It was like the elf could see right inside her head.

She dragged her thoughts kicking and screaming into the present.

"All right, but you can't come into the city looking like…that." She waved a hand to encompass the homespun robes, piercings and bone jewelry. "No one will believe you are Enos. And if this is to work, you have to fit in. I'm sorry but you'll have to lose the bones."

She knew she was asking a lot. Bones were at the heart of the Ebos religion. They weren't simply ornamentation, but links to their spirit realm.

"I respectfully disagree, Evani." Minna bowed her head, but her eyes never left Rowan's face. "Our primary mission is to protect you, but Omika is wise beyond his bones and breath. He wishes for the Enos of New Torwood to become familiar with our kind. He wishes them to be exposed to our ways."

"You'll scare the piss out of them."

"Perhaps. At first. But then they will see that the princess is not afraid of us and eventually our presence will be common."

"I think you over-estimate my influence. The nobles already think I'm quirky, to put it politely. They'll think of you as one more of my eccentricities."

"Perhaps. But it is a first step."

Rowan glared but the elf wasn't backing down.

"Fine. But I can't promise I'll be able to protect you if things go badly."

"Of course, Evani. We are there to protect you. Not the other way around."

Rowan turned to face the city. It was time to go home.

"This is it, Princess." Clem took Rowan's hand. She would be heading toward East Gate with Denny. They each carried a basket of wild blueberries the Ebos had picked along the way. If the keepers were searching for them, they'd be looking for a squad, not a couple of foragers hoping to sell their bounty. Clem would take Denny to Bretta's tearoom, where he would hide out for the next few months, working as a dishwasher. In a few days, Clem would report at the ranger's barracks, saying she got separated from the squad.

Rowan hadn't thought about all the goodbyes, hadn't realized how hard it would be.

Clem tugged on a strand of Rowan's loose hair and grinned. "Next time we do this, we *will* have a hair braiding party. You need it."

"Yeah, I've never been good at that girl stuff." Rowan ran a hand over her badly chopped hair. It was starting to grow back, but that only made the rough cut look worse.

"That's okay. I can teach you," Clem said. "And you can teach me princess stuff, like how to hot-wire a cat." She winked.

"Absolutely." Rowan could feel her lips trembling as she forced a smile.

Denny stood behind Rowan, his eyes fixed on the ground.

"Bye, Denny." Rowan lifted her hand to wave. Their relationship had changed and neither one knew exactly how to navigate that change.

They'd shared something strange and intimate when they'd connected with Noah to wipe Orson's memories. Their unique knacks had linked in a way that Rowan suspected had never been done before. Denny's empath knack had latched onto Rowan's and Noah's and sent them deep into Orson's mind. Noah's knack had steered her to the thera in Orson's blood and bones, and Rowan had used her galvanic magic to shatter it. The whole procedure had taken hours. Cell after cell, they'd stolen magic from the scribe, leaving him, not mindless, but empty, like a vessel that had been dumped of its contents and was ready for refilling.

Noah had almost died in the process. The hot emotion his knack induced had forced him to take a blade and try to plunge it into his own heart. Luckily Clem's shot never missed and she knocked the blade from his hand with an arrow. Conall tackled him and sat on Noah's chest until Murdoch had sedated him.

All in all, it had been a team effort.

And now, that team was scattering.

Denny rushed forward and gave her a short, tight hug.

"Bye," he whispered. As he hurried away, Rowan felt something in her left hand. She looked down to find she was holding a ratty piece of knotted string.

She watched Clem and Denny walk off, wishing she wouldn't have to wait so long to know they were safe.

The rest of Squad 54 headed toward North Gate. The keeper on watch took one look at the bedraggled crew and told them to wait in an anteroom in the guard tower.

They waited over an hour. No one came to offer water or food. There was only one small table with two chairs in the room. By unspoken agreement, no one sat in those chairs. The furniture was clearly set up for interrogation purposes. Instead, Conall and the others rested on the floor with their backs against the wall. Rowan paced. Minna and Ferlan stood guard on either side of the door.

"We won," Lena said quietly. It had become their mantra over the last miles. They were alive. The monsters sent to kill them weren't.

"Keep that in mind, whatever comes next," Conall said.

Finally, the door was flung open and a man walked into the room. Rowan didn't recognize him, but he wore a ranger uniform and had the five stripes of a general on his shoulder.

Conall rose and gave him a desultory salute. "General Teassel."

The general glared. "Commander West. I didn't want to believe it when they told me you had the balls to return."

"Yep, me and my balls just couldn't stay away." Conall grinned.

Teassel looked like he wanted to spit on Conall. Instead he headed for the table and chairs, but stopped when he saw the Ebos.

"Who're they?"

"Friends we picked up on the road," Conall said. "Princess Andula invited them to stay at the palace."

The general's eyes narrowed. He glanced at Rowan and dismissed her just as quickly. Then he looked Conall up and down again. After his last shift to wolf and back, Conall had run out of uniform jackets. He wore his civilian clothes and looked more like a raider than a ranger.

"Why are you out of uniform, Commander?"

"Had some trouble on the way home." Conall kept his tone light, like they were talking about a spot of bad weather.

Teassel ruffled a folder in his hand. They'd already given a preliminary report to the striker on duty at the gate. Teassel read that report, then closed the file.

"We expected you back three days ago."

"Ran into some storms and titans," Conall said. "Lost our cats and we had to walk back."

"Lost your cats?" His voice rose an octave. He consulted the file again, flipping pages. "And didn't you have four more rangers with you and a scribe when you left?"

Conall showed him his teeth. To his credit, Teassel didn't flinch.

"As I said, we ran into some trouble. I'm ready to make a full report."

The general held up a hand. "Save it. The council will want to hear it. I don't give a damn." He leaned into Conall until they were almost nose to nose. "I just want your shifter ass out of my city."

Conall stood upright and saluted. "I know how concerned you are about your soldiers' asses, sir! I will be leaving as soon as I report to the council."

The general pinched his lips. His face turned red and he slapped the file on his desk. He opened his mouth to berate Conall, but Rowan cut in.

"Sir, what will happen to Squad 54?"

Teassel narrowed his eyes and considered her.

"As of now, Squad 54 is dissolved. If I have my way, this whole sorry mission will be buried. Now, get out. I'm disgusted by this whole business and your pathetic excuses."

Rowan pushed herself away from the wall. She stopped him as he pushed back his chair.

"General Teassel, a word please."

The general frowned, no doubt wondering why the shy princess that most people thought was crazy or mentally infirm was actually addressing him.

She wore a rumpled and stained uniform. Her badly cut hair stuck out at all angles. She was dirty and smelled like horse. She didn't let any of that stop her.

"If the squad is done, then I am no longer Striker Andula. Do you know what that means?" She didn't wait for his answer. "That makes me Princess Andula again. My father was Reynar Andula. King Andula. That makes me heir to the throne. You know, the throne that pays your bills."

Teassel opened his mouth, but she held up a hand and barreled on. Her heart pounded. She'd never liked confrontation, but this...this just felt right.

"The way you speak to the rangers under your command is abusive. The way you spoke to me is insulting. I should have you reprimanded or brought up on charges of insubordination. But as Princess, I don't even need to go through those formal channels. I could have soldiers toss you off the wall right now. It's said that my great-great-grandfather used to do that for after-dinner entertainment." She leaned in until she could see the sheen of sweat on his brow. "I don't think I need to wait until after dinner."

The general was standing perfectly straight now. He'd lost his sneer, but she could see emotion flashing in his eyes. Dared she hope it was respect or at least fear?

Rowan lifted her chin.

"Tell Regent Atherton to wait for me in the council chambers. I need a bath and a meal. I will attend him in an hour. I expect the entire council to be there. Waiting."

"I...I will have word sent, Princess."

"No, General Teassel, you will bring this message to the Regent yourself. And you will be waiting in that chamber when I arrive to give my report too. Do I make myself clear?"

"Yes, Princess."

"Good, now leave us."

Teassel left so quickly, he knocked over a chair.

"That went well," Conall said.

"Did it?" Rowan hid a smile. "I got the feeling he doesn't like me very much."

Conall grunted. "It's me he doesn't like. Teassel was with us at the Algid Pass. He knows about General Naylor. And he knows I had no choice but to take him out. He just doesn't like it because that means generals can't hide behind their stripes."

"He should learn from the scribes," Noah said. "I hear they're sacrosanct." He didn't even quirk a smile, but there was a light in his eyes.

"So I hear." Conall shook Noah's hand. "What will you do now?"

Noah ran a hand over his short hair. "My military service is up soon. I thought I might wander over to Oxeye Outpost and offer my services as a physician at the thera farm."

"Dangerous work," Conall said, "but they'll be lucky to have you. It's been an honor serving with you, Maven."

"You too, sir." Noah nodded, then turned to Rowan and took her hands in his. "I hope you're right about this."

"I am," she said with more confidence than she felt. "Thank you for… well, for everything."

Noah squeezed her hands then let them drop. He tapped his head with one finger.

"You're still up here, Striker. I suspect you always will be."

"I know." She felt it too. It was like he'd left part of himself inside her brain. Like a memory, only more solid, more real. She hadn't felt that close to anyone since her brother's attack.

"Stay safe, Noah." She leaned in and kissed his cheek. "And you know how to get a hold of me, if you need to." They'd all agreed that Bretta's tearoom, the Fox's Cup, would be their gathering place. Rowan would try to visit once a week and any messages for her could be left there.

Noah nodded and headed out the door toward the mess hall. Conall dismissed the rest of the squad.

Lena shook Conall's hand, then Rowan's. "Thank you for everything." She hugged Noah fiercely before heading out the door.

Murdoch waved and left without a word.

Elias saluted Conall. "Sir!"

"At ease, Tracker," Conall said.

Elias beamed at his new rank.

"It was a pleasure riding with you, sir." He waved shyly at Rowan, blushed when Minna threw him a kiss, then scampered after Murdoch.

Rowan fought back irrational tears. Squad 54 was breaking up, but in her heart, they would always be a family. Already, she looked forward to her first visit to the Fox's Cup.

Conall was another matter. He'd told the general he was leaving. She didn't want to think about that.

"Come on." She hooked her arm in his. "I need a bath before facing the council." She leaned in to sniff him. "And so do you."

Conall sniffed himself and shrugged. "You're such a princess."

Rowan laughed. "I really am."

Rowan HELD ONTO CONALL'S ELBOW AS she led him to her suite of rooms in the palace. Minna and Ferlan followed behind them. Roger scooted along at her heel and Phalian circled overhead. She usually tried to come and go with little fanfare, but there was no disguising the spectacle they made traipsing down the palace corridors. By the time they'd reached her suite in the far east wing, she felt like they were on parade.

She closed the door to her rooms and pressed her back to it with a sigh. Minna and Ferlan spread through the suite, checking every shadow and nook for possible intruders.

"I'll wait out here," Conall said. Rowan nodded and headed right for her dressing room. A bath had been laid for her already and she'd never seen such a welcome sight.

Minna checked the room and opened a door at the far end.

"Where does this lead?" Minna frowned.

"That's the servants' door," Rowan said.

"It's not safe. It should be locked."

"I'm not even sure where the key is."

Minna shut the door. "I will make arrangements."

Rowan wasn't worried about the servants. All she wanted to do was get into that bath. She stripped and let her filthy clothes drop to the floor. Even the precious black glove over her mech was discarded. There was no saving it. The water was only warm, but it soothed every scrape and ache in her battered body. She closed her eyes and leaned against the back of the tub with a sigh. She wished she could lie there all day. But the council was waiting.

Ten minutes later, Rowan emerged clean and dressed in a simple midnight blue gown. She wore a fresh black glove on her mech arm. The other hand was bare. She'd tried to tame her wild hair, and opted for a simple blue head band to hold it away from her face. She could do nothing about the bruise that had blossomed under her right eye. She cocked her head and decided it made her look older and just a little mean.

Perfect.

Conall whistled when he saw her. "You clean up good, Princess."

"Your turn."

"You have a visitor." Conall nodded toward the balcony where a slim figure stood in the buffeting wind.

Dale.

She should have known Dale wouldn't wait for their official report to the council.

"Better get this over with."

"Bath can wait," Conall said. "I'm not leaving you alone with them."

Rowan didn't bother to remind him that she wasn't alone. Minna and Ferlan stood like gargoyles beside her door. She suspected she'd never be alone again. But she welcomed Conall's presence for what might be a disquieting interview.

Dale stood on the balcony that stretched to the city wall. Wind whipped their hair. They turned as Rowan stepped outside and nodded. It wasn't quite a bow, but close.

When Conall joined them, Dale raised an eyebrow, but made no comment.

"I have only water to offer you," Rowan said. "Unless you want me to call down for tea."

"There's no time. The council is already waiting."

Rowan frowned. "Let them wait."

Dale's eyes widened.

Let them be surprised. Everyone would have to get used to the new Princess Andula and her demands. She sat on a sculpted stone bench that overlooked the Meadows and patted the seat for Dale to join her.

Dale sat, then tipped their head toward Conall and the elves who lurked by the door. "I see you had quite the adventure and you even brought home souvenirs."

"It was an eye-opening experience." Rowan's gaze reached across the

Meadows. The light was that perfect soft color that made the grass shine like gold. She had a sudden longing to be back out there.

"Tell me the truth. What happened to those scientists?" Dale spoke low and leaned in as if they might be overheard.

"They died," she said without looking at him. "Our medic examined the bodies. It was a gaunt attack. Unlucky I guess."

"Your initial report is pretty thin. The council will want more details."

"They'll have it. Maven Medic Sommerton kept detailed notes." Rowan looked at Conall as if for confirmation. Conall nodded.

Dale sighed. "It's not common knowledge yet, but they found your scribe. He's alive. He was wandering around the docks, raving like a mad man."

Rowan kept her face perfectly neutral. "That's good news. We were worried about him."

"His story will corroborate yours?"

"You think I'm lying?" She let outrage tinge her voice.

"Of course not." Dale ran a hand through their thick hair. It was naturally unruly, but their habit of pulling at it when frustrated made it worse.

"Why were these scientists so important?" Rowan asked.

Dale shook their head. "Their work is part of a big trade deal with the southern cities. You wouldn't understand. Politics and economics. Two of your least favorite subjects."

"You know, I recently discovered a new fondness for politics. And economics. I wonder if it's too late to find a tutor, someone who could catch me up to speed."

Dale looked surprised. "Of course not, Princess. I'll, uh, see who I can find."

She took their hand with her mech fingers. Dale flinched. Dale always flinched when her mech touched them. She had noticed it before but thought it was only an aversion to her disability. Now she wondered if it was more about guilt for hiding the truth from her all these years.

"I was hoping you could teach me," she said.

"Of course." Dale swallowed hard. "I'd be honored."

"Thank you. And how's Ethan?"

"The same." Dale looked down. "You should go see him. Tell him you're home."

"I will." She paused until Dale looked up again. "You know I'd really like to know more about his attack. I read the official report years ago, but there must be more to it. Files that were suppressed? Maybe an eye-witness account?"

"I..." Dale glanced from Rowan to Conall, but found no help. "You know." Their shoulders sagged. "How?"

"I remembered. Funny how running into real monsters made me realize the truth. There never were any gaunts, were there? Ethan was attacked by men. Why did you lie for all those years?"

Dale seemed to shrink. "You were so little and so hurt. I…I just wanted to protect you. And you already thought it was gaunts."

"Because we were children, play acting."

"Yes, it was play." Dale pulled at their hair again. "Hard to imagine that now. It seems so stupid. I'm sorry." Their eyes pleaded for understanding. "There were things going on…plots that frightened me into silence. Please forgive me. I was just a child too. I did what I thought was right." They held out their hands, palms up. She reached over and took them. Dale's flinch was barely noticeable.

"I know. And that's why I need you. It's time to find the truth. It's time to make changes around here."

Their eyes narrowed. "What are you saying?"

"I'm…not sure."

"Are you planning to revoke the regent's right to rule?"

His question jolted her. Revoke Atherton's rights? The idea squirmed around her gut, making her queasy. She glanced at Conall. He gave her a small smile and she was glad for the weight of his support.

"Is that even possible?"

"Perhaps. The laws are very clear, but there may be some loopholes."

"Then I need you to find them." She held up a hand when Dale seemed ready to protest. "I'm not planning a coup. Not yet, anyway. Right now I just want a seat at the table, and I might need some ammunition to force the council to accept me. Also, I need a secretary, someone I can trust." She pointed at her oldest friend.

"Me?"

"You."

Dale sat straighter. She squeezed their hand.

"Will you do it?"

Dale nodded. Their face had gone pale. "I will look into the regency laws…quietly. And I would be honored to be your secretary, but…"

Rowan held her breath. This was the moment she would learn if Dale was truly on her side.

"We need to take this slowly. If I leave the regent now, I will lose all access to the records you need. Give me a few weeks to research and to make copies of the files you want. Once everything is in order, I will be the first to kneel before you and pledge my allegiance to the new queen."

Rowan's throat tightened but she managed to thank them.

Dale rose. "I will tell the council you're on your way." They smiled. "But take your time. I think you're right. They could use a lesson in patience."

Dale nodded to Minna as they left the room.

Conall said, "Do you really trust them?"

"Yes. Dale would never betray me because that would mean betraying Ethan. Dale loves Ethan."

"So why didn't you tell them the truth about the scientists?"

Rowan paused. "I would trust Dale with my life, but I have no right to trust them with Denny's. We promised to keep our secret and I will."

Conall nodded. "You may have to trust someone before this is over. It might have to be Dale."

"Maybe."

He was standing so close to her, she could feel the warmth of his body. She felt herself sway toward him, like she was caught in the pull of a vortex.

He placed a light kiss on her forehead.

"Let's get this done, then."

She nodded, not trusting her voice.

44

A SHUFFLING OF SWORDS

Rowan STEPPED INTO THE COUNCIL CHAMBERS. There were a few chuckles when Roger rolled in behind her. The mech valet still had moss clinging to him and one antenna spun erratically. The murmurs turned to gasps when Minna and Ferlan entered the room with heads held high and bone necklaces clacking.

Conall used the disturbance to slip to the back of the room and stand beside the benches set aside for onlookers. He was glad to spy General Teassel seated on a bench. He'd taken Rowan's reprimand seriously.

The ministers were still in an uproar over the Ebos in their midst, though Minna and Ferlan seemed nonplussed by the reactions.

"What is the meaning of this?" Atherton rose from his chair. "Guards! Remove these…these savages!"

"Sit down, Faustus." Rowan pointed to his chair. Atherton's eyes nearly fell out of his head. The princess had never addressed him by his first name. His lips flapped open and closed like a fish, then he dropped into his seat.

Rowan stepped around the table, pulled out her father's empty chair and sat. The Ebos stood like an honor guard behind her. Roger spun in a circle beside her chair, the sound of his wheels grated against the silence in the room. The only other sound was the slow ticking of the Infinity Clock.

Several ministers looked like owls caught in the morning light. With an impassive expression, she met each minister's eye. Conall grinned as he watched Rowan claim her birthright.

Good for you, Princess. Let the fish squirm on their hooks.

After several moments of utter silence, she sat back in her ornate chair and spoke quietly enough that old Hayes, Minister of the Purse had to lean in to hear.

"Where are councilors Renata, Docker and Wrede?"

Atherton looked confused. "They're not here."

"When I call a council meeting, I expect everyone to attend." She glanced at Olan March. "Chancellor please make note of their absence and let them know that if they miss another meeting without a proper excuse, they will be fined."

"Yes, Princess." Olan smiled. He'd been Chancellor to her father and recognized the authority she was attempting to wield.

"You can't do that!" Atherton sputtered.

"I just did." Rowan smiled. "Now, I suppose you want a full report about the disaster at Eklridge Oasis. I'll let Commander West fill you in." She sat back with her hands folded in her lap.

Conall stepped forward. He kept the report simple. They found the camp. Everyone was dead. They were attacked by gaunts. They came home. They lost the cats in a storm.

It was a faded pastel of the truth.

When he finished, Regent Atherton leaned back in his chair with his fingers templed under his chin. He seemed to have recovered from the shock of Rowan taking over her father's chair. The other council members stared at Conall like he might shift into wolf form at any moment and rip out their throats.

It's still an option, Garou said. The wolf chafed to be away from these cold stone walls.

"It is a bitter wind that brings so much death," Old Hayes said in a quavering voice. He clacked his false teeth as he spoke, making his long white mustache jump. A sudden and vivid image of the walrus titan flashed in Conall's mind. He caught Rowan watching him with lips pursed as if she held in a laugh and knew they were thinking the same thing.

Finally, the regent spoke.

"So you have nothing to show for your mission. And you lost valuable resources including vehicles and rangers."

Conall scowled. "Rangers Augustus Paddon and Clementine Tyendi," he said. They were maintaining the fiction that Clem was lost in the Meadows for another few days. "They were people, not resources. And yes, their loss is a tragedy beyond measure. Too expensive a price for a mission that was a failure before we even left. The scientists in that camp had been dead for days. But you already knew that, didn't you?"

The regent ignored the jibe. "And the scribe? Do you have any idea how expensive it is to train a scribe?"

"Yes, I've been told they're sacrosanct."

Rowan shut her eyes and her chest rose as she sucked in a deep breath. She was trying not to laugh. He winked at her.

"Excuse me?" The regent arched one white eyebrow.

"In battle," Conall said. "Scribes are considered sacrosanct—outside of the fight. It's a shame the gaunts that attacked us didn't understand that nuance."

More silence. Atherton turned to Rowan.

"It's no secret that you didn't want a scribe with you on this mission."

Rowan smiled sweetly. "And it's no secret that he wasn't my responsibility. Scribe Orson made that clear. It's not our fault if he couldn't keep himself alive."

They had also agreed to keep to the fiction that they didn't know the scribe's fate. No one could know that Rowan was working with Dale. Not yet.

Atherton leaned in and smiled. "Oh, he's very much alive. Keepers found him in Dockside. He's a bit scrambled from a head wound but that'll soon clear up."

"That's excellent news," Conall said. "I'm sure he'll be able to fill in all the details of our mission. Now, I believe you owe me some papers to prove the bounty has been lifted from my head."

Atherton glared, but held out a parchment. When Conall stepped forward to take it, he hissed, "I want you out of my city."

"Happy to oblige." Conall yanked the paper from his hand. He read through it, studied the seal at the bottom, then nodded.

The meeting was about to break up. Rowan rose before anyone else.

"Thank you for coming. I would like to meet again on Monday. Until then, you are all dismissed."

Atherton gaped at her. She smiled sweetly then rose and swept out of the room, leaving her ministers to wonder what storm had just blown through the palace.

A storm that will shake the foundations of this city, Garou said proudly of their mate.

Conall agreed. Those poor ministers didn't know what was coming for them.

45

POLICY MAKERS AND SHAKERS

In THEIR SMALL OFFICE OFF THE regent's, Dale had listened to Atherton rant at ministers and palace officials for hours. Rowan's little coup might have been symbolic only, but it had rattled the regent and his cronies.

They were all gone now. The offices outside the council chambers were quiet. The ministers would continue their speculations at dinner tables around the city.

Dale had a few hours alone to make copies and organize the papers they needed. They weren't sure what Rowan had planned, and so they would prepare for anything.

They activated an errand mech and set it to collect and hold documents, then set mimeo mechs to copying trade agreements and promissory notes from the regent to various guilds and merchants. As the mimeos completed the copies, they slid right into the holding bin on the errand mech.

Dale found the treasurer's ledger and flipped through it. The old Minister of the Purse was diligent about filling out these records everyday. And it was all lies. Dale shoved it aside with disgust. Atherton kept the real ledger locked up. They'd have to work on getting that key. But they weren't ready to reveal their hand in that way. Not yet.

Satisfied with the night's work, Dale glanced at the new reports on their desk. The first one was from a doctor at the Temple of the Word. Scribe Orson had been found wandering outside East Gate. His memories were damaged and his cachet gone. The doctor detailed a head wound. Most of the report corroborated what Rowan and Conall had claimed. Except for the last note written in the doctor's hand that read: Trauma from head wound not consistent with complete memory failure.

Dale read that line twice more. The scribe's memory loss wasn't from his wound. That could only mean one of two things. The scribe had scrambled his own memories, or someone had done it to him. Either way, something didn't match up with the official report.

The regent should know about this. It was Dale's job to make certain he knew. But instead of slipping the report into the regent's update for the morning, Dale put it with the copies in the errand mech and closed the compartment.

"Follow," they ordered. There was one more report to secure before they could rest for the night. The mech trundled along behind them as Dale crossed the hall and fished a ring of keys from their pocket to find the one that unlocked the door to the archives.

Inside, the room was dark, lit only by one small lamp near an elevator shaft. Dale stepped into the box and waited for the errand mech to follow, then they inserted another key and turned it. The elevator started its slow, creaking descent.

The basement was pitch black and Dale's fingers fumbled with the thera lighter as they lit a lamp that had been left by the elevator. The lamp sent ripples of purple light ahead, but not enough to dispel the shadows in every corner.

Dale didn't look into those shadows. They didn't want to know what was hiding there. Instead, they took a direct route to the far corner of the archives. It was a route they'd taken many times in order to read a particular file.

They stopped at a cabinet that was labeled 310-330. The drawer squeaked when they opened it. Dale pulled one file from many. It was unmarked. Years ago, they'd taken the report about the attack on Prince Ethan from its official home in the archives. They'd transferred it to this folder and hidden it in this antique cabinet that held reports on crops and floods from over two hundred years ago.

Many nights, they'd come down here to read through the file. They knew every ink mark it contained. And now it was time to pass it on to Rowan. Dale paused with the folder gripped tightly in their hand.

She would despise them when she learned of their role in the attack. Wasn't that why they'd kept it secret all these years? And now they were just going to bring it into the light?

Yes, they were. It was time.

Dale placed the folder into the errand mech, and said "Close." The mech's compartment shut with a tinny clang. "Seal with the code *gaunts don't lay eggs.*"

A whirring sound came from the mech as it complied with the voice command, then it went dormant. Without the code, it wouldn't wake again.

Dale picked it up and tucked it behind a pile of antique crates, where no one would ever find it. Then they left with the thera lamp, leaving all their secrets in darkness.

$$46$$

A HUNDRED WAYS TO SAY GOODBYE

It was the last night they would spend together, and they squeezed every drop of passion from those few hours. Their love-making had been desperate and frantic, as if they were sensitive to the precious seconds ticking away. Then they talked all through the hours of the midnight sun. They made love again, slowly this time, committing each rasp of skin against skin to memory.

Now Conall slept. Rowan lay in his arms, her back pressed against his chest. His slow, even breath warmed her neck as she watched the window brighten with the morning sun. She wanted to freeze time in this moment, but even a princess didn't have such power.

He would be leaving today. He could never live in the city, and she couldn't leave it. Their partnership was never meant to last beyond the mission in the Meadows.

She slipped out of bed and left Conall sleeping. It was too early even for the servants to be up, but someone had laid out clothes in her dressing room. She ignored the formal dress and dug out her old tinker's shirt and overalls.

In a bid for privacy, she'd left Phalian on the dresser the night before. He woke up with a clack of metal mouse paws and scampered to her shoulder.

Roger was still in sleep mode. She woke him up.

"Roger that!"

"Hush." She glanced at Conall, but he slept on.

The mech valet stared up at her with big oxidized eyes. She touched a button on his chest and a compartment opened up to reveal her treasures: two scribe cachets and the device used to control gaunts.

Satisfied that her booty was safely hidden, she closed the compartment and patted his head.

"You stay here. You're on guard duty."

"Roger that!"

She took one last glance at Conall and let herself out of the suite. Ferlan was standing guard outside her rooms. He didn't say a word, but just followed her down the corridor. At the end, she took the stairs down to the basement and then along another dimly lit hall to her tinker shop.

Then she sorted through the boxes on the shelf, looking for the one little mech that would make parting with Conall not easy, but bearable.

Conall WAS GONE WHEN SHE RETURNED to her rooms. He'd left a note saying he was going to visit Bretta before leaving the city. She had no doubt he would return to say goodbye.

She ate breakfast on her balcony to be closer to the Meadows, and watched the sun and wind make highlights dance on the grass. Already, her time outside the wall seemed to be fading like morning mist. Her hand reached into her pocket to squeeze Denny's knotted string.

It had happened. All of it. And now she lived in a world changed by those experiences. A world where her quiet, tidy ideals no longer fit. A world that needed to be turned over and shaken until the bugs fell out, like a dusty old bin left forgotten in a shed. She wondered what other secrets would fall out with the roaches.

A notebook was open in front of her, but she hadn't written anything down. She had planned to make a to-do list, and the first three items would be:

1. Hack into illegally obtained cachets to read scribe reports.

2. Link the Theracine Corporation and the council to murder.

3. Find a way to prove the regent's treason.

With her pen poised, she realized she could never leave such a paper trail. She sighed and closed the blank notebook. She'd add learning covert operations to the list of things Dale would have to teach her.

In any case, all of it seemed overwhelming after her sleepless night, and her thoughts kept returning to Conall—the feel of his hands on every inch of her skin. Her fingers, mech and human, running over muscle that hummed with vibrancy. The heat of him inside her, claiming her body and soul—

She shut her eyes and pressed her palms against them, knowing these memories would become the new dreams that haunted her nights.

She could think of a hundred things she meant to say to him, and not one was goodbye.

Shoving the notebook aside, she got up to find a diversion. It was well past midmorning, late enough to visit Ethan. Ferlan followed her like a shadow to the prince's room, startling the few maids they passed along the way. One actually shrieked when she spied the dark elf.

Ferlan ignored the fuss.

Rowan found Ethan alone. She sat by his bed and held his hand. Did he look different? She'd been gone only a fortnight but he seemed older somehow. Or maybe she was the one who'd aged a decade in a few days.

She had so much to tell him, but she was so very tired. Instead, she simply held his hand and hummed *Ode to Joy*. Then she kissed his forehead and left.

Auntie Bella wasn't much of a morning person, so Rowan skipped her rooms and mounted the great spiral staircase to the wall.

And she waited.

She stood there for nearly two hours, watching the sky shift colors and waiting for Talos to round the bend.

"Dale said I might find you here."

Rowan closed her eyes and hugged herself without turning to face him. She'd known he would find her. She turned and smiled.

Conall was dressed for the road, with his hunting leathers and worn pack. The crossbow was slung across his back.

"I just needed to be up high. I needed to see Talos and remember where I come from."

Conall nodded and stepped forward, holding a folded note in his hand.

"Bretta asked me to give you this."

Rowan took the note and opened it. A printed poster advertised the opening of a new pub and tearoom called The Glass Boot. "Hope you can come" was scrawled across the bottom of the page.

She lowered her hand. "What is this?"

"It's Bretta's new place. She's...re-branding."

"I see that." Rowan had a sudden urge to run to Squall's End.

"Clem made it home," Conall said, reading her thoughts. "And Denny. They're safe for now."

That only made Rowan feel marginally better.

"Has Dale seen this?"

"Probably. There are posters all over lower town, and Dale probably has a network of spies in the city. And they know Bretta was on our squad, so their mind is turning over a lot of questions right now."

Rowan crumpled the paper in her hand. "I'll tell Dale. Soon."

After her morning spent plotting her next moves with the council, she'd already come to the same conclusion. She needed Dale's help and their complete confidence if she ever hoped to bring the truth to light.

"When are you leaving?" she asked.

"As soon as I can find a way out of the city that isn't tracked by the keepers. I want to keep Atherton guessing about my whereabouts." He reached up to trace the line of her jaw with his thumb.

She leaned into his touch. "Are you going to accept Omika's invitation?"

He wouldn't be able to resist the lure of learning more about his brother's death.

"I think I have to go." He smiled, but there was nothing happy in his eyes. "The rangers never gave me much information about what happened to Nathan. All I know is that he was working on some secret operation during the first year of the war. If the Ebos know more, I think I have to find them. And..." He ran a hand over her hair and tucked it behind her ear. "And I want to return to the Warren."

"Why?"

"We left in a hurry. There might be clues we missed. What will you do?" He took Rowan's mech hand and placed it over his heart. His eyes bore into hers and she had a hard time putting thoughts into words. His heartbeat thrummed through her sensitive fingertips and she couldn't help feeling like it was Garou, trying to communicate with her.

"I guess…" She pulled her thoughts back to the present. "I guess my first job is to crack the code on the cachets. I don't really have any idea where to start with that though."

Conall's hand closed over hers. His flesh felt inordinately hot against her mech fingers.

"If anyone can figure it out, it's you."

He leaned in and kissed her. She let herself indulge in the feeling of his lips on hers for only a moment, then pushed away.

"If you find anything—at the Warren or with the Ebos—you'll send word?"

She hated herself for the blatant hope in her tone.

"I'll send word."

She leaned her forehead against his chest. He kissed the top of her head.

"I feel like it was all for nothing," she said. "Augie gone. Lena and Bretta forever changed. And for what? What did we gain? What did we win?"

Conall's arms tightened around her. "We won the right to keep on fighting. Right now, there are a bunch of ministers scrambling to figure out how this will play out. Taking your father's seat was perfect. It was like you sent your galvanic magic around the table and shocked them all out of their complacency." He tipped her face towards him. "Chin up, Princess. We're still on the right side of the grass. This is a turning point for all of us. And everyone will be looking to you to light the way."

Rowan nodded. She didn't feel up to the task, but for him—for Squad 54—she would damn the saints and give it her best effort.

He kissed her, then pressed his forehead to hers so they could meet eye to eye.

"I wish I didn't have to go," he said.

"I know. I hope one day New Torwood will be more wolf friendly." She smiled. "Oh! I almost forgot." She rummaged in her belt pouch and pulled out a locket on a long silver chain. The locket was etched with vines and berries, and seemed to hang from a silver branch. Rowan pulled off the branch and used it like a key to open the locket. The insides shone with the blue of active thera.

Conall reached for it. "Is that a graphium?"

She nodded. "The smallest graphium in existence. Isn't it amazing? Look, this is the stylus." She scrawled a tiny heart on the thera screen with the silver branch, then she shut the locket and latched it. She pulled an identical locket from her shirt and opened it. The tiny heart appeared there too.

"My father gave these to my brother and me one Founder's Day. You won't be able to write much. The screens are too small. But for emergencies…"

Conall took the locket and closed both his hands around hers. He let the wolf shine from his eyes. "Thank you. I'll use it. I promise. But now I'd better cash in some favors and find a way out of the city."

"No need. Your ride's here." Rowan nodded toward the bend in the wall where Talos's copper dome was just visible above the stones. She pressed a key into his hand and folded his fingers over it.

"Take this for when you come home again. There's a door in Talos's neck and another on his ankle."

Conall looked at the key, then at the giant mech lumbering toward them. "You expect me to jump to his shoulder?"

"Yep. And you'd better hurry. Here he comes."

The wind didn't quite mask the sound of Talos's footsteps on the hard-packed ground.

Conall whipped his arm around her waist, pulled her close and kissed her.

"I love you." He let her go and saluted. "Striker!"

She raised a trembling hand to her brow.

Then he turned and ran across the wall. His free arm windmilled as he leapt across open air. Rowan's heart lurched as he landed on Talos's shoulder. He unlocked the door, then gave her one last smile before disappearing inside.

She waited ten long minutes. Talos was almost out of sight around the eastern bend in the wall when she spied a tiny figure leap off his foot and dash into the Meadows.

She saluted again. "Safe travels, Commander."

Acknowledgments

A Knack for Metal and Bone took much longer to write than I expected. It wasn't just about writing a plot—I created an entirely new world: new characters, governments, settings, weapons, magic systems, monsters, religions, and more. Many of these creations aren't even reflected in the story (yet), but they were essential for me to understand this world and the people who inhabit it. I spent a lot of time in my head while crafting New Torwood City and the Meadows—a lot of time that might have looked like daydreaming or aimless wandering around our little patch of forest. I want to thank my family—and my husband, Louis, in particular—for understanding that there was nothing aimless about it.

Part of the challenge of this book was that it's a story I've been thinking about for many years, and I had pages and pages of notes that needed to be reshaped into a new mold. Also, I stepped out of my comfort zone by writing a large cast of characters. There was purpose to this madness. While I'm not planning to abandon Rowan and Conall, future books will also focus on other characters and other knacks, so I wanted even the peripheral characters to feel fully fleshed out. I hope you'll look forward to stories about Noah, Clem, Denny, and the rest of Squad 54.

Writing can be a solitary endeavor, but connecting with like-minded souls makes it incredibly rewarding. I'd like to give a big thank-you to Elaine Jackson and Vicki Pinkerton, especially for our writing weekends, where we enjoy silent time to amble and chatting time to connect. A double thank-you goes to Elaine for editing The Knack and for pushing me to make it better when my energy flagged. My assistant Emily Alice also deserves a big hug for coming through for me when I really need it. Thank you also to my daughter, Genevieve, for being a creative sounding board—talking about books with her never gets old. Special thank-you's go to my Auntie Karen Knox for gifting me the perfect writing retreat with a view that inspired the Meadows, and to my mother, Claire McDougall, for always being my biggest fan.

Finally, I'd like to thank my Advance Review Team for their encouragement. Their excitement for this book has made releasing a new series less stressful and so much more fun.

Kim McDougall

Reviews Help Everyone

You probably know that authors love reviews, but do you know why? Reviews are important to every author, for the following reasons:

- They help other readers know what to expect from the book.
- They let me know how my books are received by readers.
- They help booksellers decide which books to show to new readers.

If you enjoyed this book I would be grateful for your honest review. It can be as short as you like. Even a few positive words will go a long way. And I'll try to make it as painless as possible. Use this link, KimMcDougall.com/Review-A-Knack-for-Metal-and-Bone to find the review site of your choice.

Be sure to sign up for the Readers' Group at KimMcDougall.com/Readers-Group to get updates on new releases. When you subscribe, you'll get two free ebooks just for subscribing.

Thank you for reading *A Knack for Metal and Bone* and I hope you'll continue Rowan's journey with me.

What to Read Next?

Magic runs the machines. Secrets run the city. And Squad 54 stands between order and chaos.

Conall thought he'd buried the past with his brother. But when a cryptic summons surfaces—tied to a long-vanished village and a wolf who should be dead—he's forced to retrace the path of the disbanded Squad 54. What he finds in the shadows could unravel not only their fate, but the fragile balance between elf and human kind.

Back in New Torwood City, Princess Rowan Andula is done playing the figurehead. With a seat on the ruling council, she's ready to fight for her family's legacy—until the city's giant mech guardian begins to fail. Talos isn't just a machine. He's the heart of the city. His collapse could bring down everything her ancestors fought to preserve.

As enemies close in and new treacheries are revealed, Conall and Rowan must face the same question: How far will you go to protect what you love?

Mech and Magic is the second thrilling installment of The Knack Series—where ancient tech, dangerous politics, and fierce loyalties collide.

Books by Kim McDougall

The Knack Series
A Knack for Metal and Bone
Mech and Magic

The Fair Folk of Mullarkey Series
Black Annis Year

Valkyrie Bestiary Novels
Dragons Don't Eat Meat
Dervishes Don't Dance
Hell Hounds Don't Heel
Grimalkins Don't Purr
Kelpies Don't Fly
Ghouls Don't Scamper
Devils Don't Lie
Unicorns Don't Cry
Worlds Don't Collide

Valkyrie Bestiary Novellas
The Last Door to Underhill
The Girl Who Cried Banshee
Three Half Goats Gruff
Oh, Come All Ye Dragons
Thorn of Vioska

The Hidden Coven Series:
Inborn Magic
Soothed by Magic
Trigger Magic
Bellwether Magic
Gone Magic

About the Author

If Kim McDougall could have one magical superpower, it would be to talk to animals. Or maybe to shift into animal form. Definitely, fantastical critters and magic often feature in her stories. So until Kim can change into a griffin and fly away, she writes dark and humorous Urban, Epic, and Cozy Fantasy from her little farm on the edge of the woods in Quebec, Canada. Kim's book series include the Valkyrie Bestiary, The Knack, The Fair Folk of Mullarkey and Hidden Coven.

Visit Kim online at www.KimMcDougall.com.

www.ingramcontent.com/pod-product-compliance
Lightning Source LLC
Chambersburg PA
CBHW061109310726
48974CB00002B/462